Romantic Suspense

Danger. Passion. Drama.

Guarding Colton's Secret
Addison Fox

Her Private Security Detail
Patricia Sargeant

MILLS & BOON

Addison Fox is acknowledged as the author of this work
GUARDING COLTON'S SECRETS
© 2024 by Harlequin Enterprise ULC
Philippine Copyright 2024
Australian Copyright 2024
New Zealand Copyright 2024

First Published 2024
First Australian Paperback Edition 2024
ISBN 978 1 038 90768 4

HER PRIVATE SECURITY DETAIL
© 2024 by Patricia Sargeant-Mathews
Philippine Copyright 2024
Australian Copyright 2024
New Zealand Copyright 2024

First Published 2024
First Australian Paperback Edition 2024
ISBN 978 1 038 90768 4

® and ™ (apart from those relating to FSC®) are trademarks of Harlequin Enterprises
(Australia) Pty Limited or its corporate affiliates. Trademarks indicated with ® are
registered in Australia, New Zealand and in other countries.
Contact admin_legal@Harlequin.ca for details.

MIX
Paper | Supporting
responsible forestry
FSC® C001695

Published by
Harlequin Mills & Boon
An imprint of Harlequin Enterprises (Australia) Pty Limited
(ABN 47 001 180 918), a subsidiary of HarperCollins
Publishers Australia Pty Limited
(ABN 36 009 913 517)
Level 19, 201 Elizabeth Street
SYDNEY NSW 2000 AUSTRALIA

Cover art used by arrangement with Harlequin Books S.A.. All rights reserved.

Printed and bound in Australia by McPherson's Printing Group

Guarding Colton's Secrets

Addison Fox

MILLS & BOON

Addison Fox is a lifelong romance reader, addicted to happily-ever-afters. After discovering she found as much joy writing about romance as she did reading it, she's never looked back. Addison lives in New York with an apartment full of books, a laptop that's rarely out of sight and a wily beagle who keeps her running. You can find her at her home on the web at addisonfox.com or on Facebook (Facebook.com/addisonfoxauthor) and Twitter (@addisonfox).

Visit the Author Profile
page at millsandboon.com.au.

Dear Reader,

Thank you for joining me on the latest Colton adventure! I've so enjoyed visiting Owl Creek, Idaho, and uncovering all the secrets in this small-yet-growing hamlet about two hours outside Boise.

Chase Colton has a problem. Several of them actually, from his father's horrible betrayal to secret siblings he never knew about to a possible embezzler at his firm, Colton Properties. Enter Sloan Presley, computer wizard and a most determined puzzle solver.

Sloan's spent her adult life building her own professional services firm, SecuritKey, and she's one of the best in the business. It doesn't take her long to suss out that there are some real problems under the surface at Colton Properties. A skill Chase then puts to further use to try to uncover the whereabouts of his aunt Jessie, who they're increasingly worried has been taken in by a local cult.

As Sloan digs into the problems that seethe beneath the surface of Owl Creek, Chase is discovering the heart he'd believed long dead was simply in hibernation. But admitting that after years of swearing off relationships may prove difficult when it becomes obvious Sloan has become the target of a group determined to keep their secrets at any cost.

I hope you enjoy another wild and heart-pounding visit with the Colton family. And thank you for taking the ride with me!

Best,

Addison Fox

DEDICATION

For our wonderful Colton readers. Thank you
for going on these adventures with us!

Chapter 1

Chase Colton stared at the men and women assembled around his boardroom table bright and early Monday morning and braced himself for the inevitable. "As I shared in my email when I called this meeting, my focus as the new CEO of Colton Properties is transparency. No questions are off-limits."

He saw a few eyebrows raised at that last bit, but resolved it would be the truth.

His legal counsel was already leaning in, the man's voice low, his lips barely moving. "Sir, I'm not sure that's the best course of action."

Ignoring Tim's concerned visage, Chase addressed the table even more determined than when everyone had filed into the room. "Transparency. Accountability. Honesty. It's how I'm running Colton Properties moving forward. So, please—" he extended his hands "—feel free to ask me what's on your mind."

"I'm sorry about your father, Chase." As first comments went, it was something of a softball, but he appreciated the warm smile that creased Sonja Rodriguez's face. His head of marketing was a gem on any day, but the clear support from such a senior member of the team was encouraging.

"I'm sure I speak for us all when I say you have our sympathies on Robert's passing."

It had been a little over three months and Chase was still getting used to the idea that his father was dead. Robert Colton had been a force in life, both as a parent and as a real-estate maven in their growing corner of Idaho, Owl Creek. Both aspects of his father's life affected Chase equally, as his son and as the recognized heir apparent to the leadership and management of Colton Properties.

"Thank you, Sonja. It's been a difficult few months. My father cast a very long shadow in life."

"Would that long shadow have anything to do with the siblings you didn't know about?" The question seemed to hold the deliberate air of a challenge. Clint Roebuck, their lead property scout, liked to play big man whenever he could—but it also made him the perfect person to ask the question. Everyone else in the room was dying to know the same, but Clint's pugnacious tone would hopefully make the rest of the crowd sympathize with Chase.

"It's true that since my father's death my brothers and sisters and I have discovered a half brother and half sister. We're dealing with that as a family."

"And we're dealing with it as a business," Clint pressed. "You can't tell me that if someone wakes up one day and finds out they're related to a bigwig like Robert Colton they don't want a piece of his empire?"

Chase had walked into this aware it wouldn't be easy, but Clint's taunting tone was like sandpaper over the raw feelings he hadn't yet dealt with.

Feelings he wasn't sure he ever would.

Keep cool, Colton.

"While my family is working through equitable division of assets for my additional siblings, the succession plans for

Colton Properties have been in place for a long time. I've worked at the company since getting out of college and am the best Colton for the job."

"But your newly discovered siblings could make things difficult. Here. For us."

"Clint," Sonja hissed. "I think Chase has been pretty clear on next steps for the business."

Clint looked about to argue when their office manager, Althea, wheeled in replacements for their coffee service. A table full of eyes stared longingly at the refreshed carafes and Chase figured it was as good a time as any to take a break. There'd be more questions—it was inevitable—but the break for coffee and another round of pastries off the sideboard would give people more time to loosen up and figure out how to frame those questions that might be difficult.

"Why don't we get fresh cups of coffee and a bit more breakfast and we can pick back up in fifteen?"

The dismissal provided the bell for round one and people quickly stood, their quiet murmurs filling the room as they moved toward the refreshed coffee. Although he was itching to go to his office to mentally regroup, Chase stayed in the conference room, talking to various folks and deftly ignoring Tim's efforts to catch his eye, no doubt to quietly tell him all the reasons why this meeting was a bad idea.

He leaned in when Sonja walked over to him, her dark brown gaze warm as she laid a hand on his arm. "Days like this show us what we're made of." She tilted her head toward the rest of the room. "It shows others, too. People do understand this is a difficult time for you and your family, and that you're doing your best."

"People who aren't Clint, you mean." He kept his tone even and his smile easy, but the resentment spiked hard in Chase's gut all the same.

"Even he'd admit in the moments when he wasn't trying to be the biggest jerk in the room that you're dealing with a lot."

"I can handle it."

Sonja assessed him, her fathomless dark eyes seeming to see far more than Chase was comfortable sharing. "I recognize I'm a woman of a certain age," she began. Before he could dismiss her reference, she waved a hand. "Both my kids are now married and having children of their own. It's a good place to be, Chase. Welcoming the next generation. It makes the decisions of the prior generation seem less dire."

"Decisions?" Chase asked. "Isn't that just a nice word for sins?"

"I'll stick with decisions. But you have to know I'm right. Finding someone and settling down would go a long way toward making this—" she gestured to the room at large "—feel less all-consuming."

"I'm my own man, Sonja. My father's behavior isn't about me. And the romance dance isn't for me, either. It never has been."

It was a fact his family knew—hell, the whole office knew—and, Chase admitted, it was the excuse he gave every woman he dated. He wasn't the marrying kind. Not anymore, after surviving a divorce in his late twenties that had decimated him. He just wasn't cut out for forever with someone else. Colton Properties was his life and he liked it that way.

Besides, having a partner wouldn't have made any of the fallout from his father's secret life any easier.

Sonja looked about to argue when Chase glanced pointedly at the sideboard. They'd held back a few paces from the line to keep their conversation private, but as a spot opened up, he gestured her toward it. "Please, go ahead and refuel."

She did as he asked, obviously recognizing the space wasn't conducive to their conversation, and Chase took another moment to refocus and consider his next move. He dated and enjoyed the company of women, and that was as far as it went. His focus—his *full* focus—needed to be on business.

This staff meeting was scheduled for an hour and then he'd planned a few one-on-ones with key members of his leadership team later that afternoon to go through even more specifics. While the succession plans for him to become CEO had been in place for some time, there were still the realities of his father's will. Luckily, the early feedback from Nathan and Sarah, his half siblings, was that they had no interest in being involved in Colton Properties.

But a secret family was a big deal, and so was the passing of a company's owner, no matter how well prepared or codified the man's wishes had been. Chase had spent his life training for the day when he'd take over as CEO and he couldn't afford to lose focus or let his personal shock and grief cloud what was best for the company.

He had a room full of people depending on him.

A room that suddenly seemed to shrink as a woman rushed in, her hair flying behind her as she ran smack into him.

His first thought as he suddenly held an armful of woman was how glad he was that his coffee cup was still empty.

His second thought barely qualified as one, as sheer instinct and a shocking swell of desire hit him with the force of a wrecking ball. Full, rounded breasts pressed against his chest, the delicious scents of vanilla and almond filled his senses and the softest skin he'd ever felt filled his palms.

It was only as the woman lifted her head, her deep brown

eyes going wide, that Chase felt the first stirrings of real concern.

He could have unhanded her.

Should have stepped back and let her go.

So why was he still standing here, his arms wrapped tight around her, even though her slight frame seemed steady?

Sloan Presley reveled in the strong, muscled arms that still held her and briefly considered faking a faint to ensure he didn't let go.

Which was ridiculous in the extreme.

Ridiculous, yet deeply tempting.

A temptation she nearly succumbed to when she realized she and the tall, sexy man still wrapped around her had the full focus of a room full of interested gazes.

How had she gotten herself into this?

She mentally tallied her mess of a morning. An overnight power outage had kicked her bedside alarm out of commission so that she'd only had the clanging of her mobile from across the room. Then she'd had to clean up after her sick cat just as she was about to race out the door, already late. And then, the oddly impossible parking situation when she'd pulled up to the building in downtown Owl Creek.

She eyed the man who held her. "You don't look like Arthur Ryan, the owner of Ryan Partners Marketing."

"Who do I look like?" His green eyes crinkled at the corners and Sloan couldn't deny the man's appeal. Mischief lit up that gaze, only adding to the temptation factor, along with full lips that even now twitched with humor.

"Not the man I met on an introductory video call."

"That might be because Arthur Ryan has office space in the building next door. We share the parking lot out back.

I helped him find that space myself when his firm grew large enough to upsize."

Sloan finally found the will to extricate herself, both because those arms had grown far too comfortable and, well, *hello*. Room full of interested people watching them with collectively bated breath.

"This isn't Ryan Partners Marketing?"

Those eyes did more of that sexy crinkling. "No, ma'am, it's not."

"Which means I'm not only now monumentally late for a prospective client meeting, but I've managed to be late and directionally challenged, all with an audience."

Mr. Sexy Smile glanced at the rest of the people assembled in the room before he shrugged his broad shoulders. "Afraid so."

"This isn't happening." Sloan barely avoided the small, squeaky moan that threatened to spill out.

"Again, I'm afraid to have to tell you that it is."

"May I use a private area to make a call? I need to reach out to Arthur and make my apologies. Hopefully, he'll still agree to see me."

"Chase, why don't you let this woman use your office and give her some privacy for what will likely be a difficult call? Arthur Ryan's a tough cookie." Sloan glanced at the kind face peeping out from behind the man, a broad smile on her face. "In fact, why don't you take her there yourself."

Mr. Sexy shot a strange glance, clearly fraught with *something*, at the woman before turning his attention back to her.

"Chase, is it?"

"Chase Colton," he said and extended his hand. "And you're at my family's company. Colton Properties."

"Sloan Presley." Sloan took it, his large palm engulfing

her. Warmth ran up and down her arm as their gazes met once more, that vivid, vibrant green drawing her in. "I can see you're in the middle of something. I really am so sorry to disturb."

"Nonsense," the kind woman behind Chase chimed in once more. "We were taking a quick breakfast break. Another five minutes won't hurt anyone. Go on and make your call in Chase's office."

"Yes. My call." Sloan nodded, dropping his hand as she willed herself back into the moment. A moment where she was not just late for a client meeting, but now the object of attention for nearly two dozen people. "I need to make that."

"I'll walk you to my office."

Chase Colton gestured her back into the hallway she'd not even looked at as she'd rushed in. If she had, Sloan now realized, she'd have seen the large sign dominating the wall behind the front desk declaring that this was the office of Colton Properties.

Her hand still tingled—hell, *all* of her still tingled—as she followed him down the hallway, his long strides eating up the distance. Her initial impression of a big man was accurate, but as she took in the lines of his body, she could see that he had the firm, lean strength of a swimmer, with wide shoulders tapering down to slim hips.

And a high, firm butt that was impossible not to admire as his black slacks pulled taut against his body as he walked.

Get. It. Together.

The refrain in her head kept time with her footsteps as the two of them wove toward the back of the office. Since his last name was on that sign she'd ignored in the lobby, it would stand to reason his office was something big and cushy, overlooking Owl Creek from some wide-windowed corner of the building.

"I am sorry to interrupt your meeting."

For the first time she saw a flicker of stress underneath that warm smile. "It can keep for a few minutes. Especially since our office manager just refilled the coffee."

"Those pastries did smell good. Even in my dazed haste I could smell the gloriously distinct scents of yeast and sugar."

"We'll see that you get one on your way out."

"I didn't mean—" Sloan broke off. Did it matter? "Thank you. That's very kind."

"Of course."

He gestured toward the phone. "Feel free to make your call."

She stood there, inside the wide, cavernous office that carried all the trappings of power, yet felt strangely empty. As if the man who worked there—the man she watched even now, while also trying not to gape at just how attractive he was—was somehow absent from the place.

Like no matter how much time he spent here, it wasn't quite his.

Which, Sloan supposed, was why she was here, wasn't it?

"Mind if I close the door?"

He nodded. "Be my guest."

She was closer to the exit, so she crossed the few feet to close the thick wood door, scanning the hallway to confirm it was empty. When she heard the firm snick of the latch catching, Sloan turned back to Mr. Sexy, her gaze direct.

"Okay, Colton. I think we convinced them."

Chase watched as the slim woman standing inside his now-closed office transformed before his very eyes. The haphazard, rushed form who'd collided with him inside the office conference room, running on adrenaline and the fear she'd missed a meeting, had vanished.

In its place was a force of nature. That slim frame that looked willowy and soft grew, somehow, steel straightening her frame.

"You think so?"

"I know so. The entire room watched what was going on. You did a good job with the moony eyes, too."

For reasons he couldn't name, that stung a bit. "You did a decent job yourself."

"Just like we planned."

And they had planned it, hadn't they? In a series of calls he'd taken from his home office, on his own personal communications devices, unwilling to bring this anywhere near Colton Properties.

The calls had left him frustrated at his next move, even as he knew it was inevitable. Which was why he'd hired one Sloan Presley, founder, owner and chief hacker at Securit-Key, who'd come highly recommended by his cousin Max. Max's FBI work had put him in contact with Sloan on several different projects and she fit the bill for what Chase needed: an independent party who could do some discreet hacking into the Colton Properties network and servers to ensure no one else was doing anything nefarious.

They'd hatched the meet-cute ruse because his bachelor status was widely known around Colton Properties and, even more widely, throughout Owl Creek. He'd never been great at relationships—a fact he'd proved spectacularly with his first wife—and after divorcing he'd sworn off ever attempting marriage again. But he'd also spent his adult life being told he only needed to find the right woman to fall head over heels.

Hadn't Sonja hinted at that very point in the conference room?

Which made this the best approach to keep his questions about threats to Colton Properties under the radar. People would be so focused on the idea he'd found a girlfriend they'd have no reason to question her presence or the time she spent with him. Subterfuge, yes, but they'd never have pulled it off if he'd simply hired her as an employee.

So when Sloan had questioned him about the job and whom he was trying to avoid—and the answer to that question was basically *everyone*, family included—they'd hatched the girlfriend plot. He hated lying to his loved ones, but since the news of his father's double life, he'd come to realize there wasn't anyone he could really trust.

"So much for transparency, accountability and honesty," Chase muttered. He thought he'd said it low enough, which made Sloan's raised eyebrows that much more pointed.

"You're battling a hidden force, Chase. One who can destroy your business and all you've built. Root out that dishonesty and you can go back to running the business however you'd like."

She was right. He knew that and he knew what he had to do to preserve his company. But when had life gotten so complicated? And how, in a matter of months, had his father's betrayals changed the way he thought about his family?

Even as he recognized they had in every possible way.

He was the oldest, damn it. It was his job to look out for his siblings. To protect his mother. And now, he was staring at a life of lies, churning through every conversation he could ever remember with his father, trying to find a shred of truth.

All while the answers remained elusive.

His mother's sister, Jessie, had run off, leaving her husband and four children, vanishing as if she'd never been. His Uncle Buck and his cousins had been devastated, trying to rebuild their lives after that horrific betrayal. They'd done a decent job of it, only to find since Robert's death that Jessie was not only very much alive, but also had been living a secret life with his father and the two children they'd had.

It was mind-boggling, Chase acknowledged, with the additional layers of grief, anger and deep-seated betrayal fighting for top of the heap of the emotional damage at any given moment.

It was that fact that continued to resonate deep within him, forcing his hand with the decision to reach out to SecuritKey's owner. Sloan Presley was just what he needed. A neutral third party under a signed confidentiality agreement.

He looked at her now, still positioned on the opposite side of his office. That spine of steel hadn't wavered, but it was the rest of the woman that really drew him in. Long hair settled around her face in soft, curly waves, those compelling, deep brown eyes alert and sharp. Her skin was a pretty shade of light brown that his fingers itched to trace, her long arms drawing his gaze in the short-sleeved, conservative blouse.

There was something about the woman that was captivating.

Which was the very last thing he needed to worry about right now.

So he'd ignore those sparks of attraction and force himself to forget the feel of her when she'd been wrapped tight in his arms.

They had work to do.

"We fooled them, Chase."

"No doubt about it." He nodded. "That was an award-winning performance."

"Then let's get to work."

Chapter 2

Let's get to work.

The words still rang in his head an hour later, his staff meeting wrapped after he gave one more excuse to *help* the woman in his office, as he and Sloan mapped out a plan for the week.

He had to give the woman credit—she came prepared.

Their entire contact up to now had consisted of those calls, mostly on the phone and then the final one on video. He'd thought her competent before, but seeing her in action only ratcheted that feeling even higher.

And then there was his reaction to her beauty.

He was a man who appreciated an attractive woman, but he wasn't normally this distracted. But Sloan was...

Well, she was the whole package.

Beautiful, yes, in a way that hit a man over the head. And then there were her computer skills.

SecuritKey had come highly recommended, and he could see why. Its founder was a whiz with a computer.

He would never have called himself a digital expert, but he knew how to navigate a laptop to do his work, program basic commands in their database and navigate through spreadsheets, all in service of running a successful business.

Next to Sloan, though, he felt like a kindergartner with his first computer.

The woman had some serious skills.

"I recognize this is a difficult subject, but would you walk me through the financial implications of your father's other family?"

Chase had struggled with that himself—and based on the questions this morning, his staff were worried about the same—yet something about it coming from Sloan felt different.

Up to now, he'd felt varying levels of shame, embarrassment and the sheer lingering fury of betrayal.

But with her, it was…

Well, it was okay, somehow. And he hadn't felt that way since the discovery of his father's secret life and the half brother and half sister he hadn't known he had.

Was it because he'd hired her to do a job?

Or was it her?

In the end, Chase realized it didn't matter. What did matter was working with her to uncover the problems he suspected with the books and figure out where he had a snake in the garden of Colton Properties.

"*Financial implications* is the polite term we're using now for lying to your family for decades?"

He'd meant the comment as a joke but didn't miss how flat the words felt to his own ears.

"I'm sure this is difficult. Monumentally so. But maybe we can take a slightly different tack. One that focuses on the finances and the records instead of the more scandalous aspects."

It was funny. If anyone else had framed it quite that way, Chase wasn't so sure he wouldn't have been offended.

Scandalous aspects.

The Colton family had become the hottest scandal in Owl Creek in decades.

Yet even with that public embarrassment, Chase had to admit Sloan had a point. Because separating what was happening at Colton Properties from his personal upheaval was essential if he wanted to get underneath his very real problem.

Something improper on the books was a fact.

Records that didn't add up were facts.

Rooting out a problem that had everything to do with swindling Colton Properties and nothing to do with his father's secret life was a fact.

And facts were something he'd had precious little of for far too long.

That first horrible blow of losing a parent had been crushing. But to then realize the man he'd loved and damn near revered for thirty-six years wasn't whom he'd believed he was had been killing him these past months.

On a hard exhale, he nodded. "Okay. Focus on the financials. What can I give you to move this along?"

"Access to the books is a place to start. I can do a proper digital forensics audit on the work while also searching for irregularities."

"You can do that on spreadsheets."

Her grin was broad and the words behind it held a confidence that bordered on cocky. It was…endearing. In a way he'd never have expected.

Here was a woman who knew her worth and didn't question it.

It was impressive. And deeply fascinating.

"We're also going to need to come up with excuses for me to be here. Reasons I have to log on to the network or something I need to do for my own job."

"Lie to my staff, you mean."

"Chase." He saw real compassion in her gaze, even as her voice remained strong. Soft, but still steel-edged all the same. "We've been over that part. It's lying if you do it indefinitely. I'm one person, here in a consultant capacity, to help you ferret out a highly confidential problem. When we find the problem, you can move on to running Colton Properties exactly as you want to."

"It still feels wrong. Especially with the realities of my father's lifetime of lies."

"I wish there was another way."

Once again, Sloan was the competent voice of reason. Chase realized that if he continued hemming and hawing, he would be as much a problem and an impediment to her investigation as the person attempting to swindle the company.

He sighed and looked up at her. "I'm usually far more decisive than this."

"You're grieving. I'd be a bit surprised and—" She broke off, seeming to pull herself up short.

"You'd be surprised at what?"

She shook her head, her mouth a grim line. "I'm sorry. I speak my mind far too quickly."

"I'd like to hear it."

Once again, her gaze was direct when she spoke, even if the words came a bit slowly. "To be honest, I'd be disappointed if you weren't struggling a bit. I'm deeply sorry you're going through this, but you're human. You're entitled to a range of emotions and feelings that don't all line up like numbers on a balance sheet."

"I thought the numbers on my balance sheet were the problem."

This joke hit far better than his earlier one and Chase

felt a small moment of triumph when that thin line of her mouth turned up into a wide smile.

"Touché."

"But thank you. I've spent my life being the decisive one, especially as the oldest child. My job here at Colton Properties has only reinforced that."

"Then that means your faith has been shaken the hardest by your father's actions."

For someone who spent her life staring at a computer screen, Sloan Presley was pretty damn perceptive.

And once again, Chase was right back to that list of attributes in his mind he seemed unable to stop thinking about for long.

Yes, she was beautiful. But that beauty was matched by an inner calm and serenity, and a level of *understanding*, he'd really never seen before. Or certainly not in someone so young. He didn't know her exact age, but at thirty-six himself, he figured he had at least six years on her, if not more.

Was she even thirty yet?

And did it really matter?

He wasn't dating her. And the fact that his mind kept veering back to attraction had no place in this discussion at all. The only reason they'd even hatched the dating angle was to have a reason for her to come and go in the office without anyone being the wiser.

And yet…

He kept circling around that simmering level of attraction, anyway.

On his part at least.

Since he had far bigger issues, he'd better start focusing on the task at hand and off the very beautiful Sloan Presley.

The future of Colton Properties depended on it.

*   *   *

What was she thinking?

Chase's calm attitude and his even tone as they spoke of his business seemed to have seen them through that awkward moment, but Sloan couldn't help but wonder what had possibly gotten into her.

She *never* told a client what she actually thought.

Hell, she never told *anyone* what she actually thought of their behavior.

People claimed they wanted honesty, but no one truly did. They wanted a sanitized version of their behavior that was fed back to them, reinforcing all the things they wanted to hear.

Not what they actually needed to be told.

Wasn't that why she had a job?

Human beings were capable of any number of things and her ability to ferret out those things—especially the bad things—was why she had a successful business.

They'd moved past those difficult moments when she'd analyzed the impact of his father's death and moved right on to the files she'd ultimately need to review on the business. Chase Colton was the height of professionalism and accountability as they worked through a quick list of needs and how they'd go about setting her up to review the files.

"I pulled down a few files just to give you a sense of the business. We're privately held but still create the equivalent of an annual report for our records and to share with any potential investors on projects. I've also downloaded the monthly spreadsheets I work off with Finance. We do a soft close each month and then a formal close at the end of the quarter."

It was impressive, Sloan thought, as he walked her through the various aspects of the business. Although privately held, as CEO he ran Colton Properties like a publicly held business. The files were designed to show proper reporting on the work, their investments and overall cash flow in and out of the company.

She was anxious to dig in to those monthly reports. No matter how well someone thought they had hidden their activity in the books, the month-by-month review would give her a strong sense of where to look.

"That's a really good start. I'll begin there and then let you know what else I might need."

"Of course. I've got the files already downloaded for you." He got up and crossed to his desk, then pulled a small drive out of his desk drawer. When he returned to her, he didn't sit down again, even as he handed over the drive. "So we should probably work out the fake dating part of this, too. We'll need to be seen around town a few times."

Sloan took the thumb drive, tucking it away into a small pouch she kept in her bag for work. It gave her the small moment of normalcy she needed as she considered how to play this.

Yes, the idea of posing as a couple had made sense when they'd hatched it in their planning meetings.

But now?

Seeing Chase Colton in person and realizing the man was far more attractive than even their brief video call suggested—it was a bit like having her brains scrambled.

She'd done her research, as she would for any other job, but nothing had fully prepared her for the impact of Chase Colton in the flesh.

The man had a lethal sort of intelligence that, coupled with those amazing green eyes and that broad-shouldered swimmer's build, was…well, it was sort of devastating.

Which was a serious problem seeing as how they were

going to be playacting a romantic relationship for the next few weeks.

It was a new business strategy for her—she'd never even considered it before—and now that she'd committed to it, she had to be all in.

But ever since she'd barreled into the Colton Properties conference room, Sloan had been wondering what, exactly, she'd gotten herself into.

Or why a fake dating ruse had seemed like a good idea when they'd come up with it on their last call.

"Where do you normally take your dates?"

It was a casual question, and it matched his prompt perfectly. Yet even as she asked it, Sloan felt the heat creeping up her neck.

"I have a few favorite restaurants. But there is another problem. I should have given it more thought but the talk today in the conference room made me realize I might have made a bit of an oversight."

She'd spent precious little time getting to know Chase, between their calls and now this morning's face-to-face, but she hadn't gotten the sense this was a man who didn't think through every situation in fine detail.

So his admission was something of a surprise.

"What type of oversight?"

"If we're seen for any length of time, and, based on your estimates this is going to take a few weeks, my family is going to want to meet you."

"Oh."

The Colton *family*? As in all of them?

She already knew he was one of six children who were the biological offspring of Robert and Jenny Colton. Then there were the two additional children from his father's secret life.

Whatever she'd been bracing for, the revelation that she would need to meet his family wasn't it.

"Isn't that a lot of people?"

"More and more every day." Chase grinned and she couldn't help but respond in kind.

"I thought your half siblings were sensitive ground."

His smile softened, a clear ability to add a bit of self-deprecating humor going a long way to make those god-like features seem a bit more human.

"Yeah, it is sensitive. But a few laughs can't make it any worse."

"No, I suppose not."

"But to your question, we *are* sort of a lot when we get together. There are my five siblings, and three of them have new significant others in their lives. And then, there are my four cousins. And now, there's Nathan and Sarah, who have sort of kept their distance but who are part of all this, too. And since we're getting to know them, leaving them out seems wrong, somehow."

"Of course, it is."

"They're half siblings to all of us."

"You gave me a sense of the situation on the phone, and I also know your cousin Max, but when you say 'all of us,' what do you mean?"

"My Uncle Buck and Aunt Jessie had four kids."

"But your Aunt Jessie is the mother of Nathan and Sarah?"

"Yep. She's also my mother's sister."

Sloan's head spun with the implications of it all. Two families that then crossed and created even more family.

She didn't want to judge.

Not only wasn't it her place, but she'd also learned a long time ago that people had precious little control of three things in life: what others thought of them, what others expected of them and what their family members did of their own accord.

And still, the emotional implications of all Chase and his siblings and cousins had learned in the past few months was staggering.

"Did your cousins know their mother was alive?"

Of all the various aspects of Chase and his family's situation, that aspect somehow seemed the most cruel.

"They knew she was alive but when she left my Uncle Buck it was like she divorced her children, too. She never came back or showed support for them in any way. She sent flowers for her mother and father's funerals when each passed, but that was all anyone heard from her."

"How terrible."

Sloan knew Chase's cousin, Max Colton, from the work she'd done over the years for the FBI. He'd recommended her to Chase for this job and she now thought about the man she'd worked with off and on through the years. Stoic and singularly focused on his work, he wasn't one to let his emotions show.

Had that been because he felt abandoned by his mother all those years ago?

And if that built a person's frame of reference for life, how much worse would it be to discover they'd not only abandoned you, but also gone on to make a new family?

Her own upbringing had been quiet at times, but good. She was an only child, so life was about the three of them, just her and her parents. Her Portuguese mother had come to Chicago on a nanny assignment and met her father a few months after coming to the US. They'd courted and fallen in love and her mother had never gone back to Portugal.

But she and her family had visited Europe through the years and many summers her relatives had come to them.

Add on the large family her father came from and Sloan had always felt she'd been given the best of both worlds. A solid, warm, supportive upbringing and deep roots in her extended family that ensured she was never alone.

She'd always been something of an outlier in her Chicago neighborhood growing up, with her Portuguese mother and Black father, but when she was with her large families on both sides, she was always welcomed.

Always loved.

And she'd always known who she was.

How awful would it be to have that all taken from you? Upended in a way that those roots you'd believed so strong and firm were revealed to be resting in very shallow ground.

Sloan was a difficult woman to read, but Chase could only imagine what was going through her mind at the complexities of his messed-up family. Even as those musings lingered, he also sensed she was professional enough to find a way forward.

It was his nature to believe things would work out.

Hadn't he done that after his divorce?

He'd married Leanne because he'd believed they were in love. And it had turned his life upside down to find out that he'd been the only one in the relationship who felt that way. His wife had been far more enamored with his standing in Owl Creek and his last name than actually building a life and a family together.

In the end, he'd seen her for what she was. Too late to have avoided a wedding and an expensive divorce payout, but soon enough that they hadn't brought children into the world.

For that small benefit, he counted himself lucky.

The children they'd never created even luckier.

"The files you gave me should keep me busy."

Sloan's words interrupted his maudlin thoughts and Chase pulled himself back to the here and now. He still had that lunch to get to and needed to get her out of his office so they didn't arouse so much interest that their burgeoning fake romance wouldn't be believable.

"That's good. And, um—" He broke off, not sure why the sudden attack of nerves. "Let me walk you out and when we're in the lobby I'll make an offer for dinner."

"That's a good plan. I'll get my dazzled face on."

He thought she was pretty dazzling just the way she was but held off saying anything. He wasn't a man who did relationships—Leanne had ensured that—and he wasn't about to start now.

So it was time to compartmentalize how attractive he found Sloan Presley and concentrate on her real reason for being here: the rat inside Colton Properties who was stealing from his business.

"There is something I've been meaning to ask you."

Sloan had already stood and was settling her laptop into an oversize shoulder bag. "Of course."

"You did a really good job of coming off as frazzled and late this morning."

"That's because that part wasn't an act."

They had given each other minimal prompts on how they'd set up their meeting, both deciding it would be better to let it play out, but even he hadn't been able to dismiss how real their faked meeting had felt in the conference room.

"What was it?"

"A result of a sick cat and impossible-to-find parking in your lot downstairs."

"It was damned convincing."

"I'll remember that next time I'm cleaning up cat vomit."

"My sister Ruby is a vet. If you need anything, I can hook you up."

"Thanks. I think Waffles was just letting me know he wasn't crazy about our new digs, but if he doesn't settle I'll be sure to get her number."

It was one more layer of involvement between Sloan and his family but he hated to think of any animal sick. And if his sister found out there was a distressed animal in a hundred-mile radius of her, she'd hunt it down until she found it and nursed it back to health.

Since Sloan's bag was packed and already on her shoulder, Chase had to admit he'd stalled long enough. "Let me walk you out then."

The hallway looked the same as it had a half hour ago.

So why did it feel so different?

The carpet was the same. So were the tasteful art pieces on the walls and in a few carved-out niches along the corridor.

And yet...

He was different.

He'd walked Sloan down to his office with the intent to deceive. While it was a means to an important end, that reality had stuck a hard layer of guilt in his gut all the same.

Now, as he walked her to the front of the lobby, preparing to invite her to dinner, he realized something far more important had happened in the ensuing time in his office.

The guilt had faded in the face of the reality of their plan. Her expertise and her commitment to ferreting out a problem had helped him realize this really was the only way.

Yet something new had taken up root in his gut.

He was no longer worried about Colton Properties, or

what his employees ultimately thought of his tactics to protect his business.

He was far more concerned he'd been deceiving himself.

Because no matter how he played out the ruse in his mind, Sloan Presley would be walking out that door for good once she solved the problems in his company.

And he was increasingly convinced he wasn't ever going to be the same man who'd welcomed her in.

Chapter 3

Sloan tapped a few keys and set up a small algorithm to run on one machine while she opened a browser window on another.

She'd done some research before taking the job—her standard background checks and basic vetting of her potential employer—but she hadn't done a real deep dive into the Colton family.

It was time to do that now.

Chase had been pretty forthcoming in his comments, so she hadn't walked out of his office thinking that he'd been holding back, but there were some things that would be easier to find on her own.

Even now, she could remember those layers of grief, anger and bewilderment that clouded his green gaze. They pulled at her, drawing on something she wouldn't have expected.

A not-so-subtle tug of emotion that she couldn't afford.

She was invested in this case, yes. But those emotions also left her with a concern that she was getting far too personally involved in the work.

The whole fake-dating ploy was a risk. One she'd believed herself able to handle, but now that she'd spent time in Chase Colton's company, she had to admit she might be a wee bit in over her head.

Could she handle it?

Again, *yes*.

But she'd prefer to feel no further tugs or feelings or *emotions*.

She was the investigator here, nothing more.

Which was why she was doing some digging on her own. Once she had those details, she could better frame her questions to Chase, avoiding asking about areas that were open-ended or left room for him to feel his way through the answers.

The man was still grieving his father, after all. More, he was grieving the loss of a life that would never be the same again.

In the moments when she wasn't actually thinking about the man, she'd focused on those changes. For reasons she couldn't explain, she sensed there was something in that distinction that mattered.

And if she could help Chase work through some of that grief—the portion that was wrapped around the aspects of his father's life he'd never known—she'd go a long way toward helping him through this time in his life.

Fanciful?

Yes, she admitted with a sigh.

She wasn't a person given to flights of fancy, so it was odd to realize how important this assignment had become to her.

And how quickly she'd become consumed by it.

But similar to the thoughts she'd had in his office earlier, something about this situation with the Colton family haunted her.

The idea of a mother leaving her children to go and have another family.

With her sister's husband, no less.

It truly boggled, that level of…well, selfishness.

Wasn't it?

Her children weren't at fault, but in so many ways she'd abdicated her responsibilities as a mother. Robert Colton had relinquished his duties, too.

Secret lives.

A secret family.

All wrapped up in a secret love.

Why do that?

If someone was truly in love with another, why not just leave your current circumstances and forge a new path?

Yes, it would be hard, but it would be a grief with purpose. And an endgame, of sorts.

Because these…well, these *lies* Chase and his siblings and cousins were dealing with now were far, far worse.

It was part of what always both amazed and comforted her about data. Data didn't lie. Numbers were numbers and they always added up.

But human emotions?

They were scattered and selfish for some. Profoundly felt and fathoms deep for others.

Waffles strolled into her home office, his tail switching. The little tuxedo cat had found his way to the doorstep of her apartment in Chicago about a year ago. After a quick internet consultation on how to handle a stray, she'd given him some water and can of tuna. The fish must have seemed a feast because he'd stayed, and after getting him checked out by a vet a few days later, Sloan had become the proud owner of a cat.

It had been a novel experience and she was pleased to see whatever had agitated his stomach this morning was long gone as he rubbed himself against her legs.

"You inadvertently added to my cover this morning,

young man." She scratched beneath the chin he'd lifted for her. "So I thank you for that, even as I'm very glad you're on the mend."

Waffles purred under her touch and seemed oblivious to her worry over his health, or her gratitude.

Such a simple response, Sloan mused as she lifted him onto her lap. No emotion necessary. No lies. Just a sort of simple existence, day to day.

For all their seeming evolution, humans found it far more challenging to live in the moment.

As she gently brushed long, full strokes over his back, she continued clicking around a search window for more information on the Colton family.

The same details on Colton Properties came up threaded through the results, but since she'd already been through those, she focused instead on the ones that detailed the family.

Owl Creek, Idaho, was a small town, about two hours away from Boise, but Robert Colton had had a vision for the place. A respite from the city and a place to vacation and get away. The area was rich with water sports in summer, the main lake in town wide, deep and full of options. In winter, they weren't far from ski resorts that offered cross-country skiing, snowmobiling and tubing down snow-covered slopes.

He'd obviously played on the same sorts of wide-open offerings that had made Jackson Hole in Wyoming and Bend in Oregon so appealing. And by all accounts, Robert had succeeded. Owl Creek had grown in reputation, with more and more visitors every year for the past two decades.

For a man with that sort of vision and focus, how hard would it be to add on not just the demands of one family, but two?

She clicked into an article that was more than a decade old, coming across a picture of Robert and Chase, standing side by side in the very conference room she'd stumbled into that morning.

The resemblance between father and son was evident, even as Robert's body had softened with age. She gave herself a moment to study Chase, his broad smile and even broader frame suggesting a sort of comfortable competence and raw strength. What she saw, though, was something even more profound when it was matched with the ensuing interview beneath the photo.

Chase's smile was proud, but it was his words that really struck her. About all he and his father had planned and envisioned for the future of Colton Properties. It spoke of an excitement for the work and what lay ahead.

With the passage of time and the revelation of secrets, Sloan now knew the man who stood proudly beside his son, echoing his words in the article about their grand, ambitious future, was hiding secrets.

From his son.

From his family.

From everyone.

Chase handed over his credit card as he ordered a Scotch on the rocks for himself and a tequila-and-soda for his cousin Max. They'd agreed to meet and Max's text that he'd pulled into the parking lot had ensured his drink would be ready when he sat down.

The bar was relatively new in Owl Creek, established the year before and quickly becoming a favorite of the young professionals in the area. As a real-estate man, Chase liked the town's newest entertainment offering. As a frustrated amateur detective, he liked the atmosphere even more for the low lighting and ability to have a private conversation.

Just what he needed for this meeting with Max.

His cousin walked in just as the bartender placed their drinks on the bar and Max gave him a small wave as he headed in from the front door.

Chase stood to give his cousin a quick hug and a hearty slap on the back.

"You're looking good, cuz."

Max smiled, that quick, flashing grin at odds with the lingering grief Chase knew the man carried, just like him. "What can I say? Life with Della agrees with me."

It certainly did.

Max's work hunting serial killers for the FBI had put him in contact with K-9 tracker Della Winslow the month before. Her skills were extraordinary, and it was her search-and-tracking work with her K-9, Charlie, that had led to the discovery of several dead bodies in the mountainous area not too far from Owl Creek.

The work had been dark and rather grisly, but Della had held up under the pressure. Even though the last body discovered had belonged to her cousin, Angela Baxter. Max had gone all-in on the case, determined to get answers, but ultimately decided his career hunting for depraved murderers had run its course.

Especially after he and Della realized they had feelings for each other.

Chase had always admired his cousin's dedication, but it was only now, when he saw a lightness in the man he hadn't seen for years, that he realized the real toll that work had taken on Max.

He was damn glad the man had decided to move on.

"Love and retirement from the Bureau look good on you."

"Everything's different. I can't believe just how different—" Max took a sip of his drink "—but I'm not questioning it."

"I appreciate you taking the time to talk to me."

"I wanted to hear how things were working out with SecuritKey and, well…" Max put down his glass, wiping a small bit of moisture from the lip. "We've all been through a lot these past few months. Your dad dying. Finding out he and my mom had a family. Meeting Nate and Sarah. It's…" Max trailed off, before seeming to regain his voice. "It's a lot."

Hadn't Chase said something similar to Sloan just earlier?

What he, his siblings and his cousins had all dealt with was more than Chase could have ever imagined, but he'd also gained enough perspective to realize that it couldn't have been any easier for Nate and Sarah. They might be viewing the situation from the opposite perspective, but it wasn't really any better, knowing their parents had kept such a huge secret from them, too.

"We both know what each other's going through, Chase. And if there's anything I've learned, especially after finding those bodies of the young women who will never get a chance to live their lives to the fullest, it's that we need to support each other."

"I keep thinking I'm going to wake up. That this is just some strange, extended dream and it'll all be over." Chase took a sip of his own drink. "But it's like, surprise! You're wide-awake, pal."

"It helps that Nate and Sarah are so great."

"Yeah, they are. And I want to give that a chance. A real chance. They're brother and sister to us all. And they're no more responsible for this weird situation than any of us are."

"No. You can lay that squarely at the feet of our parents."

Chase stared into his drink, seeking some semblance of wisdom from the amber liquid, even as he knew that was as futile as wishing his father had been a different man.

"You think it'll ever get easier?"

"Yeah, I do." Max nodded, his gaze thoughtful. "Finding Della and talking to her about it all has helped. But more—" He broke off, that wide grin once again spreading across his face. "She's made all the difference, somehow. Even though I know I have to put in the emotional work and find a way through this, it's better." He shrugged. "Not easier, but somehow smoother that there's someone there with me. And I'm grateful for it. Damn grateful."

Unbidden, an image of Sloan from that morning in his office rose up in Chase's mind.

To be honest, I'd be disappointed if you weren't struggling a bit. I'm deeply sorry you're going through this, but you're human. You're entitled to a range of emotions and feelings that don't all line up like numbers on a balance sheet.

She'd been so honest and, even more, she'd been fair. To him. His emotions. And all that was swirling in his heart, his mind and his gut.

To a point, he'd recognized she was a bit embarrassed by it, but she'd risked the words, anyway. And with that risk, Chase realized, he'd taken her words to heart. He'd felt better that she'd acknowledged he didn't have to be some automaton, pushing his way through the situation without care or regard for the pain.

"I'm happy for you." Chase raised his glass, clinking it in a light toast with his cousin. "For you both."

Max took a sip of his drink, the smile clearing as he settled into the conversation. "Tell me what you think about Sloan Presley."

"The woman's sharp. Smart. And I think exactly what I need to do the digital-forensics work at Colton Properties."

"You worried there are more irregularities than you first thought?"

Max's FBI work and their close, lifelong relationship had made him the one person Chase had trusted to discuss what was going on at Colton Properties. It wasn't that he couldn't tell his siblings, but he didn't want to panic anyone. And with a family his size, he couldn't risk someone potentially saying something, even in passing.

So Max was the only one who knew he was concerned about the financials.

And once Chase had answers, he'd share all he'd learned and come clean with everyone.

"I think I want Sloan to scour everything top to bottom and tell me what she sees. I'm too close to it all. Which is why I know something's off but can't decipher exactly what."

"She's the best. Her company only takes jobs through referrals and still has a shocking amount of work, all the time. That's how good she is."

"Good is what I need."

Max's gaze was sharp, speculative and even as he asked, "How are you playing it for the office?"

"She's my unexpected and brand-new girlfriend."

Max's eyes widened as he let out a low whistle. "No kidding!"

"We hatched the plan as we worked through the details of what needs to be done. It's the only way we can get her in and out of the office with an easy reason for being there."

"You do realize the irony in it all?"

"Irony?" Chase wasn't sure where Max was going, but the man's pointed smile had him immediately curious.

"You're the great bachelor of Owl Creek. Surely you can see the joke in all this."

"I'm a divorced man. That hardly makes me a bachelor."

"You're wealthy, single and you never date a woman more than twice in a row. Trust me, people notice that." Max leaned over and patted Chase on the back before signaling their bartender for one more drink. "And you're the one who needs a fake girlfriend to get underneath the problems at your business."

Chase wasn't sure he saw Max's humor with regard to his current situation. His cousin's words haunted him long after they'd wrapped up their second drink and their conversation.

He'd walked back to the office with the intention of getting a bit of work done, but after an hour of staring at his computer screen and intermittently checking sports scores online, he decided to call it a night.

As a man used to work and action, this strange, lingering malaise he hadn't been able to fully get rid of since his father's death had been endlessly confusing.

You're entitled to a range of emotions and feelings...

Again, Sloan's quiet and compassionate diagnosis was front and center in his mind.

He wasn't one who gave in to his softer feelings. Hadn't he even taken pride that he'd focused on work all the way through his separation and the months that came after as he and his ex-wife wrangled over the dissolution of their marriage?

Divorcing Leanne had been the worst time in his life. Or had been, until this situation with his father and the man's secret family. Chase hadn't gone into marriage expecting he'd end it two years later, but his wife hadn't been who he thought she was.

The woman he'd believed himself in love with had revealed herself to be a grasping, unfaithful partner, and after discovering her affair—what had been revealed to be one of many—he'd walked away.

Was that part of his problem with his father?

His bad marriage aside, his father's death and the revelation of his secret life would have been a horrible experience, regardless. But to add on his experience with Leanne?

Was he that poor a judge of character?

Did he see what he wanted to see instead of what was?

Was there anyone he could trust?

Those thoughts had swirled these past few months, stealthily creeping in at odd moments. He'd tried to ignore them, but the questions were there all the same.

More, the self-doubt had become crushing at times.

Add on the problems at Colton Properties and Chase had been forced to reconsider his ability to properly assess those around him.

It's why you've hired Sloan.

He mentally shook his head as he shut down his computer. It was why he'd hired SecuritKey.

He had to stop thinking of this job through the lens of the woman and start thinking of it through the work she did. He'd hired her for her skills.

Even if he found himself continually imagining the soft sweep of curls she'd brushed behind her ear, or those sharp, fathomless brown eyes.

Which was how he found himself ten minutes later heading across town to the apartment complex where she was renting a small one-bedroom.

He'd suggested the location himself, the reality of needing her close by in Owl Creek for the duration of the job ensuring she'd be too far away to stay at her own home in Chicago.

The apartment complex was only a few years old and had been another expansion in town directed by Colton Properties. The location boasted long-term rentals as well as a handful of furnished, short-term options for those who wanted a place to stay in Owl Creek longer than a hotel stay.

He'd pushed for the short-term options with the property owner, helping the man round out his vision of what his investment could truly become.

As he turned into the complex's entrance, Chase was happy to see the place looked well-kept, and its parking lot was full.

"You might suck at reading people, Colton, but you've got damn good instincts for real estate," he said to himself.

Brimming with that subtle sense of satisfaction, he got out of his car and headed for the building that housed Sloan's apartment. Windows were open and he heard the strains of oldies music pumping into the air.

Instinctively, he knew the sound of Chuck Berry was coming from Sloan's place and at the same time, he recognized how the music fit her.

She was an old soul.

One with knowledge and understanding layered through her words and actions.

He walked up the exterior concrete steps to the second floor and knocked on her door. The music was louder now that he stood outside her apartment, and he knocked again. When the knocking still went unheeded, he waited for the last strains of Chuck's voice to wane before pounding on the door a third time.

Only to hear the rushing of feet before a bemused Sloan stood on the other side of the open door.

"Chase. Hi."

"Hey. Am I bothering you?"

"Sorry, no." She shook her head, before stepping back to gesture him in. "I was working and had the music turned up a little loud. Were you out here long?"

"Just a few rounds of knocking."

"I'm sorry."

Chuck Berry's rocking voice gave way to the familiar strains of Ritchie Valens's guitar and she raced across the room to snap off a high-end portable stereo with built-in speakers.

The room quieted immediately and Chase could only smile. "I would have pegged you for Madonna. Maybe Janet Jackson or Pink."

"Oh, when the mood strikes I can definitely get into the groove. I was feeling the fifties tonight."

"Old-school."

"Definitely."

They both stood there. He knew it should have felt awkward, but instead it just felt…right.

Complete, somehow, to be here with her at the end of the day.

Since that only reinforced his earlier inward admissions that he needed to get his fanciful thoughts *off* Sloan Presley, Chase pointed to the couch. "Mind if I sit?"

"Sure. Can I get you anything?"

"No, I'm good. I met up with my cousin Max for a few drinks."

Sloan brightened at the reference to his cousin. "How is he?"

"He's good. He's left the FBI, you know."

"I'd heard rumblings from a mutual friend but wasn't sure if it was rumors or fact. That's a big change."

"A good one, I think." Chase thought about the happy man who'd sat opposite him in the bar. "Hunting serial killers is grisly work."

"It's terrible work. Necessary, but terrible." Sloan shuddered. "I think his calling was admirable, but it must be soul-sucking."

Chase had often thought the same, and even in the very short time Max had been away from it, he'd seen a difference in his cousin.

A welcome one that reduced the unceasing shadows he'd always seen in Max's eyes.

"I agree, which is what makes it great to see him so happy."

"That same friend who'd shared those rumblings was more descriptive about Max's last case. Those murders are awful."

Chase didn't know much more than what had been shared in the news—none of them seemed to—but the case had definitely captured local attention. Max, with Della and her K-9's help, had uncovered the bodies of seven dead women the prior month. An eighth victim had escaped and been placed in protective custody as she healed in the hospital, but a blackout had left her vulnerable to an attacker, who'd killed her.

Max had killed that man, but they hadn't been able to get any more details about the murders or why that woman had been targeted, either.

"The extensive loss of life has been a shock."

"Rumors say it's that strange Ever After Church." Sloan visibly shuddered. "Though *church* feels like a bad term for them."

"You know of them?"

"I did a bit of research after you emailed me, saying Max was our connection. I've spent my entire adult life looking into the weird, unexpected and flat-out off. Heck, I've made a career out of that work."

Sloan's comment hung there and Chase picked up on it. "Yeah?"

"Anything I've tried to dig up on them? It's all strange and oddly bucolic on the surface, yet feels deeply false at the same time."

"Max certainly thought so."

"I keep wondering why no one has followed the money because something's definitely not right there. Their nomadic lifestyle. Those bodies that were discovered. And then that poor woman in the hospital?" Sloan looked thoughtful as her cat jumped onto her lap, and she absently ran a hand down his back. "I know it's wrong to assign blame until actually proven guilty, but something isn't right with that group."

Chase considered Sloan's comments and once again recognized just how skilled the woman was. Her success at her work went far deeper than her computer skills, which were obviously expert.

But she had sharp instincts, too, and that couldn't be dismissed as anything other than a key part of her success.

Suddenly coming back to herself, she grinned over the top of her now-purring cat.

"Sorry. I got lost in my head there for a moment."

"I was just thinking it was an impressive skill." When her deep brown eyes warmed, Chase continued on. "You're observant and aware. Obviously, you know your way around computer code, but I think you've been successful because you apply considerable smarts over that."

"Oh." Her hand fumbled against the cat's fur before she lifted her gaze to his. "Why, thank you."

"You're welcome."

"I—" She broke off, then muttered, "What the hell?"

Intrigued, Chase avoided saying anything, giving her the room to continue.

"Most people find my curiosity annoying."

"You mean your intelligence," Chase corrected.

"I meant curiosity, but we can add on intelligence if you'd like."

"Let's add it."

She stilled for a moment, her hand settling on the cat's back, before she continued on. "I learned early that people don't like all the tech talk. They come to me when they want their computer fixed or are having some issue with a file, but no one loves the idea I can dig into databases and find information."

"Sounds like their problem."

"Maybe yes, maybe no. We live in a digital world and someone who can dissect all those ones and zeroes is threatening."

"To people burying something nefarious in those ones and zeroes, maybe." Chase shrugged. "I still say it's their problem. One of their own making, too."

"Yes, well, most men, well, really all men," she amended, her brow crunching into the cutest frown lines. "What I do is seen as aggressive, for some reason. And each time I've shared my business and my work with a man, he's gone running."

"Sounds like you've had some really crummy dates in the past."

"Are you being deliberately obtuse?"

"I'm processing what you're saying and discarding it as loads of BS that has been heaped on you."

"It's not a skill people appreciate."

"I appreciate your skills. In fact…" Chase shifted to the edge of the couch, leaning forward to look into her eyes.

"*In fact* what?"

The slightest catch in her breath warmed him clear through and Chase felt the air around them ignite.

"I appreciate them so much I've invited you into my home and my work to help me get to the bottom of my little professional problem."

"I'm here to help."

Chase sat back, suddenly realizing how effortlessly she drew him to her. "I appreciate it more than I can say."

It was so simple to sit here with her.

To breathe the same air and talk about the day. He'd shared more of his life with her in less than twenty-four hours than he'd shared with most people of his acquaintance for the past year.

Even knowing there was nothing at the end of their time together other than a disappointing revelation about someone he presumably trusted, he couldn't seem to keep his mind on that fact.

Because he was more intrigued by Sloan Presley than he could have ever imagined.

Chapter 4

It had been close.

No, *they* had been close, Sloan amended to herself as she got into her car to drive over to Colton Properties, just as she'd corrected herself all morning.

They.

With their heads bent together in her living room, Chase's compelling green gaze had drawn her to him like a lodestone.

He'd been the quintessential gentleman, checking on her, asking how she was settling in and talking with her about his visit with his cousin.

She'd felt…connected.

And he'd complimented her with one of the nicest things anyone had ever said to her, she thought as she turned onto the main road that would take her into downtown Owl Creek.

While she was deeply appreciative of her own gifts as a human being—and valued what others brought to bear as well—her intelligence had often alienated people. Never intentionally, but the distance had been there all the same, especially when it came to dating and discussing her career with the men she was seeing.

It was never overtly mentioned, but any enthusiasm she

brought to discussing her work was typically met with polite smiles and blank stares. So she'd learned to push it
down and suppress it, recognizing that what interested her
and drove her wasn't get-to-know-you date conversation.

Yet with Chase, she not only didn't have to do that, but he
also seemed to celebrate her professional accomplishments.

Not that they were dating.

Sloan shook off that thought.

Firmly.

They were *fake* dating and that was an entirely different
matter.

Those confused yet utterly pleasing thoughts had rattled through Sloan's mind all morning, as she ran around
the small reservoir in the center of her apartment complex.

They had vexed her as she'd come back and fed Waffles
and made herself coffee and oatmeal.

And they'd haunted her as she'd showered and gotten
ready, slipping into business attire for her trip to Colton
Properties.

She was not a woman who got rattled, vexed *or* haunted,
so it was all a novel experience.

"Just a little fanciful moment, that's all. And why not,
with the change in time zones and living space and the job
to be done?" she asked herself as she checked her reflection
in the rear view mirror and used the moment as an abstract
sort of pep talk. "Your body clock is upside down and this
job is important to you. That's all it was."

Satisfied she'd finally explained it away, she grabbed
her work bag, got out and locked her car, and headed for
the building that housed Colton Properties.

In spite of the ruse they'd concocted to have their "meet
cute," Sloan had legitimately been running late to the meeting because of Waffles's unceremonious delivery of his

breakfast back to her. So she gave herself a few more moments this morning to catch her breath, all while taking in her surroundings.

Owl Creek really was beautiful. She'd never been to Idaho before this job and while she knew the weather would turn cold before long, September had a lot going for it. The morning breeze was fresh, and the sky was a vivid blue that made Sloan think of endless possibilities.

She'd been intrigued by this job. Although Colton Properties was smaller in scale and scope than the clients she usually took on, the business had real promise. And the change of pace from her usual workload was a plus. She'd recently worked a string of government contracts that, to borrow a description she'd used the night before, had been soul-sucking.

There had been several money-laundering jobs, drug trafficking and, most recently, a human-trafficking case that still managed to give her nightmares.

The opportunity to get out of Chicago for a few weeks and do some work that was decidedly less fraught with human suffering had been appealing when she'd gotten Chase's outreach email.

It had been humbling to realize that even with the more streamlined, business-focused work, there was still a fair amount of suffering. The Colton family was going through a real trial, and she was oddly glad she was here.

She might not be able to change Chase's personal situation for the better, but she could solve his business problem for him. And somewhere down deep she felt that the work mattered extra, somehow, because of it.

"There really is something to be said for all that clean mountain air."

She whirled at the voice, only to come face-to-face with Chase.

Had she conjured him up?

Quickly regrouping, Sloan fought for something to say, even as she could still feel his liquid gaze from the night before and those intense moments of closeness they'd shared.

"I haven't seen any mountains."

"Owl Creek is less mountainous than other parts of the state, but overall we can rock the fresh mountain air with the best of them. There are over three thousand mountains in Idaho, with the highest being Borah Peak at over twelve thousand feet."

"Wow." She considered what she'd read before coming. "The northern Rockies come through Idaho, yes?"

"Yep, on their northward climb to Canada. Which means we've got great ski weather in the winter and fantastic trails in the summer." Chase grinned, the look boyish and appealing in the bright morning sun. "And I sound like a walking advertisement for the tourist board."

"You sound like a man who knows where he lives and knows how to sell it."

He shrugged before gesturing her forward. "I'll take it."

They walked across the parking lot toward the building, and she scrambled for something to say. "I'm a little early but I wanted to get started."

Chase pulled the door open for her, his gaze appreciative. "I'd say you're right on time."

It was only a reference to her arrival, yet as she stared up at him before crossing the threshold, Sloan couldn't help feeling his words meant so much more.

Why did this all feel so right?

While that inward sense would radiate out to others and

help keep their dating ruse intact, she knew well enough to realize these thoughts were dangerous.

This was a job.

There wasn't room for it to feel *right* or *wrong*—she just had to do the work she was being paid for.

With that sobering thought, she moved through the lobby and headed for the elevators that led to Chase's floor.

If he sensed her lack of equilibrium this morning, he didn't mention it, instead following her and holding the elevator doors as she stepped in. After the doors swooshed closed and they were ensconced in a small moment of privacy, he finally spoke.

"I can set you up in my office and give you the access you need into the systems. I think you should work off of my extra laptop so it looks like you're doing your own work, but you can access files through my log-in."

"You don't mind? That's still your personal workstation."

He shrugged but the ease that had carried him into the building had vanished.

"I don't have anything to hide. And I'm committed to finding the person who does."

"That will make it a bit easier for me to get in, especially initially. I can clone your access points and transfer over to my machine without IT being any wiser if you're okay with that, too?" Despite his complete lack of response to that offer, Sloan rushed on. "I can show you exactly what I've done and then show you how I'm removing it from my workstation when we close this job."

"I trust your work, Sloan. You've been clear about the skills you bring to this and I need your services. Do what you need to do."

And there it was again.

That endorsement of her and her work that held nothing back. No conditions and no excuses.

And maybe even better, that saw those parts of her as something to be trusted.

Chase couldn't explain it to himself, but something about Sloan Presley made him feel calm.

Centered.

And *interested*, despite all his better judgments.

Even as all that interest kept his senses heightened and his awareness of her became something he hadn't experienced in…well, ever.

He'd loved Leanne, that hadn't been a sham. They'd dated and when they'd connected quickly, he'd continued to press the relationship forward, carrying them along toward forever.

Had things been perfect?

No, but things had been good.

And he'd assumed that it would be enough to see them through forever.

It had crashed and burned in spectacular fashion. But whenever he thought back to their origins, Chase had always carried that clear personal admission that he'd progressed their relationship so quickly toward marriage because it had felt like it was time.

Like the big clock in his head that told him he was meant to grow up, be successful in business and start a family like his father, was ticking away.

Or counting down, more like.

So he'd found Leanne. She was an attractive companion, able to fit into any situation, be it social or business. She was full of sparkling conversation and pretty smiles, and he'd felt a deep sense of satisfaction knowing she'd fit the bill.

One that lived entirely in his head and was of his own making.

Whatever resentment he'd carried for her and her actions since the dissolution of his marriage, the one area he took full blame for was that unchanging truth: he'd searched for a wife that fit a set of criteria, not someone whom he loved simply for who she was.

It was part of why he'd sworn off marriage so completely.

He'd made his personal life a business transaction and he simply couldn't be trusted to chart a path forward with someone else. Colton Properties was too important to him, and, in the end, he'd accepted that about himself just as he'd accepted his role in the failure of their marriage.

Despite the scars he carried from his divorce, he had moved on. He didn't think about Leanne every day, or frankly, even most weeks. She'd even called him a few years back to tell him she was remarrying and that she was happy, and he'd been happy for her.

No lingering remorse or anger. Just acceptance.

So why had she occupied his thoughts so heavily these past few weeks?

Even as he asked himself the question, Chase knew the truth.

It was the woman he was currently ushering into his office.

Sloan.

He followed her through his office entryway before leaving the door open so anyone passing by or stopping in to discuss the day's business would see she was here with him.

With her bag stowed at the small meeting table he kept in his office, she crossed over to the individual coffee brewer on his sideboard. After selecting a coffee pod, she settled a mug in the serving tray and started the machine whirring before turning back toward him.

"You sure I'm not in the way?"

"Not in the least. Work through what you need in here and when the usual parade comes in this morning for meetings and updates, people will be sure to see you."

"It sounds like your day will be busy. I want to strike the right balance between starry-eyed new relationship and *not* looking like a leech sucking up time in your office."

She set a new cup down on the brewer for him before hunting for the container of cream he kept in the small fridge built into the base of the sideboard.

Chase wasn't sure why, but something in that small domestic act pulled him up short. He'd have missed it if he hadn't looked up at just the right moment from logging in to his own computer, but he *had* looked up.

Had seen that simple gesture.

And realized he hadn't shared coffee with anyone in a long time.

"Chase?"

Her soft smile and expectant gaze pulled him out of his reverie.

"Oh. Yeah."

"Do you want cream or sugar?"

"I can fix it." He jumped up like a cat who'd been doused in water and crossed over to her. "You don't have to make my coffee."

She shrugged before stepping away from the machine with her mug. "Shouldn't I know how you like it?"

"Technically, we just met yesterday. You'd probably get a pass on how I drink my coffee."

"Fair." She appeared to consider for a moment, tapping the side of her mug. "We are going to have to figure out what conversations we would realistically have at what stage of things. To your point, coffee would be new, but would I know how many siblings you have? Or what's currently going on with your family?"

If the switch to business had something sour settling in his stomach, Chase ignored it as he lifted his mug and pasted on a smile. "Black with two sugars."

"Noted."

"But the situation with my family isn't a secret. You could just as easily hear it from me as anyone in this office."

His tone—the one he'd determined would sound as cheerful as possible—instead sounded like he'd been chewing nails with his coffee.

"I'm sorry. I keep bumbling over the same difficult ground." She moved closer and laid a hand on his forearm. "I do recognize this is a trying time."

"It's not your fault."

"No, but I could be a little more delicate. We're investigating your business. I need to leave your family situation off the table."

"It's hardly off the table, Sloan. Nor is it something that people are whispering about." He thought back to the conference-room discussion the day before. "People are talking about it with bullhorns in hand to amplify the message."

He saw the unmistakable sympathy in her eyes and something about that stuck in his gut.

Hard.

"I don't need you to tiptoe here. Do what you need to do. That's why I hired you."

Although he'd stand by every word he'd just spoken as truth, his tone was harsh. Unyielding. It bordered on obnoxious-bastard territory.

"Got it."

"Sloan, I—"

He was stopped by the arrival of Clint Roebuck and the lead of retail properties, Jamie Hunt. "Colton. Do you have a minute?"

Sloan glanced over at the two men, a beaming smile firmly in place. "You gentlemen discuss what you need to. I'm just going to get caught up on some email over there."

If the men were surprised to see her there, they hid it well, save for Clint's glance toward the small table where Sloan busied herself settling in, popping in earbuds before facing her computer.

"If now's a bad time, we can come back."

"Not at all." Chase pasted on a grin of his own, gesturing toward the coffee maker. "Help yourself and let's get down to what's going on. I'm betting you're here over the Lake Road property."

"It's a mess, Chase," Jamie began, waving off the coffee. "We've had a deal for some time, but the owner is balking now. Says he doesn't want a retail center marring the pristine lake environment."

Chase wanted to kick them both out and apologize to Sloan, but he had a part to play.

They both did.

And they'd all been working on the Lake Road deal for months now. It had been one of the last deals his father had initiated before his stroke.

Business as usual, Colton.

It's what he had to do.

More, what he had to focus on.

His thoughts had been full of fake dates, corporate espionage and all the damn problems that seemed to define his life right now.

Yet as he'd so eloquently told Sloan, that's why he'd *hired* her.

Chase Colton didn't do relationships. He'd learned that a long time ago.

But business deals?

Those he could see through in his sleep.

Sloan hunted through files, downloaded what looked important and ultimately mapped herself a digital back door into Colton Properties. Chase had given her extraordinary access to his company and while she was grateful for his trust that she'd do her job, she had to admit the man had—literally—handed her the keys to his kingdom.

From files on property deals, to business expansion plans and audit histories, there wasn't much she couldn't learn about the company. And even though she still smarted from their coffee conversation—she was hired help, after all—she couldn't deny her fascination all the same.

Do what you need to do. That's why I hired you.

Over and over, that specific part of their conversation had looped through her mind. And because those words had stuck, Sloan once again reminded herself of the plain truth.

She was here to do a job.

One she'd been hired for.

That didn't mean she was "hired help" in a derogatory way.

Yet even with the admonitions to herself, the discussion stuck.

Because nothing about this job had helped her maintain the professional distance she was known for.

Was it the fake-dating situation?

While she'd like to blame it on that—and the odd,

swirling feelings for Chase she couldn't quite blunt or blot away—she knew it was something more.

Something about what the Colton family was going through pulled at her. It had flipped a switch she hadn't even realized she possessed.

And yeah…there was that incendiary chemistry, no matter how much she wanted to avoid it all with her inward commentary on how this was a job.

But it was also the family.

She knew who her parents were. Her extended family, too. And while she'd never dare to think that she was privy to every thought any of them ever had, she was quite confident that her father and mother were who they'd shown her to be. After a lifetime of knowing them, she knew the good and bad about them, their charms and their quirks.

But she also *knew* them.

How terrible must it be, then, to realize your parent wasn't just something other than you'd believed, but someone with a whole other life?

And a whole other family?

The very idea of it haunted her.

She was someone who worked in data. Things she could see or create, in and with code. It was part of why she was as good at her job as she was. Everything she did was about hunting for information.

But that information *existed*.

It wasn't about feelings or emotions. It was about finding the truth.

The knock on the door pulled her attention from her computer and Sloan quickly locked the screen.

"Hello?"

After the parade of people who'd trooped into Chase's office, she'd ended up moving to a small conference room off the front entrance. She figured she'd lasted long enough doing the "girlfriend show" and she needed some quiet, focused concentration to get through the setup of her digital back door.

"Yes, hello." She smiled, thinking about the dreamy, slightly unfocused look she'd practiced in the mirror.

"We're ordering in some food for lunch and Chase suggested I ask what you're hungry for."

"Oh, that was sweet of him." She pushed a bit more dreaminess into that smile, then added, "I'm fine with whatever he wants."

The words felt like syrup on her tongue but the woman clucked happily. "We're planning on pizza and a big salad." The woman stepped farther into the room. "I'm Althea, by the way. I'm the office manager."

"Oh, it's lovely to meet you. I'm Sloan."

They exchanged basic pleasantries for a few minutes, but Sloan recognized two key facts beneath the chitchat. Chase might be the head of Colton Properties, but Althea ran the place.

And she was dying to get more information on the new woman in the boss's life.

Since this was the exact sort of opportunity Sloan was looking for, she leaned in.

Hard.

"I hope you don't mind my hanging out here. Chase said I could and then we could go straight to dinner from here later and, well—" She broke off, pleased to see the happy smile on Althea's face. "He's just such a wonderful man."

"Our Chase is wonderful. Can I tell you a secret?"

"Oh, you don't have to do that."

Althea waved a hand. "It's a secret in so much as the men around here pay little attention. But all the women here in the office have been hoping Chase will meet a great woman."

"We just met and—" Again, Sloan pasted on that loopy smile. "Do you think he likes me?"

"I've no doubt of it."

"Well then, I'll share a secret of my own. I like him, too. And it's just so fast, I'm not quite sure of myself, but I do know I like him. More than I could have imagined."

"Honey, when you know, you know. The night I met my Ben I was out with two girlfriends. I told them both that was the man I was going to marry."

Sloan's mom had often told a similar tale about her father, and while she'd thought it a sweet story, she'd never put all that much stock in it.

People didn't fall in love with a glance across a room or, even if their own response was strong enough to make them feel that way, there was no way of knowing with certainty the other person felt the same.

Since she worried she wasn't quite good enough as an actress to sell her agreement, she opted for an adjacent topic. "How long have you and Ben been married?"

"Thirty-three years next month." Althea beamed before she seemed to come back to herself. "I'd better get that pizza and salad ordered or we won't have it in time for lunch. I'll see you later."

"Do you need me to move somewhere else?"

"Not at all. I went ahead and booked the room for you in our conference-room system. It's yours for the rest of the day."

Althea turned to go but stopped just shy of the door. "There is something, if you don't mind my saying."

Sloan tilted the lid of her computer so that she could fully focus on Althea. "Of course."

"Be gentle with his heart. He pretends toughness but I've known him a long time. He feels a lot more than he lets on."

"I have no intention of hurting him."

Althea didn't say anything else, just nodded and left.

But it was long minutes later before Sloan lifted her computer screen back up and got back into her work flow.

Even longer for her to put those words out of her mind.

Chapter 5

The week sped by in a blur. Chase wasn't quite sure how it had happened, but he'd gotten used to Sloan's face. She didn't come into the office with him every day, but kept a good balance of popping in with a surprise lunch one day and then a big show of dragging him out to play hooky for the afternoon.

He'd spent the other day making his own show out of rushing out the door at the stroke of five to meet her for drinks and dinner.

And now, here they were on Friday afternoon, staring down a weekend.

He'd monopolized her time, between the work itself and their endless parade of dates to put on a show around town, and he recognized the woman deserved a break.

Even if he was surprisingly loath to spend the evening alone.

He'd gone out on a property tour a few towns over and had just cleared the front door of the office when he heard the commotion.

His sister, Ruby, and his brother Fletcher's new girlfriend, Kiki, were in the lobby, along with a puppy and what appeared to be half the office.

Sloan was there, too, on the floor with the pretty shepherd mix, her work bag abandoned near her feet.

"Hi." Chase said.

"Chase!" Ruby rushed for him first, the growing roundness of her belly pressing against him as she leaned in for a big hug. It still amazed him that his little sister was having a baby, but he was happy for her. Especially since she'd found forever with Sebastian Cross.

They'd all known each other since they were kids, with Sebastian and their brother Wade going into the marines together. Wade had stayed in the service until he was injured, but Sebastian had come back to Owl Creek after completing his tour of duty. They'd all recognized Sebastian was a changed man, but it was only once they got together that Ruby realized how much his time in the military had affected him.

Their work placing dogs with PTSD training to veterans was a passion project for both of them and Ruby donated her veterinarian services while Sebastian volunteered the training. But when something had ultimately sparked between them, Chase and his whole family had recognized just how perfect a match they were for each other.

He'd also never seen his sister so lit up inside.

"I'm always happy to see you," he murmured against his sister's cheek, "but what's going on here?"

"Kiki and I are training this little girl for service. We were downtown so thought we'd stop in. It's good for them to experience elevators as part of their training."

Chase almost pulled back when Ruby whispered heavily in his ear, "And you've been holding out on us about Sloan. She's great!"

Since there was no way they could continue this conversation in the middle of all those people while locked in a whisper war, Chase stepped away from his sister and turned to the team. "Looks like it's time to get an early head start on our Friday. Once you've had your puppy time, feel free to get your weekend going a bit early. Thanks to everyone for a good week."

The offer was enough to get people moving and after a few more polite smiles and oohs and aahs for the puppy, the crowd began to thin, leaving him, Ruby, Kiki and Sloan, who gently handled the puppy as she got to her feet.

"She's adorable. Such a sweet girl," she said, bending to give the gangly puppy one more pat on its soft brown head.

"Fancy's coming along," Kiki agreed, then turned to give Chase a hug. "Thanks for letting us intrude. We weren't sure how she'd take to the elevator but she's a champ."

"I'm always happy to see you all. And let me introduce Sloan."

"We met," Ruby said quickly, her smile broad. "I'd heard some rumors you two were spotted out and about this week."

Although he hated lying to his family about why Sloan was really in his life, he couldn't deny his reaction was pure truth. "We're having a good time."

"Which means you can have an even better time this evening at my place. Kiki and I decided we needed a cookout tonight before it gets too cold to enjoy grilling."

He glanced at Sloan, but she seemed okay with the plan he suspected had already been presented to her. "What prompted this informal gathering?"

Gathering intel on his love life, Chase had no doubt. Information that would be spreading around the family like wildfire the moment his sister could text out of his line of sight.

But Ruby stood there, innocence personified, and Kiki was quick to back her up. "She claims the baby's hungry for a steak, so we figured that was as good a reason as any. Plus, we haven't had much time with Nate and Sarah, and this is a casual way to all be together."

"Did you invite Mom?"

He liked Nate and Sarah and did want to get to know his half siblings, but discussion of them still gave him concerns for his mother, too.

For the first time since his arrival, he saw his sister's smile tighten, her green eyes, so like his own, clouding with those same concerns. "She already had plans tonight with her book club so isn't able to join us."

So he wasn't the only one looking out for Mom.

In fact, it was probably his mother's plans that had made it so natural to press for this evening's impromptu get-together.

With one last glance at Sloan, which she greeted with a happy nod, he said, "Then count us in. And let me know what we can bring."

"You've been working all day. Bring a few bottles of wine or a twelve-pack of beer and we'll be all set. We'll see you at seven."

As quickly as they'd rolled in, Ruby, Kiki and the now-sleepy Fancy rolled out and he was left in the lobby with Sloan. Althea was looking on from the small office that had a direct line of sight to the front area.

He avoided glancing that way, well aware they were the center of attention, and instead used the moment to his advantage, leaning in to press a soft kiss to her cheek.

"Hi."

"I probably would have said it, anyway, but the puppy inspired me." She smiled and Chase realized that warm visage packed enough punch to nearly make him forget his name. "Fancy meeting you here."

She kept her voice low, breathy almost, and Chase had one of those abstract thoughts that had become more and more distinct over the past few days.

Why did this feel so real?

He knew it wasn't, but between having her here and now the dinner with his family, it was getting harder and harder to remember that.

When she only kept up that conspiratorial smile, he tilted his head in the vague direction of his office. "I need to get a few things and then we'll start our weekend, too."

"Sounds like a plan."

He heard a happy little sigh from the direction of Althea's office as they progressed down the hall and it wasn't until they were inside his office, with the door closed, that Chase turned with a quick apology.

"I'm so sorry for my sister. And my brother's girlfriend. Though, if I know Ruby, Kiki was innocent in plotting and planning this."

"It's fine."

"Yeah, but you didn't get a lot of choice there."

"Chase, really, it's fine. I'd like to meet your family, and to be honest, that steak Kiki mentioned sounds like a lovely end to the week. Especially with the merlot I have in my apartment that I will plan to bring along."

"You don't have to bring anything."

Her face fell at that statement, and he sensed he had overstepped, even though he couldn't fully figure out why.

"I can pick something up. You don't have to go to any trouble."

"It's not any trouble and I'd like to."

Although the subject of the wine seemed to have been figured out, he couldn't dismiss the feeling he'd mishandled the conversation. In fact, he'd felt that way a few times this week whenever he shifted into business.

The friction vanished almost as fast as it came, but it was there all the same. That subtle sense that talking to her about the work she was doing was insulting, somehow.

Even as he considered that angle, Chase had to admit it wasn't exactly right. She sent him an update at the end of each day, and they spent time on each of their "dates" talking through what she'd learned or was working on.

So really, work wasn't the actual problem, was it?

He nearly asked when she tapped on the edge of her shoulder bag. "I do have a few things to share with you. If you'd like to pick me up a bit earlier than we need to get over to your sister's, I can fill you in."

"Yeah. Sure. That makes sense. Is it bad?"

"I want your thoughts. You may see something I don't."

She didn't answer the question and Chase figured it was the tip of the iceberg. His gut had told him something was wrong. Whatever digging Sloan had been doing must be reinforcing his concerns in some way.

With a heavy heart at the realization that someone he knew was at the center of it all, he just nodded.

"Alright. How about if I get to your place around six?"

"I'll see you then."

Before they could engage in any of the comfortable conversation they'd had before, Sloan was already headed for the door.

And as she left, he couldn't help but wonder if there was more truth in her words than he wanted to admit.

You may see something I don't.

He wasn't so sure about that. Especially because there was something standing right in front of him, and he hadn't seen it yet.

Worse, he had no clue what it even was.

"It's just a bottle of wine."

She'd muttered that to herself, or some version of it, including "get it together," "stop being a drama llama," and "get your head out of your butt" since she'd walked in the door.

Even Waffles had grown tired of her, his tail waving in the air as he'd headed for his favorite spot in the corner of the living room, where she'd set up a small feline entertainment center for him.

With the small sting of that kitty disdain still lingering, Sloan admitted to herself that it really was time to get her head out of her butt.

And really, *why* did she keep getting herself bent out of shape when Chase's comments suggested he had his own head on quite straight and was operating with the full knowledge they were working a job?

It didn't matter they'd had a great week together. Their dinners had been enjoyable, always professional, but human, too, full of easy conversation and shared thoughts.

It was the conversations that made her feel good.

Heard.

Understood.

But it still didn't mean there was any room for the emotions sparking all over the place on her side.

What did matter was that Chase had hired her to look into problems at the company.

And while she hadn't pinpointed the culprit yet, she'd dug deep enough to know there were problems.

Someone was very good at covering their tracks and at hiding the data, but the files were off.

Dates didn't match up.

There were small discrepancies that, once dug into and added up, led to an overarching larger issue in each month's financial close.

And a strange set of expenses she couldn't find fault with, yet couldn't connect to any major job, either.

Aware she wasn't going to figure it out standing there staring into space, she headed into the bedroom to freshen up. There wasn't time to bother with another shower, but she did want to look good for Chase's family. Where Kiki had been a bit more subtle, Ruby hadn't been able to hide her interest. Just like Althea earlier in the week, she seemed particularly happy that her brother was in a relationship.

It was interesting, Sloan mused as she added hot rollers to her hair and redid her eye makeup. That steady stream of everyone wanting to see Chase settle down. Although it wasn't talked about, there was that subtle hum in the air that suggested his first marriage loomed large in his life.

Which meant they were going to be hit with an awfully big bomb of disappointment once the case was over, and he wasn't "dating" Sloan any longer.

"A problem for another day," she muttered to herself as she walked back into the bedroom to get the slacks and thin blouse she'd already laid out.

Waffles looked up at her from where he groomed himself on the end of her bed and she sat down beside him, pulling him close. "You don't know how easy you've got it. Sleeping and eating and finding some warm spots in the sun. It's a pretty good life."

Waffles purred under her attention, and she rubbed her cheek against his soft head. "It's us humans who manage to make life far harder than it needs to be."

When he simply purred louder and pressed himself into her, Sloan figured it was worth taking a few minutes to snuggle her cat and resettle herself.

Maybe she was making this harder than it needed to be.

She was a professional and she'd taken this job with the intention of seeing it through, just like all the other work she'd ever done.

The ruse she and Chase had to concoct in order to get to the end was a necessity. While she'd admit to losing her way for a bit, it was time to reset. Tonight's visit with his family would be good, in fact. She could prove to herself that she could handle this and mentally move on. Put these pesky sparks of attraction in a box—where they belonged— and focus on getting the work done.

Based on what she'd discovered, she figured she'd have a breakthrough in another few days of work. Then she could go back to Chicago and on to whatever came next.

And if that thought sent a small shot of sadness winging through her, then it was all the more reason she needed to buck up and face the truth.

A quick glance at her bedside clock let her know she'd dawdled longer than she had planned, and Sloan settled Waffles back onto the bed and rushed to finish dressing. She'd just stepped into her heels, adjusting the cuffs of her pants so they fell just so over the back of her shoes, when the doorbell rang.

She'd set up her computer on the small table in the kitchen and already pictured how she'd walk him through the information as she headed for the front door.

Straightforward.

Fact-based.

And life-cratering, she acknowledged as she reached for the door.

Later, she'd tell herself that advance preparation was a wise move. At the moment, however, the man who stood on the other side of the entryway practically took her breath away, all while managing to detonate a few brain cells along the way.

He was magnificent. His broad shoulders were perfec- tion in a gray button-down shirt he'd left untucked over dark jeans. He'd obviously taken time for a shower, as his normally light brown hair was darker at the tips, where it curled.

But it was his eyes…

Those green eyes of his seemed darker. More focused and full of a personal history she wanted so desperately to explore. When Sloan finally realized she'd been staring into that captivating green a bit too long she waved him in. "Come on back. I have everything set up at the table."

He followed her through the small apartment, and in a matter of moments they were in her kitchen, which suddenly seemed a lot smaller with him standing inside of it.

"Can I get you anything to drink?"

"How about a soda? I'll wait and have something to drink at dinner."

"Sounds good. Why don't you sit down and read what I've got teed up and then I can answer any questions and walk you through it."

He did as she suggested, and Sloan busied herself pouring them both something cold. After placing his glass down next to him, she took a sip of hers when she sat down.

"You've been busy this week."

"You read it already?"

"It was a quick scan, but your executive summary was pretty straightforward." His gaze narrowed as it flicked back to the screen, then returned to her. "I've got someone in the company who's been skimming for quite a while. Especially since you've noted irregularities as far back as a decade ago."

"I'm sorry, Chase."

"Yeah. Me, too."

"So it really is true then."

Chase knew it was—Sloan had documented it all in

black and white—but still, the gut punch of it all was shockingly real.

One more in a line of nasty surprises these past few months.

First his father's death.

Then the news of his half siblings and his father's secret life.

And now this.

Was anything in his life solid anymore?

"I'm sorry that it is. I don't know who yet, but I'm confident I can keep following the various threads and will get you the answers you need."

"Just like we planned."

He knew Sloan had found something. She'd told him as much before walking out of his office earlier.

And somehow, even with the knowledge the news wasn't good, the information that practically blinked at him off her screen was worse than he'd imagined.

A decade?

How could something so bad—something so nefarious— have gone on for so long?

"What questions do you have?"

"How was I so stupid, for starters. I've been groomed to lead this company for damn near twenty years and I've had no idea a snake's been inside the walls for more than a decade?" He slammed back from the table, the chair wobbling but somehow staying upright.

"But that's not your fault."

"Not my fault? It's fully my fault. I'm the leader of the company."

"That doesn't make you all-knowing. I can walk you through the data I've found, but whoever's doing this is good and they've had a lot of practice covering their tracks."

Since he was already standing, Chase turned on his heel and headed for the living room. The urge to pace was strong, and because of it, he found a spot near the window and stared out over the common area beyond.

Owl Creek was in that space beyond the limited view from the window. His home. Where that thought would have given him peace in the past, all he could manage was a solid breath.

Inhale.

Exhale.

This he knew. Real estate. Land. Building. The urge to create something that would last long after he was gone.

He knew that work in his bones and he loved it.

But all the rest?

It was a stark reality to have spent more than three and a half decades on the planet and realize he still knew very little.

"Chase? Please talk to me."

He turned from the window, oddly grateful that she was there. He needed to get his head together and stop reacting each time he got news he didn't want.

"I'm sorry you're stuck with my reactions, whiny and immature as they are."

"Whiny?" Her mouth actually dropped a bit before she seemed to catch herself. "Is that actually how you see yourself?"

"Isn't it accurate?"

"Hardly. Chase, you've had to face more in a matter of months than most people experience in a lifetime. It's okay to have some messy feelings you can't fully reconcile. That would be true regardless, but you're trying to process it all."

"Or am I giving it all too much power?"

The question sort of hung there, like a live wire sparking in the midst of a storm.

"It does have power."

"Yes, but not over me. I can't let that happen."

"Then why are you fighting so hard against telling me how you feel? I'm a safe space. Even if I wasn't contractually unable to say anything, I won't. I've got the benefit of an outsider's eyes and, with the work I'm doing, digital ears. Lean into that."

It was an enticing thought. One he'd had more than once since embarking on this project with Sloan and SecuritKey.

Only now, standing here, Chase realized something. He'd let the fake-relationship aspects of the work dominate his thoughts, but now, at her words, he had to admit she had a point.

Talking to her wasn't fake.

Telling her how he felt about his business and his work and, hell, his life, wasn't made up.

She was that safe space she spoke of, but she was also a sounding board. And if he could get past the endlessly frustrating emotions that had dragged and pulled at him since the day his father had had his stroke, he realized Sloan was the one person he could speak to freely.

His siblings were all dealing with the matter in their own way. His cousins, too. And Nate and Sarah had an even bigger set of challenges to address, with the understanding that the very life created for them by their parents came at the expense of the rest of the Colton children, both Robert's and Jessie's.

What a mess it all was.

"Do you want to go tonight? If you don't, we can blame it on me and a sudden case of nerves to meet your family."

There it was again, that subtle sense of protection he'd felt from her from the start.

He was her full focus and it was...

Well, it was extraordinary.

"Thank you for that." He moved closer to her, taking her hands in his. "Truly, thank you. It's kind and thoughtful, and I appreciate it more than I can say. But I do want to go tonight. I think it'll be good to go and get away from this for a bit."

She glanced down at their joined hands before looking back up. "If that changes, just give me a signal."

Chase smiled at that, the first one since he'd read that dispassionate overview on her laptop. "You mean a couple signal."

"A what?"

"You know. That standard signal most couples have when one of them wants out of a situation. A story they both know to tell or a preplanned fib in the event of a quick getaway."

When she still looked stumped it made Chase wonder—more than he should have—about her past relationships.

Had she never experienced that paired camaraderie that came with being coupled up with someone?

"So what is our story?"

"We'll fake an early start to the day and a long week. How about that?"

She nodded, her expression sweetly serious. "That makes sense. And it's not untrue, which makes it even better."

Chase squeezed her hands once more before letting them go. "Right. It's not a lie."

Even if every other thing that was going to come out of their mouths that evening was a lie. A big one he was keeping from his family.

He trusted them. Whatever he thought about the problems at Colton Properties, he didn't believe his sisters, his brothers or his cousins were involved. But with all that was going on in their lives—and the knowledge that Ruby had invited Nate and Sarah as well—Chase wasn't ready to give the real reasons Sloan was in town.

They'd hatched the dating scenario as a proper cover, and if there was one thing he'd learned from his various family members in law enforcement, you don't break cover.

Ever.

It was stunning, then, to realize a few minutes later as they walked to the car to head to his sister's, that his father had taught him the same thing, albeit for entirely different reasons.

Robert Colton had spent a lifetime keeping his cover as a doting husband to Jenny and, as they now knew, as an equally doting husband to Jessie.

And he'd never broken cover.

Not even once.

Chapter 6

There were a shocking number of Coltons.

That was Sloan's constant thought as she roamed around the backyard at Ruby Colton's home, a large place she shared with her fiancé, Sebastian Cross.

The property the couple lived on, Crosswinds, was gorgeous. Rolling land, dotted areas of woods and even a stream burbling in the farther reaches of the place. It was so beautiful as to be picturesque.

The party's start at seven had given her enough time to still see the land in the light. She'd taken it all in, while Chase had navigated the long driveway into the vast property, and had loved every bit of it.

That easy, quiet time had also given her both the head space to think about all they'd discussed in her apartment, as well as be able to brace herself for the conversations to come that evening.

She knew how these things worked. She was the new "girlfriend," and everyone would want a few moments of her time to size her up. The same puppy she'd met earlier was one of the first to greet her and she'd dropped to a crouch, giving Fancy a big dose of affection. The introductions had followed on quickly from there.

She'd met three of Chase's five siblings, which meant she

now knew Ruby, Fletcher and Frannie. She'd also met Nate and Sarah, who both seemed as shell-shocked as she was.

It was only when Chase made a polite excuse to move Sloan on to more introductions that Nate winked at her. He offered a small, wry smile and whispered, "My sister and I thank you for taking a bit of the heat off of us tonight." Sloan got the sense Chase's half siblings might be settling in a bit, but were still nervous.

The fact that Jenny Colton was at her book club likely helped, but Sloan figured it was a bit of a relief not to be the center of attention tonight.

The grill was smoking away, the most divine scents rising into the air, as Sloan and Chase mingled through the crowd. She'd ultimately won the battle on the merlot and was drinking a glass as Chase nursed a beer, continuing with the introductions, clearly determined to have her meet each and every person there.

It got a bit tricky when they got to Max, but the man played off their meet-and-greet like a pro, no one any wiser that they already knew each other.

"This is my cousin Max and Della." Chase gestured to the large athletic man with twinkling blue eyes who stood with the woman who'd captured his heart, Della Winslow.

Della also worked at Crosswinds as one of the K-9 trainers and she had a dog by her side as well. Although older than Fancy, Sloan could tell by the large body and lithe grace that the dog was still young and very much in his prime. Della had introduced him as Charlie and Sloan found herself nearly as smitten with him as with Fancy when the black Lab had given her his paw.

Next to Della was another cousin, Greg. As she stood up from giving Charlie praise and his proper due in shaking his hand, Sloan could see the clear resemblance between him and Max as brothers. Where Max was a bit taller and leaner, Greg had a solid, thicker build. When Chase had added on that Greg was co-lead at the Colton Ranch, Sloan could see how that sort of work had shaped the man's physique.

"Welcome to the melee, Sloan." Greg smiled as he shook her hand.

"Thank you." She smiled back, keeping her tone light. "Though I have to say, you all have a certain sort of orchestration to your crowd. Some cook. Some make drinks. Some keep the conversation lively. I'd definitely say it's more shindig than melee."

Greg's smile was broad, and she got the sense her comment had been met with a quiet sort of approval, even as Chase let out a distinct cough beside her. When she turned to see if he was okay, she saw nothing but a stoic calm.

She'd have questioned him if they were actually dating, but they still didn't really know each other. And since it was a party, she vowed to ignore his reaction for now and think on it later.

Chase had filled her in on the Colton Ranch on their drive over. Worked by his Uncle Buck for years, two of the man's four children, Greg and Malcolm, had followed their father into the business, while Max had chosen the FBI and Buck's only daughter, Lizzy, was a graphic artist.

Just like Chase's determination to do right by his siblings with Colton Properties, it struck her that this was a close-knit family whose lives were intertwined in their relationships as well as in their work.

"How did you and Chase meet?"

"At his office. I was late for a meeting and ended up rushing into not only the wrong office, but the wrong conference room, too."

"She actually barreled right into me." Chase put an arm

around her shoulders, looking down at her with distinct notes of attraction, and her breath caught.

So much so that she had to think for a minute to recapture her train of thought.

"It was the first time in my life I found benefit in my clumsiness."

"Looks like Chase is the beneficiary." Greg was all smiles, but she didn't miss the distinct tightening of Chase's arm around her shoulders.

Before she could say another word, Della gestured toward the back porch. "Sloan, would you care to join me? Sarah looks a bit lonely over there."

Sarah had at least three other women fluttering around her, but Sloan recognized the lifeline and reached for it. Something strange had occurred between Chase and his cousin, and a bit of air would be welcome. She was oddly grateful no one asked what business she was in that had even brought her to Colton Properties, but that tension between the two men blotted out the relief.

"I'd love to."

The two of them headed off, Charlie trotting beside them and Della smiling as they went. It was only when they were fully out of earshot of the men that she spoke. "If they were two of the dogs I train, I'd tell you to watch out or you'd get marked."

"What?" Sloan nearly bobbled her wineglass at Della's bold remark.

"Oh, yeah, you heard me. That was definitely two men circling around each other. I figured we should get out of their way so they can do it properly."

Although she got the basic gist of Della's comments, Sloan struggled to understand why. While she had gotten the obvious notes of male appreciation from Greg, what did it actually matter? She and Chase weren't dating.

And it wasn't like Greg had been outwardly inappropriate. A little flirty, sure, but nothing that required the emotional equivalent of marking territory.

"What are they circling around?"

"You, my dear."

"But that's silly."

"No, that's men. And it's interesting, too, because the two of them normally get along very well." Della glanced over, her smile growing even bigger. "We've all been hoping Chase sees the light and finds someone. It looks like a little healthy competition might be just what he needs."

Sloan had never been a good dater. She'd dated from time to time, but her work and her focus on it usually scared off men before things progressed very far.

Which made the idea of being stuck in a tug-of-war between two men mind-boggling.

"I'm sure it's no big deal."

Della glanced back to where Chase, Max and Greg still stood in a conversation circle near the grill. "I wouldn't be so sure, but let's stay here a bit. I'm feeling the need for a bit of girl talk."

Since a bit of girl talk would give her a chance to get a broader sense of the Colton family, she was more than happy to oblige Della's whim.

And since it was also nice to just spend some time in the company of other women her age instead in front of her computer, well, she'd take that, too.

Chase and Greg were a year apart. They'd played together since they were in diapers and Chase considered the man one of his closest friends on the planet.

And right now, he'd happily punch his cousin in the face.

A fact, Chase knew, Greg was well aware of.

In fact, his cousin could have used a trowel he was laying it on so thick.

"Things sure are moving fast between you and Sloan. You met on Monday?" Greg's question was casual but there was as much interest stamped in his eyes as Chase had seen from every other family member tonight.

When you know, you know.

The words were actually on the tip of his tongue before he pulled them back.

It might have been an appropriate response, but that the thought felt as natural as breathing caught him up short.

"It's been a bit of a whirlwind but we're enjoying ourselves."

"And you're already bringing her to family dinners." Greg let out a low whistle. "Something's brewing, cuz. I'm looking forward to having a front-row seat."

"You're awfully interested in Sloan."

As comebacks went it was a lame one, but Chase couldn't shake off this frustration and annoyance with his cousin.

"She's a beautiful woman. Who wouldn't be interested?"

Max had given them room to circle each other but he used that moment to interject. "Greg, it looks like Sebastian could use a hand at the grill. Why don't you go help him?"

Greg gave him one final look before reaching over and giving Chase a hard slap on the shoulder. "I want you to be happy, Chase. Don't forget that."

He watched his cousin walk away and Max waited until his brother was across the yard before jumping in. "You're awfully touchy about Sloan."

"I'm trying to make sure Greg doesn't get *touchy*." The comeback was harsh to his own ears and Chase tried to soften his attitude. "The woman is here to help me and instead has been subject to constant scrutiny, raised eyebrows and veiled questions and now an impromptu family party. It's a little overwhelming."

Max glanced in the direction of the women, all seated in a circle talking and laughing on the back porch. "She looks like she can handle it."

Chase's gaze found Sloan immediately, and just as Max had said, she was talking and laughing and obviously fitting in. It warmed him to see her so comfortable with his family and whether it was fair or not, he couldn't help but remember the first few times he'd brought Leanne to family functions.

She'd settled in after a while, but those initial get-togethers had been tough. Facing his parents, his own five siblings, his uncle and his four cousins had been a lot for her.

But Sloan seemed unfazed by the same.

He took the moment to look at her—really look at her—without her noticing. The long dark hair she normally kept back in a tight updo was down, an ocean of pretty curls framing her face. She was beautiful, her light brown skin glowing under the soft yellow lights strung around the back porch. Her smile was warm, and as he watched her, she laughed at something Kiki said before bending down to pick up the tired puppy who'd curled up at her feet.

"She looks like she's been there forever," Max murmured, and Chase was already acknowledging the comment when he caught himself.

"Don't you start in, too. She's a guest and she's here on a job."

"Doesn't mean she can't look natural laughing and getting to know our family."

Recognizing he was in danger of overplaying his hand, Max smoothly changed the subject. "Has she found anything yet?"

"Unfortunately, yes. She's as good as you said, and it's only taken her a matter of days to uncover several irregularities."

Max's eyebrows slashed down over his light blue eyes. "Do you know who it is?"

With one last glance at Sloan, he shifted his full attention to his cousin. "Not yet, but it's only a matter of time."

"And then what?"

"Then I'll come clean with the family."

"Is your little charade with Sloan working?"

"Beautifully. The entire office is so caught up in my being besotted with her that they haven't noticed she's found some reason to be there several days this week."

"Be careful there. Someone who's been covering their tracks for this long will know to look for irregularities."

Chase considered that warning and thought back over the various interactions he'd had this past week at the office. Although, he couldn't think of a single person who asked questions more than usual or seemed to be acting out of the ordinary.

But really, what did he know?

This problem had festered for damn near ten years and he'd been oblivious.

"I know that look."

Max's stare was as tough as his words.

"What look?"

"The one where you carry the weight of the world on your shoulders, along with your belief that you must carry every member of this family, too."

"It's not like—"

"Oh, no?" Max challenged. "Let me see how close I can get. The problem you're dealing with at Colton Properties shouldn't even be happening. You should have known there was an issue. Not only should you have known, you should have rooted it out quite some time ago because you believe you should have some sort of omniscient superpower."

"I don't do that."

Max took a sip of his beer, the epitome of practiced cool. "How close did I hit the mark?"

"Damn it." Chase glanced down at his beer. "I should have known."

"I hate to break it to you, but that's why people get away with stuff far longer than they should. Because they do know how to cover their tracks. They know how to blend into society. Criminals doing bad things don't wear neon signs." Decidedly less calm, Max took another sip of his beer. "It'd be a hell of a lot easier if they did."

They were no longer talking about Colton Properties or someone committing fraudulent practices against the company. Max's experiences—taking down serial killers for the FBI—was proof that no matter how bad a situation seemed, there was always something worse to be found.

And his cousin had spent a lot of years running down and catching *worse* for a living.

At what cost?

"The job doesn't leave you, does it?"

Max smiled but there wasn't a trace of humor in it. "No, it doesn't. But I'm coming to understand that with the love of a good woman it's a lot easier to deal with."

Chase watched his cousin as the man's attention drifted back to the circle of women, his gaze unerringly settling on Della.

Although they weren't prone to diving into their feelings,

Max had said something to him years ago, when Chase was going through his divorce with Leanne, that had always stuck in his mind…

"Hell," Max had begun as he shook his head, "people like to romanticize a significant other with a cause. It's all well and good until they see the toll it takes up close."

"Come on, Max," Chase had replied. "What's that supposed to mean?"

"It means people are quick to call you a hero, but they don't want to know you have the ability to delve into the mind of a killer. It's that old adage—no one actually wants to know how the sausage is made."

"You do a good, honorable and brave job."

"And I will be forever alone because of it," Max had replied, ending their conversation…

Chase had been lost in his own misery at that time, dealing with the end of his marriage. Add on the bottle of whiskey they'd shared that night in the kitchen at the Colton Ranch and he hadn't had the wherewithal to ask Max what he meant.

But he'd tried the next day. When Max had shut him down, Chase tried again on a few other occasions, only to get the same response.

Whatever had triggered Max's honesty, be it Chase's own pain or the liquor, Chase had never known.

But it had stuck.

He might not hunt killers for a living, but he did have ambition. A good job and a big family and responsibilities to both. He'd let Leanne behind the curtain into his world and she hadn't been interested in what happened when the fancy dinners and the courting stopped.

She hadn't wanted to live with the reality of a man who spent long hours at the office and demanded they also spend time with his family nearly every weekend. So when things had gone south, he'd recognized it for what it was.

And while he might not be hunting killers, Chase had realized then he was as ill-suited for a relationship as Max had been.

Because unlike his cousin, who eventually did walk away, Colton Properties was his life.

And a woman couldn't be expected to sign up for that.

Jessie Colton stared dreamily at her swooping, swirling handwriting and wondered if she'd ever been happier.

Jessie Colton
Jessie Colton Acker
Jessie Acker

Oh, sure, she'd told herself she was happy with Buck all those years ago, but she'd learned soon enough it was simply a lie she'd told herself to mentally breeze past the fact that she'd really wanted to marry Buck's brother, Robert.

But her saintly sister, Jenny, had set her cap there and managed to land him first.

So she'd taken Buck and told everyone how happy she was and how perfect her life was being a rancher's wife.

Perfect?

Hardly.

Ranch life and four kids certainly hadn't agreed with her. She did love her children, but they were a lot of work, and they were always underfoot. And rowdy. Oh, goodness, had they been a handful. She'd had three boys in a row until she finally got her girl.

She might have stayed for Lizzy, but it was only after she was born that Robert had finally come to heel. He'd realized which sister he was truly in love with and they'd started a family of their own.

It had been such a happy time. She'd shed a few tears over leaving her kids, but life with Robert had been wonderful and they'd quickly started a family of their own.

It had truly been a blissful existence. For a few years, she had all she wanted.

Only to have Robert freak out about having two families before he finally ran off, leaving her with two young children. Sure, he sent money and kept them in a nice home, but he'd abandoned ship.

Left them and gone back to Jenny and their six kids.

And while it was still better than being stuck out in the middle of nowhere on a ranch, stuck was stuck.

She'd given up her life for those kids. And with Robert finally dead and their secret relationship out, she would have thought Nate and Sarah would have more regard for their mother.

More, that they'd be ready to take what was rightfully theirs.

Why should Robert's other six kids get all the family money and property and business? How was that fair?

Only, Nate and Sarah really didn't care.

She'd asked herself the same question over and over, but simply couldn't see it any other way. How was it possible they didn't care their father had essentially abandoned them?

And her?

Nate and Sarah both kept telling her they were happy with their lives, they didn't want any more of their father's money and that Robert had left them enough already, having set them up with his guilt money while he was still alive.

Couldn't they see they deserved more?

She'd struggled with that, trying so hard to work her way through her problems, finally turning to the Ever After Church for guidance. And still, she was no closer to understanding the children she'd begun to think of as ungrateful.

Thank goodness for Markus.

He'd been so wonderful and caring and patient, helping her process it all.

Jessie stared down at the name she'd looped over and over on the page.

Jessie Acker.

They would be married soon and that would be her name. She'd finally rid herself of the Colton moniker once and for all, moving on to something so much better.

Because Markus really was a wonderful man.

He loved her and he was preparing to make her his wife. Oh, they'd been careful, and he'd stressed to her that they couldn't go public with their relationship just yet. Too many single women in the Ever After Church had set their sights on him and he didn't want to ruffle feathers.

Great loves, after all, were a gift from God.

Hadn't he told her that, over and over?

That love needed to be nurtured and given room to grow in private, away from prying, spiteful eyes.

She'd agreed with him, and she did understand his point, even if it was getting a bit tiresome keeping their relationship all to herself.

But, oh, how she wanted to shout it to the world.

"Soon, darling." Markus would whisper those words against her temple each time she pressed him. Then he'd take her in his arms and kiss her, and she'd forget for a while that she wanted something more.

In the moment, all she needed was him.

She knew he felt it, too. Hadn't they confessed that to each other almost from the first?

All her life she'd been looking for a transcendent love. And now, she had it.

Markus had been so sweet. So vulnerable. He'd told her that he'd been seeking the same. That all his life he'd been willing to go where a higher power willed him to, all while giving up his own dreams of a family of his own.

He was doing good work, but, he'd confessed to her, it was lonely work.

But now, they had each other.

Jessie stared down at her looping signature once again. Soon, they wouldn't have to hide their great love.

Soon—so very soon—everyone would know.

Chase carried the last set of folding chairs from a small shed about fifty yards off the back of the house, settling them into place along the big tables already covered with plates, napkins and serving spoons.

Ruby had put him to work, asking him to get a few extra chairs to supplement the ends of the tables so they weren't overcrowded on the picnic benches. He'd just set the last chair into place when he heard his name over his shoulder.

"Chase, I'm sorry. I could have given you a hand with that."

He turned to find Nate, the man's hands full of two fresh beers.

"Is one of those for me?"

His half brother smiled and extended one of the cold bottles. "You bet."

"Then consider yourself having helped."

They stood there in companionable silence for a few

minutes, the *shindig*, as Sloan had called it, moving in full, orchestrated force around them.

And while they hadn't hit one-hundred-percent attendance this evening by his siblings or cousins, Chase figured any event that got more than eighty percent of his family out and together was a pretty solid hit rate.

Even as he was silently grateful his mother was one of the ones who'd stayed away.

He didn't need to protect her. Jenny Colton was doing just fine and had managed to develop a sort of equilibrium with the news of her husband and her sister's betrayal. She'd always focused on her children, and her nieces and nephews, and nothing was going to change that, she'd assured him just a few weeks ago.

And still…he couldn't help the overprotective streak he felt toward her.

Her feelings.

And the reality of the life she'd lived for almost four decades.

"Do you have a few minutes? I won't keep you long since we're all ready to dig into those steaks."

Chase recognized Nate's obvious sense of discomfort but gave his half brother props for pressing forward, anyway. "Sure."

Nate drifted a bit so they were still part of the party, but far enough away to have a private conversation. Chase's curiosity grew at what the younger man might want.

They hadn't spent much time together, as Nate and Sarah had only been introduced to them a few weeks ago. Even with their limited interactions, Chase had recognized them as good people.

Honest and caring and as churned up over this situation as the rest of them.

"I owe you an apology."

"For what?"

"This life." Nate gestured toward the grouping of family. "Your family. All you never knew about Sarah and I."

"That's not your fault. It's no one's fault but our parents'."

"I keep telling myself that. Sarah keeps trying to tell me, too. But the truth is, I knew."

"Knew what?"

"About you. About all of you."

"You what?"

Nate shook his head and the bitterness that thinned his lips and hardened his jaw was unmistakable. "We knew our parents weren't married. And because she'd been married to Buck, Mom was already a Colton and could easily give us the Colton name. As small children we didn't understand it, but Sarah and I both figured it out later."

If he was honest, Chase had wondered about that aspect. Whatever power his father had amassed over a lifetime, it never would have protected him on a charge of bigamy.

"How did you know about us?"

"Dad and Mom 'divorced'—" Nate added air quotes on the word *divorce* "—when I was about ten. He'd always traveled a lot. Or that was the excuse they told us for when he was here in Owl Creek. I'd always known something was a little off, but by then I was old enough to do some digging after he left. A few computer search queries and it was all too easy to find evidence of his other life."

Nate was a police officer in Boise. When they'd first learned of their half siblings, Max had done some digging of his own. He'd easily discovered Nate was a good cop, both by the cases he'd closed as well as the reputation several of Max's contacts shared. Tenacious. Focused. Willing to dig for the truth instead of accepting things at face value.

It was obviously a personality trait, because here he was, basically confessing he'd known about Robert Colton's secret life for close to two decades.

All while Chase had known nothing.

"I'm sorry. And more than that, I'm sorry I didn't talk to you about it from our very first meeting." Nate glanced down at the grass before his gaze lifted, that vivid blue direct and focused. "You deserved better than that. You all did."

Chase wanted to be angry. A very large part of him was angry, but oddly, it was an anger that sort of seethed with amorphous edges, swirling around yet having no place to land.

Would he have liked to have known this information sooner?

Of course.

Would another month have made a difference, seeing as how he'd spent a lifetime in the dark?

No, not really.

Am I giving it all too much power?

He'd asked Sloan that question earlier, in her apartment.

For all his confusion, anger and raw fury at his father's selfishness, Chase had genuinely begun to wonder about his own role in it all.

In what came next.

His father was dead. The image he'd crafted of the man was riddled with holes, all now visible in the light.

He could resent it and allow it to rule his actions, or he could find his way to some level of acceptance that every member of his family had the same disservice done to them as he had.

Which also meant he had a choice.

A very clear one, Chase knew, that he couldn't lay at Robert's feet.

He could turn on them, his newly discovered siblings most especially.

Or he could build something real and true in spite of his father's actions.

As he stood there beside his brother, his family laughing and shouting and enjoying one another across the expanse of lawn, Chase knew what he wanted.

Placing a hand on his younger brother's shoulder, he turned toward Nate. Their gazes met, and Chase saw clear traces of himself in the younger man.

The deep need to hold it together.

The feelings of responsibility.

And the determination to be strong, even when the world around them was cracking in half.

"We deserved better, Nate. We."

"Yeah, but I—"

"Not I, brother. *We.* This here—" He gestured toward their family. "That's us. All of us. And we all deserved better than what Robert and Jessie did."

"It's not that easy."

"Maybe it is. If we choose to make it that easy, we can have what they never dreamed of."

"What's that?"

"Family."

As that last word lingered between him and his youngest brother, Chase felt his first moment of peace since this all began.

He had a family. A rock-solid one.

And there was nothing he wouldn't do for each and every one of them.

Chapter 7

A carefree bubble of laugher filled Sloan's chest as Fancy shot straight up from her position on her lap.

One minute the puppy was conked out, sleeping like the dead, and the next one, Sebastian had gotten close enough with a huge platter of steaks that the dog was launching herself off her thighs so she could follow the man like he was the pied piper.

"Training is a process," Kiki sighed as she watched her small charge racing around Sebastian's feet.

"She'll get there," Della assured her before standing. "But it's probably time to get her and Charlie settled in their crates."

As she and Kiki went off, and Ruby and Frannie headed into the kitchen to get the additional sides to go with the steaks, Sloan found herself alone with Sarah.

"Have you and Chase been dating long?"

Sarah's smile was sweet, and Sloan had observed how hard the woman had worked to fit in that evening. She'd been kind and a bit deferential, obviously still trying to figure her place in the Colton family.

"We met on Monday."

If Sarah thought less than a week of dating was fast, she didn't show it and instead only nodded. "It might be cliché, but it's surprisingly accurate. Life really does turn on a dime."

"With respect to romance, it's one of my mother's favorite sayings. She met my father and six weeks later was engaged."

"And things worked out?"

"They celebrated thirty-two years of marriage back in April, so things seem to be going okay."

Sarah laughed at that before something seemed to crumple in her face, tears welling in her eyes. "I'm sorry. I swore to myself I wasn't going to cry and then something triggers it. I—"

"It's okay." Sloan moved closer, angling her body so she and Sarah faced each other on the patio furniture. "I hope you don't mind my saying, but Chase told me about what you've all been living through. His father's death and then the discovery for all of you that you had siblings you didn't know about."

If it was possible, Sarah's visage twisted up even more. "That they didn't know about. We knew. Nate and I. It was all of them that didn't." Sarah swiped at tears, even as more spilled over her fingers. "Surprise!"

It was uncharted territory—Sloan figured on some level she was a handy listener, and on another she was safe since she was an outsider. But regardless of the reason, she was here and Sarah needed someone to lean on.

"You were children. How could you have known how to handle something like that?"

"They're my brothers and sisters."

"Who share parents with you. Parents who had a far greater responsibility to tell them the truth of their lives than you did."

"They're a family and we're just the interlopers who have turned it all upside down."

Whether it was her rapidly fading objectivity on this case, or just the sheer indignity over Robert and Jessie Colton's behavior she couldn't quite get past, Sloan wasn't sure.

But she refused to sit there and let Sarah take this all on herself.

"You're part of a family, no qualifier needed."

"I *was* part of a family."

"Please don't do that to yourself. It's not past tense." She reached for the woman's hand, putting hers over top of Sarah's. "I've watched you all tonight. There's genuine effort and care there. Between you and Nate and all your siblings, too. It's hard and no one's saying it's not, but you and your brother are welcome here."

"Everyone has made me feel welcome. Even Uncle Buck, who probably had the biggest right to feel otherwise, has been so kind to me. To Nate, too."

Although Buck was absent this evening, just like Chase's mother, Jenny, Chase had filled her in fully on his whole family. Buck was his father's brother and had been married to Jessie, the two of them bringing Greg, Malcolm, Max and Lizzy into the world before Jessie up and left when Lizzy was three.

How shattering would that have been?

For Buck, yes, but for his kids? To lose one's mother like that? A woman who was an essential aspect of a child's stability and foundation, to just vanish?

She may not have died, but Buck and Jessie's children lost her and they'd still all found a way to move forward.

To forge ahead.

Jessie might have gone on to a new family, but that also meant Sarah and Nate were now dealing with the reality of who their mother was. Any illusion they might have had about her character had to have taken a hard blow with the obvious proof she'd walked away from four children.

It was difficult and convoluted and a terrible example of what atrocities people could commit to those they claimed to love.

But it didn't have to define Sarah and Nate's future. It didn't have to define any of their futures, not if they didn't want it to.

"Your brothers and sisters want to get to know you."

"I keep telling myself that. And most of the time I can feel it. And then I stop and look around and all I can think is why? Why would they want to welcome us into their lives? The two people who are the living proof their parents perpetrated a lifetime of lies."

"You and Nate are dealing with the consequences of that choice as much as anyone else."

Sloan was under no delusions that a few well-meaning moments could erase what the woman was feeling, but she did take heart when Sarah brushed away the remaining tears and glanced toward the large picnic tables set up about ten yards off the back patio.

"I do think I'm hungry."

"Why don't we go get some dinner then? The steaks smell wonderful, and it looks like Frannie made enough potato salad to feed an army."

Sarah glanced around at the assembled people throughout the backyard. "We're sort of a small one when we're all together."

"Fair point."

Chase had crossed over to the porch and came up to the two of them, his smile broad even as Sloan saw a distinct gentleness in his green gaze.

There was a subtle haze of sadness, too.

"We're definitely an army. And our drill-sergeant sister, Ruby, will see to it that we all get into a line to fill our plates."

"I'd best get to it then." Sarah headed off and it left Sloan and Chase briefly alone on the patio.

Chase waited, watching until Sarah picked up a plate and began talking to Fletcher, who was already in line, before he spoke. "I overheard a bit of what you said to her. That was incredibly kind."

"It's true."

"It's still nice to hear." Chase looked around at the large group of people filling the yard, laughing and talking under the lights strung around the space. "And when we're here, together, it's easier to remember. It's when we scatter back to our lives it's a little harder."

"You've all dealt with a major trauma as a family. Everything about your life has been upended and changed. That takes time to process, and from this outsider's view, you're all handling it admirably."

Chase moved in, putting his arm around her and pulling her close. The move was casual and it wasn't especially romantic, but it was intimate. And as his well-muscled arm held her against him, Sloan felt her heart kick hard in her chest.

She placed a hand on his chest, looking up into his eyes.

Once again, that distinct sense of sadness was pervasive, even as he seemingly fought to keep his smile bright.

"Maybe even more important, Chase, you're all trying. I think that says all I need to know about this family."

Chase still hadn't figured out how Sloan had managed it, but in a matter of hours she'd charmed his entire family, become the adoring subject of two dogs and had somehow managed to make him even more enchanted with her than he already was.

And based on how hard he'd tried not to look at her with anything but professional attention in their private moments, that was saying something.

But, wow, the woman was amazing. She had a quality, he'd quickly come to realize, that was the epitome of effortless grace.

Most of all, he acknowledged, she was *there*.

With him.

With his family, each of them fighting a battle to understand what had made them.

And all desperately trying to forge a new path forward.

He didn't need to be looking at her this way—needing her close—but heaven help him, he couldn't look away.

Even earlier, when he'd gladly have punched Greg, he'd understood his cousin's interest. Sloan was beautiful, yes, but that beauty went so much deeper than the surface.

A few hours had passed since he'd come upon her and his half sister on the patio, but even now he could hear her kind words running through his mind, and how she'd comforted Sarah.

What he hadn't expected was how comforting *he'd* personally found her sentiments. Especially with his own conversation with Nate still ringing in his ears.

He'd meant what he'd told his brother, even as the heavy weight of Nate's knowledge of their father's secret life pressed on him.

They *all* deserved better.

How much easier was it to accept that truth when he was with his family, talking, laughing and being together?

And how much easier was it with Sloan?

When he'd hired her, his only goal had been to uncover

the rat at Colton Properties. Yet, now knowing they were close, that the answer to that puzzle would be solved soon, Chase found himself at odds about something else.

He wasn't ready for her to leave.

She made it all smoother somehow. Like what he was dealing with was something he could handle.

Like he had a partner.

It was the last thing he'd expected, and that depth of need scared him.

All while it lifted him up.

Up to now, he'd struggled with the concept of his father's secret life. His mind knew Nate and Sarah were as innocent of their family drama as his other siblings and his cousins.

But his heart had struggled with that reality, the betrayal a visceral blow.

Somehow, Sloan's presence—and her absolute lack of judgment or disdain—made it easier.

Better.

"I keep saying I can't eat another bite and then something even more wonderful comes out of that house." Sloan grinned beside him as Kiki and Frannie marched out of the house with desserts. "It's like a clown car of food. Every time you think there can't possibly be more, there is."

Her comment pulled him out of his wandering thoughts, and he caught sight of the platter in his sister's hands. "I can promise you that you do not want to miss Frannie's pound cake."

"Then, somehow, I'll persevere."

Although the table was crowded, with shouts, laughter and conversation flowing from one end of it to the other, Chase couldn't help but feel this moment was somehow just theirs.

A tender moment in an oasis of happy chaos.

One he was loath to let go, the seeming spell she managed to weave around him keeping them tethered.

He wanted to kiss her.

It would have been okay. More than okay, Chase admitted to himself, as he recalled any number of kisses shared by the couples around the table. Sebastian and Ruby, after hiding their feelings for each other for so long, made no effort to hide their affection now. The deep glances and lingering touches and the big, smacking kiss Sebastian had laid on Ruby as he'd finished up the steaks had made everyone smile.

Fletcher and Kiki, Frannie and Dante, and Max and Della were the same.

The Coltons weren't quite so single any longer and everyone was more than welcoming of the fact that Chase had brought a significant other to the party.

Which made it a special sort of torture to hold himself back.

"Your family is special." Sloan's voice was low, her observation meant only for him. "I'd initially expected this many people all in one place would be overwhelming. Especially when we drove up and I saw all those cars. But—"

She broke off, seeming to gather her words. "It's not that they aren't overwhelming, because there are certainly a lot of people. But there's a warmth there. And a sense of welcome. Like every person you meet is happy you're here. Just as you are. Just for yourself."

Wasn't that the core of it all?

Somehow, with that easy and rather lovely compliment, Sloan had gone to the heart of what he was so determined to puzzle through and make sense of.

His family was warm. And welcoming. And for all their size, there was a congenial camaraderie they all shared.

Even Nate and Sarah had that quality and had shown it to full effect in a matter of visits.

Yet for all their generation knew how to care for one another and accept one another, it had all risen out of a cauldron of secrets each and every child of Robert or Jessie Colton had spent a lifetime oblivious to.

It was the seesaw of emotion he hadn't fully figured out how to manage.

He'd *worked* with his father. For years. And somehow, in all that time, he'd never known the man had a second life somewhere else?

How did a person live a life so completely separate that it was invisible to his loved ones?

That had gnawed at him for months now, and yet, when he sat here with Sloan, he was better able to accept it. More, he could settle himself in a way that he acknowledged it was his own father's choices, not anything self-directed.

So when her hand came over his, resting there in a show of support, it was incredibly easy for him to shift so that their palms touched. Almost of their own accord, their fingers linked together.

A solid bond as well as an outward sign to others.

He knew he shouldn't lean into that support. But here, with Sloan, surrounded by the family who did help him make sense of who he was in the world, Chase knew his first moments of peace since his father's death.

It was small and simple, and the outside world still awaited him.

But in that moment, it was enough.

Sloan felt herself slipping back toward the passenger seat headrest and fought to keep her eyes open.

It would be so easy to close her eyes and revel in the

warmth of an enjoyable evening and the company of a wonderful man.

Which were the exact reasons she needed to remain
wide-awake.

She had to stay alert. Sharp. Focused.

More, she had to stop this lovely, drowsy feeling from
taking her over.

Because it would be so easy to sink into those feelings
of warmth and protection and *couple*dom she'd been trying to fight all evening.

She and Chase weren't a couple. It didn't matter they'd
shared those moments of awareness when they not only
felt like partners, but where it was also the two of them
against the world.

Those flashes of awareness and attraction had happened
in his office as well as on the dates they'd faked throughout the week. But tonight, with his family, it hadn't just felt
right, it had felt real.

Deeply real.

Whatever she'd expected going into this job, never, not
in a million years, would she have said she was at risk of
losing her head or her heart over Chase Colton.

Yet here she was, imagining herself in his arms and
tossing all personal *and* professional restraint to the wind.

"My family really liked you. My phone's been going off
since we got in the car and I suspect it's a string of texts
from my sisters telling me how awesome you are."

"They're pretty great, too." With those lingering thoughts
of professionalism still running through her mind, Sloan
added, "Glad to know we did such a good job of fooling
them."

The temperature in the car changed immediately and
Sloan was happy to see the turnoff for the street that ran in

front of her apartment building. She was more than willing to own the fact that she'd tossed their professional relationship at him like a hand grenade, but really, what other choice did she have?

Sitting here, nestled all snug and warm in his car, was hardly the way she needed to behave with a client. Better to keep it business.

All business.

"We certainly did."

His voice was flat, a sure sign she'd hit the nerve she was aiming for. That her shot had ricocheted back and was currently doing a bit of damage inside her own chest was the logical outcome.

Just something she'd have to deal with.

It was also an important reminder that she needed to stay engaged in the work.

Chase said nothing more, and in moments was turning into her parking lot, navigating to the row of spaces in front of her building. He'd barely put the car in Park when she was unsnapping her seat belt and pushing out of the car in one burst of speed.

She needed to get away from him and all this misplaced emotion and just get inside.

Once she was inside, she'd be fine.

She could regroup with her computer and her files and her work and put all of this out of her head.

It was a good plan. A solid one, if only she had the ability to move more quickly.

But suddenly Chase was there, standing in front of her as she rounded the front of the car.

He was big, somehow seeming even bigger as he blocked the stretch of sidewalk she had to navigate to get to the stairs for her second-floor entrance. Yet for all his size, there wasn't anything threatening about him.

Instead, all she saw was about six feet two inches of hurt. Oh, he kept it leashed—coiled, really—but she saw it there all the same.

The man was in a vulnerable state, with the changes in his life upending everything he thought he knew.

And it was for all those reasons she had to get away. She couldn't let that vulnerability sneak beneath her own defenses. Nor could she let herself think that this temporary reprieve they were taking from their normal lives to play-act a relationship, as well as hunt down a criminal inside his company, was real.

Or maybe, more importantly, had a pathway to *becoming* real.

He'd created this facade specifically because he didn't want romantic entanglements in his life.

"Thank you for a lovely evening. I really did enjoy meeting your family."

"I can walk you to your door."

"It's just up there." She pointed toward the stairs. "I'm fine. Really."

He nodded, but she wasn't sure he'd heard her. Instead, he continued to look at her, full of that vulnerability and awareness that had shaken her to her core.

"You said something. Earlier."

She'd said a lot of things, so instead of responding, she just waited for him to continue.

"When I overheard you talking to Sarah. She told you that she felt like an interloper. And that why would I, or any of my siblings, really, want to have a relationship with someone whose very existence proved the lies we were told."

Whatever conversation she'd expected him to bring up,

her discussion with Sarah wasn't it. Those moments she'd spent with his half sister had been a surprise, for all Sarah had been willing to discuss with a virtual stranger. But they'd also given her a better sense of what the entire family was dealing with.

Like a kaleidoscope, they all were crystals in the same lens. But shifting through each perspective painted a different story.

"She did say that."

"But it was what you said in return that meant something. That she and Nate were dealing with the consequences of our parents' secret as much as anyone else."

"It's true. I think it's because I have the benefit of distance, but I can see the terrible disservice done to you. To all of you. I can't imagine the pain or the raw fury of it all. And it makes me angry for you."

She sighed but pressed on. "Despite the fact that it's not my place to feel that way."

"Not your place?"

An evening breeze whipped up, proof that the days might be warm, but the Idaho nights were rapidly cooling. She wrapped her arms around her waist and tried to convince him she was right.

"This is a job. One you're paying me to do." Sloan pointed once again in the direction of her apartment. "You're even putting me up and paying my expenses. It's very much a job."

"You're human. You've got eyes and ears, and you're entitled to build opinions based on what you see and hear."

"No, actually, I don't. In the confines of my work, I have to find answers. That's all I'm entitled to."

"That's BS."

"No, Chase, it's the truth. I have no right to an opinion

on your circumstances. Whatever else this is, I have no il-
lusions about that."

Wasn't that what she'd been trying to tell herself from
the start?

That she didn't have a right to an opinion. About what
Robert and Jessie did to their families. About how their
children handled what came after that terrible revelation.
Not even about how it affected each of them, collectively
or individually.

But now, she'd crossed a line. Sure, she'd gone this evening at his request and under the ploy they were perpetrating
to get beneath the issues at Colton Properties, but now that
she'd gotten to know Chase and some of his family members,
it rankled—that decision they'd made to lie to everyone.

More than she could ever have guessed.

She was here for work.

A *job.*

Each time she'd chafed at his words that suggested the
same it had been because she'd forgotten that.

His brush-off about her bringing wine.

Or that feeling that she was staff.

Even tonight and what his family had unknowingly
shared with her.

Somehow, that had been the worst. Because they'd spoken to her with openness and honesty, and it would be one
more betrayal when it all came out she was there at their
family function as an imposter.

"Of course, you have a right. Our situation is on full
display."

"Your situation is one you didn't make. It's a problem
created by others that you, your siblings, your cousins—"
she waved a hand "—have all had to clean up. More, what
you all have to find a way to live with."

He moved closer, and where she expected their disagreement to continue, he reached out instead and pressed a hand to her cheek.

"You're so compassionate. And strong. And you make me feel like we will get through this as a family."

"You will." She put her hand over his, knowing she had no right to lean into the warmth, yet unable to pull away. "You all will."

"Thank you for being here."

It's a job.

This isn't real.

These moments can't be.

Each of those thoughts bombarded her, yet even as they did, Sloan knew the truth.

She could no more pull away than ignore these growing feelings of attraction.

And for however long she was here—and realistically, she knew it wasn't long—she couldn't deny her attraction to Chase.

As he lifted his other hand, cradling her other cheek oh-so gently, she accepted that truth.

And when his lips came down over hers, a small sigh escaped from the back of her throat.

She could argue over and over that this wasn't right, or smart, or professional, but she could no longer say it wasn't real.

Chapter 8

Sloan.

Chase pressed his lips against hers, something so profoundly right welling up in his chest as her mouth opened beneath his.

He wanted her.

It no longer mattered how she got here or why she was here. Nor did it matter what secrets they were trying to unearth.

Right now, there was only one secret that mattered.

Discovering the woman in his arms.

Questions had haunted him for months now. About his life. His family. His very foundation.

All of it cracked and crumbled and faded to dust as he pulled her closer, taking the kiss deeper.

Sloan responded, her mouth opening beneath his. Her arms came around his waist and he pulled her even closer. The feel of her in his arms, pressed against his chest, was deeply satisfying after nearly a week of fighting how he felt.

She was everything he'd ever wanted in a partner. Responsive. Engaged. And deeply in the moment with him.

It was a soothing balm after so many months of questioning all he believed.

And it was an exciting push forward with a woman who

both challenged him and helped him see his way to the future.

And…

With a sudden tug of awareness, Chase pulled back.

What was he thinking?

Yes, he wanted her. He'd be lying to say otherwise. But there was so much unsettled in his life. So much to still figure out.

He'd spent the better part of a decade actively avoiding relationships and suddenly he was thinking differently.

Acting differently.

And forgetting that there was nothing to be gained from traveling down that relationship path other than pain.

Sloan stared up at him, the depths of her dark brown eyes nearly black in the light of the overheads that dotted the parking area.

"Chase, I—"

"I'm sorry. I shouldn't have done that."

He glanced down, realizing that he still had her pressed to his chest, and hastily moved back.

"*I* shouldn't have done that. You're my client and it was unprofessional of me and—"

He cut her off, laying a finger to her lips. It shocked him how much that small touch cost him, the desire to pull her back against him and continue their sensual exploration of one another raging through him like an inferno.

But he held himself back.

"You're not unprofessional and you don't need to apologize. It's been a busy week and it was an intense evening. Maybe we can chalk it up to a moment of indiscretion and leave it at that?"

She seemed to consider his words as he dropped his hand back to his side, before coming to a decision.

"I've lost my objectivity."

"Sloan, don't do this. You haven't lost anything."

She shook her head, her smile soft. "I have. And I'm not quite sure if that's good or bad or just a new experience. I've always kept a distance with my work, keeping the case firmly in place in my mind. And with you, with your family—"

She broke off once more, obviously searching for the words before pushing on.

"I care about you and your family. I care about what happens to you all. Your situation is unique, and I can't help but feel that you deserve better, Chase. And I feel the same for your siblings and your cousins, too. You all deserved better."

"I'm working on that part myself."

"I know. Which is the real reason I'm sorry. You need the proper distance to process what's happening. We set up this plan with a specific goal in mind. Allowing me to hide in plain sight."

Chase remembered their discussions as they'd set up her assignment at Colton Properties and had to admit to himself just how shortsighted he'd been.

It was the plan they'd hatched, yes. But it was also the whole situation, requiring him to spend time in close proximity to a woman he found fascinating.

He'd forgotten how lovely it was to enjoy an evening with someone, sharing conversation over dinner. Or sitting beside someone at a family event, laughing through stories and ordinary, everyday conversation.

Or even the simplicity of driving home with someone.

He'd spent so much of his adult life alone, keeping his "relationships" to nothing more than lone evenings, sharing a few hours of time and intimacy. It was only now, when he experienced that real intimacy of day-to-day life, that he acknowledged all he'd been missing.

Moreover, it was about all he'd shut himself off from.

He'd chosen his bachelor lifestyle for a reason. He wasn't cut out for marriage. He'd proved that to himself quite clearly with Leanne.

He didn't feel anything had changed—he still wasn't cut out for forever with anyone. But Sloan's arrival in his life had shown him just how much he'd been missing.

And it only sharpened the ache that had settled deep inside at the knowledge she'd soon be gone.

Saturday morning dawned dark and rainy, and Chase was surprised to realize how neatly it fit his mood.

He'd walked Sloan up to her apartment the night before—he'd do nothing less no matter how awkward those few moments after their kiss had become—and then high-tailed it for home.

But the distance from her hadn't helped.

He'd fought against the lingering taste of her on his lips, yet no amount of inward admonishment *or* the glass of Scotch he'd had once he got home could erase it. And the sensation of cradling her in his arms, their bodies pressed together, seemed to have imprinted on his skin.

He could *feel* her.

When he'd dreamed of her, too, leaving him raw and achy at five in the morning, he'd realized sitting around the house by himself all weekend wasn't a smart idea. But for the first time in a long while, he had zero interest in going into the office and working off his frustration.

Which meant he needed to get out of the house and go *somewhere*.

After a quick shower and breakfast, he headed out, calming a bit as he drove through the entrance to the Colton Ranch.

The ranch had been like a second home growing up. Even the simple act of driving up to the ranch house had given him a few moments of ease from his unsettled thoughts.

Greg stood out on the front porch, drinking his coffee beneath the overhang, and waved as Chase pulled up.

In a matter of moments, Chase was running up the front steps, trying to minimize his exposure to the rain.

"Good morning!" Greg smiled and Chase didn't miss the small shot of knowing in the man's brown eyes.

"Hey there."

They shook hands and at what must have been a longing stare at Greg's coffee mug, his cousin gestured him toward the house. "I need a refill and you look like you need a cup. We'll catch up inside."

"How'd you know I want to catch up?"

"Because it's barely nine o'clock and if you were okay, you'd be at home with Sloan instead of looking like a grizzly bear here with me."

Chase considered making an excuse, one nearly falling off his lips, when he stopped himself.

He was tired of the lies.

And he was tired of how his current situation had made him question what he could or couldn't say to his family.

Sloan was close to figuring out what was wrong at Colton Properties and maybe it was time he eased up a bit and talked to someone he trusted.

And despite his wholly inappropriate streak of possessive jealousy last night, Greg was one of his closest confidants.

"She's at home, exactly where she belongs."

Greg glanced over from where he'd pulled another mug from the cabinets. "Why does she belong there?"

"Because she's not my girlfriend."

Greg's eyes widened, the slight thunk of the mug on the counter his only response.

"She's an independent contractor I've hired to look into some problems at Colton Properties."

Greg recovered quickly, filling the fresh mug along with his second cup before speaking. "So you started dating and you broke up?"

"No, the dating's a fake-out to allow her to come and go at Colton Properties."

"You can't just give her a key?"

A small smile twitched at the edge of Greg's lips and for the first time Chase had to admit what had seemed like a solid idea when they'd hatched it did have elements of the absurd.

"This isn't funny. And if I let the office know she was there on a job, people would want to know what for."

His cousin gestured them toward the kitchen table, then took a seat. "I can see that. I might not have any interest in riding a desk all day, but I can see where someone coming into that environment would get asked questions." Greg took a sip of his coffee before something serious replaced the smile. "But why us? Why lie to the family?"

"There are a few more of us lately. I didn't—"

Chase stopped, unwilling to take the easy out.

"No, that's not fair. It's wrong to lay it at Nathan and Sarah's feet. I didn't want to tell the family because problems at Colton Properties are on me. And I'm embarrassed that I've got a potential financial problem and have been oblivious to it for who knows how long."

There.

It was out.

The real reason he wanted to hide Sloan's investigation.

"This isn't on you, Chase."

"How can you say that? It's entirely on me. I'm the head of CP and what happens there happens on my watch."

"People are capable of some pretty bad stuff. That doesn't rest on you."

Once again, there it was. It was that same push Max made last night. But how did he explain this?

Even if he could see his way to the point that he didn't own every action of the people around him, he was still the leader of the company. He'd made it his life, damn it, and shouldn't there be some benefit to that?

Some proof that all his time, effort and energy had created a company that was more than the sum of its parts?

Only he didn't say that.

He went with the easier truth. The one that demonstrated responsibility and accountability.

Not one more oblivious failure in what was shaping up to be a list of them.

"I'm the head of the company. If it doesn't rest on me, Greg, who does it rest on?"

Greg remained quiet, obviously thinking. For all his earlier teasing, the only thing that remained in the man's dark brown eyes was concern.

And the clear traces of stubbornness Chase recognized lived in his own eyes.

"I think you're confusing responsibility with deliberate action."

"Hardly."

"Hear me out. Then you can go back to being a stubborn ass. But seriously…" Greg paused. "Will you promise to listen for a minute?"

"Alright. I will."

"I've been thinking about it all a lot lately. We can thank our parents for that."

That same wry smile was there, but it was tinged with something decidedly more sober.

Grief.

"And I can't say I have it figured out, but I do think there's a space there."

"A space where?"

"Between responsibility and action. I might take responsibility for my own actions, but I can't own others'. And it's a tougher pill to swallow than it initially seems."

Chase wasn't entirely sure he understood where Greg was going but he knew the man sitting opposite him.

He was like a brother.

They'd spent their whole lives together and Chase knew Greg wasn't prone to fits of deep thoughts. He wasn't a callous man, or a superficial one, but his sense of himself was innately tied to the land he worked, each and every day. With that came a certain sort of centeredness that didn't depend on the opinions of others, *or* much worry or bother about what they thought.

So when the man spoke of those deep thoughts and the things he'd spent time working through in his mind, Chase recognized a kindred spirit.

He'd believed work—hard work—was the key to getting through it all. Hadn't he done the same to get through his marriage? And then to get through life postdivorce?

Work and effort and focus had seemed like the only answers he'd needed.

So how jarring to realize that doing those things—using work as the balm—was one more way of just running away.

And the things that hunted him always found a way to keep up.

"So what you're saying is I need to cut myself a break?"

"Yeah, you do. But more than that, you need to find a way to separate that innate sense of responsibility from feeling that you need to own every problem. They might rest heavy, but you didn't make the mess, Chase. You're just stuck cleaning it up."

They sat there quietly, drinking their coffee, Greg's words of wisdom filling the air between them.

Chase might not be fully ready to accept his circumstances, but perhaps he could see his way toward loosening the tight grip he had on that sense of responsibility as the oldest Colton. Maybe he could even relax a bit further and accept that for all the pain in their lives, they were forging a path to something new, too.

Something that included a new brother and a new sister, two completely awesome people in their own right.

And when the smile returned to his cousin's face, Chase realized they'd come to some sort of an unspoken agreement.

"Now we move to the most important part of our discussion. The beautiful woman you're parading around town as your girlfriend."

"Watch it, cuz."

"You see—that right there." Greg's smile only grew wider and far more mischievous. "That tells me she means something to you."

"Sloan's an amazing woman and an incredible professional. She's damn near solved my problem at Colton Properties and did it in less than a week."

Greg only smiled more broadly.

"What?" Chase pressed. "What are you trying to say through that stupid grin?"

"Your obsession with being the de facto head of the

family and taking care of everyone. It's an admirable trait most of the time, even if you can't take us in your confidence and trust we can support you." Greg's smile faded, his tone laced with more heat and frustration than the man normally worked up in a year. "But right now? You're confusing responsibility with shortsighted idiocy."

"Gee, thanks." Chase fought the urge to get up and pace the room, Greg's words settling over him like an ill-fitting jacket. "What am I being an idiot about?"

"You're talking like you're going to let that woman walk away without a fight."

"She's got two legs and a mind of her own. She can walk wherever she'd like." Even with each word of that statement being totally true, Chase felt heat creep up his neck at being read so easily.

"Yeah, nice try, but I'm not buying the crap you're peddling here."

"She's a contractor, doing a job for Colton Properties."

"Yeah, and she's amazing to boot. And you look at her like you can't stop looking at her."

Chase realized he hadn't taken his gaze off his coffee mug, so he looked up to face his cousin.

Because there it was.

The truth he couldn't run from *or* hide from his loved ones.

Sloan Presley was under his skin and had been from the moment she'd barreled into his office.

And it didn't seem to matter that he didn't want a relationship. Nor did it seem to matter she was only there in a professional sense.

"If you let a woman like that just walk away without even trying to get her to stay?" Greg shook his head.

"That's major-league stupid and I've never taken you for that. Ever."

Chase hadn't taken himself for major-league stupid, either.

But lately his life had been bound and determined to convince him otherwise.

Sloan had thought about calling Chase about a half-dozen times, but firmly tamped down on each wave. Calling led to talking, and talking could lead to seeing each other, and she needed distance.

Desperately.

Especially because that kiss they'd shared hadn't left her thoughts for longer than about eighty-three seconds at a time.

"Pathetic much, Presley?"

Sighing, she pushed back from the kitchen table and crossed to the fridge to root around for a midmorning snack. The rain hadn't let up and there was a gloomy feeling to the dark light seeping into the kitchen that made her think of something rich and decadent.

Which had then made her think of the leftover piece of Frannie's pound cake she'd stashed in the fridge last night.

Each time she'd been victorious against one of those urges to communicate, she'd forced herself instead to work through the irregularities she'd found in both the books as well as the record-keeping systems at Colton Properties.

This go-round she'd assuage it with some delicious butter and sugar.

With the cake and a fresh cup of coffee, she returned to her computer and figured it was worth trying a new tack on the hunt into Colton Properties. There were some particular irregularities, and she was curious if she could tie them by date to any specific happenings in town.

Sloan took another bite of cake, closing her eyes briefly in bliss at the perfect blend of sweet and buttery, before typing in the most recent date of the anomalies she'd uncovered from the prior month.

And she leaned in toward the screen at the page full of articles.

While each was written slightly differently, the headlines all said much of the same thing and she clicked into the one that was the most succinct.

Seven Women Found Dead in Wake County

How had she overlooked this?

It wasn't directly tied to the situation at Colton Properties, but it was pretty gruesome news.

Leaning forward, she read through the article and remembered she had gotten a few of these details before coming to Owl Creek, the biggest of which she'd forgotten. Max had worked this case. He hadn't spoken of it, but Chase had referenced it very briefly on their first call when he'd given her the information that his cousin had been the one to recommend her firm.

Goodness, how did a person live with doing that work?

She admired Max, his skills and his willingness to do the very hard work, but she couldn't imagine the toll it would take, day in and day out.

Her work brought her close to crimes, but she still had the safety of a computer screen and the distance of reading about something, not actually being there when a body was found or a killer's most depraved acts were discovered.

She scanned the article quickly, as was her habit, and read about the initial search-and-rescue and the discovery of the bodies over a period of days. But it was the link at the bottom of the article that caught her attention.

Law Enforcement Seeking Connection Between Serial Killer's Victims

"I guess I'm in now," she muttered to herself, following through to the linked article.

This one was full of speculation, she thought. There simply didn't appear to be any concrete facts for them to follow, but the enterprising reporter who'd written the story focused on the comparable ages of the women, their general similarity in appearance and the time period of their expected deaths.

"Just over two years." The shiver that skated down her spine was impossible to ignore. "What senseless deaths."

She was about to click on another link at the bottom of this article, leading her to the latest details, when her phone lit up with a text from Chase.

Come outside.

She smiled in spite of herself as three dots appeared on the screen, followed by another message.

It'll be worth it.

It was ridiculous to feel this shot of joy at the texts, but they did make her happy, the grisly articles quickly forgotten in favor of the man waiting outside.

And if that was a problem?

Well, she'd deal with it later.

Whatever had happened last night—and she'd tossed and turned endlessly trying to figure it out—was last night.

It was time to see what he had up his sleeve right now.

She slipped into a pair of sneakers she'd left by the couch and was almost to the door when an impish impulse hit her. Opening up the text string, she shot a quick text of her own.

Who is this?

The text went winging away as she opened her front door and she was just in time to see his reaction as she looked over the second-floor railing. His hair was tousled and his head was bent, but even from above she could see the way his mouth thinned into a straight line as he stared at his phone screen.

"Serves you right!" she hollered down, unable to fight the bubble of happiness that welled in her chest.

He glanced up then and Sloan had the wildest impulse to race down the stairs and into his arms.

"What serves me right?"

"Summoning a woman out into the rain!"

He smiled up at her before extending his arms. "Am I wet?"

Sometime between her last look out the window and now, the rain must have let up, even though it was still pretty gloomy.

"Come on down. I want to show you something."

She didn't skip, but Sloan figured she could have moved a bit more sedately down the concrete steps that led to the first floor. It was only as she got close that Chase reached out, snagging her hand and pulling her up close to him.

"There. Look."

She followed the extension of his hand as he pointed to

something up over the roof of her building, a small gasp spilling from her throat as she took it all in.

"It's a double rainbow!"

"I had to show you."

"It's gorgeous."

She followed the distinct lines of the rainbow, each color coming to life in the sky in vivid relief. The second rainbow, a short distance from the first, had the expected fading, more pastel-hued in each color than the first rainbow, but equally beautiful.

And, in that moment, it was like a small piece of magic just for them to share.

"You really didn't know it was me texting?"

Sloan hadn't believed that bubble of happiness could grow bigger, but at the anxious expression on his face, she realized that it had.

"I was teasing you. We've been texting for three weeks now."

"Right."

"Chase." She poked him in the chest before putting her palm against those firm lines. "It was a joke."

"Sure. Of course."

It was one of those small moments of vulnerability that simply melted her.

Did he realize how adorable he was?

And how hard he made it for her to keep her distance?

Here was a formidable businessman and yet he could still be stymied by a silly text.

It was…oddly sweet.

And one more chink in the armor she was desperately trying to protect herself with.

"I'm sorry."

The apology was out of place, especially seeing as he'd

called her out here to see something so spectacular. "For what? The double rainbow is amazing."

"For last night. I was out of line, and I am sorry."

Sloan weighed her thoughts and realized there were two ways to play this. She could play dumb and pretend last night hadn't happened and that she hadn't actually spent most of the time since thinking about it, or she could push for what she wanted and stress her interest in having it happen again.

"You weren't out of line." She lifted up on her toes to press a kiss to his jaw. "And I don't need an apology." She shifted to kiss his chin. "But I really would appreciate it if you'd do it again."

This time, she pressed her lips to his.

For a fraction of a second, she thought she'd overstepped and misread the cues, his lips firmly closed and his jaw still unmoving.

But then he opened his mouth, their lips suddenly locked in a delicious battle of wills.

And it was the moment his arms came around her, pulling her tight against his chest, that Sloan realized she'd won the battle.

Chapter 9

Markus Acker stared at the text from his second-in-command, Winston Kraft, and felt a shot of pure satisfaction light him up from the center of his chest straight out to the very tips of his fingers.

Their latest scheme and tentative partnership with a new launderer had gone off without a hitch and their money was clean.

That quick hit of endorphins was short-lived since it hardly solved all their problems. Still, it was a step in the right direction.

He'd managed to grow his flock considerably in the past few years, and with their devotion came their money. He had to find ways to funnel it into the Ever After Church without all those dirty strings attached.

Speaking of attached...

He rolled his eyes as he thought of Jessie Colton. Easily manipulated, yes, but she had a certain streak of determination he was finding increasingly annoying. She wasn't nearly the subservient lamb he'd initially thought and her attitude of late had become downright demanding.

And, damn, the woman had quite a life story.

He'd believed he'd done a fairly decent job playing on her latent guilt. Since she'd left her four children to run off with her husband's brother and have two more in secret, it had been easy to subtly shame her, especially when she first came into his flock. But of late, he'd questioned just how effective he'd been.

His lamb had sprouted a few fangs.

The death of Robert Colton was tricky. She'd loved the man, well enough to leave her first marriage and her young children to take up with him. But Robert's subsequent leaving a decade later to go back full-time to his first family had left some wounds that most definitely hadn't scarred over.

No, Markus thought as he headed for the cabin they used in the woods outside the Ever After compound in Conners. That wound still had a lot of raw, seething pain in it.

Which still left him with a tool to manage her, but he did have to be careful. Overchanneling that anger in the wrong direction could backfire if she erupted like a loose cannon.

Up to now he'd focused on the two biological children she'd had with Robert.

Nathan and Sarah.

Both seemed rather oblivious to the benefits to be gained from their newfound family. But Markus innately knew that was the right button to push.

They were abandoned children.

Another family had received the majority of Robert's love and affection in life.

And now, most pressing of all, if they didn't act, those other children would receive Robert's wealth after his death.

Robert had set up Jessie and his secret children well and Markus already had designs on that money, but there was always a need for more. He wouldn't rest until Jessie had squeezed every last drop out of the rest of the family.

They'd already discussed their approach and how she

needed to position her abandoned family to maximize their sympathy and, therefore, her children's inheritance.

Taking a deep breath, he prepared himself for the evening. At first, she'd amused him, but things had grown tiresome of late. Especially with the constant requests to marry. What had started as a murmur had moved to a fevered crescendo in the months since Robert had died and he hadn't fully settled on a dismissal that would work.

The jealousy from the rest of the flock had worked for a while, but he knew that excuse was wearing thin.

He rapped lightly before opening the door. Even with the fact that several women had been found dead in the area, Jessie was oblivious to any risk to herself.

She almost flouted it, truth be told. Walking around the compound and trying to meet him in the more deserted areas of the property as if nothing amiss had happened to other women out alone.

"Darling!"

Jessie flung herself at him and he braced for impact as he suddenly had his arms full of woman. Ensuring his next eye roll was a mental one only, he cooed back at her, "Darling, how I've missed you."

"It's been forever." She practically mewled the words against his chest and Markus held her in place there, his chin propped against the top of her head.

He'd just left her this morning, but he could play the besotted swain with the best of them. It was one of many in his bag of tricks.

"It's felt like ages, my darling."

She sighed against his chest before staring up at him. "It's agony. I can't wait until the day when we don't have to live in secret any longer. When the whole world will know I'm Mrs. Markus Acker."

"I wait with bated breath."

"Can we do it soon? I've been thinking, and really, my love, there's nothing to be done for those selfish, silly leeches who will be jealous of me. Of our love."

It was further reinforcement that the jealousy-of-the-flock argument was losing its power.

He cycled through any number of responses, initially floundering before the perfect one filled his mind.

"I know, darling, and I feel the same. The women who will be jealous are going to be no matter what. But there is another issue. One that worries me even more."

Jessie's gaze narrowed, her clear irritation at being put off once more filling eyes that had grown far less adoring. "Now what?"

"It's Nathan and Sarah."

That gaze brightened right up. "Well, that's no problem. They won't be jealous."

"Of course not. They love you. I'm more concerned with pushing one more layer of upheaval into their lives. They're still grieving their father and meeting all those new brothers and sisters." He waved a hand. "I'd hate to give them any more emotional pain. I want them to celebrate our love right along with us and I fear that won't happen if we try to marry now."

He mentally applauded himself for the quick thinking and had to admit the point had merit. Even if he had been wildly interested in marrying their mother, her children were grieving the loss of their father and adjusting to a new family, all at once. A marriage at this time was hardly ideal.

He pressed a kiss to her forehead, keeping her close and practically willing her to his way of thinking. But as he pulled back, determined to keep his visage calm, his attitude easy and serene, he saw her start to wear down.

A sort of acceptance seemed to fill her eyes before she nodded.

"You're right, my darling. A little while longer. Nathan and Sarah have been through so much."

So very much, Markus thought as he pulled Jessie against him once more, his hands drifting down over her spine before settling low on her back.

He was still determined to use the way Jessie and Robert had brought their two youngest children into the world to his advantage.

Because there was no one serene enough or centered enough to overlook the slight of being excluded from an inheritance when the rest of their siblings got something.

He'd spent a lifetime reading human behavior.

And he'd bet his life he could work those two to his advantage.

I'd really appreciate it if you'd do it again.

Her own words ran over and over in her head as the kiss with Chase spun out and Sloan wondered how quickly she'd changed in so short a time.

When had she become so brazen?

And why did it seem so natural to kiss him beneath a rainbow-laden sky?

She should pull away.

There was no way she could get used to this. She was so close to uncovering the answers at Colton Properties. And once she did, she'd be gone.

But it was because of that very fact she stayed where she was.

She'd have to leave soon, and she needed to soak up every single moment of this. Wrapped up in Chase's arms, kissing him and exploring this magic between them.

Chase nuzzled her lips before gently lifting his head. "Does that mean you liked the double rainbow?"

"I like the man under the double rainbow. The beautiful sky was just a side benefit."

They stood there for several heartbeats, their gazes locked before Chase seemed to come to some decision.

"I can't say I'm sorry, but we shouldn't be doing this. Your work's impeccable and much as I hate the outcome, I know you'll have my problem fixed in a matter of days and be headed back to Chicago."

He was right.

Every single bit of it was fact. And yet...

Why did the thought of leaving make her sad?

Yes, she was attracted to Chase, but they'd only formally met less than a week ago. Even if she added the few weeks they'd spoken on the phone, Chase Colton had been part of her life for less than a month.

So why would completing a job and going home be something to be upset about?

"I will be."

"I—" Chase's hesitance was something of a surprise, especially when it was matched by him stepping back. "I can't thank you enough for all your help."

Those small embers that had sparked to life in the past, when he'd firmly put her in the professional box, were nowhere in evidence this time. Instead, she saw the cracks around the frayed edges of his control.

And with it, she laid a hand on his shoulder, willing him to understand that the challenges he faced now weren't permanent. They were earth-shattering, but they *would* pass.

"You and your family are going to get through this, you know." She held his gaze steady. "All of you. Together."

"There are some days I believe that. Like last night."

His whole demeanor relaxed a bit, some of that tension that had lit him up as he'd stepped away fading. "When we're together I do believe we'll get through it."

"That's what you need to focus on, then. That there is a future for all of you and it's a good one. And it's built on a solid foundation."

"Oh, sure, rock-solid."

It was meant as a joke and she knew that. But as Chase said the words, she realized that there was something there worth digging underneath.

"There is, Chase. Think about it. Your mom and your Uncle Buck were there. Always there, for all of you."

As Sloan considered it, she realized there really was something there.

Something well worth celebrating.

"I haven't met either of them, but their presence was clearly felt last night at the barbecue. The way everyone spoke of them and whenever anyone shared a funny story, the names Jenny and Buck were at the center of it."

"They're good people. We've often joked quietly among all us kids that those two should have been the ones who got married."

"They built your foundation."

"I guess they did."

"They gave you the tools to get through this. The depth of your relationships with your siblings and your cousins. The understanding of the importance of family."

"It's a wonder how Nate and Sarah got that at all," Chase said on a sigh. "Especially seeing as who they got as parents."

"You'll see to it that they get the full benefit of being Coltons from here on out."

"You make it sound so simple."

"Maybe it is. Maybe for all the complications in all your lives, what your mom and what your Uncle Buck gave you is solid. Unshakable."

"I want to believe that, Sloan. You have no idea how badly I want to."

"Why can't you?"

"What if I'm wrong?"

His question sort of lingered there between them. One more sign the man he believed himself to be had somehow vanished in the events of the past few months.

Those unassailable qualities about himself he'd have said were unbreakable had, in fact, broken.

"Maybe it isn't about being right or wrong, in this case."

Sloan's words had been spoken in a low, soft tone and Chase found himself caught up in that quiet, lilting quality.

Moreover, he was snared in the promise she offered.

"How can it be about anything else?"

"You have to find a way forward for yourself. Based on what I've observed, I believe your family will, too, but in the end it's their journey."

He'd bet on every one of his brothers and sisters and cousins in a heartbeat.

Why was he having such a hard time betting on himself?

Sloan glanced toward the fading rainbow before her gaze resettled on him. "Take me for a drive."

"Where?"

"Here. Around Owl Creek. A bit beyond if you'd like. I want to see what you do."

"You want to see real estate?"

"I want to see the home you love and the land you love. Show it to me." She spread a hand outward. "Whatever else has shaken your foundation, this is yours."

It was a unique sort of encouragement but as they exited her apartment complex grounds fifteen minutes later, Chase had to admit it was the perfect balm for all that had been bothering him.

Crisscrossing through Owl Creek, he pointed out various landmarks, silly things he'd done as a kid down at the town lake and even a piece of land on the edge of town that was his dream property.

"What's so important about it?" Sloan asked.

"I've believed for years we could sustain a resort here. A real one, that people plan trips around. We'd bring a significant amount of tourism along with a heck of a lot of industry and jobs."

"What's stopping you?"

"The land's the easy part on this one. Getting the right backers. Working with the right company. It's far more complex than a typical build and I haven't quite found the right promise to investors."

Chase pulled into a small gravel lot near the largest lake in Owl Creek. He put the car in Park and cut the engine, about to get out when Sloan put a hand on his arm. "You'll get there. I know you will."

"I'd always believed it."

"Then keep believing it."

Old habits died hard, and Chase knew more than a decade of choices couldn't be undone in a matter of days. But Sloan had changed something.

He didn't want a relationship. He'd been so firm on that count, quite sure heading down that path again would destroy him.

It was a mistake he had no interest in making again.

And even with all that *certainty*, Sloan had snuck through his defenses.

He kept fighting it but his reaction to Greg's interest in her had been a flag. The special combination of excitement and ease he always felt in her presence was another. And the fact that he wanted to share this dream with her was yet another.

In what felt like much too short a time, she'd come to matter.

And he wasn't quite sure what to do about it.

Which made the frown that subtly marred her lips a surprise he keyed in on immediately.

"What is it?"

"I have no way of making this sound better than I mean it, but I was sitting here looking at all this beauty and couldn't help but question those dead women discovered last month." A small shiver rippled through her shoulders. "It's terrible."

It had been horrific, and Chase knew the case had shaken a lot of people in Wake County. The brutality of it all and the sheer number of women who'd been killed had been staggering.

That another young woman had then been killed in the hospital, after seemingly escaping from captors, had only added to that underlying sense of unease folks had been feeling.

Although they'd spoken briefly about the Ever After Church before, Chase elaborated on what he knew.

"Max worked that case. It's where he met Della."

"I got the sense something dark had drawn them together based on a few things that had been said at the barbecue," Sloan said. "But I didn't feel last night was the right time to ask."

Chase caught her up quickly. He told Sloan how Della had been training her K-9, Charlie, in a new-to-him mountainous area, and while tracking, had found a dead body. Max had been called in as the FBI lead to work the case.

"Horrifically, they found seven bodies in total and then another woman who'd been badly hurt who died later. One of the seven was Della's cousin, Angela Baxter."

"That's awful."

"It really shook Della up, as you'd imagine. But she was committed to seeing it all through."

"Those articles I read? One reporter seems determined to link it to that local church we talked about."

It was Chase's turn to frown at that description. "Ever After?" When she only nodded, he added, "You hear things, working in real estate. They seem to move from place to place and have laid claim to a property a few towns over in Conners."

"Laid claim? Don't churches have actual structures? Buildings they use? A place they actually settle and develop?"

"My thoughts exactly. I've always been one to let people live their lives because you see a lot in real estate that's not really your business. Who wants to build a survival camp, or who's decided they need to carve out a ditch in the woods for a fallout shelter."

"People still do that?"

"They most certainly do." Chase shook his head. "But there's something about that church that isn't right. Max's mother has dabbled in that group and it's worried him."

"Jessie Colton's a part of that?"

"Appears so. My cousins all think it's a bad idea, but she's not exactly been a part of their lives and I don't think they know how to engage her on the topic." Chase shrugged, recognizing a deeper truth. "I don't think they know how to engage her on anything."

"What do Nate and Sarah think?"

"I'm not entirely sure but I don't get the sense they put too much stock in their mother's choices."

"One more choice in a long line of poor ones," Sloan murmured.

"What do you mean?"

"Leaving her children and her husband. Putting on a married facade with a new man who also happens to be her sister's husband. Now she's caught up in an *entity* that is under a cloud of suspicion. Those are some seriously questionable decisions."

Chase had never put much stock in the stories of his Aunt Jessie. Any woman who'd run off on her children—his cousins, who had become, through a lifetime together, some of his best friends—had never seemed worth his time or attention.

The fact that his cousins had gone out of their way to avoid speaking about her—a point his mother mimicked—had made Jessie a sort of ghost in his life. Someone who hovered on the periphery but wasn't really visible from day to day.

"It does make you wonder."

And now that Sloan had made the point, it actually had him wondering quite a bit. He had the details on the property in Conners the Ever After Church was purported to live on.

Maybe he'd do a bit of discreet digging.

It really had nothing to do with him, and yet…it had everything to do with him because it was about his family. Max, Greg, Malcolm and Lizzy were as close to him as his siblings.

He'd spent enough time wallowing in the things he hadn't considered or had the foresight to recognize, Chase realized.

But this he could look into.

This he could understand better.

If his Aunt Jessie really was making yet another poor decision in a long line of them, wasn't it important to understand that?

Because maybe if they did, they'd all take a big step forward in putting the past firmly behind them.

Sloan wasn't sure what had prompted her suggestion to drive around Owl Creek but was glad for whatever impulse had struck. Their afternoon had been…restorative.

And it had given her yet another glimpse into the fascinating man Chase Colton was.

His love of this deeply beautiful part of Idaho was evident, as was his knowledge of real estate and the business of making a property a successful enterprise.

Even their discussion of the dead women had been laced with his knowledge and understanding of real estate, property management and the basic requirements to use the land.

And how odd to know that his Aunt Jessie—already suspect to Sloan's way of thinking—was part of that creepy group.

Although it was a distraction that she didn't really need to indulge, she knew herself well enough to know that she'd be doing a bit more digging later into the Ever After Church.

In the meantime, she was sharing an afternoon with a handsome, interesting man. It was time to start paying attention to that instead of the sad mystery that had spiked her curiosity.

"How long would something like that take?" she asked. "Building an entire resort?"

"Why don't we get out and we can walk along the shoreline? I promise not to be so boring you're tempted to jump in the lake to escape my incessant droning."

The wry humor combined with his captivating green gaze was all the encouragement she needed. Sloan scrambled out of the car, eager to hear all he wanted to share.

Although she was honest enough with herself to admit she was a bit besotted with Chase, a half hour later all she could see was the vision of his resort. It was coming to life in her imagination, rising from the land surrounding the lake.

"So really," he said. "It's not about just creating everything all at once. You could do it in phases."

"I'm not a real-estate expert, but I am a human being who enjoys a vacation. What you're describing is incredible. From the spa to the outdoor activities to the hotel itself?" Sloan ticked off just a few of the images Chase had described for her.

She stopped, circling a full turn before coming back to where she started so that she could look up at him. "It's special, Chase. This place is special. Welcoming and bright and deeply restorative."

"I was thinking the same thing about you."

"Chase, I—"

He shook his head before holding up a hand. "Please. Let me say this."

The change in his demeanor was so swift, so immediate, she could only nod.

"I'm a bad bet when it comes to relationships."

"Chase, I'm sure that's not true."

"It actually is. And I've not only been content with that truth, but I've actively reveled in it." He laughed but the sound fell hollow before floating away on a light breeze.

"It's why we've been so successful at the office with our little show we've been putting on."

Since she heard the brush-off coming, Sloan felt her spine stiffen, already bracing for it.

Which made his next words so earth-shattering.

"You're the first woman I've met since my divorce that has made me realize I've shut myself off from living."

"I..." She stopped, realizing a truth of her own. "I don't know what to say. But I do have a sense of what you're feeling."

"Oh?"

"I've put everything I am into building SecuritKey. And I don't regret it, in any way, but I've come to realize that I have used it as an excuse at times."

"Why?"

"Lack of successful relationships. A personality that's innately more comfortable behind a computer hunting for data than going out and engaging with others. Take your pick."

"You did well with my family last night."

"And that time made me realize that I've been hiding a bit. Perhaps more than a bit these last few years as my business has really taken off. It's easy to say there isn't time for a relationship, or that I'll work on it later when there's something else occupying my time. But I think I've been marking time instead."

It was a stark realization, but it was true all the same. It had been easier than she ever could have expected to use her job as the reason she wasn't in a relationship. Or, worse, why she'd slowly given up on trying, especially these past few years.

The number of dates she'd been on had dwindled. The number of second dates, after those few first dates she did have, had become nonexistent.

"What do you want to do about it?" he asked softly.

"I'm not sure. But I do know I've enjoyed the time this past week in your company."

She considered all that stood in their way, a few key details still glaringly obvious.

She lived in Chicago and he lived in Idaho.

She was here on a job only.

And most of all, despite his confession that he'd been running from relationships, he wasn't exactly seeking one out with her.

"I've enjoyed this time with you, too."

Chase reached out and brushed a wayward curl behind her ear. His hand lingered briefly against her jaw before he pulled away.

It wasn't much, Sloan admitted to herself. Not a declaration of interest or a request to see where things could go.

By either of them.

But it was a step forward.

An admission, really.

And despite her confused sadness at the reality that she was leaving as soon as she wrapped up the work for Colton Properties, she couldn't deny how sweet it felt to actually say the words.

It was even sweeter to hear them.

Chapter 10

Sloan spent the rest of the weekend with work.

Yes, it was a bit of slinking back to her corner where she was most comfortable, but it was also the work she'd contracted to do. SecuritKey maintained its commitments, no matter how moony its owner was.

And she did manage to carve out a bit of time to herself. Time that wasn't spent obsessing over Chase Colton, thank you very much.

She'd driven around Owl Creek a bit more, retracing some of the roads they'd taken the day before while also finding a few more herself. And she'd taken a relaxing run around the lake she and Chase had visited.

She might not have been in the best frame of mind Monday morning as she opened a package of food for Waffles before making herself some scrambled eggs, but she wasn't in a bad place, either.

And, damn it, she was so close to figuring out the thief inside Colton Properties.

She'd dug hard the day before, forgetting to eat dinner until Waffles had squawked at her from his perch beside the makeshift desk she'd set up at the small kitchen table.

The irregularities in the books were subtle and very well done, but there was a pattern she'd nearly figured out.

It wasn't the same day every month, or the same week each quarter. Nor was it a specific amount, but more of a vague skim that never exceeded more than about two percent off a transaction. But she sensed there was something specific to the timing all the same.

She'd made a mental note to ask Chase if there was any specific payment schedule for his properties. Perhaps the way they collected on income or when they removed monies for tax assessments would give her a clue.

Regardless, she was close to the answer. And she'd effectively ruled out both the sales and marketing teams from any nefarious doings. Although that encompassed quite a few employees, she was hesitant to question those who were left.

Although few understood what she really did for a living or how she did it, Sloan had always been careful to rule people out, but avoid casting aspersions on those she hadn't yet eliminated. Proof was the only way to approach potential criminal activity and she was acutely aware she could ruin someone's life and reputation if she was wrong.

So she'd keep digging.

It was the only way.

She'd worked until about midnight before deeming herself suitably tired enough to sleep. Even then, she'd still tossed and turned a bit before finally drifting off.

Why hadn't he called?

Wasn't she glad he hadn't called? How else was she supposed to make a clean break when she went home to Chicago?

And why hadn't he kissed her, right there beside the lake?

I do know I've enjoyed the time this past week in your company.

Chase's comment had lodged in her thoughts, lighting up her senses with each and every restless turn in bed.

She enjoyed his company, too.

And Sloan instinctively knew they had moved into dangerous territory admitting that.

She didn't live here. And he didn't do relationships. It would be a really bad idea to form some sort of attachment under any circumstances, but especially when she was so close to cracking the culprit at Colton Properties.

She told herself all these things and had finally drifted off to sleep,

And then her eyes had popped open bright and early, and no amount of telling herself to go back to bed had worked. She finally got up, put in another hour and a half on the financial files and then cleaned up to head over to Chase's office.

It might have only been a week, but the Colton Properties offices never failed to inspire her, Sloan thought as she pulled into the parking lot. Chase's SUV was already there, and her heart gave a hard thump knowing she'd see him soon.

Frowning as she got out—really, was she a fourteen-year-old with a crush?—Sloan pulled her work bag from where she'd stowed it behind the driver's seat and put both the image and the anticipation of seeing Chase in his dress shirt and sharply pressed slacks firmly out of her mind.

And stared up at the building that housed Colton Properties.

For all the negative thoughts she'd had about Robert Colton and his actions to his families, both the one he publicly acknowledged and the one he didn't, she had to give the man credit for his vision. What had begun as the Colton hardware store when Robert first started his business had grown, expanded and flat-out evolved into what was now the family enterprise.

They'd managed to leave the original hardware-store layout as the first floor of the building, while adding to the place by going up. Colton Properties sat above, as modern and business-focused as the old store felt small-town and folksy in the very best sense of the words. The shelving and cash registers were still on the first floor, but the merchandise had long been removed. In its place were various stations full of photographs of properties in the surrounding areas, both for sale as well as those that had already been developed.

It was impressive, Sloan acknowledged as she headed for the elevators.

Vision was something she always respected.

And it was awe-inspiring to see how that vision had found a place in Robert's son, unwavering and true.

Althea was already standing in front of the elevator and Sloan smiled at the office manager as she moved up beside her. "Good morning."

"Oh." Althea shook her head, obviously startled by the greeting. But she quickly regrouped, even as she pressed a hand against her chest. "I'm sorry, dear, you scared me. I was wool-gathering about all I need to get done today."

"I'm confident you can do it all," Sloan said as she gestured the older woman into the open elevator. "You're certainly getting a good head start on your Monday."

"I could say the same for you," Althea said, and though there was a light tease in her words, Sloan didn't miss the clear signs she really was frazzled.

"I wanted to see if I could drag Chase out for a quick cup of coffee and maybe a little breakfast. Then I need to get some work of my own done."

"What is it you do again, dear?" Althea asked as she stepped off to the main floor of the business.

"I'm a consultant."

"Which is?"

The first question had seemed a bit off, the words strangely sharp even as Althea's tone held a flat quality. But Sloan quickly deciphered the real question underneath the continued probing as they walked into the open lobby of Colton Properties.

And in that moment she had a flash of those dates and stealthy withdrawals she'd reviewed, over and over, all weekend.

It hadn't been the dates in each month.

It had been the time stamp.

Each and every one had happened before eight a.m.

She glanced down at her watch before aiming a big wide smile, full of teeth, at Althea. "I take on clients who have need of digital-forensics services."

"What are those?" The light titter that skimmed beneath the question only reinforced the sudden shot of awareness and *certainty* flooding Sloan's veins.

"It's an ability to dig into digital files and understand that all elements are managed properly. Finances. Profit-and-loss statements."

"Why ever would anyone need that?"

"A variety of reasons, but it's the quickest way to suss out embezzlers."

Chase chose that moment to come into the outer office and Althea smiled at him, all cheerfulness and sunshine. "Chase, good morning! Your girlfriend and I rode up the elevator together."

Chase's smile was equally broad, his "good morning" winging back through the lobby area.

Sloan didn't know why she moved, but something about

the entire tableau playing out in the lobby keyed her into one very important point.

Althea was about to run.

Without questioning it, Sloan moved into position between the older woman and the door.

And cleanly intercepted her when she made a run for it.

"Get off me, you bitch!"

Chase stared at the scene unfolding before him and lost about three seconds simply trying to process what was happening.

And then he moved.

Sloan had captured Althea in a tight hold, locking the woman's arms at her side.

Although Althea had Sloan by a solid thirty pounds, Sloan had youth and strength on her side and kept a firm hold on the woman, refusing to let go of her quarry.

"What's going on?"

"This is your embezzler," Sloan grit out around the struggling woman.

Chase stepped forward, reaching for Althea by the shoulders in hopes of calming her down.

Or that's what he'd tell himself later when the woman freed an arm and decked him solidly in the left eye.

"What the hell!"

A lifetime spent with brothers and male cousins had taught him how to fight. And an equal amount of time with two wily sisters and a female cousin had taught him how to use finesse while still taking hold of a dangerous situation.

He'd never hit a woman, regardless of Althea's attack. But he had no compunction about placing a stronger hold around her arms to keep her in place.

He didn't have to hold her long when the hissing and spitting devolved into hard sobs as she curled into his chest.

"I'm sorry, Chase. I'm so sorry."

He glanced at Sloan over the woman's head. She only nodded, affirming what he'd quickly pieced together.

"Why, Althea?"

"Ben. It's my Ben."

As Sloan called the police, Chase escorted Althea into the conference room off the lobby, closing the door behind them. She continued to sob while Chase crossed to the small fridge beneath the side counter Althea always kept stacked full and pulled out a water.

He unscrewed the cap and handed over the water, then took a seat next to her. "Tell me what's going on."

Through fits and starts, and quite a few more tears, Althea told him of Ben's health problems and the increasing cost of his treatments and his medicines.

Chase didn't want to feel compassion, but he recognized the pain and couldn't quite help himself. He'd known Althea most of his life and he knew her family.

And he'd known Ben had "off days," as she'd mention from time to time, but he had no real understanding of just how bad things were.

His employees' personal situations were their business, but he could have helped. Could have found some way to help her manage this burden.

Or he believed he could have. But ten years? He'd been growing his influence but ten years ago his father was firmly involved in Colton Properties.

Would Robert Colton have been so understanding?

Would he have helped?

"Why didn't you come to me?"

"I—" She stared down at the hands folded in her lap. "You've had a lot going on."

"Not for ten years."

"Your father before you did." Althea hiccupped, then added in a low voice, "That's what made it so easy."

"Made it easy?"

"I knew, Chase. About your father's secret life. His other family. And I used his distraction and his willingness to keep piling responsibility and system access on me to my advantage. I figured if the great Robert Colton could keep two families, I could at least take a little bit to help care for my own family."

It wasn't logical, but as he sat there, staring at the woman he'd believed he knew, Chase had to admit he could see how it had happened.

Fifteen minutes later he'd made his statement to his brother Fletcher and his partner from the Owl Creek PD. Fletcher's partner left to take Althea down to the station, and Chase dropped his head in his hands.

"Ten years, Fletcher. Ten."

"It's a long damn time." His brother's green eyes, so like his own, were filled with a mix of compassion and anger.

A look, Chase suspected, he'd find in his own if he only had a mirror.

"Do you believe it? That Dad's secret life was why she did it? And it was those secrets that made it all so easy."

Fletcher nodded, tapping at the small notebook he'd written in while Althea had told her story. "I heard it. And for what it's worth, she's backpedaling an awful lot. She found an excuse she's comfortable with to make her own sins not seem so bad."

"Her husband is sick."

"And we'd have helped her. Somehow, we'd have found a way. But she stole from us instead. Don't forget that."

"I guess."

Fletcher moved closer, his hand settling on Chase's shoulder. "She made a choice, Chase. A bad one. Don't lose sight of that."

They said their goodbyes and Chase watched his brother leave. He was not at all surprised when Sloan showed up at the door, slipping in and closing it behind her.

"People must be wondering what's going on?"

"Yeah, they are. I told everyone to get settled in the big conference room in about a half hour and you'd let them know you'd be out to talk to them."

"And tell them I've missed an embezzler for the past decade."

"And tell them you *caught* an embezzler who's covered her tracks—well—for the past decade."

Sloan's emphasis was in all the right places and still, Chase couldn't help but feel the spin.

"One more excuse. Just like Althea's."

"I'd call it the truth."

He heard the steel in her tone and saw it mirrored in the hard set of her features, her jaw fixed in place.

It should have been harsh, but instead…it was compelling.

And a reminder that he'd wanted answers and had gotten them.

This was never going to end in a good place. He'd called in Sloan and her expertise specifically because there *was* a problem with the books.

It was hardly the time to get angry at the messenger.

Which made the explosion that much worse.

"You can call it whatever the hell you want, it doesn't

change the fact that a woman was just escorted out of here, broken by life."

He picked up Althea's half-full water bottle and hurled it at the far wall.

The move wasn't particularly satisfying, but the anger roiling through him softened a bit with the action.

In the desire to move and rant.

To somehow shed this rage that had filled him at the discovery of his father's secret life.

Yet Althea's excuses—one more dark mark in a column full of them—only made the thick miasma of it all heavier.

A weight that seemingly grew as each day passed.

Sloan didn't deserve any of it.

She'd helped, but in seeing her standing there, more than willing to shoulder the burden of her discovery, Chase knew a sense of shame.

And anger.

And a deep sort of fracture that separated the life he believed he had from the one he actually did.

It cratered through him.

And Chase wondered if he would ever be the same.

Sloan was tempted to just walk out.

Leave Chase to his anger and his need to process it, and head home.

She'd solved the case. It was time to pack up and head back to Chicago.

She nearly did all that, actually turning on her heel to head out the same way she'd come in, before something stopped her.

This wasn't directed at her. Oh, she was handy, but she wasn't the real target. And whatever she was seeing now had nothing to do with the raw, aching fury that was raging through him.

With calm, purposeful movements, she crossed to the sideboard and picked up a roll of paper towels, then went over and cleaned up the water. She'd sopped up the first seeping puddle when she felt a large hand on her back.

"You don't have to do that."

"It's fine. I can—" She didn't even finish her sentence when Chase was gently pulling her to her feet, taking the roll and the sopping handful from her. "It's my mess. I'll do it."

He tossed the wet handful in the garbage and already had a fresh length pulled off when Sloan laid a hand on his arm.

"Why don't we both do it and we'll get it done in no time?" She couldn't resist adding a smile. "Your aim was solid, and you even cleaned that window there."

The tease had its desired effect and he let out a laugh when he saw the streams of water dripping down the window that overlooked Main Street. "Side benefit."

Chase handed her the paper-towel roll and within minutes they both had the room back to rights, the floor and the window dry once more. He resettled the considerably smaller towel roll back on the sideboard before turning to face her.

"I'm sorry."

His green gaze was bleak, but his voice was firm.

Solid.

And underneath it all, she could hear that Chase had regained some of his equilibrium.

"Apology accepted."

"Althea's been here for so long. She's part of the Colton Properties family."

Sloan didn't want to add to his pain, but she'd done enough work through the years to know that his thinking was a fallacy. Colton Properties, no matter how well-meaning, was a place to come to work. Althea's family was separate and always had been.

And when push came to shove, her focus and her bad decisions were in service to her own family.

Although she said nothing out loud, Chase must have seen her lack of agreement. "You don't think we could have done something different?"

"Harsh truth?"

"Give it to me," he said on a resigned sigh.

"I think this is your family business, but I think this is a job and a place to come to work for everyone else."

He nodded. "I suppose you're right."

She wanted to go to him—to touch him—but because she did, Sloan stayed right where she was.

"It's not a bad thing, Chase. In fact, if you can channel that properly, which I believe you have, you create a place where people want to come to work. Where they want to devote their lives."

"To steal from me."

"To build a career. To partner with you on your vision. To live a good life, with purpose and commitment every day. It doesn't have to be a family. A job can be a good thing. It can matter, just for itself."

Her own words felt a bit hollow as they echoed in her ears.

Hadn't she done the exact opposite?

She might have begun SecuritKey with purpose, but it had become something of an all-consuming mission, especially these past few years. She'd felt that all too starkly when she'd considered her dating life, but if she extended it even outside the realm of dating, she had made her job her life in all aspects.

Perhaps it was time to pull back on that a bit.

Whatever else this job was meant to be in her life—and meeting Chase Colton was obviously a part—maybe he wasn't the whole story.

And maybe this assignment had come at the perfect time to make her wake up and realize she needed to build a life that was more than work.

More than something to fill her days.

"I should get into the big conference room and update everyone on what's going on."

"Why don't I come with you? I can explain my role and why I've been here."

"You don't have to do that."

"I think I do. You said it to me from the first. That you didn't like foisting a ruse off on your employees and lying to them. I can explain what I did and what I've turned over to you."

"There've been way too many lies up to now."

"Yes, there have been. And because of it, let's tell them the truth. Push it all into the light and let everyone know how you're going to fix it."

Markus sat with Winston Kraft in the luxurious trailer they used as an office and watched the numbers scrolling on the large computer monitor in front of them.

"We need her to come to heel. That Colton money will help solve some of these shortfalls." Winston pointed to three areas on the screen, all tied to recruitment and some payoffs they'd needed to do to manage the dead women.

Dead women who would have stayed buried if it weren't for those damn K-9 trackers.

He'd always hated dogs. They found more than they

should and uncovered the stuff that needed to stay beneath the surface.

And wasn't it bad luck Jessie's son had been engaged in the case?

He'd guilted her about it and managed to buy himself a few extra weeks without her nagging him incessantly about marriage. How Max had turned to such dark life's work because she'd left him as a child.

He'd been subtle about it, Markus smiled to himself, but it had been an effective ploy. And the added benefit was how much he could then press her about her relationship with Nathan and Sarah and how much love and devotion she'd shown them.

Shouldn't they *want* to support her? Shouldn't they want more of their fair share of Robert Colton's money?

Despite manipulating her to the situation, it hadn't changed the fact he'd had to pay out to keep a few county officials quiet.

It had been necessary dollars out the door, but they were operating in a deficit and would be fully in the red if Jessie didn't figure out a way to get her kids on board.

"How much time do we have?" Markus asked.

"Another month. Maybe two if we can squeeze a bit more out of the current patrons."

It wasn't much time. Markus considered how he'd approach some of his followers, who still hoarded some of their own money they thought he didn't know about.

He had a few tactics he could employ there. But the truth was, Jessie Colton's money would go a long way toward not just keeping them solvent, but putting them in a position to invest more. There was a trafficking ring in Boise he wanted a piece of and there were a few other big fish he'd had on the line he wanted to try and reel in.

They were skeptics, but prettying up his enterprise would go a long way toward getting those fish into his growing pond.

"She still at you to get married?" Winston asked as he shut down the program, tapping in the additional layers of passwords and encryption he insisted on.

"With damn near every breath."

"You know you may have to do it?"

Markus eyed his second-in-command. Winston had been with him for years now and the man was a slimy bastard, but effective and committed to the grift.

"I don't see you lining up to do it."

Winston flashed him a dark grin and batted his eyes. "I'm a married man myself. My sweet little wife is a good-natured follower and is eager to have children to increase our flock."

"How's that working out?"

Markus hit his friend with the dig on purpose. He knew it had been a serious bone of contention that Winston's young wife wasn't pregnant yet and he'd always found those well-placed barbs kept a person in line.

And ensured they realized Markus saw far more than his benevolent demeanor might suggest.

Winston's eyes had grown dark, and he pushed away from the computer. But when he spoke, he was his even-toned self. "In due time."

"Don't you have grandkids you could foist off on her?"

Winston didn't keep up with his first family. His estranged son, Rick, was unwilling to be a part of his father's life. Winston had always seemed okay with that, if not actually somewhat relieved not to have the baggage of his adult son nosing around in his business.

"Rick's not eager to have a family reunion, but I keep tabs on them."

Markus kept a few tabs of his own but held back from saying anything more.

It always paid to know the comings and goings of your flock.

Even when it was a lifelong friend.

Perhaps especially then, Markus thought.

It was a cold world and even the closest of friends could turn on you for the right incentive.

Which was why he'd always ensured he kept a stack of information at the ready.

Knowledge was power in every way. Sure, weapons and fear were endlessly effective tactics, but knowledge and the secrets most people held close to themselves were the foundation of a healthy enterprise.

The Ever After Church was the latest incarnation of that power, but it would be temporary, just like all that came before. Another year, maybe two, if they could keep reeling in the big fish, but that would be all. He and Winston would suck this part of Idaho dry before moving on, but they *would* move on.

It was inevitable.

Shaking off thoughts of what came next, Markus focused on the here and now, their budget spreadsheet vividly tattooed in his mind.

He needed to go talk to Jessie. It was time to amp up the pressure campaign for Robert Colton's money.

Every last cent he could get his hands on.

Chapter 11

Sloan watched Chase work the conference room, full of Colton Properties employees, from the initial speech he gave outlining what they'd uncovered about Althea's embezzling, to the real reason Sloan had come to Owl Creek, to then answering questions. He remained respectful of Althea's privacy, even in the midst of her destructive behavior, before directing everyone's attention to the future.

Even as he painted that vision, he was quick to answer each and every question, most of which dwelled on the past.

He was even quicker to take responsibility and outline how he and his family would absorb the costs of Althea's damages, going so far as to confirm everyone's bonus structures and salaries were safe.

It was hard work, that sort of dedicated leadership and willingness to helm the ship, but he did it well.

And when the last person had filed out of the conference room, Sloan's heart did a hard bump in her chest at the look of sheer exhaustion that painted his features.

And it wasn't even noon yet.

"That started the week off with a bang."

Chase reached for the center of the table and snagged a fresh bottle of water among several someone had thoughtfully put out earlier.

He swigged down almost half of it before looking back up at her, his smile wry. "Don't worry. I won't throw this one."

"I'm not worried about the water."

He glanced up after taking another large pull on the water. "Oh? What are you worried about?"

"You."

"Yeah, well I'll be fine."

"You will be. But right now, you're entitled to be angry and hurt and frustrated."

"Like I've been for the past four months?" Chase shook his head. "What's the point any longer? As difficult as today is, it's finally a step in the right direction. Finally a step forward, not wondering who's out to harm the business.

"I'm sad. But today's not the day to worry about me. I finally have some answers."

She didn't want to doubt him, but she knew how grief worked. Hadn't her mother always said that it comes in waves? No matter how well in hand you thought you had things, a rogue wave knocks the wind out of everyone.

And make no mistake about it, Chase Colton was grieving.

It was the second biggest point she kept returning to, over and over.

The first point she returned to was about herself.

Because she couldn't quite get past—or even begin to process—how naive she'd been in taking on this job.

She'd taken the work believing that it would be easier, somehow, to uncover secrets for a small, family-owned business.

Instead, she'd discovered that this betrayal took as large a human toll as a lot of the work she'd done for the FBI. The stakes were different, but pain was still pain and she hadn't really braced herself for that fact.

With the FBI, her work helped to uncover killers and brought them to justice.

With this work for Colton Properties, she'd uncovered yet more secrets that caused Chase pain.

"You do have answers." Sloan nodded, anxious to get out of there.

She'd changed lives today. Althea's was ruined. Chase's beliefs in an old friend had been shattered.

And she desperately needed to get away from the suddenly crushing weight of her work.

One moment she was there and the next she was gone.

Wisped away like smoke was all Chase could think as Sloan made an excuse to leave and three other people walked into the conference room to talk to him.

Because even with a morning as wild as theirs, the work still had to go on.

He vowed to call Sloan later and then switched his focus to the evolving negotiation for a piece of property just outside of Conners. That was followed by a conference call he set up with his siblings, including Nate and Sarah, to fill them in on Althea's arrest. The call had gone well, but as they were wrapping up, Nate had asked if he was free to meet for coffee later that afternoon and Chase had agreed.

Chase used a visit to the property out toward Conners as the basis to set their meeting point and suggested Nate meet him at a small coffee shop he favored there. It cut a bit of time off his brother's drive over from Boise and gave Chase an opportunity to walk the property in question once more.

It also gave him a chance to replay all that had happened that morning during his time alone. Sloan's work had been impeccable—she'd laid out a clear trail and Althea's history of embezzlement was damn near impossible to dismiss.

His office manager's crimes were long, and he had every expectation the Owl Creek PD would match what was taken from Colton Properties to deposits into Althea's accounts. Fletcher had recused himself from the case based on his personal proximity to the family business. But his partner would see this one through and help secure the evidence.

And Chase's siblings had all agreed that they would support Althea's husband's treatments for as long as he needed them.

None of it meant they weren't prosecuting Althea for the crime.

He hated it, deeply, but he wasn't excusing her behavior, either. Especially when so much of her rationale for her actions was that his father had done bad things, so she felt it was okay.

It wasn't okay.

Hadn't that been the root of their collective frustration and upset these past several months at the news of his father's misdeeds?

The man they'd all believed to be a strong, upstanding citizen and businessman hid terrible secrets.

"Those look like some pretty dark thoughts." Nate stepped up to the small table Chase had snagged when he walked into the bustling shop. "I hope it's not the coffee."

He glanced up at his half brother, dressed in a sport coat, pressed shirt and slacks. As a detective for the Boise PD, Nate no longer had to dress in uniform. But as Chase considered the younger man, he realized that uniforms came in all shapes and sizes.

This one said, *I'm in control and don't you forget it.*

Chase gestured to the cup he'd ordered and set on the other side of the table. "Nah, the coffee's great. Even my mood's not bad enough to spoil it."

"You sure about that?" Nate's smile was measured as he took his seat.

"It's been a hell of a day."

"I am sorry about that," Nate said, "I'm really not familiar with what you do, but I understand how important it is to you and I appreciate you including Sarah and I on the call earlier. A betrayal like that's hard to take."

"You're a part of this and you deserved to know like everyone else." Chase took a sip of his coffee, the bitter brew oddly soothing. It matched the unpleasant taste he hadn't been able to wash out of his mouth all day. "More than twenty years, Nate. She was with my father since he got big enough to need a real office manager and staff."

"And it allowed her to fly under the radar as a trusted employee."

"Every damn day for more than a decade she was stealing from us." He set down his coffee for fear his grip would crush the paper cup. "More secrets."

"You've had to deal with far too many of them. Which is why I wanted to meet with you. I wanted to make sure you heard this from me and know it for truth."

Although they'd only met recently, Chase had felt an affinity for Nate from the start. Smart. Strong. Upstanding. And a man who held a clear willingness to do right by others.

As Robert Colton's oldest son, Chase took his responsibilities to his family seriously. And as Robert's youngest son, Chase already knew Nate felt the exact same way.

"We don't want shares of the business, Chase."

"No, but you and Sarah are entitled to them. I've never questioned that, and I don't believe anyone else has, either."

Nate took a sip of his coffee, considering. "It's like we've both told you. Sarah and I don't need or want shares. Our mother doesn't believe us or agree with us, but I sure wish you would."

Although Chase knew precious little about his Aunt Jessie, Nate had mentioned the same early on. That Jessie had expressed heated, self-righteous fury that her children with Robert should be entitled to the same shares in Colton Properties as his six children with Jenny.

Chase didn't disagree they were entitled to something. But he recognized his brother and sister had their reasons.

What he hadn't expected was the steady layer of heat and vitriol Nate carried toward his mother.

"What's her reason for continuing to push it?"

"I'm increasingly thinking it's that damn Ever After group she's a part of."

It was Nate's turn to scowl and Chase knew it was for a number of reasons that didn't include the coffee.

"They call themselves a church," Chase said.

"Whatever else it is, *church* isn't the right word. The founder spews a lot of angelic, beatific bull. But he seems deeply engaged with the financials and little else."

"How so?"

"My mother's let it slip once he asked her about her inheritance as well as mine and Sarah's, then clammed up when I pressed her on it. It reinforces what I've heard rumor of. That the man has very little engagement with the souls of his flock, but a heck of a lot of it with their wallets."

"It has to be an expensive enterprise." Chase considered it, trying not to jump to an immediate assumption of guilt. "Don't they try to house their people, too? That takes money. Resources."

"More of what bothers me. Why can't people go home each week and live their lives? What's the point of having them all on the property like a commune?"

Chase had really only looked at it through the lens of the property needs. But adding Nate's description to the conversation he'd had the other day with Sloan, Chase had to admit things definitely sounded...off.

"Has your mom said anything else?"

"Nothing about that group she's a part of. She's been relentless with Sarah, though, pushing for her to take her inheritance. I think she's given up on me."

Not for the first time, Chase struggled against the dark feelings that swirled inside of him for his aunt. He'd spent years simply practicing disdain when it came to the subject of his mother's twin sister, but these past few months?

Jessie Colton was a problem. Beyond the betrayal of her family, she somehow had a way of getting herself into bad situations.

And now, to press her children over something they didn't want?

"I don't think I realized how bad it was."

It was Nate's turn to quiet down, and in the man's stoic features, Chase saw a match for himself.

"We'll get through it. I never put much stock in my mother's flighty ideas and neither does Sarah. In fact, my sister is the only reason I'm sticking close now. She shouldn't have to bear the heat all by herself."

"We're here for you. Both of you."

"I know and it makes all the difference."

Chase thought about his brother's words on the drive back into Owl Creek.

They *were* here for each other.

Not out of duty or requirement, but by choice. As a family. And that mattered.

Wasn't that what Sloan had tried to impart to Sarah the other night at the barbecue? The Coltons were a family. No matter what their misguided parents had done to them, the children were rock-solid.

His conversation with Nate had gone a long way toward reinforcing those feelings and he'd be damned if he was going to stop now. Whatever it took to ensure Nate and Sarah knew they had a family and that they belonged was his only goal.

Which made the discussion about Jessie so troubling.

Shouldn't their mother be their biggest champion? A part of him believed that to be the case. That her focus on ensuring they get a piece of Robert Colton's estate was, at its core, a mother's desire for fairness.

But why keep pushing if her children said they were fine?

His father had provided for Nate and Sarah, both while he was still alive and in other property allocations he'd ensured would go to his children with Jessie. So really, her complaints that her kids were missing out were more tied to the settling of succession and the assets of Colton Properties instead of any real sense they'd been left out.

Was it this church she was a part of?

Sloan's disdain had been a match for Nate's. Even as an outsider, with minimal knowledge of the area, she'd keyed into how strange the Ever After Church was.

Furthermore, how their practices didn't seem to actually fit the mold of a church.

And now that Nate had shared Jessie's interest in the money, Chase had to wonder if he'd been too lax in his initial thinking.

Especially when Sloan's comments about his Aunt Jessie came winging back into his thoughts, like tumblers falling into a lock.

One more choice in a long line of poor ones.

*Leaving her children... Putting on a married facade...
Now she's caught up in an* entity...

Those are some seriously questionable decisions.

Whether it was his discussion with Nate, or the morning's evidence that even people he thought he knew could make bad decisions, Chase wasn't too sure. But Sloan's comments from the other day had taken hold of his thoughts and he wasn't ready to let this go.

The vague thought he'd had the other day that he wanted to look into the Ever After Church had just gotten a lot clearer.

All he needed to do now was ask Sloan if she was interested in joining him.

With *pastel de nata* cooking in the oven, her mother's special recipe, Sloan tried to take solace in the comforting smells and *off* the still-roiling thoughts in her head.

Hadn't she grown up with this scent filling the kitchen? The rich custard tart her mom would sprinkle with cinnamon fresh out of the oven and then she'd eat it with a tall glass of milk. As she got older, her mother allowed her to make a latte to accompany the pastry.

It was only in the last few years that she'd gotten into the way her parents ate the treats—with a shot of espresso accompanying the dessert.

God, she missed her mom.

They normally spoke every day, but her parents had gone to Portugal for a month on a family visit. If she tried to call her now her mother would only worry.

The sweet treats would have to stand in for her soothing words and perfect hugs.

It had taken a good portion of the afternoon, but Sloan had finally calmed down a bit.

And had forced herself to honestly assess what had happened at Colton Properties.

She had done the job she was asked to do, but once she'd seen the impact of that work, she'd fled. Not only did it not make sense, but it also wasn't something she'd ever done before.

Which had only left her with more questions.

And the rapidly rising suspicion that she was far more attached to Chase Colton than she wanted to admit.

They had an attraction, one they'd both admitted to this past weekend. But her unhappiness at seeing him dealing with the outcome of her investigation?

It had cut shockingly deep.

The timer went off just as the doorbell rang. Chase was the only person she knew, so she figured it would be him. But she took the few extra moments to pull out the tarts before heading for the door to check.

And opened it to find Frannie and Ruby on the other side.

"Oh, hello."

Both women smiled at her, but it was Ruby who instantly moved forward, her attention already focused on the kitchen. "What is that divine smell?"

Frannie shrugged, but a smile twitched at the edges of her lips. "I'd like to say it's because she's pregnant, but Ruby likely would have done that, anyway."

"Well, come on in." Sloan waved Chase's other sister inside before turning for the kitchen. She'd just cleared the doorway when she let out a small cry at Ruby. "You'll burn yourself!"

Ruby stepped back, the hands wrapped around her pregnant belly quickly moved behind her back. "I'm not touching."

"You're going to burn your nose if you get any closer," Frannie admonished as she came into the already small kitchen and took a seat at the table. "Despite my big sister's manners, we didn't come here to eat."

"But we can once they cool!" Ruby quickly insisted.

Frannie shot her a dark look before continuing. "We spoke with Chase earlier and figured the lunkhead still hadn't come over to check on you."

"He's been at work."

The two women exchanged glances before Ruby gave a firm nod, then took a seat of her own. "Stupid lunkhead."

"Isn't that term a bit outdated?" Sloan asked before going to the fridge and pulling out a pitcher of iced tea. "It's decaffeinated," she added, directing her comment to Ruby, before crossing to get some glasses.

"Lunkhead was all our mother allowed when we were kids and it sort of stuck," Ruby said.

Since she was an only child and woefully ignorant of sibling politics, Sloan just nodded at the answer and went back to pouring iced tea.

"So what is that you just made?" Ruby asked.

"They're my mother's recipe," Sloan said as she set glasses on the table before each of Chase's sisters. "*Pastel de nata* are traditional Portuguese pastries."

"They smell amazing." Frannie shot a pointed look at her sister. "And I'm sure they'll be delicious once they cool."

"We can have one in a few more minutes. In the meantime, why are you upset at Chase?"

"We're upset at his *stupid* behavior," Ruby stressed.

Frannie shot her a dark look but didn't correct her sister, either. "We were just concerned. Chase called a family meeting after he'd finished speaking to his staff and we noticed you weren't on the video call."

Although she didn't have siblings, Sloan was absurdly touched at Ruby and Frannie's concern. She was surprised they'd even noticed she wasn't there.

"I figured out who was stealing from Colton Properties and it was time to leave. Chase had things well in hand."

The look that passed between the two sisters didn't give much, but it was enough to pique her curiosity. "You don't agree?"

"I think Chase has believed he has everything well in hand for a long time. And in business, he's great. In real life?" Ruby rolled her eyes. "He's spewed some ridiculous nonsense for years that he's not cut out for a relationship."

"I'm not sure I can say one way or the other, to be honest. We're not really dating."

"Yeah, he mentioned that, too, on the call." Frannie waved a hand, the gesture more dismissive than Sloan would have expected. "No one's buying it."

"I'm afraid it's true. We needed a plausible excuse so I could be inside the offices at unexpected times. That was the story we used."

The two women exchanged glances once again and Sloan held up a hand of her own. "I don't have any brothers and sisters, so forgive me if I'm missing what's underneath all this. But can you please just tell me what you think?"

Their loudly silent communication came to an abrupt halt as both women stared at her, guilty expressions lining their faces.

"We think you're perfect for him," Ruby said.

"And we love how the two of you are when you're together," Frannie added. "Watching each other when you think the other one doesn't know."

Sloan abruptly jumped up from the table, hoping the delicious sweet treat of the *pastels* would divert some of the attention off her rapidly heating face.

Because she did look at Chase when she thought he wasn't watching.

But to know he did, too?

She put the tarts on a plate and dusted them lightly with cinnamon before returning to the table. "The traditional way to eat these is with coffee. I can make some if you'd like but I don't have any decaf."

Both women brushed it off. "The iced tea is fine," Frannie quickly assured her. And since neither of them kept on with tales of their brother, Sloan took her first easy breath as she set down the serving dish on the table and then passed out small dessert plates.

It was only once everyone had taken a tart, Ruby already oohing and aahing around her first bite, that Sloan realized her mistake.

She'd just taken a bite of her tart, the creamy egg custard filling her taste buds with the comforting memories of home, when Ruby spoke.

"So tell us. What will it take to keep you here?"

Chapter 12

Chase pulled into a parking spot in front of Sloan's building and saw what looked like his sister's car a few spots away. He almost shook it off when something had him thinking better of it and he crossed over to the parking spot.

Only to look in and see Ruby's signature mess of doodads littering the cupholders.

His first thought was to ask why his sister was here, rapidly followed by a mental curse that his sister had decided to pay Sloan a visit.

"Why?" He moaned as he took the outer stairs up to Sloan's floor. "Why, why, why was I given a meddling younger sister?"

He nearly barreled through the door but stopped himself at the last minute and knocked.

Only to find a flustered Sloan answer on the other side.

She grabbed onto his arm and dragged him into the apartment without saying a word.

"Hi, Chase!" Ruby's voice filtered out of the kitchen, followed quickly by Frannie's slightly lower register.

"Hello, big brother!"

"Both of them?" he asked Sloan.

"Yep."

Since she didn't elaborate, he figured his sisters' arrival was both unexpected and, at minimum, slightly harrowing as Ruby and Frannie could be when they decided to gang up.

Thank goodness, they hadn't brought Lizzy along, too.

Three Colton women all in one place, all on some mission of their own making, was the very definition of scary.

"You have to try these!" Ruby said with her mouth full all while gesturing to her currently empty plate.

"What are you doing here?" he asked, attempting his stern-older-brother tone. It hadn't worked on them when they were ten and six and he was sixteen, and it sure as hell wasn't working twenty years later, but he gave it the old college try all the same.

"They're delicious," Frannie added, completely ignoring his question.

"Well, what are you eating?" he finally asked.

"The most amazing Portuguese pastries." Ruby gestured vaguely. "Tell him, Sloan."

Sloan already had a fresh plate out of the cabinet and had set it, along with a napkin, at the only empty spot at the table.

"We're eating *pastel de nata*."

He'd never eaten what looked to be dessert tarts but the kitchen smelled incredible, so he did what any sane man would do when faced with his nosy younger sisters, a woman he had increasingly strong feelings for and a plate full of pastries.

He took one.

And nearly fell off his chair as the subtly sweet, rich taste hit his tongue.

He'd never considered himself a man led by his stomach, but in that moment, he could have gotten down on one knee and proposed to Sloan. Or to the dessert.

At the exquisite taste exploding on his tongue, he wasn't entirely sure any longer.

"You made these?"

"Well, yeah." Sloan nodded.

"Today?"

"They're still hot, aren't they?"

"Wow, these are amazing."

"I told you!" Ruby said enthusiastically. "And it's not even the baby making me hungry."

"The baby can't be the excuse for everything."

Ruby grinned at her sister. "It will be when I take one more *pastel de nata* for the road. Come on, let's go."

His sisters flew out as quickly as he assumed they'd flown in, even Ruby's increasing size not slowing her down in her quest to leave them alone.

And exactly four minutes after he'd sat down and tasted one of the best pastries of his life, his sisters had departed Sloan's home.

Sloan stood between the table and the doorway to the kitchen, a slightly dazed expression on her face. "It's really quiet once they're gone."

He mumbled his agreement around another pastry, and she pointed at him. "Don't eat them too fast. You'll get sick."

"It'll be worth it."

She shook her head at that. "I'm afraid Ruby won't think so in about fifteen minutes."

"Why were they here?" He heard himself and quickly continued, "Not that you can't entertain whomever you'd like. But it was something of a surprise to find them both at your home."

"They came to talk to me about their lunkhead brother."

He'd heard the term since they were kids and was well

aware it was not a term of endearment. "What did they accuse me of now?"

"Not coming over here soon enough."

"And?"

"And nothing. That's all I got out of them before everyone dived on the tarts and told me that you and I seem to have a case of staring too hard and long at each other when no one is watching."

And there it was.

That remarkable truth serum she seemed able to wield with effortless grace.

Which meant it was only fair to give it right back to her.

"I *do* do that, but I didn't realize I was quite so obvious about it."

"Me, either." She let out a heavy sigh. "It's embarrassing. To be so transparent."

He stood then and crossed the small space to her. Without checking the impulse, he pulled her close and pressed a kiss against her forehead. "It may be transparent but it's not embarrassing. Never that."

The feel of her in his arms was like a soothing balm at the end of a very long day. Like the exquisite tarts, Chase savored the sensation.

He wanted her.

He could keep running from that fact, but it didn't make it any less true. Nor did it make the feelings any less intense, this ache deep inside he'd never felt before.

But what to do about it?

She was leaving in a matter of days, and he wasn't crass enough to ask her if she wanted to sleep with him as a going-away present.

Which meant he needed to keep his interest in check.

Yes, he wanted her. But he wanted her leaving Owl Creek with good memories.

And good thoughts of him.

"I'd also have told them that you weren't being a lunkhead for staying at work and doing your job, but we got distracted by the tarts. They'd finally cooled off enough so that Ruby could try them."

His sister had always been a champion sweet eater and he suspected that had only grown more pronounced with her pregnancy.

"I'm surprised she didn't try to eat one hot."

"Oh, she did, but Frannie stopped her."

Chase laughed at that, their antics as children still something that defined them as adults.

Which only brought him right back around to Nate and Sarah, and the laugh died in his throat.

His father and his aunt had taken that away from him. From all of them. A chance to grow up together. A chance to know one another.

Heck, in the case of himself, his full siblings and his cousins, even knowing Nate and Sarah existed.

"What's wrong?"

Chase stepped away, taking a seat at the table and reaching for the mostly full glass of iced tea where Frannie had been sitting. "I met up with Nate earlier. He wanted to make sure I was okay after what went down today."

"He's a good man and he wants to be a part of your family."

"So much so he's maintained his position that he wants nothing to do with the settlement around Colton Properties. Sarah, too."

"That's great, isn't it? The full transfer of the CEO role to you can happen now."

"Not if my Aunt Jessie has anything to do with it."

That subtle frown—the one that just slightly marred the edges of Sloan's mouth—struck like clockwork with the mention of his aunt.

He suspected she wasn't even fully aware she was doing it, but each time he saw that thin veneer of disgust he was oddly heartened.

Here was a woman who had his back. His family's backs, too.

And there was something special in that.

Something that made him keep wishing there was a way things could be different.

Because Sloan Presley had made everything different.

Sloan busied herself putting on a pot of coffee and then came back to the table. She had no doubt they'd nibble a few more of the *pastel de nata* and she'd rather have hers with coffee. She'd also ensure Chase got the full experience of the sweet tarts.

His arrival had been welcome—added on to his sisters' strange yet oddly wonderful visit—and it felt good to have him here.

When he was with her, she found it a lot harder to remember all the reasons she wanted to leave.

Or any of the reasons she'd fled Colton Properties earlier.

"Start from the beginning. What did Nate say about his mother?"

Chase caught her up on his coffee meeting in Conners and it struck her once again what strange circumstances Jessie Colton managed to find in her life.

An affinity for drama?

Or an inability to read other people because she was so steeped in her own selfish desires?

What could she possibly see in this so-called church that had popped up here in Idaho? And then to press her kids about their inheritance, seemingly to give it all to the organization?

"Nate doesn't seem to have a lot of regard for his mother?"

"No," Chase replied, taking another sip of Frannie's iced tea. "I get the sense he's there more out of duty and a deep need to protect Sarah more than any real feelings for Jessie."

"That's sad."

"In every way. I think that's what I'm coming to realize more and more. The choices Jessie and my father made... they weren't just selfish, though that's a big part of it all. But they've created this legacy of anger and mistrust in all their children. Their actions have erased the good feelings and left nothing but duty, or this lingering sense of obligation to care for their memories."

"I am sorry for that. Maybe more than anything else since I've been here."

"What are you sorry about?"

"I've hated watching all of you suffer for the deeds of your parents. It's not my experience." Her gaze drifted to the tarts and Sloan recognized that truth on an entirely visceral level.

Here she was, comforted merely by making a dish of her mother's. Chase, meanwhile, was left to pick up the pieces of his father's secret life.

It didn't seem fair. And even the word *fair* felt like too small a description of what he was going through.

"Why did you leave earlier?"

His question broke through her musings, and she realized the answer was really quite simple. "Because it was time for me to go."

Chase nodded at that but didn't say anything more.

The last gurgle of the coffee maker echoed in the silence, indicating it was done brewing, and she jumped up to get them both mugs.

It was only as she came back to the table, steaming mugs in hand, that Sloan realized she owed him a better answer than that.

"That's only part of the truth. I was sad this morning after you spoke with your employees." She stared down at her mug. "I was more than sad, actually. I hated that my work put you in that position."

"It's what I hired you to do. You fixed my problem."

"I ruined someone's life today."

"No, Althea ruined her life. She could have made other choices, but she didn't. Just like Jessie ruined hers. Just like my father ruined his." Chase reached for her hand, his fingers tracing the back of her knuckles.

"I'm done blaming myself or my siblings or my mother or uncle for things we didn't do and never saw coming. The people who chose a bad path. That's on them. There shouldn't be guilt because you shined a light on it. Brought it out of the darkness."

Chase stopped that warm, sweet tracing over the back of her hand and instead covered it fully with his. "Which is why I wanted to ask a favor of you. And you're under no obligation to say yes."

"What sort of favor?"

"I'd like you to look into Jessie and this church she's a part of. Something's not right there. You sensed it the other day with those articles about the dead women found in Wake County. And Nate's certain his mother is involved in something bad."

Sloan had never been able to resist a challenge, but this was a tall ask.

She knew digital forensics, but digging into the Ever After Church would likely require some hacking, too. Her coding and computer programming skills were strong, but she'd never had a real reason to go after private citizens.

Especially without the auspices of the government, who normally funded that sort of work with her.

"Do you think it's a good idea?"

"I think there's reason to look into these people and we can do it without warrants or raising suspicion." He grinned, the look boyish and appealing.

So appealing Sloan felt the attraction pulling low in her belly, her interest in following him down this path both academic *and* wholly steeped in attraction.

"Well, *you* can do it. I'll watch and cheer you on since I'm lucky I know how to reboot my computer each time I have to do a software update."

"There are risks. The members of the Ever After Church are private citizens. The church is technically a protected organization."

"Nate doesn't even think they're a real church."

"A technicality if they're incorporated as one, but…" She trailed off and Chase's gaze never wavered.

"But what?"

"That might be the perfect place to start. It's all a bit suspect on my end but if they're not legally a church entity we might be able to make an argument later if push came to shove on the technicalities. Especially since you've got reason to believe your business is threatened based on what Nate shared with you."

They were very thin lines and Sloan recognized full well

she was crossing them, but something inside of her recognized it was the right thing to do.

She felt it.

More than that, she *knew* it.

And it wasn't because of her attraction to Chase.

The Coltons deserved to know the truth.

Whatever else she'd uncovered over the past week, that lone thought whispered over and over in her mind, taking shape as she imagined how she could get in and out of the Ever After files without anyone knowing.

She had the skills to help them find answers and she wasn't going back to Chicago without trying to get them.

It was shockingly tedious, hard work to hack into computer files.

That thought had struck Chase hard around two that morning when he'd gone nearly bleary-eyed watching Sloan for the better part of six hours.

Even as he wanted to drop his head on the table in exhaustion, she kept on, her attention laser-focused on her laptop screen.

"Do we have any more coffee?" she asked before letting out a short, quick curse and tapping a few more keys.

"You've had enough coffee."

That was enough to get him a rather harsh side-eye when she glanced up from her screen. "I think I'm old enough to know when I want coffee."

"And I think you're a demon insomniac who's lulled me into thinking we're doing work when what you're really trying to do is suck my brains out my ears."

"You know that's technically impossible."

"Hardly." He made a show of slapping the side of his head and pretending something was falling out the other side.

It was enough to get a laugh out of her and pull her attention off that damn screen. Which meant he needed to act now and drag her away from the table.

"You've been at this long enough. Give it a rest and we can start in the morning."

"I'm close."

"You said that two hours ago."

"Which means I'm closer now than I was two hours ago."

The woman was relentless.

Had he ever seen anything more attractive?

She'd pulled her hair up hours ago and he was fascinated by the way small curls had broken out along her hairline. They made him want to reach out and wrap one around his finger, just to feel how soft they were.

Since he had no business touching her, especially since his *thoughts* of touching her had grown increasingly heated as each hour passed, he did what he was astoundingly good at. He pushed a serious overload of *obnoxious big brother* into his tone.

"Sloan, give it a rest. I didn't come over here to push you into indentured servitude to your laptop. We'll dig more tomorrow."

"I want to see where this takes me."

"See where it takes you tomorrow. It'll keep."

"I just—" She stopped, her eyes lighting up as her gaze remained totally focused on her laptop screen.

"What?"

"I'm in."

"In where?"

"The files at Ever After. It's locked down and hard to break through, but I'm in."

Chase leaned toward the screen, not sure what he was

looking at but able to read details of member names, contributions and what looked to be attachments on each person.

Dossiers?

On church members?

"What is that?" He pointed toward the linked files. "Can you click on one of them?"

She tapped around, not clicking directly but looking like she was attempting to make a copy when the screen went black.

Another low curse tumbled from her lips. If the moment wasn't so serious, he might have laughed at her inventive string of words.

"Was it supposed to do that?"

"Not at all."

"Got it."

He stood, stretching his muscles and working the kinks out of his neck while she futzed and fiddled with her keyboard. A few minutes later her screen came back to life, but her frustrated exhale suggested things still weren't right.

"I need to back out of this and run a full diagnostic on my machine."

"Why?"

"I think I hit a trap."

He turned at that, dropping his arms in mid-stretch. "Sloan, I'm sorry. I'm the one who pushed you to do this and—"

She shook her head. "I hate to break it to you, but this is hardly the first time I've had that happen. It means I'm close and we're on the right track."

Since she looked damn near giddy with the news, Chase wasn't sure what to do.

Was a high five appropriate in this instance?

And what level of delirium had he hit if this was what he was worried about?

"It's going to run for a while so let's leave it. I can pull out the couch for you. That way you don't have to drive home."

She seemed to catch herself, her own arms stilling in midair as she stretched, her dark brown eyes going wide. "I mean, if that's okay and you don't mind staying."

"I'd appreciate it."

Although he was dog-tired, Chase couldn't let the moment go, something mischievous sparking to life. "Unless, of course, you're worried you can't keep your hands off me, in which case I'll head home. It's not too far a drive."

She let out a hard snort at that. "In your dreams, buddy."

"What would you know of my dreams?" Pleased to see her flustered once more, Chase's grin only grew broader. "Or maybe I should ask about yours."

"I don't dream."

"Never?"

He moved closer, the exhaustion in her gaze fading as something sharper moved into its place.

Chase recognized it—*felt* it—because it matched what he knew she saw in his own eyes.

Barely banked need.

Heated desire.

And a confused, push-pull of emotion that kept seesawing between giving in to that desire and knowing that where it led might be disastrous for both of them.

So he stayed where he was. He didn't pull her into his arms or think about kissing her.

Instead, he reached out and traced a line down her forearm, her pretty, light brown skin so soft to the touch he nearly ached with the sweetness of it.

Of her.

And resigned himself to the fact that all the want and need in the world couldn't change the gravity of the situation.

She wasn't staying.

And he wasn't a forever sort of guy.

It had nearly driven him mad, like the ceaseless dripping of a faucet or an endless alarm he couldn't quite turn off as it raided his dreams, but he needed to accept the truth: he wanted what he could not have.

Was it cosmic payback for spending most of his adult life in the steadfast belief that love couldn't touch him? More, that it wasn't for him?

And why was the thought of love even crossing his mind?

Why had the idea of it steadily presented itself, over and over, rattling around his mind and taunting him as he spent more and more time with Sloan?

Love. Marriage. A family.

He'd decided long ago, well before his father's betrayal, that those things were for other people. He'd tried and ultimately been a failure at something most people found easily as they moved into adulthood.

His failure with Leanne had been bad enough. But now that he knew what horror lived in his own genes? How truly broken his father had to have been to live his double life?

It only reinforced all the reasons why there was no good end to this.

Because whatever else he wanted for Sloan, it was something good. She deserved it and he well knew he wasn't ever going to be the man to give it to her.

So he gently traced her skin once more, reveling in the feel of her and knowing it would have to keep him warm in his dreams for years to come.

Then he dropped his hand and backed out of the kitchen, leaving her to her computer and her notes and the untainted goodness he wanted for her.

And he didn't look at her, not even once, as he pulled out the sofa bed and settled himself for the night in her darkened living room.

Chapter 13

Sloan wasn't overly experienced in love, but she'd had enough relationships to understand attraction, interest and desire.

She'd had varying levels of each in her past with the men she'd dated. There had been the one who'd attracted her yet bored her to tears. And another one who'd been fascinating to talk to but had been such a horrible kisser she didn't even contemplate having sex with him.

None of them had come close to what she was feeling.

And not one of them had been worth a damn in the practical-experience category. She didn't know how to deal with such an infuriating, sexy, irritating, mind-meltingly attractive man like Chase.

The real surprise was that despite having all six sexy feet of him a room away, she'd still slept like the dead.

Because while a half-nighter wasn't quite as exhausting as an all-nighter, she'd also struggled to sleep all weekend—again, damn you, Chase Colton. And all the digging into the Ever After Church had simply used up every bit of mental energy she possessed.

None of which seemed to matter as she was lying on her bed, staring up at the ceiling.

Now that she was awake, she'd become quite aware of

the fact that she had to walk back into the living room, and who knew how Chase slept.

Shirtless?

Pantsless?

Fully naked?

A warm glow suffused her as each image grew progressively hotter and she sat up, forcing the images from her thoughts.

He was a good, respectful man. He no doubt was still wearing what he'd worn yesterday. She was the one with the flights of fancy imagining him naked.

Which made the fully dressed, coffee-in-hand man who greeted her in her kitchen ten minutes later something of a surprise.

Especially since she'd only managed to throw on an old sweatshirt with her college logo emblazoned on it and brush her teeth.

"Good morning." Chase smiled over his mug. "I hope you don't mind I started coffee."

"Not at all."

As if to stress that very point, she crossed to the coffee maker. Instead of falling on the brew like a rabid dog, she offered him a refill first.

He extended his mug and, although he was a few feet from her, she couldn't deny how close he felt in her small kitchen. Brushing off the sudden attack of nerves, Sloan filled his mug and moved right on to filling hers, easing slightly when he settled himself against the sink.

"I fed the cat, too. I hope you don't mind."

She turned at that, mid-sip, and nearly bobbled her mug. "Um, that's okay."

Why would she mind?

She woke up to fresh coffee and a well-fed cat who was

even now licking his paws in the corner, seemingly uninterested in them even as he kept darting a curious eye toward the humans.

"Did you sleep okay?" Sloan finally asked, willing the caffeine to make her a semi-human, gracious hostess. "I haven't slept on it, but the couch looks pretty comfortable."

"It was fine."

"Good. Um, I'm glad to hear it."

Whatever lusty images had assailed her as she'd been lying in bed, Sloan realized a fully clothed, stubble-jawed Chase should have been in her mental list.

The man was lethal in the morning.

And this quiet little domestic scene between them was doing something to her. She'd never claim particularly well-ordered thoughts in the morning—she was way too much of a night owl for that. But she was definitely feeling out of sorts and knew he was to blame.

Or her hormones were.

Taking another sip, she decided she'd push that blame back on him.

She simply didn't share her morning coffee with a man who'd slept at her place. One more depressing fact that reinforced all she'd given up for her job these past few years.

No, Sloan mentally corrected herself. It was time to stop blaming the job.

She'd chosen to ignore that aspect of her life.

And now, here she was, twenty-nine years old and feeling like an immature teenager. It was rather overwhelming to have an attractive man in her kitchen at 7:00 a.m. who knew how to fend for himself *and* sort of care for her, all at the same time.

And…she was flustered.

That really was the only word for it.

"I realized we didn't talk about it much yesterday, but when I asked you to take on the digging into my Aunt Jessie and that group of hers, I'd be happy to extend your contract. I fully expect to pay you for your time."

Sloan couldn't quite say why—perhaps it was the flustered feelings—but something about Chase's offer to pay her waved in front of her like a red flag to a bull.

"How benevolent of you."

"It's hardly benevolent to ensure you're compensated for your work."

His eyebrows slashed over those glass-green eyes but his tone remained even. Measured.

And in that moment she had a sense of why he was so good at his job.

This wasn't a man who'd ever let an adversary across the negotiating table get the better of him.

"Yes, well, maybe I'm interested in solving the mystery of your aunt's weird group and don't want or need your money. I can take a few vacation days or, you know, work on whatever I want to."

"Sloan, why are you getting prickly about this?"

The question was fair.

If she wasn't in such a weird frame of mind it was entirely possible she'd have glossed over the entire conversation without giving it a second thought.

But she *was* in a weird frame of mind.

And suddenly his question seemed entirely *un*fair.

"For reasons that defy logic you kiss me or talk to me of private matters with your family and then in the blink of an eye you're talking about paying me and giving me work to do. What is it that you want? Am I your employee or your…friend?"

She nearly stumbled over the last word but caught herself at the last minute.

Because no matter how out of sorts she felt, it would have been mortifying to have said the world *girlfriend* by mistake.

Chase knew the signs of a fight.

He'd grown up with five siblings and four cousins who were close as siblings. Time spent together was as likely to be full of laughter as it was arguments and, as the oldest Colton, he'd learned early how to pick some and how to mitigate others.

And Sloan was spoiling for a fight.

The real question was, why?

When they'd finished up for the evening, she'd seemed fine. A little awkward as they'd decided he was going to sleep on her couch, but if he was honest with himself, he was a bit nervous, too.

And now this?

"What does paying you for your professional services have to do with our friendship?"

"I care about what happens to you and your family. And what your aunt did to all of you is wrong. I know it's not my place to judge but I can't get past that fact."

"Observing a lifetime of crappy behavior to others isn't judgment, so I appreciate that. More than I can say, actually. It doesn't change the fact that I'm taking up your time on a task you do as your profession."

He should have expected it, *especially* after his pedantic response, but the explosion still caught him off guard.

"I don't want a contract for this, Chase! I want to help you!" She slammed her mug down on the counter, the sound reverberating through the room. "I care about you. And for the past week I've watched you question yourself in every way."

The heat that carried her through the verbal explosion quieted as she reached for her mug once again, staring down at the ceramic as if surprised she hadn't broken it. "You need answers. And this is something I can give you before I leave to go home."

And there it was. That lingering reality that drove everything personal between them.

She would be going home.

Because she might be willing to do the work on her own time, but that time had an expiration on it.

"Do you honestly think this is going to make the situation better?"

Sloan's gaze lifted from her mug, direct and with a distinct fire burning in its depths.

"The way Jessie's own children don't agree with what she's doing and have actively taken your side over their mother's when it comes to matters of inheritance and the family business? I think it matters quite a bit. And I don't think you're going to have peace until you have some answers."

"While I don't disagree with you, that's not actually what I meant."

"Oh?"

The genuine confusion that stamped itself over her features was a match for all he struggled with inside.

"I meant the situation between us."

He went with instinct and a genuine need he was increasingly unable to ignore.

Moving in close, he took her mug, as surprised as her it wasn't in pieces on her counter. He set it down gently, followed by his own, then pulled her into his arms.

"We can't fight our way out of this, Sloan."

"It's damn inconvenient." Although her angry tone had vanished, she kept her arms firmly at her sides.

"It is."

"And it can't have a happy ending."

He lifted a hand and brushed a wayward curl that had slipped out of her ponytail back behind her ear. "Probably not."

"So what are we doing?"

"Giving in."

Chase bent his head, capturing her lips with his. She was so warm and welcoming, her mouth opening beneath his as her arms came around his neck.

The lingering taste of toothpaste and coffee flavored her tongue and Chase found himself utterly intoxicated. She was all warmth and welcome, and as he pulled her closer in his arms, he fought the very reality she spoke of.

How could this feel so right, even as he was so sure it would end? Soon.

The big part of him that had spent a decade protecting his heart knew it was a bad idea to keep giving in. But the part of him that wanted her so desperately—those emotions that grew bigger and bigger by the day—simply wanted to revel in her.

In what was between them.

So he took.

And gave.

And wildly, wonderfully, gave in.

Markus quickly scanned his text messages before dropping his phone back into his pocket. He had about twenty minutes before the first members of his flock would arrive in the small clearing they used as a morning meeting area.

He'd been thinking about what esoteric words of wisdom he wanted to share today and had landed somewhere on the difficulties of managing to the practicalities of the world and avoiding greed, all as a mechanism to get his members to dig a bit deeper into their wallets.

He took several deep breaths of the fresh Idaho air, centering himself and testing a few of the tonalities he wanted to use.

Always soft and easy.

Never accusing. Never mad.

This was a welcoming place. *He* provided a welcome space. Like a father tutoring his young, the wisdom of the universe was channeled through him for their benefit.

He believed he'd settled on just the right cadence. He was mentally flipping through the order of his message for the morning guidance when Winston appeared at the edge of the clearing, stomping toward him in a way that suggested his hard-won inner peace was about to evaporate.

"Brother Kraft," Markus intoned when Winston stood before him.

"We've got a problem."

"No 'Brother Acker'?" Markus said quietly, even as steel threaded underneath his words.

"You know I hate that crap but—" Winston bowed, his hands at his side "—good morning, Brother Acker."

"Excellent. You know we can't risk one of the flock observing us in anything but prayerful solitude."

"Yeah, about that."

Winston was his right-hand man specifically because he handled problems, but Markus didn't miss the clear agitation that rode the man's features. "What?"

"Someone's nosing around the files. I picked up a flag this morning that the firewall I have in place was breached."

He paid Winston handsomely to avoid any mistakes like this. As news of an intrusion sunk in, all thoughts of calm, centered welcome vanished, a dark red haze of anger taking its place.

"Who?"

"I don't know, but I do know they're good. I wouldn't have even seen it if I hadn't been in myself checking the protections, which I do every morning. I noticed the breach, but it wasn't enough to trigger any automatic alarms."

"Find them."

"I need some time."

"Then take it," Markus growled. "And report back as soon as you have news."

"I'll miss morning reflections."

"Get out of here and get some answers."

Markus watched Winston walk off across the clearing, greeting members who'd begun the walk over to the field. He struggled to get his beatific visage back in place, even as he muttered to himself, that haze of red still edging his vision.

"And start praying if you don't find them."

The kiss spun out, at times wildly erotic and at others deep, soft and precious.

It was an endless ride of emotion. Sloan wasn't sure how she'd gone from steaming mad to being kissed mindless in her kitchen, but she wasn't going to argue.

And wasn't quite sure she had the brain cells to argue, anyway.

So it was a bit of surprise, despite reveling in being in Chase's arms, that she was the one to pull back.

"I, um…" She trailed off, marshaling her thoughts. "I'm glad you're here."

"I'm glad I'm here, too."

"But I should probably check my computer and see if that program I ran overnight did its job."

His gaze consumed her, and Sloan was half convinced they'd fall right back into another kiss, but something obviously held him back when his focus moved to her computer and where it was still perched on her kitchen table.

"Let's take a look."

She should have been relieved.

Realistically, that was the only feeling she should be having. And yet…

Sloan could admit to a solid wash of disappointment that he'd agreed to go back to work that quickly.

And then took her seat to get down to business.

Nothing had changed between her and Chase.

This attraction had nowhere to go and she couldn't afford to forget that. Especially because she was increasingly worried that if she forgot that truth—if she really allowed herself to give in—she'd end up regretting the decision beyond measure.

Your life's in Chicago, Presley. Don't forget it.

Since her life *was* somewhere else very far away, she put her full focus on her computer programs and off the way her lips still tingled.

The way she could still feel the heat of his body, pressed to hers or the feel of his large palm, splayed across her lower back.

Every one of those delicious sense memories fled at the reality of what she stared at on screen.

"Oh, no."

"What?"

"No, no, no." She tapped several commands in rapid succession, each one producing the same feedback. "This can't be."

"Sloan. What is it?"

"I've been made."

"What?"

"My program? All that searching I did. The firewall on the other side knows there was a breach."

"You're talking about it like it's a human being."

She glanced up at him, suddenly aware there was another person standing in the kitchen with her.

"There is, Chase. A real live human sits on the other side of the machine I was trying to hack into. And he or she knows I was poking around."

His eyebrows slashed over those vivid green eyes, now dark with clouds. "Do they know it was you? Sloan Presley or SecuritKey?"

"I need to find out."

Everything faded from view once again as Sloan focused only on her screen and whatever information she could find to assess the damage. She spent the next several minutes tapping in commands and using various security programs she'd either purchased or designed herself.

It was nearly an hour later when she finally surfaced.

"What'd you find?"

Sloan blinked, bringing Chase back into focus. As she came back to her surroundings, she realized he'd fixed a fresh pot of coffee and placed a steaming mug beside her at the table, and had also found some way to freshen up because his hair was obviously wet from a shower.

"Um, sorry."

"For what?"

She forced a smile, even as a wave of embarrassment flooded her veins, her pulse pounding in response. "For disappearing on you."

"You look pretty here to me."

"I mean—"

He put a hand over hers. "You had work to do. Work I asked you to do, by the way. It would hardly be fair to then criticize you for it."

Whatever else she'd thought or wondered or learned since coming to Idaho, in that moment, Sloan knew—*knew*—that she'd been changed.

And it was all because of this man.

No one ever looked at her descent into computer land as anything other than an oddity and a quirk. Even her parents, who loved her and supported her in every way, tolerated that aspect of her personality with wry humor and gentle smiles.

But not Chase.

He accepted it.

All of it.

And didn't seem to even bat an eyelash, let alone want to tease her about it or stare at her in bemusement.

"Thank you for your support."

"What did you find?"

"Best I can tell, the Ever After Church monitored my intrusion into their files but hasn't traced it back to me."

"So that's good?"

"Yes, but it's still not great. They know someone's nosing around."

Chase tapped a finger on the table, obviously considering something, before he spoke.

"You were pretty close to something last night. Do you think you can get back in before they lock everything down or move it?"

"That's what I've been doing for the past hour."

"I thought you were checking the firewalls or something?"

It was her turn to smile before pointing to the screen.

"I checked those first and then pulled down all the data I could."

"What'd you find?"

"The financials definitely look odd. A lot of deposits and multiple line items that seem to say the same thing yet don't add up."

"What's the same?"

"My guess is line one is where it's dirty and line two is after they've made it squeaky clean."

"Money laundering?"

"On an impressive scale."

"Let me guess," he added. "The squeaky lines are the only ones that add up."

"You bet."

Sloan moved the computer around so Chase could see what she'd managed to download after securing her laptop, files and any potential intrusion into her own systems.

"Look here." She tapped a few places on the screen. "They're even keeping a list of their big donors."

"Is my aunt on the list?"

"I haven't seen her name anywhere, but I've only scratched the surface."

Chase's attention was on the screen before his gaze narrowed. "Who's that? Winston Kraft?"

"His name comes up a few times. Best I can tell he's an employee of some sort."

"I know that name."

"You know someone affiliated with the church?"

"No, but I'm pretty sure that's the father of a friend of my cousin."

Not for the first time did Chase's extensive family and exhaustive network—in Owl Creek and well beyond—impress her. The Colton family seemed to know everyone.

And it wasn't hyperbole to say so.

"Do you think your friend's involved?"

"It's my cousin Greg's friend, Rick Kraft. I don't know him well, but met him and his wife a few times through the years over at the ranch. He's a good guy. Has two small kids. I can't see him being involved with something like this at all."

"We could call him. See if he knows anything or if he knows if your Aunt Jessie's involved in anything."

"A visit might be better." Chase stared at the screen once more before seeming to rethink his suggestion. "Is it worth trying to get a bit more information? Is that even possible?"

"My intention is to keep digging and get as much out of their systems as I can before they shut me down." She thought about the man Chase mentioned.

She trusted his instincts—and the friendship he'd mentioned between his cousin Greg and this man, Rick. But Sloan couldn't help but think it would be worth having a bit more information before they talked to the man's son.

"Tell you what. I'd like to keep going as far as I can and see what else I can find in the databases I have access to. Why don't I let you get back to work and I can update you later?"

Chase grinned at that. "Kicking me out?"

"Actually, giving you a chance to escape. Watching me tap away on the keyboard has to be about as interesting as watching paint dry."

"Lady, you have no idea what it's like to watch you work."

His eyes had grown dark and sultry with the compliment, and Sloan was trapped in that gaze, caught once more in that seductive quicksand that he seemed able to trap her in so effortlessly.

She nearly gave in—nearly threw caution to the wind and simply took.

But something in all that data on her computer screen held her back.

Something deeply wrong was going on with the Ever After group. And if she didn't act quickly, she was going to miss the opportunity to dive into their systems.

So she dragged her gaze from Chase's and focused on the task at hand.

And when he bid her goodbye a few minutes later and slipped out of her kitchen, she waited until he was gone before she turned to look at the empty doorway.

Chapter 14

Chase attempted to use work to stop thinking about her.

He called meetings with his direct reports, read an environmental-impact study on a property they were developing and focused on getting through the emails he'd ignored over the past twenty-four hours since the discovery of Althea's crimes.

And still, Sloan filled his thoughts.

What had happened to him?

Work had always been his salvation in the past. When his marriage dissolved, he'd thrown himself into work.

The outcome?

He'd closed six major deals in the quarter following his separation. He brokered five more the next quarter, solidifying his position as heir apparent to the CEO of Colton Properties.

When his father had died and after all the devastating news that had come since?

He'd pushed through Robert Colton's agenda for the company, driving his team and the organization to greater heights.

So what was it about this one woman that had suddenly made him lose focus? Or, worse, *interest* in what he was doing?

"Chase?" Sonja Rodriguez stood in his doorway, her

soft smile and earnest face a welcome change from his dour thoughts.

"Come on in."

As his marketing lead, he'd requested an update earlier on the new property they were highlighting at the edge of town. It was a tricky spot, the location a good one for the right buyer but close to the highway, with an odd spit of land that wouldn't ideally be developed with office space.

It would take the right client with the right vision for what they could put there.

Which made the spreadsheet Sonja slid across his desk a huge surprise.

"You've had fourteen interested buyers tour the property?" Chase looked up from the paper. "And three more who want to come back?"

"Yep."

Although he knew Sonja was worth her weight in gold with her impeccable marketing skills, the work on this was something of a professional miracle. "How?"

"We used a social strategy to build the property up slowly. A few ads highlighting the business district it was still part of, along with the other businesses you pass exiting Owl Creek. Then we did follow-ups, identifying the new housing development that was moving into its second phase of construction less than a mile away. And then…"

She left the words hang there for a moment, obviously enjoying his focus on the work.

"Yes?"

"We presented a simple yet precise vision for the space that succinctly outlined the steady stream of traffic predicted in the civil-engineering reports as well as the real and specific need for shopping, restaurants *and* a coffee house."

"Amazing."

"Never underestimate coffee addiction as a solid selling point." Sonja pointed toward the single-brew coffee maker on his sideboard. "Speaking of which, do you mind if I snag a cup?"

"Please, help yourself."

Chase scanned the sheet once more, specifically homing in on the vendors she'd highlighted.

"You do realize Sharon over at Hutch's diner might railroad you out of town for diverting her coffee business?"

It was only when Sonja turned from the sideboard, a cat-in-the-cream smile on her face, that Chase put two and two together with the name he'd read off the spreadsheet.

"It's Sharon's granddaughter who wants the space."

"You bet it is."

"You're a wonder."

Sonja took a seat opposite him, the self-satisfied smile fading, a look of motherly pride replacing it. "Susan's worked so hard in college, getting her hospitality degree at Idaho State. I think she has an even bigger vision of developing that property adjacent into a local attraction with an art focus as well as a children's activity center, but she wants to start with something she can build on."

"I'd be willing to hold it for her."

"The property?"

Chase considered it, realizing there was a significant benefit to the community, to keeping entrepreneurs in Owl Creek *and* to supporting his fellow business professionals.

Wasn't that part of his job?

Moreover, wasn't it why he'd stayed local, wanting to become a real member of the Owl Creek community instead of heading off to Boise or even farther afield after school?

"I think we can work out an arrangement. If she buys in

where she is and is willing to give us a soft commitment of formal consideration in twenty-four months, I'll hold on it."

"Chase, that's amazing."

"Let's get Finance to run some quick numbers and we can have sales put together a formal offer." Now it was his turn to smile. "And I'd like you to work with them and present the deal."

"Chase!"

"More important, I will ensure you get a cut on the sales revenue once she says yes."

"I don't know what to say."

"I hope it's yes because it's your vision for the property and your unique way of positioning it that has put us here."

"Thank you."

"The thanks are all mine."

Sonja's happily shell-shocked expression never wavered, even as she shifted into mother hen-mode. "Where's Sloan today?"

"Working. She's helping me with a small project before heading back home."

"Home?" Sonja's eyes narrowed. "She's not local?"

He'd filled in the office on why he'd hired SecuritKey, but at Sonja's question recognized he'd given minimal details about the woman herself.

"She's based out of Chicago. My cousin recommended her and we're fortunate she was willing to take on the contract so far from home."

"How's she finding Owl Creek?"

"We've kept her chained to the project so I'm not sure she's seen much." A vision of the two of them standing at the edge of the lake on Saturday filled his mind's eye. "Though I did get a chance to show her a bit of town."

"No one shows off Owl Creek quite like you."

"I've spent my life driving this town from one end to the other. It's not hard to highlight the good parts."

Sonja studied him across the desk, and it should have made him uncomfortable.

Hell, if it had even been a few weeks before it likely would have.

But something had changed since he'd directed the project to uncover Althea's bad dealings. Since he'd fully taken the reins of Colton Properties.

Since Sloan had arrived.

And suddenly he realized that people had been looking at him his entire life. The oldest Colton son and heir, and the one who Robert entrusted with his life's work.

He'd seen himself that way and it was only in the past few weeks that he'd begun to realize that it was his own legacy to create, not simply a continuation of his father's.

"I'd say it's even rather easy when you're showing off the place you love to a special woman."

Sonja's look was direct—challenging, even—but he saw beneath it.

Saw the genuine care that she brought to everything she did.

"She has to go home, Sonja. In a matter of days."

The older woman shrugged, and despite her casual expression, the unmistakable mix of passion *and* compassion was evident in her dark brown gaze.

"Maybe she already is home."

Winston Kraft stared at his computer and forced himself to take slow, deep breaths.

He'd had a breach last night, of that he was sure. And despite going over everything, from lines of code, to his firewall protections, to the review of all his files, he couldn't find any other evidence someone had been there.

Yet he knew.

Markus might consider him paranoid, but his healthy sense of paranoia had kept them in business all these years.

And someone had breached his systems.

Who was after them?

And who had the skills to bypass his advanced security measures and encrypted files?

Those weren't ordinary skills. They took practice and knowledge and an impressive ability to maneuver through layers of security protocols, built like a web to avoid intrusions *and* to detect the intruders before they realized it was too late.

But why hadn't his trap sprung?

He'd worked long and hard on that sticky, digital web and expected it would work if ever needed.

Yet here he was, facing a breach from a very clever adversary.

Rubbing his eyes, Winston cycled through the events of the past few months, considering who might be looking their way. And quickly came up with more than a few ideas.

He'd told Markus over and over the dead girls were a problem. And despite how deeply they'd buried them, ensuring there was no way they could be linked to Ever After, those secrets had still come back to the surface.

Dumb luck that stupid reporter had been making a connection between the girls' "devout faith" and a local religious group.

It was infuriating, really.

But was the reporter really the problem?

Or maybe it was the feds? The dead girls had occupied much of local law enforcement's time as well as the federal team assigned to this backwater region, so it was a real possibility.

Yet even as he turned that one over and over in his mind, he had to admit it didn't quite fit, either.

No one from law enforcement had nosed around lately. And the four new members of the Ever After flock they'd acquired in the past few months had checked out clean.

So who was looking?

He and Markus had run this con repeatedly and this one had been working like a charm. They'd ironed out some of the kinks that had stymied them in the past and until their recent need to switch money launderers, things had been going well.

But now, they'd had a string of problems and Markus refused to see it. He was so focused on landing the big fish that was Jessie Colton that he refused to pick up stakes and get the hell out of here.

It made him antsy because he always trusted his instincts, Winston thought.

Always.

Initially, he'd been apprehensive to move back to an area so close to his son, Rick. Damn boy was a do-gooder through and through and had never appreciated his old man's entrepreneurial spirit. But Markus had convinced him the open yet relatively secluded space in Conners was perfect for them. Add on the area was ripe for some "spiritual instruction" for its wealthier denizens and they'd seen their coffers build.

Then a damn dog found the dead girls and it had all started to unravel.

Winston flipped through a few of his files, his son's smiling face filling the screen, his arm around his wife. Their son stood in front of him, looking like the very image of Rick when he'd been a kid, and the little girl was in his daughter-in-law's arms.

A shot of irritation filled him.

They were a good-looking family and they'd be a huge asset to him and Markus if they'd only get on board. But Rick had sworn him off years ago, even before getting married, and refused contact.

Little did he know his dear old dad was a computer whiz and kept tabs, anyway.

He'd fallen off checking in on Rick of late, but it might be worth looking back in on his son.

He had no reason to think this breach had anything to do with Rick, but one could never be too sure. Especially when his own kid had made it readily apparent he thought his dad was the scum of the earth. Rick had never done anything to make Winston think he'd go to the cops, but he'd hedged his bets all the same.

It had been sheer dumb luck Jessie Colton was such a bad mother. The first time she'd visited, at Markus's invitation, Winston had nearly run out of the meeting room for fear of being recognized. His Rick had been best friends with her son, Greg, since they were kids.

If Jessie had stuck around Owl Creek, she might have known that, but she'd ditched her family the moment she got the chance. He'd even nosed around a bit when it was clear Jessie was becoming a more permanent fixture in their flock. The woman wasn't just uninvolved with her adult children in Owl Creek—she actively avoided talking about them.

It had served Markus well as he reeled her in, preying on that absence every chance he got.

Shaking off thoughts of Markus's new squeeze, Winston reviewed the files he had on his son. Rick's address and employment information had been easy to procure, so had his cell phone number. The rest had been harder. His grandson's preschool was solidly locked down, any information impossible to get at. He hadn't even bothered trying for hospital records after his granddaughter had been born.

But thanks to a social-media habit, he'd gotten a heck of a lot more once his daughter-in-law, Wendy, had gone full-bore on her posting. Pics of the kids, family pics, even a shot of their SUV in the background of one photo had paid dividends and he'd collected it all.

He quickly flipped through those photos, considering his next steps. It might be worth hacking into his son's phone records, just to see what the kid was up to.

He could even drive past the house and see if anyone was out playing in the yard in these waning days of warmth.

The odds that his latest problems were tied to Rick were slim. But Winston had believed his computer systems were solid, too, and he'd obviously been wrong.

It was time to turn over every stone and check hard under every rock he could think of.

He was also going to put a trusted minion on Rick for a few days. See what his son was up to and what he'd been doing while Winston dug a bit more through his son's digital footprint.

And maybe it was time he started convincing Markus that the Ever After Church might have outlived its usefulness.

Over coffee and a few slices of toast, Sloan reviewed all her files and considered her and Chase's next move. He hadn't come back to her apartment the day before and a part of her was relieved.

She was…*confused* as to how she felt.

Not the attraction part. That was crystal-clear.

But what to do about it? *That* was an entirely different matter.

A big part of her wanted to throw caution to the wind, take the few precious moments they'd have together and go home to Chicago the better for it.

Yet even as that enticing vision pulled her in, the more practical part of her knew it was a fool's errand. She wasn't a love-'em-and-leave-'em type and giving in to her feelings for Chase had disaster written all over it.

Since she'd vacillated between those two options the entire time she'd been investigating the Ever After Church and its leaders, she knew she was in emotional danger.

So she'd taken the time to also get some needed distance from Chase, keeping their communication the day before to text only.

They'd agreed to meet today, go over all she'd discovered and then talk to Rick Kraft.

A big part of her was tempted to simply turn everything over to the feds she'd worked with in the past. But she was equally aware she'd dug into this information illegally and without the protection of a government-issued search warrant.

By choice.

And when Chase had seemed willing to talk to his cousin's friend, Rick, it felt like the right solution to continuing to pursue the inquiry alone.

They might not find a thing. She hoped they wouldn't.

Even as she worried she'd ruin the man's life in the process.

Because whatever else she thought they were sitting on, two things were abundantly clear. The Ever After Church was more of a cult than any sort of real church.

And Winston Kraft was their digital mastermind.

How could they break that to the man's son?

Oh, sorry, I come bearing bad news?

Do you know what's been lurking in your family tree?

Talk to your dear old dad lately?

Any way she'd spun it in her mind, nothing felt right. Nor could she erase the subtle sense of dread that even though she and Chase might need to talk to Kraft and share all they'd found, they also risked hurting the man beyond measure.

Nothing in her line of work was worse than a lose-lose situation, but that's where they found themselves.

She'd also done a bit of hunting on the "church's" leader, uncomfortable with what she'd found there as well. Markus Acker was Kraft's apparent partner, but the details were fuzzy and had a quality that made her think whatever information was out there about him online had been tampered with.

It wasn't impossible to do, but it did take skill. Based on the weird dead ends she kept running into as she tried to look into the man, her experience suggested there was something deliberate in the way Acker's image had been crafted in the digital world.

One more sign things were not right with this Ever After group.

She'd just finished cleaning up her breakfast dishes when she heard the knock on her front door. Fighting back the sudden excitement that leaped in her chest at the reality that Chase had arrived, she moderated her walk to the door to avoid appearing too eager.

And opened it to find both Chase and his cousin Greg on the other side.

"Oh, hello."

Greg's smile was broad and slightly mischievous as he leaned in to press a kiss against her cheek. "Nice to see you again, Sloan."

Suddenly bemused at the thunderous expression that filled Chase's face, Sloan put on her brightest smile. "Welcome to my home."

Both men filed in, and Waffles shot out of the bedroom, making a beeline for Chase to weave around his legs.

"You've got a friend there." Greg pointed to the small feline form currently rubbing fur all over Chase's dress slacks.

"What can I say, he's got good taste."

Greg snorted but avoided saying anything further as Sloan gestured them both toward the kitchen.

"I went to talk to Greg first," Chase began. "I filled him in on wanting to talk to Rick and share some of our concerns about his father, Winston."

"Chase said you've found some incriminating stuff," Greg added as the two men gathered around her as she took a seat in front of her computer. "About Rick's dad. Possibly about my mom, too?"

Sloan recognized the emotional land mines in the question and stepped carefully. "My focus has been on the Ever After Church. I haven't found much about your mother beyond the fact that she appears to be a member."

"That's hardly a surprise."

Although they hadn't shared much more than those few minutes of conversation at the barbecue last Friday evening, it was impossible to miss the man's pain, Sloan thought.

And the very real proof that no matter how far into adulthood Jessie Colton's children got, they'd always carry the realities of abandonment inside.

Something about that thought both broke her and solidified all the reasons she was doing this.

The flouting of privacy rules.

Even putting her heart at risk for Chase.

The Colton family deserved some sense of closure, as

well as answers. And she had the professional skills to help them.

All of which she'd wrap around herself like a cloak to hide the deeper feelings that swirled inside her.

Although the kitchen wasn't large, something about having both Colton men in the room and hovering behind her suddenly made it feel quite small.

And made her realize just how big both of them were. Chase might have that attractive, broad-shouldered swimmer's build, but Greg had the tight, strapping build of a man who spent his life working outdoors and that had a distinct appeal, too.

Her feelings might be increasingly directed toward Chase, but since she still had breath in her body, she could admit his cousin cut an attractive figure. All the Colton men did.

One more aspect of Owl Creek to miss when she went home.

"Rick never did have a good relationship with his dad," Greg stated. "It was difficult when they were young, his father in and out of his life a lot. And then as he got older, he saw through the old man's veneer of big smiles and flashy talk."

"What does that mean?" Sloan asked, curious as it matched her opinions even though all she'd done was sift through a large digital footprint.

"Winston Kraft is always after his next mark, trying to run whatever his latest big con is. He's a huckster." Greg frowned, his expression narrowing with a thin layer of barely banked fury. "Or he was. Rick doesn't talk about it much, but I get the sense that things have turned darker."

"Darker how?" Chase asked. "A flashy salesman is one thing, but what you're suggesting sounds far worse."

"It's just a sense I get. Rick and I are good friends, but

something about his dad's always been off-limits. So I listen on the rare occasions Rick brings him up and leave it alone the rest of the time."

Greg's discomfort at the conversation was clear, but there was something else there, just hovering beneath his words, that Sloan couldn't ignore. "Do you think Rick's afraid of his father?"

"He'd likely want to punch me if I said that to him, but yeah, I think so. Maybe he never was before, but now that he's got a wife and kids? I think he sees his father's life and choices in a whole new light."

"One that puts his family at risk?" Chase probed.

"Exactly."

It would be so easy to dismiss Greg's light-hearted humor and cocky smile as vapid and uncaring, but in that moment, Sloan saw just how much the man cared. About his friend and the things that had shaped Rick's life. "Are you okay if we go talk to him?"

"I am. I don't know how happy he'll be about it, but he should know about your suspicions. More—" Greg shook his head "—he deserves to know."

"I appreciate it," Chase said, putting a hand on his cousin's shoulder. "I really think we need to understand this group and what they're up to."

The joviality Greg had walked in with had vanished, replaced with a grim man carrying a heavy weight. "And how my mother's involved."

Neither she nor Chase said anything as Greg pulled his phone from his pocket. "Let me go give Rick a call. Let him know you're heading his way."

Sloan waited until Greg was in the living room, engaged in conversation with his friend, before speaking. "I wish there was an easier way."

"I do, too. One that didn't involve destroying families. Or at least adding a painful reminder into an otherwise ordinary day."

"It's not just Rick Kraft," Sloan said. "Your cousins are facing a hard road here, too."

"I know." Chase dropped his head before looking back up at her, a bleakness in his eyes she hadn't seen since they'd started working together. "I know we need to see this through, but it's really hard to feel we're making the right decision."

Since his comment so closely mirrored her earlier thoughts, she could only agree. "I know."

"And then I remind myself that the elder generation functioned with secrets and lies, and we need to get every last one of them out in the open."

"Do you think this Ever After group is going to harm your family?"

Although she should have questioned that before, it was the first time Sloan actually felt a genuine shot of fear.

Was the Colton family at risk?

Was Chase?

"I don't know what to think, but it's not a big leap to see the awareness and press my father's death has received and make a connection with my aunt. She hasn't exhibited the most rational decision making. Now she's a part of that group?" The question seemingly hung there as Chase obviously weighed his words. "I think it's entirely possible she's at risk simply by being a member."

"And the family?"

"If we're not in danger, by extension we're at least at risk."

"Of what?"

"Having a very large target on every Colton back."

Chapter 15

Rick Kraft and his wife, Wendy, sat opposite Chase and Sloan at their kitchen table, a visible sense of nervousness arcing between them. They held hands on top of the scarred oak, an obvious unit as Sloan laid out for them all she'd learned in her digging into the Ever After Church.

"I am sorry to have to share this with you," Sloan added after walking through each piece of data she'd uncovered. "But we feel you should know and, if you're willing to talk to us, wanted to see if you can shed any light on the church."

"First and foremost, don't call it a church. Ever." Rick's tone was low, but it quivered with a barely leashed fury that Chase could practically feel beneath his skin.

Wendy's hand tightened over her husband's, clear support and strength in their hold. "Churches aren't meant to manipulate their people."

"The Ever After group does that?" Chase asked.

"All that and more," Rick said. "My father has been hooked up with Markus Acker for years. They're men of death. To suggest what they do is a church intimates something holy and I can assure you God has no play in any of it."

"Have you been in contact with your father?"

Sloan was compassionate and while he knew she was as determined as he was to get answers, Chase was again impressed by her deep well of kindness as she spoke with the couple.

Yes, she wanted those answers.

But even more, she obviously wanted to provide as much kindness and support as she could to Rick and Wendy.

It was one more facet of her that both impressed and humbled him, all at the same time. She put others first and she did it so naturally—so intuitively—that it was a part of her.

Although he was obviously shaken by the need for the conversation, Rick had agreed and had answered every question they'd posed to him. He didn't shirk away from giving a response, even with such a direct question.

"I avoid my father at all costs and have for more than a decade now. He and I never saw eye to eye on anything, and if it were a simple matter of differences, I could find a way past it."

"But it isn't?" Chase asked, aware now more than ever before in his life how challenging and potentially tenuous father-and-son relationships could be.

And at the same time, he recognized a strange sort of grace as well.

For the past months, his memories of his father had all become clouded and warped by the realities of Robert Colton's decisions around his family and his secret life. Yet as awful as it had been, he'd never seen his father as a monster.

A misguided man, yes.

But one he feared? No.

"I don't want my father anywhere near my life and I most especially don't want him anywhere near my family."

"We have two children," Wendy added. "Justin is four and Jane is fourteen months."

"How sweet," Sloan murmured. "Do you have photos?"

It was the right question and Wendy's obvious pride in her children was evident as she pulled up a photo on her cell phone.

The firm line of Rick's mouth never softened but Chase could clearly see the pride in his gaze as he stared down at his children.

"Nothing is more important than them. Then Wendy." Rick shifted, wrapping an arm around his wife's shoulders. "And I'd like nothing more than to see you put an end to this once and for all. My father and his crony, Markus Acker, have been getting away with this for years. Creating these fake church groups, bilking people for money and doing far worse. They've always been able to outrun the law and I have nothing I can definitely pin on them, but I can promise you they're guilty."

"Thank you for agreeing to talk to us. We're committed to seeing this through," Sloan assured the man.

"Greg was clear on that point, and I know that now. It's why I agreed to talk to you."

"We're going to uncover what they're doing. I'm not letting this go," Chase said.

And as the words left his mouth, Chase not only recognized them for truth, but also as something even deeper.

He knew them for the vow they were.

"Rick's scared, just like Greg said."

Sloan spoke as they drove away from the Kraft's home, their conversation with the couple filling her thoughts. She'd recognized Greg's frustration for his friend that morning, but even she hadn't fully prepared herself for the deep anger and terrible fear that Rick Kraft obviously carried about his father.

It sat on his shoulders, as clearly as a physical weight.

"What's clear is that this has changed for him. At some point it shifted from anger and disgust with his father's choices to genuine worry for his family," she added, thinking through all the man had shared with them.

"It must be a terrible weight."

"The person who should care for you the most is seen as your greatest threat? It's nearly impossible to fathom."

She'd seen difficult things throughout her career. The work she took on—and the ways she used her talents—had ensured she was regularly exposed to some of the worst sorts of humans.

But this?

A man who preyed on people, weaponizing their faith? And doing it in a way that scared his own son?

"Are you okay?" Chase asked as they drove the increasingly familiar streets through Owl Creek.

"I wish I could say yes, but no, I'm not. I keep thinking I can't be surprised by the choices people make, yet once again, I'm shocked at the darkness that lives inside of some."

"Rick's father is bad news."

"Everything about that Ever After group is bad news. I can't help but think your aunt is in danger."

Sloan recognized it was quite a departure from her negative thoughts up to now about Chase's Aunt Jessie. But after all Rick had shared, she had to believe that the woman was in trouble. Jessie Colton might not know it, but how could she possibly be a part of that group and not be at risk?

Especially if she'd come to their attention because of her relationship with Chase's father and the wealth and power the man had wielded in life?

In fact...

"Chase? When Nate spoke to you about his mother, he

also brought up that she wanted him to press for his inheritance. That he should be determined to take more. Do you think she's getting pressured by these Ever After people?"

"You mean she's being manipulated rather than being a direct part of it all?"

"It would play, wouldn't it?" Sloan turned the idea over in her mind. "She's been a conniver, but she's also been a product of her misguided thinking her entire life. Leaving her husband and children for her own sister's husband? That's..." Sloan trailed off, looking for the right word. "Well, it's small in so many ways."

"Small?"

"Yeah. She doesn't have the best interests of others at all. Not her children. Not her husband. Not her sister. But more than that, she also didn't go looking very far with her choices. If she were that unhappy with her life, wouldn't she have gone farther afield? More, wouldn't she have sought out a life that she could live without the secrets and having to remain hidden away? She and Robert weren't even able to marry, despite the deception of looking like they were a couple."

Sloan wasn't entirely sure where she was going with this theory, but something about it rang true.

Jessie Colton had jumped at whatever was in front of her. It was destructive, but it also didn't scream a sense of thinking things through with any degree of cunning or calculation.

Rather, it appeared as if she was simply being dragged along by whatever impulse was directly ahead of her.

"So if we play out your way of thinking, she's being manipulated by Winston Kraft?"

"Winston or the guy he works with, Markus Acker. She's easily fascinated by a bright and shiny promise placed in her path."

"Her children certainly don't seem to have been enough to keep her priorities straight."

"No, they weren't." Sloan thought again about what she'd managed to dig up on the Ever After Church and its leader, Acker. Everything rang patently false about the group, their leader most of all.

"I think that might give me a new line to tug."

"On what?"

"Rick's information was helpful, but his father, for all his power and influence, is functioning in the role of support staff. Keeping the computer. Cleaning up any messes. I think I need to dig deeper into the leader. Markus Acker."

"I thought you had details about him in your files?"

"I did and a lot of impressions about him that seemed off, somehow. Like a sanitized, polished version of him was all I could find online."

"You think it's fake?"

"I think it could be. And with some of the information Rick gave us, I'm going to do some more digging to see if I'm right."

"We have a very important job for you, Brother Jasper."

Markus kept his tone level and easy, pushing the lightest touch of urgency under his words as he sat in the clearing. His crossed legs and prayerful position belied the anger at their current situation roiling deep inside.

He was gratified to see that urgency was working when Jasper shifted his position, nearly squirming to get closer, his pale blue eyes lighting up with the fervor of the believer.

"Of course, Leader Acker. How can I help?"

Jasper was one of his true believers. He wasn't wealthy, but he was useful. Markus was well aware he needed both types of followers to make Ever After the success it was.

A point that had been proven in spades when Jasper had helped with the disposal of a few of those dead girls.

"It seems Brother Kraft's son has been speaking ill of our work."

"Ungrateful boy." Jasper practically spat the words.

"Ungrateful *betrayer*," Markus said with emphasis.

Winston's son had always been a bone of contention between him and Winston, the man's willingness to sit back and leave the boy to his own devices concerning. Sure, Rick and his little family kept to themselves, but it was a problem to have such a threat out roaming free.

And now that threat was visiting with Jessie's family.

There was no way it was a coincidence.

Winston had managed to tap into his son's door camera earlier that afternoon and found the proof standing on the other side of the porch.

"How can I help you, Leader?"

"I believe Winston's ungrateful son has been spying on us. Talking about us. And telling others that our peaceful life is fake."

"But it's not!" Jasper's agitation spilled over as the man leaped to his feet. "We're a peaceful sort. We do our work quietly and away from prying eyes. It's only the betrayers that must be silenced! Like those girls."

"You know how to work quickly and quietly. I need you to confirm Rick's actions and assess if the threat to our peaceful life grows too great."

"I will, Leader. I can do that."

Markus slowly got to his feet, the motion meant to convey serenity to his obedient follower. He'd learned long ago that ability to project a certain untroubled tranquility often did far more good for advancing his goals than any other tactic he possessed.

People liked calm.

They liked order.

And they responded to someone who competently wielded both.

He came to his full height, looking deep into Jasper's eyes. "I'm so grateful I can count on you, Brother Jasper."

"Of course, Leader. Ever After must be protected from that rabble."

"I know you're right." Jasper had nearly turned away, happy to head off to his task, before Markus added one final admonition. "I'm sorry to say his wife is a problem, too. I believe she's contributed to the darkness in Brother Kraft's son."

"I'll keep watch, Leader," Jasper promised, that fervency in his eyes like a form of desire. "I'll see that they can't do us any harm."

Chase paced Sloan's small living room, updating Greg on their visit the day before with Rick and Wendy. He'd meant to get to his cousin sooner but after their visit he'd had to race back to Colton Properties for an emergency meeting to make an offer on a property they were at risk of losing. Sloan had headed back here to her place to tug more lines of information they'd received from Rick.

Beyond a few text messages and missed phone calls between him and his cousin, a full day had passed until he'd been able to provide updates.

"I know this is hard for Rick and Wendy. I appreciate your willingness to talk to him on this. He wasn't happy to see Sloan and I, but he was a real help."

"He knows what a problem his father is. He—" Greg broke off, his sigh traveling through the phone line. "It was one of the things that bonded us young. His dad. My mom. Rick was the one friend who understood what that betrayal was like."

"I'm sorry, Greg. More than I can say."

"For what?"

"For never realizing just how bad it was. For not realizing how deep the hurt was. It's only now, after knowing what my own father did, that I realize how much I never said. Or understood."

That truth flowed out, a product of years observing his cousins. He'd always known Greg, Max, Malcolm and Lizzy had struggled with their mother's abandonment. But he'd never had the words before.

It was only as Sloan walked into the room, setting a small tray on the coffee table full of cheese and crackers, that he finally understood why he could say them now.

Sloan.

She'd come into his life for a difficult purpose. But she'd found a way to help him through all the things he'd never had the words for.

His cousins' pain of abandonment.

His own frustration and loss after his marriage dissolved.

And then the deep, cavernous pain of betrayal at his father's actions.

Sloan had seen it all and she'd had the compassion to help *him* see that they might be facets of his life, but they didn't have to define him.

"We were kids, Chase. You didn't have to say anything. You were there for me. For my brothers and my sister. So was your mom and so were *your* brothers and sisters. We got through."

A level of certainty filled Greg's voice that humbled Chase.

Here was a man who'd faced a lifetime of challenges—

and was still facing them—from the actions of a parent. Despite it all, he didn't blame others or lash out.

"I'm still there for you. I hope you know that."

"Right back at ya, cuz. Now. Get off the phone with me and get back to that lovely woman who's dumb enough to spend time with you."

"I'll be sure to tell Sloan you said that."

Whatever seriousness had laced their conversation had vanished, Greg's normal level of mischief and good humor firmly in place. "See that you do."

Sloan glanced up from where she settled the snack, a broad smile on her face. "Tell me what?"

"Greg says hello, in his own inimitable way."

It was a facet of his cousin's personality, one Chase was finally coming to understand had been forged in the fires of his mother's abandonment.

Smile. Laugh. Joke.

Wonderful traits in their own right, but also weapons that could defend, deflect and protect one's emotions.

He hadn't really understood it before now, but hadn't he done the same when it came to relationships?

Avoiding anything serious—on the surface—looked like a carefree lifestyle. But it was only now, when faced with someone who had truly begun to matter to him, that Chase realized all he'd done was hide behind his own emotions all these years.

Because Sloan had come to matter.

No matter how much they both had tried to disregard that fact, it had become increasingly impossible to avoid.

Or ignore.

"Sloan." He reached for her hand, oddly pleased when she not only took what he offered, but also gave his hand a light squeeze. "I'm glad you're here."

"I'm glad I'm here, too."

"I mean really here. In this moment. In Owl Creek." He stared up at her, his heart racing. "With me."

She moved closer, her free hand settling on his shoulder. "I'm glad I'm here, too."

"It's inevitable, isn't it?" He murmured the words as he stared up at her, gratified when he saw the same acceptance in her eyes.

"I think it is." She nodded.

"What should we do about it?"

She stood there, staring down at him for several long moments as she seemingly came to some decision.

"I don't know if this is a good idea."

He wanted her, of that he was certain. But he couldn't deny the reality of their situation. Or the risks that no amount of want could get them to the other side of this attraction. "Me, either."

"But increasingly, I've come to realize it's the only idea."

Before he could respond, she bent her head and pressed her lips to his, a world of want and need and sheer desire in the play of her mouth over his.

Chase placed his hands on her hips, pulling her close until she tumbled into his lap.

And as she fitted into his arms, cradled against his body, he asked the question they'd been leading to from that very first moment in his office.

"Let me stay with you."

Her gaze never left his, those fathomless depths of the deepest brown pulling him in.

"Yes."

Yes.
Such a simple word.

Such an easy agreement.

And yet, for all the simplicity, Sloan thought, there was power in the acceptance of all that was still to come.

Their kiss on the couch had spun out, delicate and urgent all at once. And it was only now, as she held his hand and led him to her bedroom, that Sloan recognized everything up to now had been leading them here.

The attraction between them was undeniable.

But the need to be together physically had become an ache she could no longer ignore.

More, she no longer wanted to ignore it.

She was a woman in full possession of her faculties and her will.

And every bit of both wanted Chase Colton.

The back of her legs brushed the side of the bed, both stopping point and decision point.

Continue to go further on this journey?

Yes.

It pounded through her in lockstep with her heartbeat as Sloan reached for the hem of Chase's dress shirt, dragging it from where it was tucked neatly into his black slacks. The man was well-dressed, sharp and natty, and all she could think of was messing him up.

Of getting beneath that refined look to the man who was flesh, blood and beating heart.

The man she loved.

That awareness hit hard and fast and Sloan stilled her movements to stare up at him, drinking in the moment even as it scared her beyond herself.

Love?

Was she really there?

Or was she confusing the overwhelming need to give

in to passion with feelings that had her dreamily thinking of forever?

There was no way to really know. But dissecting her feelings in the dimming light outside her bedroom window seemed rife with the potential to miss the moment.

She'd think on it later. Then, she could turn it over in her mind to her heart's content.

But right now, she'd take.

With renewed focus, she finished undoing the row of buttons that ran over his chest, stripping the thin material of his shirt over those impressively broad shoulders. His T-shirt quickly followed and as she ran her hands over the wide planes of his chest, she reveled in the feel of him. The light dusting of hair beneath her palms. The wide, flat nipples that were sensitive to her hands, his green eyes darkening at her touch. And the thick bands of muscle over his stomach, solid and firm beneath her seeking fingers.

He was impressive. So hot and so responsive to the lightest touch.

But it was the thick length of him as she slipped her hand beneath the waistband of his slacks that drew her in. Beckoned her toward all that was still to come.

And that had her quivering in anticipation when he growled against her mouth before pulling her fully against him.

She was killing him.

Slowly. Determinedly. Exquisitely.

And he'd never been more ready to give in and simply accept his fate.

Sloan was a marvel, his own personal miracle. And as he mimicked her earlier motions, slipping her now-open blouse from her slim shoulders, Chase took a hard breath.

She was beautiful.

High, rounded breasts spilled over the lacy edges of her bra, while that small rib cage tapered down into a flat stomach and the secrets that still lay beneath her jeans.

Secrets he was determined to uncover, one achingly slow moment at a time.

With her blouse removed, he shifted his attention to her bra, unhooking the delicate material and taking in his fill as it followed her blouse to the floor. With firm hands, he cupped her breasts, his thumbs playing over her erect nipples, her skin so soft he wondered if he'd ever touched anything so perfect in his life.

He'd wanted before.

Needed before.

But never had he been so overwhelmed by a woman so as to forget everything but the pure magic of the moment. And she was so responsive—so achingly beautiful as her eyelids dropped with her pleasure—that Chase gave himself the joy of simply watching her take the pure power of what was between them in physical form.

A need that pushed them harder, faster and more greedily toward a finish line that waited in the distance.

A finish line they'd cross together.

With that temptation awaiting them both, Chase laid her down on the bed, his gaze never leaving hers, as he took the final steps of removing his slacks, then reaching for her to pull her jeans and panties down the slim lines of her legs.

And then, it was just the two of them, naked bodies pressed together as he stretched out beside her on the bed.

Her pretty brown skin practically glowed in the soft, end-of-day light that filtered through the window as he traced his fingertips over her flesh. She followed suit with gentle traces of her own, from the surprisingly sensitive skin on the inner curve of his elbow, to the achingly hard length of him she returned to with fervent strokes.

They shared it all, there in the dying light of day. As the lazy discovery turned more urgent—as the need for her that had overwhelmed him from the start grew so intense he could think of nothing else—he positioned himself over her.

She'd already sheathed him in the protection he'd retrieved from his wallet and as her thighs opened for him, Chase touched that endless sweetness, her slick folds waiting and ready for him.

She reached down to guide him into her, her body drawing him in, closer.

Deeper.

And in the most erotic moment of his life, they began to move. The rhythm was fast, hard, exquisite. Pleasure built in his body, the magnificent force building behind his eyes even as he desperately fought to keep his gaze level with hers.

More, as he wanted to watch her the moment she was as consumed as he.

The moment her world exploded in starlight.

He didn't have to wait long, and when she cried out in pleasure, he let himself go.

That final race to the finish.

The final driving beat of body into body.

The beauty of—finally—falling over the edge into the soul that waited for his.

Chapter 16

She shouldn't feel this decadent.

This wanton.

This wrapped up in Chase.

But that's where she was and had stayed for nearly twenty-four hours.

It had been a sharing unlike anything she'd ever known. An erotic, sexual feast that at times was so intense she'd never imagined she could feel like this, and at others so warm and intimate and funny she couldn't find her breath.

How could two people experience such a range of emotions?

And how had she lived so long without it?

Sloan had done her level best to keep herself in check, avoiding those types of mental wanderings in favor of taking the pure joy of the hours spent with him. But despite all her efforts, those thoughts kept creeping in.

She had to give this up.

In a very short time, she'd be heading home.

And while he'd been attentive and so thorough, there were moments she'd wanted to cry at his aching tenderness, Sloan admitted the truth, if only to herself.

He hadn't told her he loved her. Or that he wanted her to stay. Or that this meant more to him than these special hours together.

And it was that truth that she tried to focus on as she watched him walk back into the bedroom, the plate of cheese and crackers in his hands.

"Is that from last night?"

"I'd hardly be a gentleman if I poisoned you on rancid cheese." Chase bent over and pressed a kiss to her lips before setting down the plate. "This is fresh from the fridge."

"I'm starving."

"I figured this would hold us over and we could think about going out for dinner." His gaze drifted down over her nakedness as he settled in beside her. "Or maybe we order in dinner."

She reveled in that warm appreciation. "Maybe we will."

It had been like this since the day before. That intense awareness of each other and an inability to remain apart. As if they were both trying to absorb all they could in this brief interlude together.

Sloan reached for a cracker, settled a piece of cheese on top and nibbled a small bite. "We haven't talked much about the Krafts. Do you think it's worth pulling your family in and talking about the discussion we had with them?"

Chase swallowed around a bite of his own before responding. "It's worth filling everyone in on what we've discovered so far, but we don't have a lot to go on. Rick and his wife's fear is real, and I don't want to underestimate that. We can put my family on alert as well, but there's nothing specific we can call on other than keep a careful watch if my Aunt Jessie reaches out."

"It's interesting she's only pressed Nate and Sarah so far. Not her other children."

"I suspect she knows her antics won't be welcome."

"Perhaps." Sloan shrugged and finished the small square of cheese, something tugging at the back of her thoughts.

That conversation they'd had, about Jessie's actions being small and a product of whatever decision was right in front of her, struck Sloan once again.

It was instinct, nothing more. She didn't know the woman, nor did she have a sense of how Jessie Colton would behave in the real world. The sum total of Sloan's impressions was tied to past behavior and the few things her family had said about her.

And yet…

"Those look like some very serious thoughts." Chase pressed a gentle kiss to her cheek. "Want to share them?"

Sloan surfaced from her musings, only to glance down to see her half-nibbled cracker still between thumb and forefinger. "Sorry. Habit."

"Not at all. Walk me through it. What are you thinking?"

"Jessie's been pressuring Nate and Sarah. And from Nate's feedback to you, he and his sister aren't budging."

"Not at all, based on my read of him."

"Then how long will it be before she goes after her other children?"

"Go after them how?"

"A pressure campaign to get them on board. To either use them to influence Nate and Sarah or to pull them into her narrative that her children deserve a share of the Colton money."

"Everyone's doing okay in life. My father was the wealthier brother in terms of income, but my Uncle Buck has done fine with the ranch. More than fine," Chase added. "The money isn't what drives us."

"But your aunt doesn't know that."

"I can see something's there, something that you're working through, but I'm not following the same thought process as you. My cousins are grown adults. Max is former FBI, even. They can handle themselves if their mother comes back calling on them."

"Yes, but does this Ever After group know that? What resources do they have? Or worse," Sloan said, thinking of those dead girls dumped in hand-dug graves. "What if that church has set their sights beyond Jessie."

"To my family?"

"Exactly. What if the Colton family is the endgame here?"

It was a sobering thought, going from a day of nonstop sensual pleasure to talk of his family's lives at risk.

But Chase was rapidly catching up.

He'd like nothing more than to stay right here, keeping the world at bay with Sloan, warm and responsive in his arms. Only the real world had intruded, and he knew they needed to follow her concerns.

"Looks like it's time for another Friday-evening family meeting."

Sloan was already out of bed, heading for the en suite bathroom to shower. Chase watched her beautiful body as it was backlit from the light of the bathroom doorway.

Even more, he now knew that body matched the beautiful heart that beat in her chest.

He'd seen that from the first, her compassion and care such obvious traits. But now, after spending these hours with her, he recognized how deeply it ran in all she did. She was a warm, generous lover, but it was an extension of the warm, generous person that she was. And even now, her mind was rapidly processing, wanting to ensure his family was okay.

Her thoughts were always focused on others.

Hadn't Max said that in their very first conversation, when his cousin had recommended Sloan for the job?

How foolish he'd been, Chase realized, not to recognize the real risk to his heart it would be to bring in someone so competent and so deeply caring as she translated difficult work into help and support for others.

But he'd been so foolish and so deluded. He'd thought his life would continue the way it always had, indefinitely in limbo, always able to keep his heart protected.

In reality, he'd only been protected because there'd been no one worth falling for. No one who mattered so much. No one who'd truly put his heart at risk.

Until Sloan.

The sound of the shower had him imagining joining her, even as he knew there was work to be done and a family meeting to plan, when his phone went off on the bedside table. He saw Greg's name painting the face of the screen and connected to the call.

"Chase."

That flat use of his name and the odd urgency that transmitted through the phone lines in a heartbeat captured him immediately.

"What is it?"

"It's Rick and Wendy. They were in a car accident about an hour ago. Both were pronounced dead at the scene."

"Walk me through it."

Despite his whirling thoughts and the sheer impossibility that the healthy, vibrant people he and Sloan had spoken to a few days before were now dead, he forced himself to concentrate.

To *listen* to the words Greg spoke.

To accept that no matter how much this looked like an accident on the surface, there was no possible way it was.

This was all part of the swirling, writhing evil that the

Ever After Church was capable of. And he and Sloan had brought the wolf directly to Rick Kraft's door.

It was worse than he'd imagined, Chase thought two hours later as he sat in the kitchen at the Colton Ranch.

Rick and Wendy were dead, and Greg had headed off with Wendy's best friend, Briony Adams, to pick up the couple's children. They'd been sheltered at a day-care facility that had been watching the children through the madness of trying to sort through the accident, but Briony and Greg had both been designated as caregivers in case of emergency.

And this qualified in the worst of ways.

"You okay?" Max sat down next to him, fresh mugs of coffee in hand. Chase wasn't all that interested in drinking anything, but it was something to do in the endless roiling of his thoughts. A strange sort of anchor as his hands wrapped around the heat of the mug and his senses took in the heavy, rich scent of the coffee.

"I did this."

"What's that supposed to mean?" Max's demand was quick, the narrowing of his eyebrows into slashes over his light blue eyes even quicker.

"I asked Sloan to dig into the Ever After Church. Into Winston Kraft. There's not a chance in hell that accident was really accidental."

"We don't know that."

"Oh, no?" Chase glanced up from where he stared into the depths of his coffee, anger at himself eating a path from throat to gut. "Can you honestly sit there and tell me you think this is just a massive coincidence?"

"Until proven otherwise, we have to keep all reasonable

options open. People do have car accidents. It's sad and horrible and ruins lives, but it happens."

Chase wanted to believe that. In every way, he wanted to believe that it was simple coincidence that he and Sloan had met with the couple, and two days later they'd lost their lives.

But something deep inside refused to accept it.

Because something equally deep recognized something far bigger was at play. It was the same sense he'd had that there were issues at Colton Properties.

Something was *off.*

And Rick and Wendy Kraft had paid the price. Their young children would pay an even higher one for the rest of their lives.

"Since I can see you don't believe me, walk me through it." Max held up a hand. "Not the guilt-ridden version where you have to hold the responsibility for the whole world, but the one that your gut's telling you."

"Two people are dead, Max. This isn't me playing overbearing big brother."

"No, but if you are correct, you're taking responsibility for the actions of a killer, which isn't right or accurate. *If,* and it's still an *if,* Rick and Wendy were murdered, then that responsibility sits with the person who did it."

Chase wasn't so sure about that—they'd never have been in danger if not for his poking around—but he saw Max's point all the same.

And a killer on the loose was a danger to them all.

"At my request, Sloan's been digging around the Ever After Church."

"Speaking as a former representative of the US government and a law-enforcement professional, surely you understand why that's a problem?"

"Yes."

Max's gaze was direct. "Do you?"

"Max, come on. These people are corrupt in every way. And—" He stopped, well aware he was treading into very dangerous personal territory. "Your mother's involved with them. We needed to know what we're dealing with. Sloan had the skills to find the answers we needed."

"What the hell, Chase?" Max practically spit out the words. "You do realize this is a massive violation of privacy and could backfire on you both? She could damage her incredibly stellar reputation."

One more point of guilt to add to all the others.

And while Sloan might have been a willing accomplice, this was all his doing.

"I'm the one who pushed for this, Max. I want answers."

"I want them, too, but we're not going above the law to get them."

"And if this church is doing some dangerous things?" Chase knew he had responsibility here, but he couldn't quite rid himself of the importance of that point. "Things even the government hasn't been able to find?"

"That's a low blow."

"Not a low blow. It's the reality of the situation. They've shielded themselves so much that they were nearly able to bury the story about those dead girls. If you hadn't been on the case, I believe they *would* have buried it. They've got skills and some clout, and we need to fight fire with fire."

"A handy excuse until you get burned."

"Rick and Wendy sure did."

And there it was again. That steady drumbeat he couldn't see past. It suggested his insistence on the truth and on cracking open the details on the Ever After group was tainted with danger.

"Walk me through what Sloan has found. Step by step."

"You do understand she did this for me?"

"Yeah, I get it." Max shook his head before crossing to a small drawer near the fridge and pulling out a pad of paper and a pen. He sat back down and flicked the ballpoint. "Tell me what you've found."

Jasper Thomas Miles.

Sloan tapped a few more keys, hunting through her databases to see if anything popped on the man. It was a long shot, but she'd been digging for hours and still wasn't sure if she had anything or if she was going in big, tired circles.

But if this person, Jasper Miles, had anything to do with the Krafts' deaths, she was determined to find it.

He'd popped up when she'd followed a trail from the Krafts' accident report Chase's brother, Fletcher, had been kind enough to share. The driver on scene, a Mike Arnold, was responsible for the car that hit Rick and Wendy. He'd been taken into custody for driving under the influence and everything about the situation had seemed run-of-the-mill. A real and tragic accident that had resulted in loss of life.

But something about the timing of the accident and the fact that she and Chase had just seen the couple had her digging further.

Because no matter what, she couldn't shake the feeling it was made to *look* like an accident, even as it was deliberate, intentional action.

She'd hunted through Arnold's social media and uncovered two interesting things. A social post where he'd checked into a local bar and tagged a friend who was meeting him there, one Jasper Miles.

When she'd clicked into Jasper's account, she'd seen several photos of him out in the wide-open air that looked like this part of the country. He had also posted spiritual quotes about the "ever after way" and "building a life to last ever after, even past his last breath."

Odd phrasing? Yes.

Actually incriminating? It was hard to say.

But it bothered her, especially the use of the words *ever after* in his language.

So she continued to dig. And was finally rewarded late in the day with a clear and obvious hit.

Jasper Miles spent two years in prison more than a decade ago for a violent incident. He was ultimately released on good behavior after finding his faith in prison and went on to preach to his fellow inmates.

One of whom was Mike Arnold.

Parole-board testimony for both men made the connection along with the matched timelines of their incarceration. Sloan recognized there was way too big a relationship to simply brush this off.

Or call it a coincidence.

She texted Chase with the news, only to get a text message come winging back.

Max said send over the details and he and I will go visit Mike Arnold in jail.

She quickly wrote up the details and emailed both men, texting back once it was done.

Call me or come over after you're done. Too much coincidence here. Just sent you and Max all the details.

As work went, she was satisfied with what she'd found. There was a connection there—a clear and evident one—

and she'd peeled back layers of the onion that was the complex and convoluted actions of the Ever After Church.

What she couldn't quite peel back or wish away was the strange way she felt, texting with Chase as if nothing was out of the ordinary.

As if they hadn't had sex and slept together for nearly twenty-four glorious hours before the news of Rick and Wendy's death reached them.

Where had that intimacy gone?

He hadn't even sent an assurance back that he'd come over after visiting Arnold in jail.

It was one more sign she needed to hold tight to her common sense and even tighter to her heart.

She'd gone into this with her eyes open and still had managed to fall in love, anyway.

Maybe it was time to acknowledge that was a fantasy. One steeped in mutual attraction, but not destined for anything more than the time she was slated to spend in Owl Creek.

Chase watched Max navigate his way through Owl Creek, the past several hours still lodged in his chest like a deal gone sour.

He'd worked through specifics with Max all while Sloan had hammered away at potential suspects. Based on the information she'd managed to uncover in a short period of time, they should all feel *very* good.

They had a lead, and he didn't need to be a law-enforcement professional to understand it was a strong, solid one.

But even with that encouraging news and the very real possibility they would have answers about Rick and Wendy Kraft's death in no time, he felt strangely empty.

He wanted to solve this and figure out what was roiling underneath the surface here in his home and with his family.

And he wanted Sloan to stay.

He might want that most of all.

"Do you think this guy's actually going to talk to us?" Chase asked Max, willing away the sense of malaise and frustration.

He'd talk to Sloan about staying later. Sure, he had a reputation for being averse to relationships, but things had changed and it was time to approach this head-on.

He'd talk to her and see what she wanted.

And he'd put himself on the line. All the way, no half measures. Not like with Leanne, when he told her he wanted to marry her and move onto the next stage of their lives simply because some magical list of check boxes had been ticked in his mind.

He'd focus on what Sloan wanted as much as his own needs and desires. On what it would really look like if they tried to have a relationship, even if it was long distance at first.

His life was in Owl Creek and that wasn't all that easy to untangle. But he'd already found himself imagining how he could juggle a life in Idaho along with one in Chicago, managing his personal life and his professional life across two places.

For Sloan. And for the relationship he believed they could have together.

They'd work it out because he wasn't making the same mistake this time. He was committed to talking through how he felt.

But in the meantime, he had a bigger problem staring him in the face.

"We've put you in a really difficult position, Max. I'm sorry."

"Less difficult since I'm out of the FBI, but yeah, you really need to leave this sort of work to professionals." Max side-eyed him before continuing. "Not the professionals we hire for jobs, either. Sloan should have left this alone."

"We both should have."

"While it pains me to say this, because you're both outside the law, your nosing around has opened a few avenues law enforcement can't quite as easily breach."

"So you're okay with it."

"I'm making the best of it."

Max couldn't quite hide the smile and Chase figured he'd passed some invisible hurdle. He wasn't off the hook, but his cousin was determined to help them.

"While you're doing that, could you ask Sloan to stay off her computer?"

"I think we both came to that conclusion on our own."

"Yeah, well call her and stress the same. We'll visit Mike Arnold in jail and can come straight to her place to fill her in."

Chase was just ready to do that as Max turned into the entrance for the prison. Flashing lights filled the parking lot and an ambulance was parked near the front door of the facility.

"What's this all about?" Max hit the speaker on his phone, giving voice instructions into his device to call one of his contacts in local law enforcement as Chase scanned the lot for any clues to what was going on.

"Owl Creek PD. Will speaking."

"Will. It's Max Colton."

The two men exchanged quick pleasantries, then Max said, "I'm over at the prison hoping my former FBI status gives me a bit of an okay to talk to a suspect. There's a lot going on over here."

"A lot," Will agreed. "I'm manning things here at the station, but the chief sent over a few squads. EMS is on high alert as well."

"For what?"

"An inmate died. He was brought in earlier and was found unconscious about fifteen minutes ago."

"Did his name happen to be Mike Arnold?"

Will hummed as he checked his information, the sound of computer keys tapping in the background, before his grim voice filled the SUV.

"Michael Arnold. EMS confirmed death ten minutes ago."

Max said his thanks before pulling into a space and turning around. It was only as he was headed back out of the lot, the prison filling the rearview mirror, that he finally spoke.

"What was that I said earlier?" Before Chase could even ask, Max added, "About some accidents just being accidents?"

"Yeah?"

"No way in hell this is an accident."

Chapter 17

"You did well, Brother Jasper." Markus's voice remained soft and calming as he spoke the words.

This was a delicate time and any misstep in his handling of Jasper could lead to a problem.

They'd nearly had a situation with the girls a few months before, but Jasper had come around. He'd calmed at Markus's gentle words and the reassurance that he'd had to do the deed. That the killing and burial of several of the women had been necessary.

More, as Markus had told Jasper, he'd had to protect the flock, assisting the leader with the difficult work of culling the bad seeds who'd infiltrated them.

It was the same technique he'd use now, but he needed to work up to the approach. Jasper *was* a true believer, but he'd struggled when the girls were discovered. It had taken several personal sessions to calm him down and Markus had even begun to wonder if the man had outlived his usefulness.

Winston didn't seem to think so, but Markus wasn't so sure.

Nor was he convinced the events with Winston's son couldn't have been avoided with a bit of planning instead of rash action. The problem had been handled. But the death of a young couple with two adorable children was not going to go unnoticed.

Which made Winston's arrival in the small cabin they used as an office a few minutes later an opportunity to regroup.

"Brother Jasper…" Winston bent his head. "Hello."

Jasper nodded. "It is done, Brother."

Done?

Markus watched the exchange between the two men, increasingly connecting what they were talking about. He'd understood that Jasper had acted, but had believed it the man's inability to control his more violent impulses.

But to discover it was at Winston's direction? "What is done?"

"My son was poking into our work. He met with one of Jessie's family after my computer was hacked. He was a problem."

Markus struggled to keep himself in line. Although he'd been more than willing to show Winston his temper over the years, it was a display he avoided in front of his followers except in extreme circumstances.

People talked and they remembered when a person administered harsh words.

So he fought to keep himself in control, his words careful. "He's kept his distance from us for all these years. Surely you overreacted with this course of action?"

"I don't think so." Winston's gaze was challenging to read, as if the reality of his son's death was finally sinking in. What Markus didn't miss was the subtle sense of satisfaction that broke through. "And it was Brother Jasper's quick thinking that ensured we didn't have a bad situation on our hands."

"Computer hackers." Jasper shook his head. "It's devil-ish, invading others' privacy with those devices."

Markus nodded, adding his reflections to Jasper's, even as he kept a steady eye on Winston.

His right hand had acted alone, and it left him with a bothersome problem. Should he address it? Or take heart that the man stepped in and solved a situation before it be-came a problem.

If he was convinced that was all, perhaps he could have settled himself, but this was a bit much to take in.

The man had seen to it that his own son was killed.

He hadn't plotted or planned, but he'd taken swift ac-tion the moment he'd felt threatened. The two of them had worked well together for a long time, but this would take some reflection and review.

"Brother Jasper, you've earned a quiet night in private quarters. Why don't you go lie down in the Ever Rest hut and I'll see to it that a nourishing and restorative steak din-ner is brought to you."

Jasper's smile was eager as he took in Markus's direc-tion, and he was gone shortly after, on his way to the small, richly furnished hut they kept for special rewards. Markus waited until the man was fully out of hearing range before he turned on Winston.

"What the hell? Your son! Are you insane?"

"It needed to be done."

"Needed to be? Do you hear yourself? Do you have any idea what a mess you're going to bring down on us with this? Your do-gooder boy has a reputation and friends in connected places."

"Which is why he was dealt with. It's a Colton nos-ing around in our business, Markus. One more freaking Colton."

"That's who hacked you?"

"A woman Robert's son hired, who has the skills, is the one who did it. I nearly overlooked it. But I found a small signature she likely doesn't realize she left and it was enough for me to circle back and find her. She's been digging in places she has no right to."

"Why?"

"I haven't figured that out yet. Did Jessie talk to them? Say something that might make them start wondering why she wants Robert's money so bad?"

"Jessie hasn't left the property in days."

"No calls then?"

"Nothing. I've gently asked if she's spoken to her children, and she's maintained that they're ungrateful and she needs to regroup before she tries to deal with them again."

"The Coltons are a problem."

"They're the big fish we need before we pull up stakes here."

Winston's mulish expression suggested he didn't agree, but he held back.

"I want the Colton money and then we poof. We have our normal exit plan in place. It'll be a simple matter of quickly executing it once Jessie gets the money."

"And if they find us first?"

"Clearly, you're quite adept at quick thinking and getting rid of threats, *Brother* Winston. I have every confidence you'll handle any nuisances from Colton quarters, too."

"Mike Arnold is dead?" Greg sat at the table at the Colton Ranch as he ran his fingers through his hair. "The guy who got into the accident with Rick and Wendy?"

He'd asked a series of similar questions, about what they knew, who the guy was and how it came to be that he could have died so quickly after the accident, especially since he'd walked away unscathed.

"I keep pressing my contacts at the Owl Creek PD, but they don't have a lot of details yet." Max sat next to his brother, an encouraging voice in the midst of the chaos that seemed to have descended in the middle of their lives. "The situation's still developing."

"But you think it's all related to the group Mom's involved with?" Greg asked. "The one Rick's dad is a part of?"

"It all seems to stem from the same."

"There are two children at Briony's house right now who've lost their parents. Increasingly, it's looking like they were murdered. By their grandfather?"

"That's the connection we don't have," Chase interjected, happy to have something to contribute. "All Sloan found is the strange link in social-media posts between Mike Arnold and a man she believes is part of the Ever After Church. It doesn't mean Rick's father was responsible."

"But he's the link. He has to be."

While Chase had long stopped believing in coincidences when it came to this situation. A man had his son killed? One he'd left alone for the man's entire adulthood?

It seemed…extreme.

Yet the more they uncovered, the more it seemed the Ever After group operated at the very edge of extreme.

"There has to be enough evidence to take Winston Kraft into custody," Greg said.

"I've asked." Max's jaw set in a hard line, a match for his brother. "There's not a single thing linking Winston Kraft to Rick and Wendy's deaths."

"But he did it."

"Not according to the law."

Chase watched as Max tried to explain it, step by step, even as it was clear Greg was having none of it.

And how could Chase blame him?

Everything about this situation suggested the Ever After Church—and by extension one of its heads, Winston Kraft—was involved.

But the person who'd actually killed Rick and Wendy was now dead and unable to reveal secrets, no matter how badly they wanted them.

"So who killed Mike Arnold?"

They'd circled around it earlier. But it suddenly dawned on Chase that uncovering that piece might get them what they needed.

"Owl Creek PD's digging in but nothing's popping on the prison cameras. One minute Mike Arnold is alive and well in his cell, and the next an alert's going out and the ambulance is getting called."

"He didn't just die, Max," Chase argued. "Something happened."

"Which is why I keep telling you to give the police the time to do their work."

It felt so useless to argue and so endlessly depressing to just sit there.

Helpless.

Which shifted his attention to even darker, more dismal places.

"How are the children?" Chase asked.

"Briony's very good with them, but Justin is really confused and keeps asking for his mom and dad. Jane's too small to fully understand, but she gets upset each time her brother gets upset. It's heartbreaking."

One more sin to place at his feet, Chase thought. Guilt,

anger and utter sadness for the Kraft family became a noxious brew in his blood.

But he knew the truth. Max could argue all he wanted about the person responsible for Rick and Wendy's deaths, but Chase had been an unwitting accomplice.

He'd pushed this course of action, desperate for answers.

And got several he never could have imagined.

Sloan pulled item after item out of her closet, folding each piece of clothing into a neat pile on the bed. The room still held Chase's scent, a lingering reminder of what they'd shared.

She didn't have much, just what had fit in her suitcase, and the exercise didn't take overly long to complete.

But it was done.

It was time she left Owl Creek.

She'd known this was coming from the first day of her arrival, a return ticket—albeit open-ended—in her possession.

This was a job and while she'd fought to remember that specific point, she'd still managed to lose her head, anyway.

A small glint of metal reflected off the bed and she realized it was one of her many GPS tags. She'd learned after losing one of her electronics to put the tags with her equipment, and even her luggage, to ensure she could find them should they go missing.

The flash of a message floated over her cell-phone screen, alerting her to the tag's proximity and still-active status, and she turned to slip it back into her luggage when a small form slipped into the room. She dropped it into her pocket, then bent down and picked up the cat instead.

The rest of the packing could wait.

"I've made a mess of this, Waffles."

The cat's only reaction was a small meow and Sloan rubbed her cheek against his head.

She'd spent the better part of the afternoon thinking about her next move. But now, as she looked over the bed, her sense of action faded, her spirits plummeting.

Why hadn't she protected herself? She was a smart woman. She ran a successful business. Would it have been that hard to resist the abundant charms of Chase Colton?

"If he'd simply been charming, yeah, it would have." She murmured the words against the cat's soft fur, realizing it for the truth. "But he is so much more than that. He's…everything."

If this had only been about simple attraction, it would have been so much easier. Either ignore it for the duration of the job or give in, but the outcome would have been a still-whole heart and a readiness to go home at the end of the job.

Instead, she'd fallen for the man, hook, line, sinker, heart and soul.

"What other dumb clichés can I come up with?" she muttered to Waffles as the heavy knock came from the front of the apartment.

After gently setting the cat back on the bed, she headed for the front door. It was probably Chase, which meant it was time to tell him that she was leaving.

She had the door open, words nearly spilling out of her mouth to that effect, when she realized it was a man standing on the other side of her door in maintenance clothing.

"Oh, I'm sorry. Can I help you?"

"Yes, ma'am. I'm here to fix things."

The man had a sweet if dull look about him, his salt-and-pepper hair wisping out over his ears from beneath his navy blue cap, a small tool belt slung about his hips.

"Fix what?"

"You."

The swift strike against her shoulder was the first clue she was in trouble. He'd been prepared for her response and his arms were surprisingly strong as they wrapped around her.

Despite her struggles, she was no match for his hold or the obviously practiced movement that had a cloth going over her face.

Sloan fought to hang on.

Fought to hold her breath.

But the natural, desperate need to take in air took over and as she breathed deep, she felt her world go black.

Chase was still thinking about Rick Kraft's small children an hour later as he paid the delivery service for several large pizzas.

How were they going to get by?

Greg had suggested he and Briony had some sort of guardian status but what did that really mean? Rick's estranged relationship with his father meant there wasn't support in the form of grandparents and Greg had confirmed Rick's mother was long gone. Wendy's parents were both dead as well.

One more layer of circumstance that felt so sad.

And terribly, horrifically bleak.

Pushing away the sadness and vowing to talk to Greg later about what he might need and how he could help, Chase set the pizzas on the kitchen counter. Then he checked his phone. He'd texted Sloan a while ago, expecting she'd beat the pizza over to the ranch, but hadn't heard back yet.

Greg stepped into the kitchen as he was wrapping up a

phone call. Della had arrived a short while before, her arm now wrapped around Max's waist.

"Thanks for this." Max gestured toward the boxes.

"We all need some food. Go ahead and dig in."

"We're not waiting for Sloan?" Della asked.

"I haven't heard back from my text yet." Even as he said it, something about the total lack of response bothered him and Chase hit the screen on his phone, reaffirming nothing had come in. "Let me go call her."

Two minutes later, with nothing but her voice mail to show for it, Chase stared at Della, Max and Greg. "I'm not sure where she is."

Greg didn't hesitate. "Let's go over there."

"She—"

Chase stopped, the swirl of fear only spiking harder in his chest. "She'll think we're out of our minds if we show up, guns blazing."

"So?" Max said, already reaching for his keys on the counter.

He'd worry later if it was an overreaction to the stress of the past few days.

In that moment, all Chase wanted was to see Sloan and hold her in his arms.

"Let's go."

The desperate need for water was all Sloan could think of as she awakened on a hard exhale.

Where was she?

That thought struck hard, with another swiftly following.

What had happened to her?

She struggled to a sitting position, her hands bound in front of her. She leaned to her side and used them as leverage to move onto her knees before struggling to stand, trying to figure out where she was.

Her stomach turned over violently and she stood still for a moment, the quick movements to stand so soon after coming awake nearly causing her body to revolt. With deep breaths, she gave herself a moment, even as her mind raced with the implications.

Who was that man at her door?

The Ever After Church.

Although she had no proof, she'd bet anything that man was affiliated with the church, even as she struggled to figure out who he might be. He wasn't one of the leaders—of that, she was certain. Something tugged at the back of her mind, fighting for her attention through the nausea, and she stilled once more, trying to remember.

The kindly face. The gray hair. The hat.

What was it about the hat?

A shaft of light streamed in through the window, the late-afternoon sun a vivid yellowish red as it illuminated the room.

Was she still in Owl Creek?

Since it had been about four when she'd headed into her bedroom to pack, she estimated she couldn't have been out that long, especially if it was still light out.

But...

"Hello."

She glanced toward the door, her pulse spiking at the intrusion.

What did he want with her? Because attacking her and drugging her in her home wasn't the act of someone who simply wanted to chat.

Which meant she needed to get as much information as she could as fast as she could, all while figuring a way out of this. Chase had no way of knowing where she was, and nor did anyone else, for that matter.

She was going to need to get through this on her own.

"Did you sleep okay?"

Sloan considered how to play this, especially since the man clutched his hat in his hands, twisting it back and forth.

"What?"

"Did you sleep okay or did I use too much?"

The pounding in her head suggested that *yes, he'd used too much*. But she heard the vague concern in his tone and decided to try and use it to her advantage.

She had precious little to fight with, so she was going to need to use her wits as much as any physical advantages she could find.

"I'm okay."

"You're a little thing. It's never easy to judge."

Under other circumstances, she'd have thought a statement like that was designed to be a compliment, but all she got from him was an overwhelming sense of fact.

And a sort of resigned purpose in what he was doing.

"Why did you do that at all?"

"You've been bad."

"I've been what?"

"You've got those fancy computers and are using 'em to spy on people."

Had he walked through her home? Worse, did he know her, somehow?

Speaking softly, she tried to delicately step her way through this one.

"I'm visiting Owl Creek for work. I needed my computer with me to do my job."

"What do you do?"

"I run a consulting business."

He eyed her suspiciously, his easy tone fading on a sneer. "Fancy words for computer hacker."

"Everyone uses computers."

"To do bad things! How'd you think I got back in touch with good ol' Mikey?"

"Mike Arnold." The name came out on a hard exhale as the puzzle pieces she was struggling to work through snapped firmly into place. "Which means you're Jasper. Jasper Miles."

Sloan suddenly realized that she'd overstepped at the use of his name.

Especially when he moved toward her, something scary and oddly fervent building in his eyes, a gun appearing in his hand.

Chapter 18

Chase stepped on the second-floor landing in front of Sloan's apartment. The panic that had spiked off and on during the quick drive over from the ranch was now going nuclear.

The door to her apartment was open and Waffles raced around the entryway, obviously agitated.

He bent down to pick up the small cat, cradling him close and trying to soothe him as Max and Greg followed him inside.

"She's gone," Max said after a quick search of the apartment.

"Taken." Chase spit out the word. "She was taken right here."

He held tight to the cat, the animal a sudden lodestone as the absolute pain of responsibility hammered his body with hard, punishing blows.

He'd done this.

He'd pulled her into this mess and put her in danger.

Just like Rick and Wendy, Sloan was going to pay far too high a price for his damned insistence on looking into the Ever After Church and his aunt's involvement.

"Chase!"

Max's tone was insistent as he stood across the room.

"We're going to find her. But first, I need you to help me look through her things. We need to find something."

Chase had never felt so helpless in all his life.

Not the day he knew his marriage was over. Not the day his father had his stroke. Not even the day he'd discovered his father's betrayal and lies.

Nothing compared to the abject pain of knowing he'd done this to her.

"I found a cell phone!" Greg hollered as he headed back out of the bedroom.

"She doesn't even have her phone?" Chase didn't know her password, but he extended a hand for the phone as Greg walked over.

"This might work to our advantage," Max said, moving closer. "Anyone who would have taken her would likely have ditched the phone."

"It won't do any good if we can't hold it up with her and use facial recognition to open it," Greg muttered.

"She doesn't use it," Chase said, one of their date-night conversations coming back to him.

"Why not?"

"She gave a host of reasons that seemed scary at the time, but she said that she only uses a passcode."

"Any chance you know what it is?" Max asked.

"No." Chase nearly tossed the phone, but something lit the face before he could heave it away.

Curious, he brought it close, his gaze narrowing in on the alert that flashed on the screen.

"What is it?" Max asked.

"I think—" Chase stilled, hardly daring to hope this was as good a sign as he thought it might be.

"Let me see." Max took the phone, his movements gentle as he tilted the device in his hand. "Damn, that woman is amazing."

The comment was part reverence, part awe, and Greg pressed for details. "We all think that. What's this about?"

"She's got a GPS tracker somewhere on her person," Max said.

Chase held the cat close, the small animal now calm. He took heart from that calmness and desperately fought to believe the cat's faith in his arrival meant he had faith he'd see his owner again, too.

He took his first easy breath as his gaze remained on the phone screen. "Which means we can find her."

"How'd you know who I was?" Jasper practically quivered where he stood, far too close for comfort in front of her. "Those damn devil devices again?"

"I only looked at your social-media pages."

"What?"

If the situation wasn't so dire, she might have laughed at his confusion. As it was, his abstract inability to link his social feed with how he was found wasn't information she was going to share. Instead, she pressed the very small advantage she had at his confusion.

"All your posts about faith and peace. They really spoke to me."

"My faith keeps me going."

"A testament to your leader, I'm sure. The Ever After Church is doing very good work."

His eyes flashed once again, that fervent madness filling his irises, and Sloan's stomach sunk.

Damn, she'd overplayed her hand.

A point that didn't play out, as he nodded, his smile wide.

"People don't understand that. They don't know all the good that our leader does. But the church is a haven. A home."

"A place of safety."

"Yes."

"Then why are we here? Why didn't you bring me there?"

"I can't allow you to soil my home."

"I—"

That deep, fervent conviction was back, only this time the menace was being telegraphed loud and clear.

"The evils of technology have you in their grip. You don't believe in us. You won't believe in us."

"You don't know that."

"Oh, yes, I do. Because if you did believe, you'd never have gone to talk to that traitor Rick Kraft."

Pure, undiluted fear beat through her body.

Whatever she'd hoped or believed, conversation was not going to get her out of this. Conciliatory remarks or interested chatter weren't the keys to her escape.

The only way out of here, Sloan knew with absolute certainty, was through Jasper and his gun.

Which was why she didn't give herself another moment to think. Whatever determination Jasper had to take her wasn't going to be assuaged by her outsmarting him.

Without another word, she charged.

Head low.

Shoulders braced.

Everything she had focused on ramming into him and dislodging the gun in his hand.

The GPS device on Sloan continued to beat, their homing beacon as Max flew through the streets of Owl Creek toward the edge of town.

Although he had no way of getting into her device, the

GPS pinged alert, appearing on Sloan's phone screen with each mile they got closer. They used a mix of the technology itself and Chase's knowledge of Owl Creek to assess where she was.

It was only as they got closer to the lake at the edge of town that Chase knew the spot.

"The old caretaker's cabin. Down along the lake."

"The one that's been up for demo for a few years?" Greg asked.

"One and the same." Chase considered the small hut. While he'd believed it an eyesore for some time, the city had control over the place and hadn't seen fit to approve its demolition yet.

He was going to kiss someone at the next town-council meeting if that lack of foresight was what saved Sloan.

Max slowed as he pulled into the graveled parking lot that abutted the lake. They saw an old truck at the end of the parking lot.

The phone flashed once more, and Chase knew they were close. "She's here."

Max and Greg both had guns, retrieved from the glove box. Chase had briefly considered asking for one of them, but knew he was a businessman, not a gunslinger. Max was well-trained and Greg carried around the ranch to ensure he was safe from dangerous wildlife.

He rode a desk all day.

Right now, Sloan needed protection and he wasn't sure he could remain steady enough, anyway.

But he was the first one out of the car, moving gently over the gravel to avoid making noise.

He needed to get to her. It was his only focus.

His only goal.

But as a gunshot filled the air, he didn't wait, or give a care for quiet.

He took off hell-for-leather for the old cabin.

Sloan struggled against the solid weight that seemed to hold her in place, nearly pushing her back, even as she pressed and drove herself into the solid mass of flesh over and over again.

Through.

She had to get through Jasper in order to get away from him.

The heavy sound of a gunshot echoed above her head, the noise so loud she nearly fell to her feet from the sheer power of it, but still, she held her ground.

Her hands were still bound, but she kicked and pushed and even used her teeth at one point to keep fighting.

To get away.

And then, there was no obstacle.

No push of flesh.

Instead, there was another loud shot as all the counterforce against her simply vanished, her foe falling to the floor.

Sloan glanced around, her gaze wild as she sought out the new threat, panic spiking once more as she took in three large forms. A scream welled just as her understanding broke through the fear and adrenaline.

Chase.

He was there.

And he'd brought reinforcements, in Max and Greg. Max was already moving toward Jasper, kicking the man's gun out of the way while Greg stood at the door, his own gun firmly in hand.

But it was Chase who came to her.

Who pulled her tight against him.

Who spoke to her through the angry ringing in her ears that seemed to fill up her head.

He was here.

And she was safe.

It was her last thought as she broke into a sob against his chest.

Chase held Sloan tight against his chest and let her cry it out. Hard, unrelenting shakes ripped through her body, and he held on, helping her through it, crooning mindless words to see her through.

To see himself through.

His own adrenaline rush was still sky-high, coursing through him in wild spikes of energy, but he held it at bay.

He'd break down later.

When he thought of how close he'd come to losing her…

And how ridiculous he'd been for all these years in pushing away the possibility of love.

He'd recognized it the moment they'd met, that first time he'd held her in his arms. And for so much of the time since he'd run from it, convinced his head knew better. Convinced he'd had his shot and ruined it.

But now, as the woman he loved huddled against him, gathering herself as the storm of emotion burned itself out, he knew just how foolish he'd been.

And how deeply grateful fate had given him a second chance.

Her eyes were red-rimmed as she stared up at him. "You came."

"I'd have hunted for you to the ends of the earth, but I have to thank you for making it a heck of a lot easier on me."

"Easy?" Confusion filled her features, then something dawned bright and clear in her eyes. "The tracker."

"You're a technology wiz, woman. It's amazing."

"I was going to put it in my suitcase and Waffles came in."

"He loves you, by the way. And he was beside himself you'd been taken."

She smiled then, and Chase knew there'd be more than enough time to tell her what had happened. How they'd come to her apartment. How Greg had found her phone and how he'd found the cat, agitated beyond measure until he knew there were people there to go after his mistress.

Later, Chase thought. There'd be time enough for it all later.

Right now, there was only time for one thing. And as he stared down at her, he felt the power of each and every word.

More, he leaned into that power and reveled at all he'd found.

"I love you, Sloan."

He saw the spark of happiness fill her eyes, even as her face remained set in wary lines. "I thought you weren't cut out for love. Isn't that why we cooked up a fake relationship in the first place?"

"Turns out I'm a dumb businessman with a fear complex over putting myself on the line. And I guess a fake relationship was just what I needed to take the pressure off."

"And now?"

"I only want what's real, Sloan. With you. Forever."

The smile that lit her eyes filled her face, transforming her before his eyes. Her smile was warm. Welcoming. And wide open to that forever he spoke of.

"I love you, Chase Colton. Make it real. With me."

"I'd like nothing more. Every day for the rest of my life."

And as he bent his head, pressing his lips to hers, Chase knew he was the luckiest of men.

He'd believed himself incapable of loving again.

How wonderful to be so utterly, absolutely, mind-bindingly wrong.

* * * * *

Don't miss the stories in this mini series!

THE COLTONS OF OWL CREEK

MILLS & BOON

Her Private Security Detail
Patricia Sargeant

MILLS & BOON

Nationally bestselling author Patricia Sargeant was drawn to write romance because she believes love is the greatest motivation. Her romantic suspense novels put ordinary people in extraordinary situations to have them find the "hero inside." Her work has been reviewed in national publications such as *Publishers Weekly*, *USA TODAY*, *Kirkus Reviews*, *Suspense Magazine*, *Mystery Scene Magazine*, *Library Journal* and *RT Book Reviews*. For more information about Patricia and her work, visit patriciasargeant.com.

Visit the Author Profile page
at millsandboon.com.au.

Dear Reader,

Thank you for continuing The Touré Security Group journey with me. I'm having a blast and hope you are, too.

We first met the Touré brothers—Hezekiah, Malachi and Jeremiah—in *Down to the Wire*, my October 2023 release. That was Mal and Dr. Grace's reunion story. I hope you enjoyed it. I loved writing it.

I loved writing *Her Private Security Detail*, too. This is Jerry and Symone's story. Jerry's impulsive and doesn't believe in planning. Symone's compulsive and doesn't trust people who don't plan. They're opposites who must work together. I love opposites-attract stories. I love reading about their differences and following their journeys. What compromises are they willing to make? Will working together change them? If so, how?

Are you ready to discover the answers to these questions for Jerry and Symone?

Thank you so much for taking a chance on The Touré Security Group series. I hope you enjoy Jerry and Symone's story.

Warm regards,

Patricia Sargeant

DEDICATION

To My Dream Team:

- My sister, Bernadette, for giving me the dream.
- My husband, Michael, for supporting the dream.
- My brother Richard for believing in the dream.
- My brother Gideon for encouraging the dream.

And to Mom and Dad, always with love.

Chapter 1

"I can't." Jeremiah Touré jogged with his two older brothers, Hezekiah and Malachi, early Thursday morning. They'd started the last of their five laps around Antrim Park in the northwest part of Columbus, Ohio's capital city.

It had been dark when the trio had started their six-mile/five-lap workout. Moisture from the air joined with the sweat forming on Jeremiah's brow, cheekbones and upper lip. The weather was comfortable—for now—but July in Columbus could be brutal.

On his left, past the bushes and down a grassy slope, lay a pond in an imperfect oval. Its serene surface mirrored the sky, shifting from black to gray and more slowly to blue. The birdsong grew louder and more energetic as the sun rose.

In front of him, the narrow dirt trail led to a broader blacktop. A row of trees and bushes lined the asphalt on both sides. Those on the right shielded the woods beyond the park. Leafy branches formed a canopy over the path, sheltering the handful of other joggers and walkers who were getting in their early morning exercise. Several had dogs or strollers. Some had both. A few were on their own.

Starting the day jogging with his brothers was the best. What wasn't to love? He was with his brothers, his friends.

They were outdoors, getting exercise. They pushed each other to keep up a good pace—no slacking!

Jeremiah and his brothers had been doing these runs since they were teenagers. Jogging was one of his favorite hobbies, which was fortunate since physical fitness was a job requirement. But opportunities for him to workout with his brothers were becoming more infrequent. Business was booming for Touré Security Group, his family-owned company. He and his siblings had inherited the agency from their deceased parents. It figured Hezekiah, the human manifestation of a killjoy, would bring up work during one of their increasingly rare opportunities to enjoy each other's company.

"You *can't* do it? Or you don't want to?" His eldest brother's response came from behind him. This part of the path was too narrow to jog side by side.

They all wore black running shorts with dark jogging shoes, but their moisture-wicking pullovers were different colors. Hezekiah's crimson red jersey commanded attention—sort of like the man.

Hezekiah had gotten his wish to expand their company to attract bigger clients, in large part thanks to publicity from a case they'd closed two months ago. They'd protected a scientist from a serial killer who'd been after her formulation. Their success had attracted a lot of new clients, from small companies to midsized businesses and larger corporations. They'd even secured a contract with Midwest Area Research Systems, the scientist's employer.

"Can't." The answer was at the same time easy and hard. "I can't take on new cases. I'm leaving the company at the end of the month, remember? I've got my hands full, wrapping up the cases I'm overseeing now. But I'll gather a few of our personal security consultants and bring them up to speed."

With their increasing client list, maybe his timing could've been better, but Jeremiah was ready to pursue his own plans. Hezekiah, however, wanted him to take on a new case protecting a high-level executive with The Bishop Foundation, but he couldn't do this anymore. He needed to walk away from the company. Staying was putting everyone and everything at risk. Leaving was the right thing to do. But, crap, did it have to be so hard?

Jeremiah took a deeper breath, meant to soothe him as he led his brothers past the first curve on their fifth lap around the pond. The air was heavy with the musty, damp scent of the earth beneath his running shoes and the sharp, dew-laden grass that rimmed the pond.

"The client asked for you personally." Malachi sounded so reasonable. The medical research scientist they'd protected, Dr. Grace Blackwell, had been his ex-girlfriend. The case had helped rekindle their romance. "They want the best."

His second-eldest brother's leaf green jersey helped him blend into the foliage. Malachi was playing to his ego. He'd give his sibling credit for that. The tactic would've worked on the old Jerry. He missed that guy. Without realizing it, his steps had sped up. It was like his subconscious knew he was running away. He made an effort to slow down. "Why does The Bishop Foundation sound familiar?"

"It came up during our case with Grace." Malachi's voice came from Jeremiah's right. This wider section of the path allowed his brothers to jog beside him. "The foundation chair contacted her for the recommendation."

Jeremiah's body filled with pride for his family and their company. Their parents had founded Touré Security

Group on qualities that were important to them: integrity, excellence, professionalism. His brothers followed the example they'd set—another reason he was quitting. He couldn't live up to those standards any longer.

A rustling from the undergrowth on his right drew his eyes to the woods beyond the park. A pair of chipmunks disappeared beneath the shelter of the nearby bushes.

"You did a great job protecting Melba." Hezekiah kept pace on Jeremiah's left.

Having his eldest brother on his left and middle brother on his right made Jeremiah feel like they were ganging up on him.

Still, thinking of Grace's grandmother, Melba Stall, made him smile. "We've kept in touch." He wiped the sweat collecting on his upper lip with the back of his right wrist and pulled together the tattered remnants of his confidence. "I know I did a great job protecting her. I also did an excellent job training our personal protection consultants. I know each one's strengths and weaknesses. We don't have any bad apples. I'll identify six of the best of our best, two agents per shift for twenty-four-hour security. I'll get the estimate to you by end of day."

"That should work." Hezekiah's sigh was louder than necessary. Typical. He was lathering on the guilt. "The client meeting's tomorrow morning. Early. We didn't expect you to guard the executive on your own, but we'd feel better knowing you were at least overseeing the job."

"The guards are well trained, thanks to you." Malachi used the back of his hand to remove the sweat from his chin. "But this is a high-profile case."

Another wave of restlessness washed over him. Jeremiah struggled to keep his steps even and his tone casual.

"All of our cases are important, Mal. Don't worry. I won't leave you hanging." *This time.*

Their silence suffocated him. He knew they didn't mean for it to. It wasn't their fault. Jeremiah blamed his guilt. He didn't *want* to leave the company. He *had* to. His brothers didn't make any secret about their concern over his decision to walk away. He didn't want them to worry about him. He wanted them to be proud of him. He wanted them to be confident in his abilities, as confident in him as he'd always been in them. He wanted things to go back to the way they'd been before he'd made a mistake that could've cost a teenage boy his life.

Digging deep, Jeremiah faked a grin. He tossed it at his brothers. "Let's sprint to the end."

Malachi groaned. "I'm too old."

Hezekiah frowned. "I'm almost two years older than you."

Malachi arched an eyebrow. His look spoke for him. *Then we're* both *too old.*

Jeremiah gave the first real laugh he'd felt in weeks. "Come on, old-timers."

He sped up, setting a challenging pace, even for himself. He took long slow breaths, straining to control his breathing. He raised his arms, pumping them as he pushed himself to take faster, longer strides. His heart galloped in his chest. Still his two older brothers kept pace with him.

"Jerry, what are you about now?" He heard his mother's voice as though she was running alongside him. He brought her image to mind. She'd stayed slim and fit his whole life. Both of his parents had. Her face had remained smooth and her hair dark well into her sixties. *"Zeke and Mal aren't your competition. They're your brothers. The only person you should compete against is yourself."*

They rounded the fourth corner of the pond and flew the final leg of their last lap. Jeremiah's feet barely touched the dirt path. Slow breath in. Hold. Slow breath out. He forgot about Hezekiah and Malachi. Now he fought to push himself as hard as he could.

I competed against myself and failed, Mom. And my failure hurt Dad's and your legacy. I can't put the company in that position. Never again.

In his mind, she frowned. It was the loving, chiding expression she'd given him when she thought he was being a fool. *But is leaving Touré Security a bigger risk to you than your staying with the company would be to your brothers?*

"You'd remove me from the foundation my family built?" Seated at the head of the long oval dark wood table Thursday morning, Symone Bishop met the eyes of each of the nine other people—all with voting power—in the small conference room, seven board members and two administrators. Most didn't—or couldn't—return her regard.

"We wouldn't remove you entirely." Tina Grand, president of The Bishop Foundation Board, sat at the foot of the table. The sixty-something woman was businesslike in her dark blue pantsuit and white shell blouse. Her cap of salt-and-pepper hair framed her round, pale cheeks. "We'd find another, more suitable position for you."

Seriously?

Symone braced the tips of her fingers on the thin black frames of her glasses. She swept her eyes over the four women and three men of the board in addition to her stepfather and vice chair, Paul Kayple, and her administrative assistant, Eleanor Press. To her left, Paul looked as shocked and outraged as she felt. Okay, so it wasn't just her. This really was a waking nightmare. On her right, Eleanor looked like she was going to sob. She could go ahead. Symone would remain dry-eyed. Tears were a luxury she didn't have time for.

Masking her anger, she held the board president's cool gray eyes. "Please explain to me again exactly why the board believes a confidence vote is necessary."

Aaron Menéndez sat at Tina's right. Of average height and build, he was in his early sixties, Symone thought. "As we explained, we've been unhappy with the way you and your mother, God rest her soul, have been running the foundation since your father's passing. God rest his soul. You've become predictable."

Symone swallowed to clear the lump of grief—and anger?—from her throat. Her father, Langston Bishop, had inherited The Bishop Foundation from his father, Frederick. Langston had died almost six years earlier after a long battle with pancreatic cancer. She'd just buried her mother less than three months ago. Odette Bishop's death after a heart attack had surprised Symone and her stepfather, Paul.

None of the current board members had served with her father, but the foundation's records showed its growth under his skillful leadership. He'd been larger than life, not just to his doting daughter and adoring wife, but to everyone who came into contact with him. His board would never have even thought about removing him.

But her board seems to have been making plans to replace her.

Symone drew a breath to calm her voice. The large, shadowy boardroom smelled like a coffee shop. She could use another cup herself. "Under my family's leadership—my grandfather's, my father's, my mother's and now mine— the foundation has been steady and successful. Is that the predictability you find so concerning?"

Julie Yeoh was midway through the second year of her first three-year term with the board. Her cool pastel business suit emphasized her large dark eyes and chin-length ebony hair. She'd taken the chair to the right of Eleanor. "The foundation's funds would benefit from taking more risks with its investments and the projects that are approved."

Symone worked to mask her surprise. "The foundation's accounts are secure while they're making a strong return on investment. Do you want me to take risks for risk's sake?"

Did the board think the foundation's investments were a game? Not on her watch.

Tina raised her right hand, palm out in a Stop motion. "No one's denying that the foundation's finances are solid, but for some time now, we have thought they could be better."

"How much time?" Symone asked.

Tina shrugged. "What does it matter? A few years?"

Keisha Lord, the third-longest-serving board member, leaned into the table. Her shoulder-length micro braids swung forward, half obscuring her elegant profile. Her ruby red A-lined dress complimented her slender figure. "'They could be better' is subjective. What level of return on investment are you aiming for? Remember, this is a nonprofit foundation."

It was as though Keisha had read her mind. What was the board's goal?

Kitty Lymon shrugged almost flirtatiously from her seat beside Paul. Her cotton candy pink figure-hugging dress clashed with her deep red mane. "The more money the foundation has, the more money it could award in grants."

Symone couldn't argue with that logic, but there was always a flip side. "Conversely, if our investments lose money, we'd have less money to award." She addressed Tina. "I respect your business background. You and Aaron both have MBAs, but my background is in financial investments. Before returning to the foundation, I worked for one of the most prestigious investment firms in the country. The foundation has a strong balance of growth and middle investments."

The newest board members, Xander Fence and Wesley Bragg, hadn't contributed to the discussion. Both men had been appointed to the board a little more than six months ago. Paul had recommended Wesley. He and the lawyer had been friends for years. Like her stepfather, Wesley was in his sixties, and of average height and build.

A former board member had recommended Xander as her replacement. The banking executive was in his fifties and was also of average height and build. But whereas Xander was like a daytime drama star with his salon-styled, wavy golden blond hair and striking green eyes, Wesley's salt-and-pepper hair and dark blue eyes seemed as somber as the evening news.

Tina sniffed. "Yes, we're aware of your background in investments, but we're still concerned with the foundation's management style. The foundation has been stagnating for the past six years. The records support our assessment."

Symone once again searched the faces around the table. Xander and Wesley avoided eye contact, as did Kitty and Aaron. Tina, Julie and Keisha looked at her expectantly. "You've stated the board has had these concerns for years. Why didn't you speak up sooner?"

Tina looked like the question caught her off guard. What had she expected Symone to do, accept their decision without debate? Not a chance.

Tina stared at the pen she was rotating between her

hands. "Frankly, Symone, Aaron and I had hoped, over time, you and your mother would update your investment strategy."

Symone didn't believe Tina's answer. For now, she'd put a pin in it. She directed her next question to Aaron, who was still avoiding her eyes. "Are you unsatisfied with the investment company? We've had them for decades. Do you think it's time for a change?"

Aaron looked up, waving his hands. "We'll leave that decision to you. You're the one who has experience with investment companies."

They were frustrated with her investment decisions but entrusted her to choose an investment partner. Were they gaslighting her? "You've said you have concerns not only about the investment strategy but also our application screening. What types of projects do you believe we should be pursuing?"

Tina repeated her deer-in-the-headlights impersonation. "Our feedback isn't meant to be taken literally. We don't have specific projects in mind, but we feel the ones you've approved have been predictable. I hate to keep using that word. It's our strong belief that the foundation should be leading the way in health care innovations. We shouldn't be following the industry. The projects we support should be more imaginative."

Symone's cheeks filled with angry heat. "This is my family's foundation. My grandfather established it before I was born."

Tina inclined her head. "And, as you know, he structured the foundation in a way that allows the board to have a guardianship role over the administration. We have the authority to replace the chair if we believe management is destructive to the foundation."

Symone unclenched her teeth. "Are you accusing my leadership of being destructive to my family's legacy?"

Tina angled her chin upward. "Yes, I'm afraid we are."

Eleanor seemed stricken. Paul appeared concerned. Aaron, Wesley and Xander continued to stare at the conference table. Keisha and Julie looked troubled. Kitty returned her regard as though trying to read her mind. Symone hoped she couldn't. This wasn't a good time for others to have access to her thoughts. People's feelings would be hurt.

She met each board member's eyes. "Are you all in agreement?"

"I'm not." Keisha waved her hand. "Like Tina, I've served on the board for less than five years. We've never worked with Langston Bishop, but I've heard he was a dynamic force." She smiled at Symone. "He must've been to rebuild the foundation's investments after several of the funds collapsed. But we're not in a rebuilding state anymore. We don't have to take risks to save the foundation. Under Symone's leadership, the funds are secure. That's what matters."

Julie tucked a swatch of her ebony hair behind her ear. "You make a good point, Keisha, but do we want to be stagnant? I mean, I wouldn't mind seeing a proposal that showed us other options. I'm not in favor of a confidence vote, but maybe it's time for a shakeup."

Keisha and Kitty nodded, murmuring their agreement.

Symone shook off her irritation. "Xander? Wesley? I haven't heard from either of you. I realize you're the newest board members, but you have a right to be heard. What do you think?"

Xander adjusted the dark blue shirt he wore beneath his smoke gray jacket. As usual, he'd forgone a tie. "The foundation is solid, but perhaps Julie makes a good point. We all might benefit from seeing a projection of what the account would look like with more aggressive funds."

Wesley shrugged. "I don't need to see that, but if the others want it, I won't stand in their way."

Symone swept her arm around the table. "If you wanted to see funding options, you could've requested that during any of our previous monthly board meetings. There's no need to bring up a confidence vote."

Tina gave a tight smile. "Let's see your proposal first."

Symone considered the board president. *What was this really about?* She stood. "I'll submit the proposal prior to the next board meeting."

That gave her three weeks to learn the real reason behind the confidence vote. In the interim, there was one thing she knew for certain. The board would have to wrestle the foundation's leadership from her cold, dead hands.

Jeremiah reread the printout of The Bishop Foundation chair's bio at his desk late Thursday morning. He didn't know why he was reading it a third time. Or why he'd printed it, much less as a color copy. Yes, preliminary client information helped assess possible threats to her security. But he'd already made notes for that. Besides, she wasn't the target. Her stepfather was.

Still… Symone Bishop. He'd committed her cool, tan features to memory. There was something in her chocolate brown eyes behind those black-rimmed glasses that made him want to take a second, third and possibly fourth look at her.

"What's really keeping you from taking this assignment?" Malachi appeared in his doorway.

After their run, the brothers had gone to their respective homes to prepare for work. Malachi preferred business casual clothes. He'd rolled up the sleeves of his crisp white shirt and left his dark brown jacket—a match to his slacks—in his office. The sage green tie was a nice splash of color. Was that Grace's influence?

Like his brothers, Jerry favored darker colors for his wardrobe, but he refused to wear a tie.

Jeremiah looked away from Symone's image to consider his middle brother's question. "I'm not taking the case because I'm leaving. Really." He hated himself for lying to his brother, but he was too ashamed to tell the truth. He couldn't bring himself to tell them—to tell anyone—that he was walking away because he didn't trust his abilities to keep people safe anymore; not after what happened with the teenage rising pop star.

Malachi took a drink from his black coffee mug. The cursive white text on the side of the mug that faced Jeremiah read, "I'm not anti-social. I'm just not user friendly." It had been a joint birthday gift from him and Hezekiah and was one of the few times he and his eldest brother had agreed on anything.

"Tell me about your plans for your consulting business." Malachi gestured toward him with his mug.

There were obstacles between him and his brother, literally. A couple of chairs had been pulled out from under the conversation table. Boxes of personnel and case files and personal protection supplies were stacked halfway to his desk. To the layperson, his office appeared to be a disaster. His brothers didn't nag him as long as he agreed to keep his door closed during client visits.

Jeremiah leaned back against his black cloth executive chair. Thinking about walking away from his family and going out on his own made his heart dive into his stomach. It was the kind of feeling you got when you think you're making a mistake. He shrugged it off and dug up a cocky grin. "Like I said, a friend of mine is a manager at a fitness club."

"Adam, right?" Malachi took another sip of coffee.

"That's right." Jeremiah had known Adam since high school. "He sold the club's owner on having me teach self-defense courses a couple of times a week to start. We'll see how it goes from there. But I'm also going to offer one-on-one fitness training."

"Sounds exciting." Malachi watched Jeremiah closely. "I'm sure you're going to be successful. You're really good at marketing. You've done ours for years, and the results have always been great. But I still don't understand why you're leaving."

Jeremiah forced himself not to squirm on his chair. "I thought you'd be happier about my leaving. You're always complaining about how much Zeke and I argue. Now you'll have the peace you're always asking for."

Malachi gave a dry laugh. "Why do you always go on the offensive when Zeke and I ask you anything personal? Or ask you anything, full stop? We're just trying to understand why you're leaving, and don't say it's because you're tired of arguing. No one buys that."

Hezekiah's laughter sounded before he appeared in the doorway beside Malachi. "That's the truth."

The eldest Touré brother slipped past Malachi and strode toward Jeremiah's desk. Along the way, he nudged the chairs back beneath the conversation table and pushed the boxes of files aside with his black oxfords.

Jeremiah swallowed a sigh. "Am I the only one with work to do?" His tone was sour. He winced, realizing he sounded like Hezekiah.

"No." Hezekiah collected the stack of files from one of the visitor's chairs, turning to place them on the table behind him. He glanced at Malachi. "Don't let the chaos and disaster scare you. It's Jer."

Despite his visible doubts, Malachi stepped forward. He cleared the chair beside Hezekiah's. "If all your files are on your floor and furniture, are your cabinets and drawers empty?"

Jeremiah had heard that question before. He closed the folder, covering the printout of Symone's bio. "All right. Let's get this over with."

Hezekiah set his left ankle on his right knee. He'd also left his suit jacket in his office. Still, in his sapphire shirt and matching iron gray pants and tie, he looked like a model for a business magazine cover. "I'm not going to speak for Mal, but I want to know what's chasing you out of the company. And as Mal said, don't try to feed us the line about not wanting to argue with me anymore."

Malachi placed his right ankle on his left knee. His eyes, so like their mother's, bore into Jeremiah's. "You know that old saying, be careful what you wish for. I left the company—left Columbus—almost six years ago in part because you guys were arguing all the time. But I came back because I missed you pains in the neck. In the end, it's about family, the good, the annoying and the ugly."

Jeremiah rested his hands on the arms of his chair. "Look, I'm sorry you guys expected a different answer from the one I'm giving you, but it's the truth." Lying wasn't getting any easier. His stomach muscles were tied in knots.

Hezekiah narrowed his eyes. "Is this because of that pop star assignment?"

Malachi frowned. "Zeke—"

Hezekiah glanced at Malachi on his left. "We need to stop tiptoeing around this." He returned his attention to Jeremiah. "Is that the reason you think you need to leave?"

Jeremiah felt his fists tighten around his chair's arms. He forced his grip to loosen. "I just guarded Melba Stall, remember? I know I'm good at what I do. There's no problem there."

Guarding Melba had been a piece of cake. First, Melba hadn't been a rebellious teen. She'd been cooperative and taken the situation seriously. Second, she'd lived in a secure senior residence where there were security procedures and guards in place. All he'd needed to do was staff up with a few Touré Security Group consultants, including himself. He'd gone undercover as Melba's godson, visiting from out of town.

Hezekiah's coal black eyes were still clouded with doubt. "Jer, The Bishop Foundation's a very important new client. They asked for you based on Grace's recommendation. We need you on this."

Jeremiah dragged his left hand over his tight dark curls. "All of our consultants are our best. I've trained them myself and oversee their annual recertification."

Touré Security Group's annual personal consultant recertification was intense. He'd created the original course with input from his parents and brothers. Each year, they reevaluated it for improvement. It was designed to cull people who didn't take the responsibility of their clients' safety with the gravity it deserved. Testing categories included physical and mental fitness, medical care and weapons training.

Malachi raised a hand, palm out. "We know, Jer. We're not questioning your commitment to the program. And we know we're going to need more than one consultant to guard this client, but you're our best. Our client expects *you*."

Jeremiah shook his head. "That won't be possible. We agreed my last day would be July eighteenth, next Friday." And he really needed this fresh start. He needed time to clear his head before he began his business. "Have you guys started interviewing the consultants I suggested to replace me as director of personal security?" He thought it would get easier to say that over time. It hadn't.

Malachi ignored his question. Not a good sign. "You haven't committed to a start date at the gym."

Hezekiah caught and held Jeremiah's eyes. "Come to the meeting in the morning—"

Jeremiah interrupted him. "Of course I'll be at the meeting. I need that information to brief the teams."

Hezekiah shook his head. "No. Come to the meeting with an open mind. Hear directly from our client before making your final decision. You might agree you're perfect to lead this detail."

Jeremiah looked from Hezekiah's intent scrutiny to Malachi's watchful regard. "Fine." Anything to get them to drop the subject. "I'll keep an open mind at the meeting. But afterward, if I believe our consultants can handle this without me, I'm leaving on schedule."

"Fair enough." Hezekiah sprang to his feet as though afraid Jeremiah would reconsider his decision.

Malachi seemed to be searching for something else to say. Jeremiah returned his regard with as much self-assurance as he could collect.

Finally, Malachi stood, stepping back toward the door. "Thanks, Jer."

Jeremiah managed a half smile. "You got it."

As soon as his brothers disappeared beyond his doorway, his smile faded. He opened the folder. Symone's image stared up at him. His consultants could handle this case without him. Besides, she wasn't the target. "You're better off without me."

Chapter 2

"What are we going to do?" Eleanor's voice was tight with worry. It exacerbated Symone's irritation—and panic.

She'd led Paul and Eleanor into her office immediately after the board meeting to debrief late Thursday morning. There was only one thing they could do.

Symone settled onto her navy blue, ribbed, faux leather chair behind her heavy oak desk and took a steadying breath. She had to at least sound as though she was in control if she had any hope of maintaining her position with the foundation. "I'll revise my annual proposal to the board to reflect their feedback, making sure it isn't predictable." She turned her attention to her assistant. The other woman was a striking figure in a sky blue pantsuit, with sapphire earrings and matching necklace. "Ellie, I'll need you to pull new figures and forecasts. I'll send you an email with the adjusted parameters."

She was pleased that she'd been able to strip her emotions from her words. It hadn't been easy.

Eleanor sat on the dark blue cloth visitor's chair farthest from the door. She typed something into her electronic tablet. "I'll get right on it as soon as I receive your instructions."

"Thank you." Symone turned to her stepfather. Paul had taken the matching seat beside Eleanor. "Could you produce a proposal of recommendations for revisions to our application process? How can we reach a broader pool of applicants? What more can we do to encourage innovations?"

Translation: *How do you suggest we get the board off my back so I can continue to protect my family's legacy?*

Paul crossed his legs, adjusting the crease in his dark brown suit pants. "What about reconsidering the application from the exercise equipment entrepreneur?"

Symone drew a blank until she remembered the application her mother had screened out of consideration. "The pitch for the enhanced aerobic cycler?"

Paul balanced his elbows on the chair's arms. "We should take another look at that application. It was a very exciting idea, cutting-edge."

Symone adjusted her black-framed glasses as she considered Paul. One of them was confused. She was pretty certain it wasn't her. "My mother screened out that application. It doesn't meet the parameters of the foundation's mission."

The Bishop Foundation was created to support, fund and encourage innovative ideas in lifesaving pharmaceutical formulations, medical equipment and health treatments. The exercise machine didn't fit any of those categories.

Ignoring her explanation, Paul's voice raced with enthusiasm. His round, brown cheeks pinkened. "But the board is looking for riskier, more exciting projects. Mark's application fits that description."

Symone frowned. "Mark? Do you know him?"

Paul's dark brown eyes slid away from hers. "Only casually. He has exciting, revolutionary ideas about health and fitness. He just needs a chance."

Her stepfather wasn't breaking any rules by associating with someone who'd submitted an application to the foundation. Even one who'd issued a veiled threat when his application had been rejected. The award process was too stringent for that. Grants were awarded only to applicants who made it through the initial screening and received the supermajority vote of seven of the nine voting members.

"Paul has a good point." Eleanor's comment refocused Symone's attention on their discussion. "The project's different from anything we've ever done. It could help generate excitement among the board."

Symone lowered her eyes to hide her alarm. Paul's and Eleanor's attitudes were the reason she had to retain her position with her family's foundation. Both were in administrative positions, which meant the board could appoint either of them to replace her. But neither Paul nor Eleanor seemed bound to the foundation's mission.

She pulled a soft cloth from her top desk drawer, taking off her glasses to clean their lenses. "The reason the enhanced aerobic cycler is different from any other project we've approved is that it doesn't meet the application criteria. It's not an advancement in medical formulations, equipment or treatment. That's the reason my mother screened out the applicant." She put on her glasses before looking first to Eleanor, then Paul. "Our mission statement is the foundation's compass. It's the reason the foundation exists. My grandfather recognized the very urgent need to support medical research to ensure quality of life. That need still exists, and that's the reason we'll continue to use the mission statement to screen out applications."

"All right." Paul nodded, but Symone sensed he wasn't convinced.

"I'm sorry, Symone. You're right." Eleanor stood to leave. Her three-inch beige stilettos pushed her close to six feet. "I'd better get back to work. I'm still archiving this year's applications."

Symone offered her a smile. "Thank you, Ellie."

Paul raised his hand. "Yes. Thanks."

Symone waited until Eleanor had left her office before turning to her stepfather. "Do you remember we have the meeting with the Touré Security Group tomorrow morning?"

Paul's eyes widened with surprise before his brow furrowed with confusion. He pinned her with dark brown eyes beneath thick black eyebrows. "I thought you were going to cancel that meeting."

Symone blinked. "What would make you think that?"

Paul rubbed his eyes with his right fingers. He always did that when he was frustrated. Well, he wasn't the only one who felt that way.

He sighed before dropping his hand to meet her eyes. "Symone, I told you I don't want a bodyguard. I don't need a bodyguard. The detectives are investigating the threats. Let them do their job."

If only it was that simple. She wished she could hand over these worries to the Columbus Division of Police. She'd then go back to worrying only about the foundation, its investments and its applications. She hadn't been able to focus on just the foundation for a long time, though, not since her mother had died suddenly and now her stepfather was receiving threats.

Symone tamped down her impatience. "Paul, the police consider stalking complaints to be homicide prevention, but the detectives said they can't do anything unless an actual attempt is made on your life. I'd rather it didn't come to that."

Paul broke eye contact. "I don't want someone following me around."

Symone raised her eyebrows. "Apparently, someone's already following you and not in a good way. A bodyguard would keep you safe."

"Fine." Paul stood to leave her office. "We'll try a bodyguard, but if this person gets in my way, the deal's off."

Symone watched her stepfather march out of the room. She owed it to her mother's memory to help keep him safe. Why was he fighting her efforts to do that?

"Someone's trying to kill me." Paul nodded toward the woman seated to his right in the Touré Security Group's conference room. "Symone and I have already reported this to the police. They're investigating so I don't think I need a bodyguard."

It was early Friday morning. Symone sat opposite Jerry at the long, rectangular, glass-and-sterling-silver conference table. She projected understated wealth and was even more striking in person. Her golden brown hair was styled in a tousled bob that swung above her narrow shoulders. Her bangs ended just above thin, black-rimmed glasses that drew attention to her wide chocolate brown eyes beneath winged dark brown eyebrows. Her dove gray skirt suit and ghost white blouse were unassuming but probably expensive. Her thin rose-gold Movado wristwatch peeked from beneath her cuff. She'd accessorized with discreet pearl stud earrings and a matching single-strand princess-length necklace. A hint of wildflowers drifted across the table toward him. Jerry couldn't help himself. He drew a deep breath.

In contrast, the man she'd introduced as her stepfather wanted the world to know he was flush. In his early sixties, he had a full head of tight, dark brown curls. He was tall and slim in a tailored blue three-piece silk suit. His gold pocket watch was redundant to his black-and-gold Rolex. His black shoes looked Italian and handmade.

On Jerry's right, Mal sat in quiet contemplation. His middle brother was good at reading people. Jerry could feel Mal's mind working as he observed Symone's and Paul's body language and considered their words. He was interested to know what his brother was thinking.

Zeke's voice from the head of the conference table pulled Jerry from his thoughts. "Mr. Kayple—"

Symone interrupted. "Please. It's Paul and Symone."

Zeke gave her a warm smile. "Thank you." He turned back to her stepfather. "Paul, could you tell us about these threats?"

Jerry breathed a sigh of relief. They were finally getting somewhere. "When did they start?"

Paul's eyebrows rose toward his hairline. "I just told you, I don't need a bodyguard." His whiny tone brought back uncomfortable memories of the spoiled pop star Jerry had attempted to protect almost a year ago.

Jerry's brow furrowed. "You don't think these threats are real?"

Paul reared back against his seat as though Jerry had slapped him. "Of course I think they're real. Why else would I contact the police?"

"You believe the threats against your life are real, but you don't want protection." Jerry cocked his head. "Make it make sense, Paul."

"Jer." Zeke gave him a pointed look.

He sat back. "Tell us about the threats."

Paul regarded Jerry with wide, unblinking eyes. His lips parted but no words came out. Jerry turned his attention to Symone.

Anger darkened her pretty brown eyes, but her voice was

cool. "There have been two threats. My stepfather received the first one July third."

"Right before the long holiday weekend." Paul sounded irritated.

Symone continued. "It was a message painted on my mother's dining room table. It read, 'Walk away.'"

"Someone broke into your house?" Mal broke his silence. He directed his question to Symone.

"It's not my house." She gestured toward Paul. "It's the home my mother, Odette Bishop, shared with Paul. She passed away in April. I've been staying in the house while I help Paul settle her affairs."

"I'm so sorry." Jerry's heart clenched. His brothers echoed his sentiment.

He empathized with the heartache and grief she and her stepfather must be feeling. Their mother, Vanessa Sherraten-Touré, a retired marine, had died of heart disease two years and nine months ago. Their father, Franklin Touré, also a retired marine, had died two months before her. He missed them every day.

Symone inclined her head, accepting their condolences. Her voice was a little huskier as she continued. "The break-in triggered Paul's security system. When we got to the house, we saw the message. It was written in red paint." She pulled her cell phone from her silver faux leather purse and went through a series of taps on its face before passing her phone to Zeke on her right. "I took a photo."

Paul picked up the story, shifting again on his seat. Waves of impatience vibrated around him. "The police searched the entire house. Nothing else was touched. They didn't take anything and the only thing they left was that message." He gestured toward Symone's cell.

"They probably didn't have time to do anything else

once they triggered your alarm." Jerry took the phone Zeke passed to him.

He studied the image of the message painted onto a black laminate dining room table. The perpetrator—or perpetrators—had worked quickly. They'd shoved the table's centerpiece and crimson-and-dark-gold runner out of the way to make room for their warning. The two-word message had been written in all caps. The letters were different sizes, but the threat covered what appeared to be a third of the midsized table. The paint had dripped during the process, forming accidental links between the printed letters. The color was a deep red, as though the culprit wanted Symone and Paul to think it had been written in blood. It was an indication of the home invader wanting to heighten the sense of danger. Jerry offered the phone to Mal.

Paul continued, adjusting his cuffs. Had he meant to reveal his Rolex? "The police dusted the table for prints and took a sample of the paint. It was still wet. That's how quickly we got home."

Jerry frowned. His eyes bounced from Symone to Paul and back. "Did you notice anyone near your home or any cars that were leaving?"

Paul sat back on his seat, shaking his head. "I didn't see anything."

"I didn't, either." Symone reached diagonally across the table to accept her phone from Mal. Frustration creased her brow and tightened her voice. "I was focused more on getting to my mother's house as quickly as possible."

Paul rubbed his eyes with his right fingers. "The second event happened when Symone and I were leaving a restaurant in Granville. It was July eighth."

"Someone followed you." Jerry's muscles tensed. His eyes settled on Symone.

"I guess so." Paul seemed uncertain. "A dark car—black or blue or gray, I don't know—came speeding through the parking lot and almost hit us. We thought it was just a reckless driver, but the next day, someone put a photo of that attempted hit-and-run in my mailbox. They'd actually taken a photo of what happened and left a message that read, 'This wasn't an accident. Walk away.' Can you believe that?"

"Walk away from what?" Jerry watched as Symone once again tapped commands against the surface of her cell phone.

She offered the device to Zeke. "I took a photo of the picture and message they left for us."

Paul's brown cheeks flushed an angry red. His eyes darkened with emotion. "I believe these threats are coming from the company that made my wife's heart medicine or her doctor or both. I'm suing them for malpractice. They were negligent in my wife's care. Obviously, they think they can intimidate me into walking away from the lawsuits." He sat back, crossing his arms over his broad chest. "Well, they can think again. I'm not dropping the suit. I refuse."

Jerry took the cell from Zeke and studied the image. Something didn't seem right to him. "You think a doctor and a pharmaceutical company broke into your house and painted a threat on your dining room table?"

Paul scowled. "*They* didn't break in. They hired someone."

"You think a doctor and a drug company hired a criminal to threaten you?" Jerry handed the phone to Mal. "I can't see a doctor or a pharmaceutical manufacturer taking a hit out on someone over a lawsuit."

"I agree with Jerry." Zeke gestured toward him with his right hand. "Recent studies have shown doctors have won almost seventy percent of malpractice cases I think, even when the evidence against them is reasonably strong."

"The odds are in their favor." Mal studied the image on Symone's phone. "They won't go to the expense of hiring someone to harass and threaten you into dropping your suit. It's unnecessary."

Paul frowned at Mal. Jerry had the sense his lawyer hadn't shared those reports with him. He made a mental note to get more information on Paul's lawyer and the case. Something wasn't right there. He owed it to his personal security consultants to tie up these threads before assigning any of them to the case. Information like this would help make sure his consultants were well prepared to protect their clients and themselves.

Paul returned his scowl to Jerry and his brothers. "So who do *you* think's behind all this?"

Jerry caught and held Symone's attention. "Who knows you've been staying at your mother's house?"

Symone shrugged one slender shoulder. "Everyone. I haven't made a secret of it." She stiffened, giving Jerry an intent look. "You can't think those threats are meant for me."

All semblance of serenity had faded as Symone seemed to bristle at the idea that someone was trying to intimidate her. Did the unflappable Ms. Bishop have a temper?

Jerry cocked his head. "Why can't I? You're the new chair of a multimillion-dollar foundation."

Symone squared her shoulders. "These threats aren't connected to the foundation. What would I walk away from?"

She was hiding something. Jerry felt it like the hair twitching on his arms. He exchanged a look with Mal on his right and Zeke on his left. Their expressions told him they sensed it, too. He caught the warning glint in Zeke's eyes. He wouldn't voice his suspicions. Yet. But her secrecy was giving him flashbacks to the rebellious pop star. He was glad he'd told his brothers he was going to pass on this case. He didn't need a repeat of that botched assignment.

Chapter 3

Symone struggled to hold Jerry's eyes without flinching. She sensed his suspicions and doubts. They were wearing her down. Somehow, he knew she was withholding information. They all knew. Were they psychic or did she have the worst poker face on the planet?

It wasn't easy to meet the skepticism darkening Jerry's midnight eyes, which were set in one of the most classically handsome faces she'd ever seen. All the Touré brothers were strikingly attractive. Their family resemblance was strong. They were tall and athletic, with sharp sienna features, deep-set, unfathomably dark eyes and strong, obstinate jawlines softened by full sensual lips.

As she met with them in their agency's conference room early Friday morning, Symone also noticed their differences. The eldest, Zeke, had an unmistakable air of authority. Mal was the quiet one who took in everything with an enigmatic expression. His personality contrasted the most with Jerry's. The youngest Touré gave the impression of a live, ungrounded electrical wire. His brash personality didn't detract from his good looks, though. It made him even more compelling.

Symone pulled her eyes from his and sent them around the long, narrow conference room. The cloud-white walls

displayed oil paintings in black metal frames. The artwork was incredible, as good as any she'd seen in muse-
ums around the world. From this distance, she couldn't
read the artist's signature, even with her glasses. The images celebrated well-known Ohio landmarks, including
the Ohio Statehouse, the Cincinnati Observatory, the Paul
Laurence Dunbar House, the Rock & Roll Hall of Fame
and The Ohio State University Oval. Sunlight poured in
through the rear floor-to-ceiling window overlooking the
front parking lot. The window framed the treetops and a
distant view of the city's outer belt, Interstate 270.

"As I said when we first arrived, the police are investigating these threats." Paul stood as though to leave. "I
don't need, nor do I want, a bodyguard."

Symone strained to keep her temper from her words.
"Paul, could you please give us a few more minutes?" She
waited for him to sit before returning her attention to the
Touré brothers. "I reviewed the estimate you sent yesterday." She adjusted her glasses before opening the folder
she'd placed on the table in front of her. The TSG estimate
was on top. "According to your description, there would be
four teams of two guards. Why two?"

"One consultant would remain with Paul and the other
would monitor the perimeter." Jerry braced his forearms
on the table. The position brought him closer to her. Symone caught his scent, a combination of soap and mint
that was oddly erotic.

Zeke's voice helped clear her head. "Our security professionals are discreet. They're trained to blend into our
clients' routines without being disruptive."

Jerry continued the explanation. "You'll have four teams
in seven-hour shifts. The hour overlap is for a more se-

cure transition. They'll monitor inside and out, even while you're sleeping."

Symone looked up from the document. "I'm moving out of my mother's house tomorrow morning." Her two bags were already packed. She hadn't brought much with her. "Your teams will only be protecting Paul."

Jerry's frown didn't diminish his good looks. Could anything lessen their impact? "It would be better for you to remain together until the police catch the stalker—or *stalkers*. They could try to hurt you to get to Paul."

Symone assessed Jerry. "Will you be stationed on-site with your consultants?"

Jerry shook his head. She thought she saw regret in his eyes. "No, I won't. But they're well trained and very experienced."

Why did she feel disappointed? This situation was serious. Lives were at stake. It wasn't time to be developing crushes, especially on someone who was so obviously out of her league.

Symone frowned. "Dr. Grace Blackwell had enthusiastically recommended *you* specifically. She said your quick thinking and excellent instincts saved her grandmother from a killer."

Jerry's cheeks filled with dusky color. His reaction surprised Symone. She didn't think someone so confident could be disconcerted by praise. His obvious embarrassment made him seem more approachable—more mortal.

He lowered his eyes to the table. "That's nice of her. It was a pleasure protecting Melba."

Symone struggled to control a smile. "I understand Melba enjoyed having you as her bodyguard."

"Our consultants will be just as effective keeping you and Paul safe. My brothers and I put them through regular, rigorous training." Jerry seemed to have shaken off his discomfort and was back to full cocky mode.

Symone glanced at Paul. She wasn't certain she could count on his cooperation. But she wasn't doing this for him. She was doing it for her mother.

She turned back to the Touré brothers and gave a decisive nod. "Let's get started."

Symone pulled into the concrete driveway of her mother and stepfather's home in Upper Arlington. It was about half an hour after her Friday morning meeting with the Touré Security Group. Paul didn't wait for her to put the car in Park before stepping out on the passenger side. Symone watched him stride toward the house as she waited for Jerry to uncoil himself from the back seat. At six-feet-plus, he'd had to sit sideways in her silver four-door compact sedan. It couldn't have been a comfortable ride for him.

He closed the rear door, then took a few moments to scan the neighborhood and the facade of her mother's home. Was he getting a feel for the neighborhood—or waiting for the circulation to return to his legs?

All the Touré men were handsome, intelligent and successful. But there was something especially exciting about the impatient youngest brother. He was built like a runner, long and lean. As he stood with his back to her, Symone's eyes traveled over his broad shoulders clothed in a sapphire blue, long-sleeved shirt. She paused on the black slacks hugging his slim hips and long legs. Jerry turned and she quickly lifted her gaze.

His loose-limbed strides brought him to her. "Beautiful house in a beautiful neighborhood."

Symone's cheeks were burning. Did he know she'd been staring at his butt? She'd never done anything like that before. "Yes. It's very clean and quiet. My mother liked living here. Most of her neighbors are—were—grandparents whose children and grandchildren visited every weekend."

Nervous chatter. She forced herself to stop and take a breath.

The houses in the area were similar. The modern Craftsman homes were dark brick with white, cream or tan siding and solid wood front doors. The lawns were in the same rich, healthy condition, which wasn't surprising considering most of the neighbors, including her mother, had the same landscape service.

Jerry tossed her a smile that made her knees tremble. "Did she use that to put pressure on you to settle down and start a family?"

For the first time, the memory of her mother made her smile. "My mother wasn't in a hurry to become a grandmother." Symone turned to lead him into the house.

Paul had left the mahogany front door open as though welcoming them in. He turned from the bay window overlooking the front yard as Symone and Jerry entered the house. Had he been watching them?

Jerry examined the locks and threshold before closing and securing the door. His eyes lingered on the security panel on the left wall. He must be trying to figure out how a stranger had gained access to a home with an alarm system and multiple sturdy locks.

Symone gestured toward the rear of the house. "The police believe the stalker got in through the door off the deck."

Jerry shared a look between her and Paul. "Thanks for letting me tour your home. I'm looking for information that could help our consultants protect you."

Paul stepped forward. The glint in his eyes was a challenge. "How do I know you're not casing my house?"

"Paul!" Symone gasped. This would be a good time for the ground to open up and swallow her. Before she could say anything else—like humbly apologize for her stepfather's piggish behavior—Jerry laughed.

His smile was genuine. Lights danced in his midnight eyes. "Are you suggesting my brothers and I use Touré Security Group as cover for a burglary ring?"

Paul squared up to the younger man as though Jerry, who looked like he worked out for fun and entertainment, didn't have at least four inches on him. "That seem funny to you?"

"Paul!" Symone unclenched her teeth. "There's nothing funny about your behavior. You're being extremely rude."

Jerry raised a hand, palm out. "No. Wait. We can give you references in addition to Grace's, if that would make you feel more comfortable about hiring us. You could even talk with Detectives Duster and Stenhardt."

Paul scowled up at Jerry for a moment longer. Jerry's smile never faltered. Finally, Paul stepped back. "No, never mind."

Symone exhaled her relief. "I'm terribly sorry about what just happened." She shot a glare toward Paul. He'd never have behaved that way if her mother had still been alive. "Grace's recommendation is enough for me. Are you still willing to work with us?"

"Of course." Jerry seemed unfazed.

Amazing. If their roles had been reversed, Symone would have been shattered. She would've walked away from the assignment without looking back.

"I'm glad." Symone's gratitude eased her tension. "Let's start that tour."

In addition to the two-car garage, her mother's home

had three floors and an attic. The main level was an open floor plan. Her mother had deferred to Paul, who'd hired an interior designer. The rooms on the main floor were heavy with crimson red and old gold accents, including wall-to-wall deep gold carpeting.

"How long have you lived here?" Jerry considered the bay window's locks and framing.

"Odette and I moved in shortly after we married almost two years ago." Paul's voice was still stiff with resentment.

Symone hadn't been surprised when her mother had told her she was selling the family home so she and Paul could have a fresh start with a house of their own. She could understand why Paul wouldn't have wanted to move into a home with so many memories. Her mother had understood as well. Odette cared enough to sell their family home to start a new life with Paul. It was out of respect for her mother's feelings for Paul that Symone was doing what she could to help keep him safe even if he was opposed to it.

She trailed the men as Paul led the tour, striding through the living room, dining room, kitchen and foyer. Jerry followed at his own pace. In each room, he examined the windows and tested their locks. He checked the entrance door in the garage, as well as the ones in the basement and kitchen. He spent extra time examining the French doors off the foyer that led out to the wide Honeywood deck.

"What are you thinking?" Symone watched as he stood outside, running his hand along the doors' threshold.

"None of your doors or windows were forced open." His attention was on the doorway. "There aren't any splinters or grooves in the wood or scratches on the locks." Jerry caught her eyes. "Have either of you lost your house keys?"

Paul's eyes stretched wide in surprise. "You think the intruder had a key?" His voice rose with horror.

Jerry reentered the house and secured the door. "I don't know how else to explain someone breaking in without damaging the doors, locks or windows."

"I've been using my mother's key." Symone turned to Paul. "You still have your key, right?"

"Of course." Paul sounded shocked. "And those are the only keys in existence, Odette's and mine. We've never made copies."

Jerry's eyes were dark with concern. "You should change your locks. Somehow someone got a copy of your keys."

Paul looked from Jerry to Symone and back. "Why didn't the police tell us this?"

Jerry shook his head. "I don't know."

Paul looked confused and suspicious, as though he couldn't bring himself to believe what Jerry was saying. Symone made a mental note to make sure Paul changed the locks.

She stepped back, preparing to leave the foyer. "We've shown you the basement and this main floor. Paul, could you take us upstairs, please?"

She followed Paul up the winding carpeted staircase. Her skin tingled with awareness of Jerry's presence behind her.

"May I ask how your wife died?" Jerry's voice was soft sympathy. Still, Symone's back stiffened.

Paul's voice was husky. "Odette had a heart condition. She'd had it for years and had been managing it with prescription medication." He reached the top floor and turned left, leading Symone and Jerry toward the room he'd shared with Odette. "Recently, she'd been feeling weaker. She'd called her doctor, who'd assured her she was fine. Everything was fine, including her prescription. Two days later, she had a heart attack and died."

"I'm so sorry for your loss." Jerry paused a moment before continuing. "You're suing her doctor because he said she was fine days before her heart attack?"

Paul crossed into his bedroom. "That's right. As well as the pharmaceutical company who made her medication. A friend who's also a lawyer and a member of the foundation's board suggested the lawsuits. He's representing me. It's taking a long time to wind through court, though, but I'm determined to make someone pay for Odette's death. This wasn't her time. She'd been taking her medication. She was exercising and watching her diet. She wasn't supposed to die now."

Jerry scanned the room before crossing to the window. "There's no way for anyone to sneak in through these windows. They'd need a ladder." He crossed to the windows on the other side of the room. "It's the same here. The intruder would've been noticed and one of your neighbors would've called the police."

Symone rubbed her arms to dispel a sudden chill. The image of intruders who were intent on harming her family climbing through their windows was alarming. "That's what we thought as well."

Jerry turned back to the room. "Did you have your mother's medication tested?"

Startled, Symone exchanged a look with Paul. "No, we hadn't thought of that."

Paul scowled, something he was doing more and more of since her mother's death. "Why hadn't Wes suggested that?"

Jerry addressed Paul. "Would you mind if I take a sample of your wife's medication and ask Grace to test it?"

Paul looked at Jerry over his shoulder. "What do you think you'll find?"

Jerry shrugged. "We might not find anything, but there's no harm in checking, is there?"

"No, there's not." Symone crossed to her mother's nightstand where she knew Odette kept her prescription. She took the bottle from the top drawer and gave it to Jerry. "Thank you for the suggestion. I'd like the tablets to be tested."

"I'll take care of it." Jerry scanned the label before putting the bottle in his front pants pocket.

"Great." Now that Jerry had brought up testing her mother's medication, Symone wanted answers yesterday. She turned toward the bedroom door, fisting her hands to contain her impatience. "If you're done here, we'll give you a tour of the foundation's offices."

The Bishop Foundation operated from a suite on the top floor of a four-story concrete-and-glass building off Riverside Drive near Interstate 670. Symone and Paul gave Jerry a complete tour starting with the parking lot before taking him into the building and up the elevator to the foundation's headquarters.

Jerry followed Symone and Paul from the elevator. What he'd seen so far hadn't impressed him. Why was security the last thing companies considered—if they considered it at all?

"There aren't any security cameras around the building's perimeter, in the parking lot, or in the lobby." He looked around the small elevator lobby between the two sets of glass doors leading to the foundation suite. Disappointing. "There aren't any here, either."

Symone spoke over her shoulder as Paul pushed open one of the glass doors. "The foundation doesn't own this building, but if you think it's important, we can address security with the property management company."

Jerry held the door as Symone walked through. "It's very important. At a minimum, there should be security cameras and guards. How many employees do you have?"

Symone paused just inside the suite. "We're a small organization. We have twelve full-time staff, including my mother, Paul and me. Well, Paul and me. There are seven board members, but they aren't staff."

Jerry paced beside Symone. She stopped several times to exchange greetings and a few words with employees. She asked after them and their family members. In response, her staff asked about her. More than one person hugged her. With each employee, her demeanor was warm and attentive as though there was nothing on her mind other than the person in front of her.

"Her mother was the same way." Paul made the comment as he watched Symone once again stop to speak with a member of her staff. "I told Odette she'd get a lot more done during regular office hours if she limited these distractions."

For some reason, Paul's words irritated Jerry. He'd noticed no one stopped to speak with Symone's stepfather. "Maybe Symone and her mother realize that these distractions contribute to employee satisfaction and the foundation's success."

The tour of the foundation's offices didn't take long. The open floor plan, bright colors and natural light streaming into the main room from the near floor-to-ceiling windows made the workplace feel like a cheerful and positive environment. The suite was laid out so the elevator lobby was in the center. This allowed people to access it by two sets of doors, one on the east side of the floor and the other to the west. They'd entered the offices through the glass doors on the east. But by walking around the office, they could return to the elevators using glass doors on the west.

Large pale gray cubicles grew up from the thin powder blue carpeting. There were four glass-and-wood-paneled offices, one in each corner of the floor. Other areas included a small kitchen-cum-lunch room, a small conference room, a large boardroom, a women's restroom and a men's restroom.

Jerry looked over his shoulder, scanning the area one more time. "Both doors to the suites should be keycard access only. People should only be able to enter through one of the doors, making the second door an exit only."

Symone narrowed her eyes as though trying to visualize the process he described. "We don't have security threats."

Jerry's eyebrows shot up his forehead. "You have one now. Think about what's already happened. The stalker broke into your mother's home without leaving a scratch. That's with a security system and all the doors and windows locked. Here, there isn't anything preventing them from getting to you and Paul."

Paul rubbed his chin. "Maybe he's right. We can do with a few cameras for our safety."

Jerry followed Symone and Paul into Symone's office. "Set them up in public spaces. Hallways, lobbies, the parking lot. But you need more than cameras. You should have security guards monitoring the grounds and the lobby. These are investments meant to keep you safe, especially since there's an active threat—"

"Symone! I was told you wouldn't be in today." A well-dressed, middle-aged white man entered the room.

The stranger's bottle green eyes scrutinized Jerry at the same time Jerry assessed the newcomer. The other man had perfect thick, wavy blond hair. Like Paul, he wore his wealth. The cost of his black Italian shoes, three-piece dark brown pin-striped suit and black silk shirt was probably enough to send a student to a four-year college.

Symone's smile didn't reach her eyes. Interesting. "Good morning, Xander. Is there something you need?"

"Hello, Paul." Xander offered Symone's stepfather a smile before responding to Symone. His grin revealed dazzling white teeth. "I wanted to ask if you need help preparing for the upcoming board meeting. If so, I'm happy to offer you my services."

Symone's smile remained fixed in place. "Thank you for your generous offer, but I can handle the report on my own."

Xander inclined his head in a gallant motion. "Well, my dear, if you change your mind, please feel free to give me a call. I know you have a lot of experience with finance and investments, but those are my areas of specialty as well. If you'd like us to put our heads together, I'm happy to brainstorm some ideas with you."

Symone stepped back from him and toward her desk. "That's very kind of you. Thank you."

"Of course, my dear." Xander turned to Jerry. His hand was outstretched. "Xander Fence."

Jerry accepted the handshake. "Good to meet you."

Xander's eyebrows, a darker blond than his hair, knitted at Jerry's refusal to identify himself. He hesitated as though he was going to say something more. Instead he released Jerry's hand.

Symone's manners were impeccable. Jerry suspected she had a reason for not introducing them. It wasn't up to him to satisfy the other man's curiosity if his client wasn't going to. Was he wrong? He glanced at Symone. Humor twinkled in her brown eyes as she observed their exchange. When she noticed him watching her, she lowered her eyes and sat behind her desk. She set her silver purse beside her keyboard.

Jerry waited until Xander disappeared beyond the doorway. "Who was that?"

Paul shoved his hands into his front pockets. "Xander's a banking executive and one of our newest board members."

Symone stood, adjusting her purse on her shoulder. "I don't have any messages that need to be returned right away. Let's—"

A woman hurried into the office. "Symone, I'm so glad I caught you." In her purple, figure-hugging, knee-length, polyester dress and three-inch, black stilettos, she looked like she'd walked out of a scene from a soap opera. Jerry waited for the theme song to roll. "There are some messages I need your input on before responding. One of the—"

Symone interrupted her. "Ellie, can those messages wait?" She checked her watch as she circled her desk. "Paul and I have an errand to run. We'll be right back."

Ellie followed Symone as she left the office. "I'm afraid they can't." She glanced over her shoulder, giving Jerry a curious look. "Hello."

Jerry inclined his head. It wasn't as gallant a gesture as Xander's. Symone didn't introduce him this time, either. Why not? He didn't think she was capable of bad manners.

Symone strode out of the office with Ellie hot on her heels. Paul and Jerry followed. "Then we'll have to walk and talk."

There was something exciting about seeing Symone in this environment where she was in charge, multitasking as people came to her with issues, comments and questions.

She'd dispatched Xander with grace and confidence. With Ellie, she was courteous and efficient.

The elevator came quickly. Ellie started talking as soon as they boarded it to return to the lobby. "There are several issues on the list."

"Take them one at a time." Symone's voice was patient.

Ellie tossed her auburn mane behind her right shoulder. "All right. The first one is those new numbers you wanted me to get." She glanced at Jerry before lowering her voice. "Are you certain it's okay to talk about this here?"

Symone frowned. "You said these issues couldn't wait. Either tell me what's going on now or wait for me to return."

Ellie shrugged. "All right." The elevator doors opened, and she followed Symone across the lobby. "The first issue is the numbers. I think the information the financial institution pulled for us is wrong."

Symone gave her a sharp look as she pushed through the exit. "What makes you think that?"

Ellie followed her from the building. "They seem too low based on the trending from the year-to-date prospectus we just received."

Symone dug into her purse and pulled out her car keys. "Ask them to rerun the numbers."

Ellie hurried to keep up with her boss. "That might delay our report and cause us to miss the board's deadline."

Symone paused on the sidewalk. "If the numbers are wrong, we can't use them. We'll worry about the deadline if it comes to that."

She was at least thirty yards away when she pointed her keyless entry device toward the tiny torture machine she called a car. Jerry wasn't looking forward to folding himself onto the back seat again. Symone pressed the device as she stepped off the sidewalk—and her car exploded.

The blast was loud enough to make Jerry briefly double over in pain. It shook the trees surrounding the parking lot. Red, orange and yellow flames engulfed the vehicle. Black smoke rose up, stretching toward the sky.

Symone gasped, jumping back onto the sidewalk.

Ellie screamed.

Paul shouted. "What the—"

Without stopping to think, Jerry leaped forward, pushing Symone and Ellie back into the building. "Come on!" His shout shook Paul from his trance.

Jerry stood behind Symone and Ellie, desperate to use his body to shield them. Was the car bomb the only attack? He didn't know, but he wasn't waiting to find out. The stalker could be close, waiting to strike while the explosion distracted them.

"What just happened?" Ellie's voice was strident with fear. "What's happening?" She kept repeating those questions as though waiting for someone to answer. No one could.

Symone was shaking. She was as pale as a ghost. Behind her glasses, her eyes almost swallowed her face.

Jerry scanned her features, neck and shoulders. "Are you all right?"

"Yes." Her response was a thin breath.

Jerry looked at Ellie and Paul. "Are you okay?"

They nodded, staring at him with wide clouded eyes.

His attention swung back to Symone as he pulled his cell phone from his pocket. "Remember I told you I thought you were the target?" He waited for her nod. "We need a new plan."

Chapter 4

"Are you all right?" Zeke crossed The Bishop Foundation's lobby late Friday morning. Mal was close behind him. Their approach was quick but stiff and jerky.

Jerry excused himself from the group he'd been speaking with and strode to meet his brothers halfway. Through the building's Plexiglas facade behind the two men, he saw the flashing red and blue lights of the emergency vehicles that had responded to his call about the explosion. Police and firefighters had arrived within minutes. He shouldn't be surprised his brothers had shown up seconds later even without the advantage of lights and sirens.

Zeke and Mal stopped in front of Jerry. Their spare features were tight. Their eyes were dark with fear, concern and anger. Both men looked Jerry over as though reassuring themselves the youngest Touré was safe and unhurt despite the danger he'd been in.

Jerry frowned at Zeke. "What are you doing here? I called Mal."

Zeke arched a thick eyebrow. "*Car bomb*, Jer? Did you expect me to sit at my desk, twiddling my thumbs?" He squeezed Jerry's right shoulder.

Mal gripped Jerry's left upper arm. "Did you think I wouldn't tell him?"

Zeke's dark eyes held him in place. "You may think you're invincible, but we know better."

Jerry felt the faint tremor in Zeke's and Mal's hands. His muscles relaxed. They were shaken, just as he would've been had the situation been reversed. He placed a hand on each of their shoulders and offered a small smile. "It's all good, guys. No one was hurt. We were far enough from Symone's car. Our clients are upset and scared, of course, but physically fine." He directed their attention over his shoulder. "Duster and Stenhardt just got here."

He turned to lead his brothers across the lobby to Symone and Paul, who waited with their administrative assistant and the two Columbus police department homicide detectives.

Eriq Duster's jaded ebony eyes twinkled and his stern, dark features eased into a welcoming smile as the Touré brothers approached. "Next time we get the band back together, let's make it a beer instead of a bomb."

The veteran detective was creeping toward retirement. He resembled an aging pugilist in his comfortable lightweight brown sports coat, pressed black pants, crisp white shirt and bolo tie with a bronze slide clip in the shape of a trout.

Zeke's smile was stiff around the edges. "I can get behind that." He turned to Symone and Paul. "We're glad you're both okay."

"I don't know if you could call us okay." Paul's tone was harsh. Anger seemed to be masking the fear that shook his words.

Eriq looked away from Paul as though giving him time to settle down. He turned his smile to Mal. Faint laugh lines bracketed his full lips. "How's Dr. Grace?"

Mal's expression brightened. "She's well. Thanks."

"Tell her we said hello." Detective Taylor Stenhardt had gathered her heavy, honey blond hair into a bun at her nape. It seemed too heavy for her long, slender neck. Her dancer's figure was clothed in a dark blue, lightweight suit.

Jerry gestured toward Ellie. "Eleanor Press, my brothers and business partners, Hezekiah and Malachi. Eleanor is Symone's administrative assistant."

Ellie seemed distracted as she greeted the elder Tourés. She hadn't been far from Symone's side since the bombing.

Eriq addressed Symone and Paul. "Is there somewhere we can talk privately?"

Symone glanced at Jerry. The uncertainty in her chocolate eyes triggered his protective instincts. He stepped closer to her.

"We can use the boardroom." She adjusted her glasses. "This way, please."

Symone led them to the two elevators at the rear of the lobby. Jerry braced his hand on the small of her back. Her muscles eased by degrees against his palm. A thick, tense silence followed them. Symone, Paul and Ellie seemed lost in thought. Did anyone have theories about the car bomb? Who would have planted it, and when, how or why?

As they waited for the elevator to arrive, Zeke, Mal, Eriq and Taylor surveyed the bronze-and-white-tiled area. He knew they were taking in the lack of security cameras and guards. At his first opportunity, he was going to talk with Zeke and Mal about submitting a proposal to the building owners for TSG's security services. He was leaving the company, but that didn't mean he didn't care about the family business any longer. Just the opposite.

An elevator arrived after a short wait. It was a cozy fit for the eight of them but a quick ride to the foundation's fourth-floor offices. Symone led them past the gauntlet of

startled, curious and concerned employees into the boardroom. She took the chair at the head of the long, oval, dark
wood table surrounded by ten cushioned dark wood chairs.
Jerry took the seat on her right, followed by Zeke and Mal.
Paul took the seat on Symone's left. Ellie and Taylor filed
in behind him. Eriq took the chair at the foot of the table.

The veteran detective opened his notebook. "Ms. Bishop,
how long had your car been unattended in the parking lot?"

"Um." Symone adjusted her black-rimmed glasses as
she took a moment to think. "Less than an hour. Paul and
I gave Jerry a tour of the foundation. As you can see, our
offices aren't very big. Then Paul and I were going to take
Jerry back to his office. So, yes, less than an hour." She
looked to Paul for verification.

Paul nodded. "I'd agree with that." He sounded much
calmer now.

Taylor's piercing jade green eyes were wide in her fair
skin. She gestured toward the large picture window at the
back of the conference room. "That would give the bomber
plenty of time to plant the device. And since there aren't
security cameras around the perimeter of the building,
the parking lot or the lobby, they could've done so without anyone noticing."

"You've reported previous threats." Eriq swung his pen
between Symone and Paul. "We'll follow up with your
wife's doctor's office and with the pharmaceutical company. Is there anyone else you can think of who might
want to harm you?"

Paul glanced at Symone. "No, there's no one else."

Eriq's eyes narrowed just a bit. The seasoned detective
seemed to sense Paul wasn't being honest. He lifted his
chin toward Symone. "What about you? Can you think of
anyone who'd want to hurt you?"

Symone blinked behind her glasses. "Me? I'm not the one being threatened."

Jerry's lips parted. From his seat on Symone's right, he shifted to face her. "You *still* think *Paul's* the target? *Your* car was the one they bombed."

Eriq waved his pen toward Jerry. "Jerry's right. Since it was your car, we have to ask who'd want to kill you. Or perhaps they want to get to you *and* your stepfather."

Symone frowned at Jerry. "The first threat was in Paul and Mom's home."

"With you in it." Jerry counted the threats on his fingers. "The second was in a restaurant parking lot after you and Paul had dinner. This third involved *your* car."

Paul interrupted. "Maybe they're right, Symone. Maybe the threats are for both of us."

Jerry had his doubts, but if the suggestion made Symone more agreeable, he'd go with it. He shared a look between Symone and Paul. "Pack whatever you need for the foreseeable future. Neither one of you is coming back here until the detectives have whoever's after you in custody."

Symone straightened on her chair. "I can't just walk away from the foundation. I have responsibilities."

Ellie leaned forward to catch Symone's attention. "Symone, really, your safety is the most important issue right now. The board will understand."

"No." Symone shook her head adamantly. "The board can't know that anything's wrong."

Mal nodded toward the boardroom door. "They've probably already heard about the car bomb." His tone was dry.

Symone scowled. Jerry sensed her mind racing. He felt her tension rising.

Ellie extended her arms toward Paul and Symone. "You both can work remotely until this stalker's caught. There's no reason you can't, and I'm sure this investigation won't take long."

Zeke addressed Jerry. "I've asked Celeste Jarrett to help us with this case."

Eriq somber expression eased into an uncharacteristic grin. "CJ's on board? That's great. She'll help you get to the bottom of this case in a snap."

Celeste was an ex-CPD homicide detective. Several years ago, she and her partner had left the department and opened a private investigation agency.

"I agree with Eriq." Taylor's tone was almost apologetic. "And I'm afraid you don't have a choice, Ms. Bishop. It's the only way to protect you."

Symone closed her eyes briefly. A red flush highlighted her cheekbones. "This doesn't make sense." She looked from Paul to Jerry. "Why would someone want to harm me?"

Jerry cocked his head. "I think we need to figure that out and fast. Don't you?"

"Welcome back, Tourés." Kevin Apple looked up from his U-shaped gray laminate reception desk as Jerry led his brothers, Symone and Paul through the agency's Plexiglas doors late Friday morning. "Glad you're okay, Jerry."

This was the twenty-something's fifth week as TSG's administrative assistant. It hadn't taken him long to fit into the company and prove his value to the team. After media coverage of the brothers' success protecting Dr. Grace Blackwell and finding a serial killer, their security company's new client intake email and phone lines had been overwhelmed. TSG wasn't the little-security-company-that-could anymore.

When their parents had launched the company, they'd replied to emails and answered calls themselves. They took pride in knowing long-term as well as prospective customers who contacted the firm were speaking with a member of the family. But after Grace's high-profile case, the brothers couldn't keep up with the flood of requests and new client inquiries. They'd needed help. Kevin was a quick study, efficient, organized and cordial. During his interview, he'd stated he wanted to be a personal security consultant. Jerry had put him on a training schedule, which was going well. TSG would need to find a new admin soon.

"Thanks, Kev. I appreciate your concern." Jerry gestured to his right. "These are our clients, Symone Bishop, chair of The Bishop Foundation, and her stepfather, Paul Kayple, the foundation's vice chair. Symone, Paul, Kevin Apple is our administrative assistant."

Kevin inclined his head. "It's nice to meet you." He looked again to Jerry. "Celeste Jarrett's waiting in the large conference room."

Jerry looked the younger man over. His eyebrows knitted with confusion. "Did you get a haircut?"

The admin had subdued his twisted high top to a curly low fade much more like Jerry's. He also was wearing a crimson long-sleeved cotton shirt with an ebony stripe down the left side. Jerry had an identical shirt somewhere in his closet.

Kevin's smile was sheepish. His cheeks filled with a hint of rose. "Yeah." He ran a hand over his tight dark curls.

Jerry turned his confusion to Zeke and Mal. His brothers shrugged their eyebrows.

Zeke turned to Symone and Paul. "This way, please." He led the five-member group down the short hallway to their large conference room at the back of their suite.

Celeste had taken one of the black cushioned chairs on the left side of the large, rectangular glass-and-sterling-silver table. She arched a straight dark eyebrow as they entered the room. "So is TSG going into investigations now?"

"Thank you for coming, Celeste." Zeke stopped in front of her and offered his hand.

Celeste took it. Her slightly irritated expression eased into surprise. Zeke's tense features relaxed. Celeste tugged free, and the moment was lost almost as though it had never happened.

But Jerry knew what he'd seen. His eldest brother had been shaken out of his comfort zone. Interesting.

Zeke took the seat at the head of the table, putting Celeste on his right. He cleared his throat. "To answer your question, no, we're not moving into investigations. That's why we're asking for your help." He made quick work of the introductions before starting the meeting.

"What's the case?" Celeste's piercing hazel brown eyes leaped from Jerry beside her to Mal at the foot of the table, and Symone and Paul across from her before returning to Zeke.

Celeste had launched Jarrett & Nichols Investigations with her former partner, Nanette Nichols. Rumor had it Celeste and Nanette had been detectives for less than two years when crooked cops had framed them for their criminal activities. They'd been kicked off the force and charged for the crimes. It had taken courage and strength of will for them to prove their innocence, restore their reputations and put the real criminals behind bars. The department had wanted to reinstate them, but the experience had been so bad, Celeste and Nanette had agreed to decline the offer and start their own investigative agency. Eriq had worked with both women. He never said much about Nanette, but he took every opportunity to talk up Celeste. He seemed almost paternal toward her.

Paul scowled across the table at Celeste. "Someone's trying to kill us."

"All right." Celeste pulled out a notebook. She looked from Paul to Symone and then Zeke.

The private investigator was dressed in a black cotton T-shirt beneath a gray blazer, black jeans and gray flats. There was a plain sterling silver ring on her right thumb.

Zeke gestured toward Jerry. "Jerry's taking point on this."

Jerry scanned the faces around the table as he collected his thoughts. Diagonally across from him, Symone looked distracted, as though she was developing arguments against Jerry's assertion that she was the real target. Beside her, Paul's frown was a indicator of his short temper. At the foot of the table, Mal's features were inscrutable to anyone who didn't know him. Jerry was certain his brother already had a strategy for the case but was waiting for everyone else to catch up. On Jerry's left, Celeste's serene expression was fake. He felt the vibrations of her impatience to get moving, to do something. Zeke sat back against his cushioned seat, waiting for Jerry to lead the discussion. Jerry brought Celeste up to speed with the timeline, the two previous threats, culminating with the bomb planted in Symone's car.

Celeste looked between Symone and Paul. "Walk away from what?"

Symone's breath was unsteady. "We'd thought the message was meant for Paul because of his malpractice lawsuit against my mother's doctor and the suit against the pharmaceutical company that made her medication." She threw a quick look toward Jerry before turning her attention back to Celeste. "But now I'm not sure." Her voice dwindled.

"We now think the threats are targeting Paul *and* Symone." Jerry's gut was telling him the threats were meant for Symone with the intent of separating her from her family's foundation. It was a theory worth looking into. "We need your help identifying who's behind these attempts on their lives. We've worked one investigation, but the scope was much narrower. We need your expertise."

"Of course." Celeste inclined her head. "You're right to be concerned." She turned her attention to Symone on the other side of the table. "The threats are intensifying. First, someone broke into your home and left behind a threatening message. Next, someone followed you with the intent of terrorizing you with their car. Did they intentionally miss you? We don't know. Today, they planted a bomb in your car while it was parked outside your place of employment. Their messages are clear. They're in charge. They can reach you whenever, wherever, however."

Paul scowled. "We didn't need you to tell us that. We figured that out ourselves." His voice was almost a growl. Jerry heard the fear underneath.

Mal spoke over Paul. "The timing's an issue as well."

Symone's eyes flickered toward Jerry before redirecting to Mal. "What do you mean?" Her question was cautious.

Mal spread his hands above the conference table. "The time between the attacks is shrinking. You received the first one July third. Five days later, on July eighth, you were almost run over. Three days later, today, your car was bombed."

"He's right." Celeste made another note in her book. "Whoever wants you to leave is getting impatient."

Paul swept his arm in a stiff, jerky motion toward Celeste diagonally across from him. "You're deliberately trying to scare us."

Jerry arched an eyebrow. "We shouldn't have to scare you

into taking these threats seriously. The car bomb should've been enough. This isn't—"

Paul cut him off. "The police are aware of these threats. They're doing their own investigation. We don't need a private investigator getting in the way nor do we need bodyguards."

Zeke's dark eyes flared in a way that people who knew him took extra care. "Celeste Jarrett will not be in the way. As you'll remember, the detectives spoke highly of her and were pleased that she'll be partnering with us on your case."

Jerry and Mal exchanged a look. Zeke had jumped to a stern defense of Celeste without hesitation. Interesting.

Symone touched the back of Paul's hand where it lay on the table between them. "Paul, they're right. My car's destroyed. We could've been standing beside it if not seated inside. The more experienced help we have to stop these threats, the faster all of this will be over, and we can get back to normal."

Her tremors were visible. Jerry's hands itched with the need to console her.

"No." Paul bit off his response. He took a deep breath and managed to regain his calm. "The message was clear. Whoever is sending these threats wants us to walk away. That's what I'm going to do. You should, too, Symone."

Jerry frowned at Paul. "Walk away from what?" The hairs on the back of his neck tightened. Why was Paul so opposed to their help?

Paul glowered at him. "I'm dropping the lawsuits. I don't want to, but they're playing hardball." He turned to Symone again. "And I'm leaving Columbus. I'm going to ask my brother if I could stay with him in North Carolina at least until things settle down here. You're welcome to come with me."

Symone's eyes were wide behind her black-rimmed glasses. "What about Mom? I thought the purpose of the lawsuits was to get justice for her?"

Jerry detected a thread of anger and something else under her words. Perhaps betrayal? He rubbed his chest, surprised by the pain that was like a tight grip on his heart.

Paul's jaw dropped as though Symone's questions surprised him. "Symone, our lives are in danger. Someone's threatening us. Do you think your mother would want that? Of course not. If we leave, the threats will stop and then you can come back or do whatever you want."

Her eyebrows knitted. "I can't leave Columbus. I have a responsibility to the foundation."

Paul glanced around the table before facing Symone again. "Your parents wouldn't want you to stay with the foundation if it was putting your life in danger. Your mother would be the first person to tell us to leave for our safety's sake."

"No, she wouldn't." Symone's objection was quiet but firm.

Jerry wondered what Paul saw as he searched Symone's face. If they were seeing the same thing, then Paul also witnessed her unwavering courage and unbreakable determination. It was in the stubborn tilt of her rounded chin and the fierce directness of her chocolate brown eyes.

Paul leaned back against the black cushioned chair. "We'll have to agree to disagree."

Symone shook her head. "My mother and father wouldn't want me to run away and abandon the foundation. They wouldn't want me to turn my back on the legacy my grandfather left us. They believed in his goal of improving the quality of people's lives." She gestured toward Jerry. "The Touré Security Group and Celeste can provide both of us with protection and help us find the person behind these threats."

Paul drew a deep breath, then blew it out. "Well, Symone, you can do whatever you want, of course, but I'm leaving."

Symone stared at him. Jerry sensed she wanted to say something more, but after several tense seconds she nodded, then looked away. Her grief drifted across the table to him.

He turned to Paul. "We could provide you with a bodyguard while you prepare to leave." He lifted his hand to stop the other man from interrupting. "The agent will be unobtrusive. He or she will keep you safe just until you're ready to leave."

Paul scanned the table. "No. Absolutely not."

"We'll respect your decision, Paul." Zeke stood, effectively ending the meeting. Jerry and Mal stood with him. He turned to Celeste. "Please send us your contract. We'll schedule a videoconference once we've secured Symone."

Celeste stood, setting her black tote bag on her right shoulder. "Sounds good." She addressed Symone. "You're in good hands with the Tourés. And I've worked plenty of investigations like yours, both on the force and with my agency. Let us do our jobs. We'll keep you safe and put this stalker behind bars."

Symone rose from her seat. Her eyes were clouded behind her glasses. "Thank you."

Celeste nodded, then turned to leave. Zeke escorted her from the conference room.

Jerry stepped away from his chair, pulling a small brown plastic bottle from his front pants pocket. He drew Mal aside and lowered his voice. "Could you ask Grace to test these pills? We need to know what's in them and what effect they would have on the user."

Mal examined the bottle. "What are they?"

"Odette Bishop's prescription medication." He inclined his head toward Paul. "He believes it might have contributed to her death."

Mal gave Jerry a sharp look. There was concern in his dark eyes. "I'll take it to Grace this afternoon. We're having lunch." He crossed to Symone, jerking his head toward the suite's entrance. "I need to get you set up with a burner cell and laptop."

Symone frowned her confusion. "I already have a laptop and phone."

Mal shook his head as he stepped back, gesturing for her to precede him. "These devices are clean. They're set up with VPNs to mask your location. That way, no one can track you while you're in the safe house."

Paul pushed himself to his feet. "And where will this safe house be?"

Mal glanced at Jerry before responding to Paul. "The location is confidential."

Paul scowled. "But I'm her stepfather. That information doesn't have to be confidential to me."

Symone faced her stepfather. "You're leaving, Paul. You have no reason to know my location. And I agree with the Touré policy to limit that information." She turned back to Mal. "Shall we go?"

Once Mal and Symone disappeared down the hall, Jerry held the door for Paul. "I'll ask Mal to drive you home. We'll meet you in the reception area. I need to get some things from my office."

He watched Paul stalk to the front of the suite before turning to his office a few steps from the conference room. He wound his way around the empty supply boxes and piles of old newspapers and magazines and supply catalogs. At his desk, Jerry shoved aside a few file folders and two dirty coffee mugs to get to his laptop. He powered down the machine and disconnected it from the surge protector before packing it into the laptop bag he'd found under his desk.

"Good grief! Is this your office?" The scandalized exclamation shattered Jerry's thoughts.

He looked up to find Symone swaying in his doorway. Her lips were parted in shock. Her eyes were wide and dashing around his office as though looking for a safe place to land.

Voices shrieked in horror in Symone's head. "How could anyone possibly work in this space?"

From Jerry's stunned expression, she realized she'd spoken that last part out loud.

"I'm in the process of packing up my office. I'm leaving the company." Jerry stopped speaking, as though he hadn't meant to confide so much to a client.

Symone stepped back in case gnats were congregating in that space. She was appalled, but she couldn't look away. The rest of the Touré Security Group's suite was impeccable, gleaming metal, polished wood, exquisite artwork. She hadn't expected to find a landfill in the center of a professional office. And what was that smell? She was going to have nightmares.

His response finally penetrated her shock. She tore her eyes away. "You're what? Why would you leave your family's company?"

Jerry jerked his laptop bag onto his shoulder. He circled his desk. Maneuvering the dark gray carpet like a minefield, he was careful to sidestep a stack of books. "We don't have time to discuss my future. We have to get you to the safe house."

Symone stepped aside, giving him room to join her in the hallway. "Are you going to be my bodyguard?" Did he hear the dread in her voice?

"That's right." Jerry stopped beside her, close enough for her to catch his clean-soap-and-peppermint scent. "Did Mal set you up with the burner tech?"

She nodded. "He said the stalker is probably tracking my movements through my devices."

"That's right." Jerry pinned her with his dark eyes. "So it's vital that you do *not* turn on any of your personal devices. Only use the burner cell and laptop Mal gave you. If you turn on your own equipment, the stalker will be able to track them again and we'll be right back where we started. You'll be in danger again—or worse. Do you understand?"

"Yes, I understand." Symone's eyes strayed back to his office. She tried to suppress a shiver. "It's just… I thought you were going to assign one of your contractors to the job?"

Jerry shook his head. "The assignment is dangerous and too complicated since it's both an investigation and protective detail." He shifted to face her. "So until the stalker is identified, we're stuck with each other."

Symone looked at Jerry's office again. *Oh, boy.*

Chapter 5

Symone's body had cried out for a nap by the time she and Jerry had entered their cabin in the wooded resort early Friday afternoon. This would be their temporary home until the police caught the stalker. But when Jerry had suggested lunch before giving her a tour of the cabin, her stomach had rumbled its approval. Either Jerry hadn't heard the noise, or he'd politely ignored it.

The safe house had stolen Symone's breath. It was a beautiful, two-story, dark-pine-and-red-cedar, post-and-beam log cabin. It stood in an idyllic spot at the back of a sprawling resort that one of Touré Security Group's clients owned. Symone had heard the pride in Jerry's voice when he'd informed her that TSG guards protected the resort's buildings and grounds. To the west and south, sturdy, old oak and evergreen trees sheltered the cabin from a distance. Symone wondered about the wildlife, fauna and hiking trails beyond the perimeter. A healthy, active river protected the cabin's eastern border. She imagined it would be a wonderful fishing spot. It seemed their cabin's closest neighbor was perhaps a mile or so north of them.

The cabin's great room was decorated in muted tones of warm tan, soft brown and moss green. An area rug in all three colors covered the pine flooring beneath the cedarwood coffee table. A stone fireplace was in front of the table. A matching overstuffed brown sofa and two chairs with ottomans were arranged around it. There was a dining area at the edge of the great room with a kitchenette beyond it. Both spaces picked up the colors from the great room.

The irony of the situation wasn't lost on Symone as she'd gazed around the cabin's warm, cozy interior when she'd first arrived. She was staying at a quiet, isolated cabin at an idyllic resort with the most attractive and exciting man she'd ever met. It would be so romantic—if someone wasn't trying to kill her.

Jerry was a surprisingly good cook. He'd made preparing their seared Cajun chicken, pasta and tossed salad lunch look easy. Symone could boil water for instant oatmeal and brew coffee, which explained her limited breakfast options. As she stared longingly at her now empty plate and salad bowl, she could still smell the sharp aromas of Cajun peppers and melted Parmesan cheese.

"I feel better now. Thank you." Symone drained the ice water from her glass and sighed. "I hate to sound like a broken record but truly, my compliments to the chef."

"I never get tired of hearing it." Jerry collected his dishes as he started to rise.

"No, please." She waved him back down. "You cooked. I'll clean. It's only fair." She stood, stacking his dishes and silverware on top of hers.

"You won't get an argument from me." His voice was thick with amusement.

Symone sensed him behind her. She set the dishes on the counter, raising her eyebrows as she looked from him to their clear acrylic glassware, which he set on the counter beside their place settings. "You won't argue. You'll just ignore me."

His grin was sheepish—and endearing. "I have a hard time sitting still."

Symone could believe it. Too bad he didn't expend that extra energy on keeping his office clean. She began packing the dishwasher. "Who do we have to thank for the groceries?"

"Zeke called the resort's manager to arrange to have the cabin opened and prepared for us with a week's worth of groceries and the rental car in the garage." He raised his voice over the sound of the running water as he scrubbed the pots and pans. His movements were confident and comfortable. Obviously, he wasn't opposed to washing dishes, just every other form of cleaning. Jeremiah Touré was a complex and complicated personality.

Symone wondered whether Zeke had made the call while Mal had taken her and Jerry to pack their bags before traveling on to the safe house. Jerry had accompanied her when she'd entered her mother and Paul's house to collect her two bags. She'd already packed her things since she's intended to move back to her place tomorrow. However, she'd been told to wait in the car with Mal while Jerry had packed his suitcase. Were those instructions for her security—or because Jerry hadn't wanted her to see the condition of his home? Would every room have been like his office? Her mind recoiled at the thought.

Jerry dried the last pan and stored it in one of the cupboards beside the oven. "Are you ready for the tour?" He waited for her nod before circling her to lead her from the kitchen. His scent, soap and peppermint, trailed after him. "You've seen this floor—great room, dining area, kitchenette. Let's go upstairs."

He swept up her two large suitcases, one in each hand,

as though they were beach towels. He held them as easily as he'd held the acrylic glass during their late lunch.

"I'll get the other bags later." His back muscles flexed beneath his amethyst shirt. Symone's eyebrows rose. Her fingertips tingled as though she'd felt the movement. She blinked, trying to break free of the sensation.

"Are you coming?" Jerry's question startled her.

Symone looked up to find him standing several steps up the staircase. He gave her a puzzled look. She blinked, then started toward him. "I'm sorry." She grabbed her laptop case, which held the computer Mal had given her.

His midnight eyes narrowed as they moved over her features. "This cabin is designed and reinforced as a panic room." Once again, in his voice, she heard the pride he felt for his family's company. She could relate. She felt the same way about her family's foundation. "There are security cameras on the cabin's perimeter and up in a few of the trees closest to the property."

"I noticed the camera above the door when we came in." She looked over her shoulder toward the entrance. "But what about the windows? Shouldn't the curtains be drawn?"

"There's a tint screen on every window in the safe house. We can see out in case someone approaches the cabin, but no one can see in." His words drew her attention back to him. "We'll be safe here—as long as you follow Mal's instructions. They're meant for your security. Don't use your personal cell phone or laptop. If you absolutely have to, you can turn them on very briefly, but don't leave either of them on for more than two minutes."

Symone paused on the step beneath his. "No electronics."

"There's a good chance whoever's stalking you is tracking you through your devices." He held her eyes. "If you leave any of your devices on for more than two minutes, they'll be able to track your signal to the cabin, which would defeat the purpose for being here."

"I understand." Her words came out on a breath as she felt the weight of his words.

Jerry held her eyes a beat longer as though reassuring himself that she did indeed understand how critical it was for her to follow those instructions. He turned to lead her up the rest of the stairs.

There were four rooms on the second floor. Jerry nodded toward the room to his right. "This is the office. All of our security systems are managed from the computers in that room. I'll go over it with you later. The narrow door beside it is the linen closet. Just a few bed sets and towels."

"Thank goodness." Symone's interjection was spontaneous. "I didn't bring any to my mother's house. I used hers."

He tossed her a crooked smile that trapped her breath in her throat. "We've got you covered." He took a few steps to the next door. "This will be my room. It's closest to the stairs."

Symone peeked in. "It's very nice."

The room wasn't very big but it seemed so comfortable. A patterned coverlet in moss green and soft brown covered the queen-size bed. It matched the area rugs that surrounded it. An ornate cedar carving of a landscape had been placed on the snow white wall behind the bed above the headboard. The bed frame, nightstand and dressing table were made of the same wood.

Jerry led her the few steps to the room next door. "This will be your room." He left her suitcases at the foot of the bed.

Symone entered the room, setting her laptop case with them. "It's also very nice. Thank you."

The room was almost identical to the one Jerry would be using. The patterned coverlet on the queen-size bed was warm tan and moss green as were the area rugs around it. The intricate cedar carving above this headboard depicted maple leaves. They seemed to be floating on an autumn breeze.

"I'm glad you like it." Jerry nodded behind him. "We'll be sharing the bathroom next door."

Alarm bells rang in Symone's head. She had a flashback of Jerry's office. There was no justification for that disaster. Would knowing he was *sharing* the bathroom with another being make him any neater?

Oh, boy.

She took a calming breath, detecting the slight scent of cedar in the room. "What are your plans for finding the person behind the threats?"

"Plans?" Jerry braced his shoulder against the threshold and crossed his arms over his broad chest. "I don't have a plan. Plans fall apart. I prefer to follow my instincts."

She blinked. "Oh." *Boy.*

Symone turned from him, pressing her hand against her chest. Her heart hammered against her palm. He didn't have a plan? How could he *not* have a plan? Wasn't it his *job* to have a plan? *She* was a planner. She had plans and schedules for every aspect of her life stretching months into the future. Plans brought her comfort. How could she face mortal danger with someone who flew by the seat of his pants?

Symone pulled the brakes on her runaway thoughts. She drew a deep breath of the cedar-scented air and reminded herself that Jerry had kept Dr. Grace Blackwell's grandmother safe in a similar—although not the same—situation.

"Why would someone want to kill you, Symone?" Jerry's question was muffled beneath the sound of the blood rushing in her head.

Symone forced herself to relax by degrees. She turned to him. "I have no idea. I hadn't even realized I had enemies."

Jerry crossed the threshold into the room. He leaned against the wall beside the door, slipping his hands into the front pockets of his black slacks. "Has anyone new come into your life? I mean, work-wise or in general." His words stopped abruptly.

"The past year?" Symone wandered to the dressing table. A simple rectangular mirror in a cedar frame balanced on top of it. "We brought on two new board members. And Ellie. But if you're implying any of those people would be behind these attempts on Paul's and my lives, you're wrong. It couldn't be them."

"Why not?"

She glanced at him over her shoulder. "We have a very reliable vendor who does background checks on all of our employees and board members."

"How many board members are there?" Jerry asked.

"Seven." Symone changed direction and wandered to the bed across the room. She trailed her fingertips over the coverlet. The cotton material was soft. "They sit for three-year terms that can be renewed. Two of our members chose not to renew this time around, but they'd already served several terms."

"The foundation does important work. I can understand their staying for multiple terms." He ran his hand over his hair. "What's changed in your life this past year—in addition to your mother's death? I'm truly sorry for your loss." His voice was thick with sympathy.

For the first time, she didn't feel as though she was experiencing her mother's death on her own. Paul had loved her mother. Symone was confident of that. But he didn't share his grief or even show it, at least not around her. The sense of isolation made losing her mother so much more painful. But the look in Jerry's eyes made her feel like she wasn't alone.

"Thank you." Her voice was husky even to her own ears. She cleared her throat as she collected her thoughts. "The only thing that stands out, of course, is the board's ultimatum. They've given me just over two weeks to develop a proposal for a more aggressive investment strategy both for the foundation's funds and the projects we support."

Jerry straightened from the wall. "What happens if the board doesn't approve your proposal?"

Symone shook her head. "They'll hold a no-confidence vote the last Monday of July. If I don't receive the support of a simple majority of the board, they'll schedule another meeting to elect a new chair."

"Really." His eyes were on her, but Symone sensed he was picturing someone or something else. "Your board would replace you. And I take it you replaced your mother."

Symone felt ice drop into her chest. Her lips were numb. "What are you saying?"

This time, his midnight eyes were laser focused on her. "It's too early to say anything. We don't have all the information. But I think it's curious that you became chair after your mother's death and now the board is trying to replace you."

"You think someone killed my mother to take over the foundation and now that same person's targeting me? That's ridiculous." Wasn't it?

Jerry began shaking his head even before she finished speaking. "It's too early to speculate. Mal's going to ask

Grace to test your mother's prescription. That should tell us whether someone tampered with her medication."

Jerry appeared to think his words would comfort her. They didn't.

Symone's skin burned as anger simmered in her blood. Had someone murdered her mother? She couldn't believe it. She didn't want to consider it. But if it was true, she swore to herself she'd bring the killer to justice—no matter what it took.

"Who would most benefit if you were to step down as chair of your foundation?" Celeste's image was projected through the laptop monitor Jerry and Symone were sharing.

Jerry felt Symone's tension as he sat beside her at the safe house's dinette table late Friday afternoon. They were on a videoconference with Zeke, Mal and Celeste. Zeke and Mal appeared in one screen as they joined from Touré Security Group's conference room. Celeste seemed to be at her desk at Jarrett & Nichols Investigations.

Hours earlier, Paul had declined their invitation to join the meeting. He'd insisted he didn't want anything to do with the investigation. The blood had drained from Symone's face when they'd read his reply. She looked as though she'd been slapped. Jerry had wanted to wrap her in his arms and assure her they'd figure this out together. Before he could speak, Symone had launched from her chair and muttered an excuse before marching from the room.

"I'm concerned about the investigation's focus on the foundation." Symone crossed her right leg over her left. She sat straight on her chair and linked her fingers over her right thigh. "I agree there's a compelling argument for it, but Paul's belief that these threats could be connected to his lawsuits deserves consideration."

Zeke's attention shifted from Jerry to Symone. "We'll look at both scenarios. Let's start with the foundation."

Jerry nodded his silent agreement. "So, to Celeste's question, who'd benefit the most if you were removed as foundation chair?"

Irritation simmered in Symone's brown eyes. "Members of the board and administration. They're eligible to be elected chair."

"People in administration?" Jerry remembered something he'd read on the foundation's website. "Paul's in administration."

"That's right." Symone nodded. "He's vice chair. As our administrative assistant, Ellie's also eligible."

Jerry shook his head. Things weren't looking good for Paul. "We need to look into both of them and your board members."

"You consider Paul a suspect?" Symone's eyes widened with disbelief. "The threats were directed at him."

Jerry searched her eyes, trying to read her mind. "You still think those threats were meant for Paul?" Was she serious? "If that's true, why didn't he agree to let us protect him? Why isn't he with us now, helping to find the person responsible for them? *Your* car was bombed, not his."

Symone crossed her arms. "My mother loved Paul very much. They'd been together for years. I can't imagine him having anything to do with these threats, especially since they put *him* in danger."

Mal's voice shattered the tense silence. "Symone, let's clear Paul's name and remove any suspicions that he could be involved."

Jerry was impressed—and relieved. Trust Mal to find a diplomatic solution for the conflict. He'd been diffusing tensions between him and Zeke for decades. But Symone seemed to need more convincing.

Her eyes stabbed him. "Am *I* going on your suspect list?"

"It's *our* list." Jerry watched the sparks flicker in her eyes behind her glasses. Mesmerizing. "And we might've added you if *Paul's* car had been bombed instead of yours."

Symone's frown deepened. "Ellie's been with the foundation for almost a year, working closely with me, my mother and Paul. We would've sensed if she was plotting something."

"Not necessarily." In some ways, the case Jerry, his brothers and Grace had just solved was similar to this one. "Sometimes people show you what you want to see."

"And you think I'd be foolish enough to fall for it?" Symone looked from Jerry to the images of Zeke, Mal and Celeste on the laptop.

Jerry shrugged. "Sometimes we see what we want to see."

Symone's full lips thinned. "There's one problem with your premise. Our foundation works with an agency to do background checks on all our applicants before we hire them or appoint them to our board. Remember?"

"That agency isn't TSG." Jerry took pride in his family's business and the quality of the services they offered: personal, corporate and computer security. The thought of walking away from his parents' legacy hurt him. He drew a breath to ease the pain, drawing in Symone's soap-and-wildflowers scent.

Symone adjusted her glasses. "None of our board members would want to hurt Paul or me. Most of them have been with us for years."

Celeste interrupted. "Symone, you just said *most* of your

board members have been with you for years. We should start with the newest ones. Who are they?"

Symone drew a deep breath, which lifted her shoulders. The action seemed to relieve some of her tension. "We have two. Xander Fence. The board member he replaced recommended him." She narrowed her eyes as though searching her memory. "He's been with us about three months." She turned those chocolate eyes back to Jerry. "You met him after we toured the foundation's offices."

"I remember." Jerry brought to mind an image of the man who'd interrupted them. "Why didn't you introduce us? He seemed curious about me or maybe about my presence with you."

"Did he?" Symone's tone was noncommittal.

Jerry's eyes narrowed. What was she hiding? "Is he interested in you?"

"Of course not." Her voice was abrupt as though his question had surprised her.

Her reaction made him even more suspicious. Surely, she knew she was an attractive woman. It went deeper than her looks, which were distracting enough. She was compassionate, taking decisive action to protect her stepfather when she believed he was being threatened. She was courageous, fighting for her family's legacy even though it could be the reason her life was in danger. And she was intelligent, although her courage and compassion were blinding her to the facts and doubts about the case and the people involved.

He tried another educated guess. "Do you trust him?"

Her hesitation was telling. "I don't have a reason not to trust him. Our screening agency vetted him and the longtime board member he replaced recommended him."

Jerry chuckled. "That's not an answer."

Mal interrupted, putting their discussion back on track. "Who's the other new member?"

Symone slid Jerry a disgruntled look beneath her winged dark brown eyebrows. "Wesley Bragg. Paul's known him for years. He's a lawyer with his own practice. He's representing Paul in his lawsuits against my mother's doctor and the pharmaceutical company that manufactures her medication."

Celeste pointed her pen toward her laptop monitor. "If Paul's somehow involved in this, they could be working together. We should prioritize background checks into Bragg, Fence and Kayple."

Jerry liked the way Celeste's mind worked. Based on the glint of admiration that sparked in Zeke's eyes, his older brother was a fan, too.

Symone's frown deepened. "I'll have the agency send you their background reports on the board, Paul and Ellie."

"That's fine." Mal nodded. "I'd like to see them, but we'll also do our own investigations. Your life's in danger. I'm not going to depend on someone else's work to identify the person behind the threats."

"Very well." Symone touched the sides of her glasses. "And you'll follow up with Paul and Wesley regarding a connection between these threats and their lawsuits?"

"Of course." Zeke leaned into the glass-and-sterling-silver conference table, bringing him closer to the computer's camera.

Symone turned her attention from the laptop back to Jerry. "If you don't need anything more from me, I'm going to my room to get some foundation work done."

"Thank you, Symone." Mal was distracted as though he'd already started on the background checks of their suspects.

"Have a good evening." Celeste tossed out the cheery farewell.

"Thank you for your time, Symone," Zeke said. "We'll be in touch."

Jerry followed her movements. He didn't need to be psychic to know she was ticked off. "I'll see you later."

"Hmm." She didn't look back as she strode from the dining area and mounted the stairs.

Celeste lowered her voice. "She's not happy that we're questioning her judgment."

Jerry frowned. "That's not what we're doing. We're questioning the character of the people on her foundation."

"And who hired those people?" Celeste's laughter was warm and friendly. "Exactly. Good luck with that. In the meantime, let's divvy up the list. The background checks will go faster."

Mal interrupted. "First, Jerry, put on your earbuds."

Curious, Jerry pulled his earbuds from his laptop case. He plugged them into his computer, then placed them into his ears. "What's going on?"

Mal expelled a tense breath. "I didn't want to deliver this news while Symone was with us. I just got an email from Grace. She's completed the tests on Odette Bishop's medication. Your instincts were right. The pills had been tampered with."

"Oh, no." Celeste gasped.

Zeke rubbed his left hand across his eyes. "I'm so sorry."

Ice filled Jerry's chest. Even though he'd thought something could be off with Odette's medicine, he didn't want to believe she'd been murdered. He looked at his brothers and saw the same pain in their expressions that he was feeling inside. He knew what they were thinking without having to ask. He had the same thoughts. A parent's death was hard enough. Learning someone had taken your parent from you before their time would be a crushing pain from which you may never recover.

Jerry struggled to clear his thoughts. "Is she sure?"

Mal nodded. The movement was jerky. "She tested it three times. Odette's pills were tainted with tetrahydrozoline. When it's ingested, tetrahydrozoline can cause heart failure."

Zeke briefly closed his eyes. "And Symone's mother already had a heart condition."

Celeste spread her arms. "How many people knew she was taking medication and who had access to her pills?"

"Paul." The name burst from Jerry's lips before he realized he was going to say it. "But there are probably others. I'll ask Symone."

Crap. He wasn't looking forward to that conversation.

Mal's eyes searched his features as though trying to read his mind. "Are you comfortable doing that? Do you want me to ask Grace to call her? She could explain her testing process to Symone."

Jerry shook his head. "I'm supposed to be watching over her." He glanced toward the staircase in the great room. "I'm her primary contact for this case. I should break the news to her. If she wants more details, she can call Grace. And she'll probably want to speak with Paul."

He wrapped up the videoconference with the rest of the team, then started toward the stairs. Every step felt heavy as though he was moving against resistance bands. Symone had been through so much already today, this year. She'd buried her mother and barely had time to grieve before someone began threatening her and her stepfather. This morning, her car had been bombed. This afternoon, she'd had to pack up and move into a safe house with someone she'd just met. She'd learned her employees and board were suspected of threatening her life.

But this news was the worst of all. He really wasn't looking forward to being the bearer of it.

Chapter 6

"My mother was murdered?" Symone didn't understand what those words meant. It felt as though she was struggling to translate a foreign language. "That's impossible. You must be mistaken."

Jerry stood just inside Symone's bedroom in the safe house Friday evening. He'd announced his arrival minutes ago with a tentative knock on her half-opened door. That was her first indication the confident, rash personal security expert was out of his comfort zone. The pain in his deep voice, tension in his midnight eyes and strain on his chiseled features were subsequent clues. He'd asked her to sit down. She was glad she had—otherwise, he'd be picking her up from the floor.

"There's no mistake." His voice was gentle, comforting. "Grace ran her tests three times."

Symone still couldn't wrap her mind around what he was saying. She wasn't getting the translation right. "Who would want to hurt my mother? Who would want her dead?" She wanted to rise from the bed to pace the room, but she wasn't confident her legs would hold her.

Jerry stepped closer. "That's what we'll need your help to find out."

Symone began to shake. *Someone had killed my mother!*

The thought screamed across her brain. Her bewilderment cleared. Her numbness thawed. Heat flooded her cheeks as rage filled her body.

Symone surged to her feet. She marched across the room to the dressing table. Her body felt stiff, brittle. "Someone plotted to kill my mother—and they succeeded. Right under my nose. I want to know who, how, when and why. They're *not* getting away with this." She clenched her fists, fighting the urge to throw back her head and scream.

"No, they won't." Behind her, Jerry's tone was hard with determination.

Symone turned to pace to the opposite wall. She pushed her words through clenched teeth. "What did Grace say? Tell me everything."

"I didn't speak with Grace." Jerry's voice came from closer inside the room. "Mal told me. He said Grace had tested the pills in the container three times. Each time, the results were the same. The pills in your mother's prescription bottle were tainted with tetrahydrozoline. We could call Grace now and ask her to walk us through her tests."

A moan escaped Symone's lips. She pressed her fist against her mouth to trap the others inside. Her eyes stung from the salt of unshed tears. She stumbled to the nightstand and pulled several tissues from the box she found there. Confusion had morphed into rage, which was shifting into soul-crushing sorrow. As her knees began to buckle, firm hands caught her elbows and held her upright.

"Why?" Her voice was muffled as she pressed the tissues against her face. "Why would someone kill my mother? Why would they take her from me?"

"I don't know, sweetheart." Jerry turned her into his arms, pressing her cheek against his chest. His voice and his heartbeat echoed in her ear.

"She's never, ever hurt anyone. She's only helped people with the foundation and the groups she volunteered with."

"I understand." Jerry's words were low.

"When they killed my mother, they took everything from me." Her voice was raw. Her tears streamed in earnest now. "My mother. My business partner. My best friend. They took everything from me and left me alone. Why? Why did they do it? They took everything."

Jerry was undone. Symone's sobs, raw with agony, ripped his heart out. He couldn't bear to see anyone in pain, physically, mentally or emotionally. Her words tore him apart. They described how he'd felt when his mother had died, as though he'd lost everything. He still had his brothers, but no one could replace his mother. Symone literally didn't have anyone, not even Paul. Her stepfather had basically disappeared from her life at the third sign of danger.

His protective instincts engaged. He tightened his arms around her. She felt fragile in his embrace. Her slight frame was battered by powerful emotions. She was so different from the woman who'd sat beside him during the video-conference. There were times he'd suspected that, if she weren't determined to maintain her decorum, she would've punched him.

Her voice grew more and more strained. She seemed lost in her misery, oblivious to their surroundings or even his presence. Through her tears, Jerry caught broken phrases, expressing her thoughts and emotions.

"It hurts…"

"They took her…"

"Why…?"

The ache he felt for what she was going through boiled his blood from equal parts anger and anguish. Jerry lifted

Symone into his arms. Two steps carried them to her bed. He laid her gently on the mattress. Taking off his shoes, he stretched out beside her. Her sobs were softer now, but still shook her slender body. Slipping his right arm beneath her, he drew Symone against him. Her head rested on his chest. After a few moments, her sobs quieted. Jerry sensed Symone slowly drifting off to sleep. As he lay beside her, he stared at the bedroom ceiling and imagined all the ways he'd like to inflict pain on the person who'd broken her heart.

Symone shifted as she slowly surfaced from sleep. The muscled arm around her waist tightened as though in reflex, bringing her closer to the hard, warm body beside her. She gasped and the scents of clean soap and fresh mint filled her head. The unfamiliar arm relaxed and dropped to the mattress. Symone pushed herself free of the broad, hard torso. She tipped her head back and looked up. Jerry smiled sleepily from the pillow beside hers.

What the...?

Her eyes dived to her white blouse—which wasn't as crisp as it had been when she'd dressed this morning—pencil-slim, knee-length gray skirt, and gray pumps.

She pinned Jerry with a suspicious glare. "What's happened?"

He arched an eyebrow. "What are you implying, Ms. Bishop? We're both completely dressed. Well, I took my shoes off."

Her face burned with embarrassment. "How did we end up in bed together?"

"You were upset." His voice was low. "I wanted to comfort you."

The memory of unbearable pain and suffocating grief

flooded back to her. Symone took a moment to catch her breath. Her eyes stung with tears at the kindness of this stranger. She blinked them back. When her mother had died, there wasn't anyone to hold her. Today, after learning her mother had been murdered, he hadn't let her go.

"Thank you." Her voice was thick.

"You're welcome." Jerry pulled his arm out from under her. He abruptly sat up, swinging his long legs over the side of the bed. He turned to face her. "My job is to keep you safe. To do that, I need you to trust me. I know that's asking a lot. We met for the first time less than ten hours ago, yet we're going to be alone in an isolated cabin for I don't know how many days. I'm going to use that time to earn your trust, which means I'm not going to take advantage of you. You have my word. Your safety depends on that. My family's reputation depends on that. Do you have any questions for me?"

Symone searched his wide, midnight eyes beneath his thick black eyebrows. He was so earnest as he waited for her response, as though her answer was vitally important to him. Her muscles relaxed. She hadn't realized how knotted they'd been. Her eyes moved over his sharp sienna features. She could trust him.

She didn't have any doubts about his capabilities or experience. When her car had exploded, he'd shielded her with his body. He'd gotten her and Ellie to safety before she'd taken her next breath. He'd directed Ellie to reassure her staff that everyone was safe, and the authorities had been contacted before she'd collected her thoughts. He'd called the detectives and updated his brothers. Yes, Jerry may be a reckless slob with no regard for a well-developed plan, but Symone was confident he could keep her safe.

She shook her head. "I don't have any questions for you right now, but I'll let you know if anything comes to me."

Jerry gave a decisive nod as he straightened his clothes. "That's fair. In the meantime, I'll get started on dinner."

Symone chided herself for watching him tuck his shirt into his waistband. She climbed out of the bed on the other side and dragged her eyes up to his. "But you cooked lunch. It's not fair to you that you do all the cooking."

"You're welcome to cook if you'd like." He bent to collect his shoes.

"I'm afraid I'm not much of a cook." Understatement. "Perhaps we could order something? My treat."

"We can't risk having strangers come to the safe house." Jerry's crooked smile made her toes curl in her pumps. He crossed to the door. "I don't mind cooking. I'll make chicken and salad."

Symone locked her knees as she watched his loose-limbed stride. "Sounds wonderful. Thank you. I'll be down in a moment to set the table."

He tossed a smile over his shoulder. "You've got a deal."

Symone watched Jerry disappear beyond the door. She exhaled as she allowed herself to drop onto the bed, letting her torso fall back onto the mattress. Closing her eyes, Symone let her mind return to the moment she'd awakened beside Jerry. Her body hummed. A sigh rose from her chest and escaped through her parted lips.

He'd given her his word he wouldn't take advantage of her. She believed him. She didn't want to be taken advantage of. But she wouldn't mind waking up in his arms again.

"That was a wonderful meal, Jerry. Thank you." Symone looked at the remains of her blackened chicken breast and salad Friday evening. She rose from her chair at the dinette table and added his plate and silverware to hers. "This time, relax while I clean up." She crossed into the bright tan and warm brown kitchenette.

"I'm fine lending a hand." Jerry's voice came from close behind her.

Symone swallowed a sigh. The scents of peppers lingered in the kitchen. "Well, I can't force you to sit still."

"You wouldn't be the first one to try, though." He watched her rinse the dishes before packing them into the dishwasher. "You don't have to prewash the dishes."

Symone shrugged. "I don't mind."

"All right." The laughter drained from his voice. He set their glasses in the sink and spoke gently. "Symone, about your mother's prescription. The fact someone tampered with it strengthens the argument that the foundation is the motive behind the threats against you. I believe someone killed your mother to get one step closer to the foundation's accounts. Now the killer's targeting you for the same reason."

"I know." Symone kept her attention on the dishwasher as though it was the only safe port in the storm.

"Tell me about your mother." He collected the pan from the stovetop and brought it to the sink.

Symone nudged him away from the counter and took his place. As she scrubbed the pan, she brought her mother to mind. "My mother's … She was a good person, and that's not a biased daughter's opinion. *Everyone* said as much. She was brilliant. Great with facts and numbers. And she had a strong personality, which was fortunate. My father was larger than life." Her lips curved with amusement at the memory. "If she'd been an introvert, he would've overshadowed her. Since they were both extroverts, they were a perfect match."

Jerry chuckled. The sound was as warm as a seductive summer evening. "Your mother and mine would've been friends."

"Your mother was an extrovert also?"

"Yes, she was. But Paul seems like an introvert." Jerry made the words a statement rather than a question. "How did they meet?"

Symone rinsed the pan. "Paul was a senior partner with Docent, Kayple and Sarchie Accounting. It's the firm that certifies the foundation's accounts. He retired in 2019. He and Mom started dating in 2020, three years after Dad died. He started proposing about seven months later. Mom said yes in 2023." She turned off the water and rested the pan on the drain board.

Jerry reached for the dish towel on the peg beside the sink and started drying the pan. "The killer would've had to have known about your mother's medication. That narrows our list of suspects. Besides you and Paul, who else knew about your mother's heart condition?"

Symone ignored that Jerry was drying the pan. Another example of his inability to sit still. She couldn't fault him. "My mother was a very private person. She wouldn't have told anyone else, not even close friends."

"Paul may have told Wesley Bragg. We have to consider that." Jerry squatted to put the pan in one of the bottom cupboards. His pants tightened across his thighs.

Symone jerked her eyes away. She wouldn't argue with Jerry about their suspect list any longer. Someone had killed her mother. As far as Symone was concerned, they could interview everyone her mother had ever known.

"We should probably also consider Ellie." She wandered

out of the kitchenette as her mind raced ahead with memories of her mother working with Ellie. "She'd been my mother's administrative assistant before she became mine. My mother wouldn't have told her about her prescription. I'll never believe that. But Ellie may have overheard her talking with her pharmacy or her physician."

Jerry hummed thoughtfully behind her. The sound sent shivers down her spine. "Would Ellie have mentioned it to someone?"

Symone stopped beside the dinette table and turned to him. "This morning, I would've said no, definitely not. But now, I don't know who to trust, or if I can trust anyone. The person who tampered with my mother's prescription would have to have been able to get close to her. My mother knew a lot of people but only a few of us would've been able to get that close—me, Paul and perhaps Ellie."

Jerry hummed again. He paced the great room as he ran his hand over his dark curls. His hair was styled in a low fade. "I believe the stalker and the killer are the same person."

"I agree."

Jerry nodded a silent acknowledgment of Symone's interruption. "The stalker was tracking you. That explains how they knew when you were home and which restaurant you'd gone to. Maybe they'd also bugged your mother's phone. That could've been how they'd known about her medication and when she'd picked up her last prescription."

"Perhaps." Symone shivered.

She was chilled to the bone. She wrapped her arms around her waist, hoping to warm herself. She was in the middle of a waking nightmare. The situation was so much worse than she'd imagined when she'd first contacted the Touré Security Group.

Jerry looked her over. His brow furrowed with concern. "Would you like some tea?" He started toward the kitchenette. "It'll make you feel better."

Symone held up her hand to stop him. "Thank you, but I can make it. I admit I can't cook, but I can boil water. Would you like some?"

"Yeah. Thanks." Jerry trailed her into the kitchenette. "I'll ask Mal to prioritize Paul, Wesley, Ellie and Xander."

"Why Xander?" Symone filled the kettle from the kitchenette's faucet. "He's new to the board and barely knew my mother." She crossed to the stove and set the water to boil.

"I can't explain it." Jerry opened one cupboard and picked out two tea bags. "There's something about him that makes me suspicious. He seemed a little too interested in my presence at the foundation."

Symone frowned at him over her shoulder. "Is this another example of you following your instincts?"

Jerry opened another cupboard for the mugs. "Yeah, you could say that."

Symone searched the nearby drawers for teaspoons. She could only hope his instincts didn't slow down their investigation. The cabin was comfortable, and their surroundings were lovely, but the homicidal stalker was an unwelcomed distraction. They needed to solve this case and secure the foundation as quickly as possible. Symone took a calming breath.

The heat from the burner beneath the kettle warmed her. "I want to be there when you question the suspects."

Jerry placed the tea bags into the two mugs. "No."

Symone blinked. His blunt refusal surprised her. "Why not?"

Jerry gave her a dubious look beneath a thick dark eyebrow. "Your mother was murdered. Someone's stalking you. A bomb was planted on your car. You'll be safer here."

Symone watched him measure honey into the mugs. "You're going to be there, interviewing the suspects. You can keep me safe."

The kettle whistled. She turned off the burner and took the mugs from Jerry.

"Yes, I could." Jerry leaned against the counter and watched her fill each mug with the hot water. "But that would defeat the purpose of what we're doing here. Why go to the trouble of settling you into a safe house for your protection only to turn around and put you in front of the people who are trying to kill you?"

Jerry had a valid point, but Symone had a compelling argument.

She handed Jerry his tea, then held his eyes. "I want a bigger role in this investigation, Jerry. Someone killed my mother. They took her from me way too soon." She blinked to ease the sting of tears in her eyes. "I'm not hiding in this cabin while you confront the suspects. I want to look them in the eye when they try to explain why they couldn't be the killer."

Jerry returned her steady stare for several silent moments. Finally, he spoke. "The answer's still no, but I'm willing to compromise. I'll record the interviews and you can listen to them in their entirety when I get back." The rigid set of his jaw was a nonverbal invitation to "take it or leave it."

"That's not good enough, Jerry. I think you can do better."

"Your safety is my priority, Symone."

She liked the way he said her name. "My priority is finding my mother's killer."

Jerry's eyes shifted from her to scan the room as though he was considering locking her in it. Could he really do that?

He sighed. "Let's be clear, *I* have the final say in this mission."

Symone arched an eyebrow. She'd let that pass—for now. But make no mistake. At the end of this impasse, one of them would be disappointed—and it would not be her.

Chapter 7

"Don't come any closer." Jerry extended his right arm, palm outward. "I probably smell pretty ripe."

He was dripping sweat as he stood behind the black vinyl, freestanding, heavy punching bag in the middle of the safe house's basement early Saturday morning. He wasn't wrong. In fact, the entire space was swollen with the sharp, salty smell of perspiration. Jerry wore a wet, smoke gray wicking T-shirt, black knee-length biker shorts, white ankle-length socks, black-and-white running shoes and silver boxing gloves. A small rotating fan helped alleviate some of the scent.

Symone had caught a whiff of the odor and heard the faint rhythmic snaps of his workout as soon as she'd opened the basement door. Curiosity had pushed her down the staircase. She wanted to know what he was doing and to see what was causing the noise. She'd only caught a few of his moves before he spied her standing on the second-to-last step.

"You really do." Shallow breaths. She softened the criticism with a smile. "How long have you been down here?" Her eyes moved over the old-fashioned weight bench, yoga mats and treadmill.

"What time is it?" Jerry used his right forearm to wipe the sweat from his brow.

Symone checked the burner cell in her right hand. "A couple of minutes before six."

"About an hour." His T-shirt had molded itself to his chest.

Symone pinched off the growing feeling of envy. "And I thought my workouts were hard." She nodded toward the heavy bag. "Perhaps you could show me a few self-defense moves while we're here? If nothing else, this experience has taught me that I have to learn how to protect myself."

"That's a good idea." Jerry removed his gloves. "Once I get cleaned up, I'll show you a few maneuvers that will help you get free in case someone tries to grab you."

"Why not show me now?" Symone stepped forward. She spread her arms, drawing attention to her outfit. "I'm dressed for it."

Jerry's eyes moved over her heather cropped yoga tank and matching midthigh shorts. Her feet were covered by white ankle-length athletic socks. His attention was like a physical caress moving over her.

Symone sensed a shift in the atmosphere, like time had stopped. Jerry's body was unusually still as though he was frozen in place. Tension leaped from him and wrapped itself around her. His eyes slowly lifted to her face. They were dark and intense. Symone reminded herself to breathe.

Jerry took a large step back and turned away from her. He set his gloves on the table in front of him. "How well can you see without your glasses?"

How anticlimactic.

Symone touched the thin black rims of her glasses. "Well enough."

Nodding, Jerry squared his shoulders and faced her again. "Maybe you should remove them. I don't want to risk knocking them off during our practice."

Symone removed her glasses and set them and her cell on one of the shelves on the other side of the room. Her vision wasn't as sharp as it was with her glasses, but they were meant mainly for reading and driving.

She turned back to Jerry—and froze. He stood about three feet from her. But his body was so still as he met her eyes. Was he planning a surprise? She wasn't ready.

Symone backpedaled. She raised her arms, palms out. "Shouldn't you demonstrate the defensive technique first?"

Jerry frowned, shaking his head. "What?"

Symone exhaled and dropped her arms. She pressed her right hand to her stuttering heart. "Oh. I thought you were going to come at me. That your teaching technique was going to be a full immersive experience."

"No." He gave her his sexy, crooked grin. "I prefer baby steps."

A relieved smile parted her lips and lifted her cheeks. Symone closed the gap between them. "Have you given other clients self-defense lessons?"

"A few." Jerry turned her around so her back was to him. "Now the key is remembering not to hurt the trainer."

Symone's chuckle sounded nervous to her ears. "Promise."

"I'm going to pretend to abduct you." Jerry's large hands rested lightly on her mostly bare shoulders. "Imagine you were working late at the office. You've finally wrapped up for the day. You're leaving the building, which doesn't have any security guards. You're walking to the parking lot, which doesn't have any security cameras—"

"All right. All right." Her laughter was much more relaxed. "I'll email the management company about providing security for the building."

Jerry squeezed her shoulders and her heart leaped into her throat.

Focus! Focus!

"Don't forget to use the laptop Mal gave you. Secure channels only." His voice was muffled under the sound of her racing pulse.

Symone nodded. "I promise." Did he notice she sounded breathless?

He squeezed her shoulders before releasing her. Symone smothered a groan of disappointment.

"You're walking to your car." Jerry started over. "Abductor comes up behind you. Grabs you around the waist to restrain you. Presses a hand over your mouth to keep you quiet. Are you ready?"

"No, but we can get started." Symone stepped forward.

Jerry came up behind her. He wrapped his right arm around her waist, pulling her back against his torso, then positioned his palm over her mouth. Even knowing what Jerry was about to do, Symone experienced a jolt of fear. It made her catch her breath and stiffen her spine. Then she remembered she was with Jerry. He would keep her safe. She relaxed back against him. His body was still warm and damp from his workout. Her skin tingled with excitement.

"Your turn. Grab me the same way I held you." Jerry released her, then turned, waiting for Symone to get into position. She'd placed one arm around his waist and covered his mouth with her hand. He removed her hand before continuing. "I'll pretend to be you. First, drive your elbow back into the abductor's solar plexus as hard as you can." He moved in slow motion to demonstrate. He tapped his elbow into the spot between the bottom of her chest and the top of her stomach. "This'll knock the wind out of them. While they're gasping for air, quickly crush their instep with your heel. The pain will cause the abductor to bend forward." Again, he mimicked the action, gently stepping on her sock-clad foot. "Next, jab your elbow this time into their face, aiming for their nose. Along with the eyes, this is the most vulnerable part of a person's face." He demonstrated the move in slow motion, stopping before he made contact with Symone's nose. "And finally, punch the abductor in the groin." Jerry didn't reenact that move. "Then run like hell."

Symone released Jerry and stepped back. Her eyebrows knitted. Her smile was uncertain. "Solar plexus? Instep? Nose? Groin? S-I-N-G. Sing. Like in the movie *Miss Congeniality* with Sandra Bullock and Benjamin Bratt?"

Jerry grinned over his shoulder. "It's a real self-defense technique." He turned to face her. "Now you try it. But remember, don't hurt the trainer."

"Promise." She tossed him a smile, then turned her back to him and waited for his arm to pull her back against him. She took a moment—just a moment—to enjoy the feeling. Then she sprang into action, pulling her punches. "Solar plexus." Jerry pretended to react, leaning forward and loosening his hold on her. "Instep." Jerry responded by releasing her. "Nose." She had to stretch for that move since Jerry was at least five inches taller than her. "Groin. SING." She spun to him on her toes. Her smile was wide and triumphant.

"Good job." He grinned his approval. "Keep practicing those moves. You could use the heavy bag. Remember, force and speed are important."

"Thank you." It was amazing how much learning those few moves boosted her confidence.

"My pleasure." He glanced at his black watch. "I should

leave so you can get your workout in before our video-conference."

The thought of the upcoming meeting to discuss their suspects' backgrounds pressed a heavy weight back onto her shoulders. "I realize we have to interview everyone who could've been involved in my mother's murder, but I just can't believe Paul could be the killer."

Jerry searched her features as though looking for clues. "How's your relationship with him?"

Symone's shrug was restless. She hesitated to speak ill of her mother's widower. "I got along with him because my mother married him, but I think you can tell we aren't close."

"I'm sorry." Jerry didn't pretend not to know what she was talking about. For that, Symone was grateful. "No one wants to believe their mother would marry a killer. If Paul's innocent, we'll clear him and it'll put your mind at rest."

Symone nodded her agreement. "I want to be there when you interview him."

Jerry sighed, rubbing the back of his neck. "Symone, we've discussed this."

She held up her right index finger. "We've had *a* discussion. Jerry, I'll be safe with you and Celeste. You and I will be together the whole time."

"No one can guarantee that." His tone was inflexible.

"I'll arrive to the interview location with you and return to the safe house with you." Symone threw up her arms. "What's the difference whether I'm with you or you're on your own?"

Jerry crossed his arms. "The difference is, if we show up together, people will know you're with me. If you stay out of sight, they won't."

Symone considered him. His T-shirt was still damp,

clinging to the muscles in his chest and abdomen. He looked so certain he was going to get his way. Poor guy. "I want to be safe, but I don't want to hide."

Jerry shook his head. "This isn't a buffet. You can't choose one or the other. It's a package deal. If you want to be safe, you'll have to stay hidden. I'm sorry."

Symone watched him stride away and jog up the stairs from the basement. She was sorry, too. Sorry he was going to be disappointed when he realized she was never giving up.

Poor guy.

"Good work as usual, Mal." Three hours later, Jerry sat beside Symone at the dinette table during their team videoconference.

He was still struggling to clear the image of her in her yoga outfit from what was left of his brain. He'd seen other women in similar outfits, but they'd never struck him speechless. Never. His mind had gone blank, and his muscles had frozen. She'd looked so different from the cool, untouchable corporate executive. This morning she'd been a warm, friendly charmer.

Symone Bishop was a collection of contrasts, and each one fascinated him.

Symone sat back. "I agree. Your reports were incredibly thorough. I wish I'd contacted you before my mother remarried."

"Thank you, both." Mal spoke from his seat beside Zeke in the Touré Security Group conference room Saturday morning. Celeste's image appeared in the box beside them. "Those are the highlights from the background checks on Paul and Wesley. The full reports have more details, of course. I'm researching Ellie now."

"And Xander." Jerry tapped the computer keys that would send Paul's report to the printer in the safe house's office upstairs. "We need to look into him, too."

Symone shifted toward him on her matching cedar chair. "I thought, for now, we were focusing on the suspects who most likely knew about my mother's prescription?"

"We should include Xander in this phase as well." Jerry hit the computer keys to print Wesley's report. His skin warmed where Symone's eyes touched the side of his face.

"Why?" she asked.

Because I didn't like the way he looked at me as though I were a threat. Am I a threat to his getting rid of you—or being with you?

But if he said that, he'd sound insane. "I told you I have a feeling about him."

Her chocolate eyes clouded with confusion. Jerry sensed her trying to decide how best to respond to his claim.

Zeke offered his insight. "Jerry's instincts are correct 99 percent of the time."

Jerry rolled his eyes. "I'd argue 100 percent."

Mal's voice was dry. "We'll give you ninety-nine-point-five."

Symone shook her head. A smile ghosted her lush lips. "All right. But I want to prioritize Paul, Wesley and Ellie. They're the ones most likely to know about my mother's heart condition. I'm anxious to find my mother's murderer."

"Of course." Celeste seemed to be behind her desk at her agency. Her camera framed her wearing a black, button-downed, short-sleeved blouse. "We understand. As Mal said, we have enough here to start with Paul and Wesley. Great work, Mal. And he's already started on Ellie's report. We won't lose focus."

Symone relaxed beside him. "Thank you."

Celeste's tone was brisk. "The killer wants to replace you as chair, presumably so they'd have total control of the foundation's funds."

Symone interrupted. "Not total control. Our bylaws mandate that our accounts are audited annually. They also allow board members to request additional audits under specific conditions."

"There are ways around that." Celeste waved a dismissive hand. "Bribes. Dummy accounts. Duplicate books."

Zeke jumped in. "I see where you're going, Celeste. If the killer's motive is money, Paul isn't our strongest suspect. He's not carrying much debt and his finances are strong."

"But his behavior's suspicious." Jerry sat back, crossing his arms over his chest. "Why doesn't he want protection? Why isn't he helping us find Odette's killer?"

These points alone put Paul at the top of Jerry's suspect list. However, he and his brothers had assigned two agents to guard him from a distance. They weren't comfortable leaving him unprotected if there was even the slightest chance his life was in danger.

"*That's* where I was going." Celeste gestured toward Jerry through the monitor. "Paul seems like our strongest suspect. No offense, Symone."

"None taken," Symone said.

Celeste counted off the strikes against Paul on her long, slender fingers. "He knew about Odette's heart condition. He had access to her prescription, and he's a member of the administration. But he doesn't appear to have a financial incentive. When we question him later today, we need to keep in mind that money may not be the motive—or at least not the only one."

Jerry nodded. "Good point."

Symone sat forward, resting her forearms on the table in front of her. "I want to be there when you speak with Paul."

"No," Jerry repeated.

"Of course," Celeste responded at the same time. She frowned at Jerry. "Why not?"

"I can't believe this." Jerry scrubbed his hands over his face. "What's the point of bringing her to the safe house if we're going to parade her in front of people who may want to kill her?"

Celeste blinked at Jerry. "To get her feedback and insights in real time. Jerry, you and I don't know these people. Symone has known Paul for years and she's worked with Wesley and Ellie for months. She can read their body language and fact-check their responses on the spot. Having her with us will make this investigation go a lot faster."

Jerry hadn't considered the points Celeste was making. They were good ones. Still, Symone was his responsibility. Her safety was his priority. And the best way to keep her safe was to make sure she was hidden away and her location a secret. He couldn't allow another one of his charges to be placed in danger. Not ever again.

He exchanged a look with her. He couldn't read her expression. Her emotions were under wraps. But he sensed her confidence growing. She thought Celeste's words would change his mind. He hated to disappoint her. He'd hate getting her killed even more.

Jerry switched his attention to his brothers. "Will you guys back me up?"

Zeke hesitated. "Celeste makes a good point. We need to identify the threat as quickly as possible. Having Symone at the interviews could help us do that."

"I agree," Mal said. "Grace helped with the interviews

while we were protecting her. You and Celeste will keep Symone safe."

Jerry read the signs of his defeat. He turned to Symone. "All right. You're coming with Celeste and me when we interview Paul later. But if I sense any danger, if there are any signs someone's following us, we're leaving you behind in the future. Got it?"

Symone's eyes glowed with satisfaction. "I've got it."

He could get lost in those brown eyes—but he would not let his attraction for her get in the way of keeping her safe.

Symone flinched when they walked into Paul's house early Saturday afternoon. Jerry followed her line of sight to the taped boxes stacked in a corner of the family room. What hurt her more, losing this last connection to her mother? Or confirmation that the final member of her family was walking away from her at a time when she needed her family most?

"Thank you for agreeing to see us, Paul." Jerry stepped aside for Symone and Celeste.

Symone was dressed in a cream shell blouse and powder pink skirt suit with matching stilettos. She'd accessorized with her pearl earrings and matching necklace. In contrast, Celeste had tucked a black, button-down, short-sleeved cotton blouse into the waistband of her slim black jeans. She wore black sneakers. Sterling silver stud earrings were mostly hidden by her cascade of wavy, ebony hair.

Jerry scanned the half-dozen boxes arranged two to a stack as he walked past them. The large brown cardboard containers looked new. They were labeled by item—clothes, linen, books. Paul must've spent most of the previous day packing, but it looked like he still had a lot to do.

Symone's stepfather led them to the dining room and sat on the carved dark wood seat at the head of the table. "I tried to call you last night, Symone. Did you get my message?"

"I sent an agency-wide email explaining my cell's turned off." Symone rounded the table to take the seat opposite her stepfather. Jerry held her chair, then sat to her left. "I'm using a secure phone until the stalker is caught."

Paul looked from Symone to Jerry and back. "And where are you staying?"

Symone's expression was unreadable. "Somewhere safe."

Jerry smiled to himself. Excellent. It was nice having a client who took her safety as seriously as he did. He once again shook off memories of the immature pop star and his high-maintenance father.

Paul's frown was disapproving. "I was expecting you to call me back."

"Was there something you needed?" Symone's voice was polished and solicitous. Had she gone to some expensive finishing school where people were taught to speak like that?

"Yes." Paul stacked his hands on the table. "When will you be able to remove your mother's things? I want to put the house on the market as soon as possible."

Jerry's fists clenched. Did Paul realize how cruel and thoughtless he sounded? He felt the impact of the other man's comment like a physical blow. He glanced at Symone to gauge her reaction. Her expression was frozen as though she didn't know how to respond. He turned back to Paul, intending to check the older man, but Celeste spoke first.

"Wow. That was harsh." The private investigator had taken the seat to Symone's right.

Paul's head swiveled toward Celeste. His lips parted. "I beg your pardon?"

Celeste jerked her thumb toward Symone. "She's a little busy right now. Someone's trying to kill her. Remember?"

"How dare you!" Paul's face flushed a deep red. "Is that how you speak to a client?"

Celeste jerked her head toward Jerry. "I don't work for you. I work for TSG."

Symone caught her stepfather's eyes. "You're not the client, Paul. I am." Her voice was cold enough to give Jerry frostbite.

He ignored Paul's simmering anger. "I see you've started packing. When are you leaving?" Jerry made a mental note to alert Eriq and Taylor that their prime suspect in Odette Bishop's homicide was making plans to leave town.

Paul drew his attention from Symone and turned to Jerry. "As soon as my brother returns from his vacation. It should be another week or so." He glanced at Symone. "In the meantime, I'm tendering my formal resignation from the foundation."

Surprise and some other emotion—grief?—swept across Symone's face. "Paul, I understand your wanting to leave the company but…can you wait until after the board votes? I need your support to keep my position with the foundation."

Jerry heard the tension in her voice. It made him even more suspicious of the older man's motives. What was behind the timing of his leaving? If it was fear for his safety, why wouldn't he accept the protection Touré Security Group offered? Or was he hoping to vanish before they connected him to Odette's murder?

"You don't need me." Paul's voice was gentle. "I know

you don't want to hear this, Symone, but maybe you should consider leaving, too. You have to take these threats more seriously. Your parents wouldn't want you to put your life at risk for the foundation."

Symone paused. She seemed to be considering both the message and the messenger. "Paul, Mom didn't die from natural causes. She was murdered."

Blood drained from Paul's round face. His dark eyes widened. His soft jaw dropped. "What? No. How?"

Symone's throat muscles flexed as she swallowed. "I'm afraid it's true. Someone altered Mom's prescription. The pills in her last bottle were tainted with tetrahydrozoline. If ingested, the drug can affect blood pressure, causing it to speed up at first, then slow down."

"This can't be happening. Who would have done such a thing?" Paul's words were barely audible. He collapsed back against his seat. His expression was blank as though the news had stunned him. His eyes landed on Symone, but Jerry didn't think he saw her.

Celeste's eyes fastened onto Paul. "How was your relationship with your wife?"

"What?" Paul's eyes wandered toward Celeste. He seemed to be coming out of a trance. "I… Wait, are you suggesting *I* switched my wife's medication? I would *never*."

Jerry considered the older man. He appeared shocked to learn his wife had been murdered—or maybe he'd been surprised that the tetrahydrozoline had been discovered. He seemed angry to have been accused of tampering with Odette's pills, but perhaps he was a good actor.

"Tell us about your relationship with Odette, please, Paul." Jerry made it sound like an invitation. "Were you happy?"

Paul turned to Symone. His eyes were cloudy with confusion. "She never told you?"

Symone's winged eyebrows knitted. "Told me what?"

Paul straightened on his seat. He set his chin at a defensive angle. "Odette had filed for a divorce."

Jerry's eyebrows leaped up his forehead. That was unexpected. He looked at Symone for her reaction.

Symone's eyes stretched wide. Her lips parted. "When?"

Paul shifted on his seat. His throat worked as he swallowed. "Three days before she died."

"She never told me." Symone shook her head. "What happened?"

Paul's shrug was restless. His shoulders were slumped. He stared at the wall behind Symone as though he wasn't able to meet her eyes. "I couldn't compete with Langston Bishop's memory. Your father was larger than life. I knew that when I married Odette. But I'd loved her so much for so long. I thought the strength of my love would be enough." He shrugged again. "It wasn't."

Symone frowned. "Why didn't she tell me?"

The pain and confusion in her voice made Jerry's arms ache with the need to comfort her. He folded his arms across his chest to suppress the feeling.

"I thought she had." Paul finally met Symone's eyes. "You can't seriously believe I would have had anything to do with your mother's death. I loved her. I was suing her doctor and the pharmaceutical company for malpractice. Why would I do that if I'd been the one to poison her pills?"

Symone didn't blink. "We had to ask, Paul, so we could clear you as a suspect. This isn't just about the threats against us anymore. I have to get justice for my mother."

"That's right." Celeste gave Symone an approving nod

before turning back to Paul. "So, Paul, do you have any serious thoughts on who might've wanted to kill Odette and why?"

Paul cocked his head as he appeared to consider Celeste's question. "Odette was a wealthy and powerful woman. She carried a lot of influence in the health care industry, at least in the Midwest. But she wasn't feared. She was respected and very well liked. She was kind and intelligent. I can't think of a motive for anyone to want to hurt her, much less kill her."

Jerry heard Paul's love for his deceased wife. But again, he could be acting. "We think whoever killed Odette is now targeting Symone. The obvious link between them is the foundation."

Paul gestured toward Symone. "That's another reason for you to leave the foundation. Someone's already committed murder because of it, which makes it more likely they'll kill you, too. You could stay with my brother and me in North Carolina at least until your mother's killer's been found."

Symone squared her shoulders. "I'm staying to help find her killer."

A glint of what looked like admiration shone briefly in Paul's eyes. "You are your father's daughter."

Jerry wished he'd known Langston Bishop. He must have been an impressive person to have earned Odette's and Symone's devotion, and the respect of an entire industry.

He shook off the regret and refocused on the case. "Can you think of anyone who'd want to take over the foundation? Someone on the board, perhaps?"

Paul was shaking his head before Jerry finished speaking. "No, no. Of course not. All our employees go through extensive screening. So do the applicants for our board. Most of them have been with the foundation for years. Wes and Xander are the most recent members. I've known Wes for years. And the member Xander replaced recommended him."

Symone arched an eyebrow at Jerry. He read the I-Told-You-So message in her eyes. He wasn't ready to make concessions, though. Paul's endorsement of the board members didn't carry any weight since, in Jerry's opinion, Paul was still under suspicion. A lot of it. He wasn't prepared to clear the vendor who did the background checks for The Bishop Foundation, either, since it appears it had approved a killer's board application.

He glanced between Celeste and Symone. "Do you have any other questions?"

Celeste tilted her head. "One last question, Paul. Did you tell anyone about Odette's heart condition?"

Paul shrugged and lowered his eyes. "I may have mentioned it in passing to Wes. But I don't recall exactly."

Symone frowned. "I wish you hadn't done that, Paul. You know Mom was a very private person."

Paul nodded. "I'm sorry. I wasn't thinking."

Jerry sent a text to the Touré Security Group agent stationed outside. "Clear?"

The reply came back. "Clear."

Still looking at Paul, Symone continued. "Call me before you leave Columbus. I don't want you to go without saying goodbye."

"Be careful, Symone." Paul stood. "I want to help find Odette's killer, too. If I think of anything else, I'll email you."

"Thanks." Jerry straightened from his chair. "And if we have any other questions, we'll call."

Paul led them to the front door. Jerry stepped out first, using his body to shield Symone. He looked up and down the broad newly paved asphalt street. A row of large, old maple trees bordered it on both sides. Everything seemed quiet in this suburban community. Two of the three cars parked at the nearby curb were empty. The third belonged to one of the agency's personal security consultants.

Jerry nodded at Paul, then looked at Celeste and Symone. "We're good to go."

They moved quickly to get Symone into Jerry's car before Celeste jumped into her own dark gray sedan.

As Jerry pointed the car in the direction of U.S. 33 East, he checked the rearview mirror and both side mirrors. No one appeared to be following them. Yet.

He glanced at Symone. She sat stiff and quiet on the passenger seat. "Are you all right?"

"I thought my mother and I told each other everything." She kept her eyes on the windshield. "Why hadn't she told me she was divorcing Paul?"

Jerry met her clouded brown eyes before returning his attention to the late afternoon traffic. "Maybe she didn't want to worry or upset you." He felt Symone's eyes on him.

"What other information did she withhold to avoid upsetting me?" Her voice was tight. "Had she known she was in danger?"

Jerry's eyebrows knitted. "That's a very good question."

Chapter 8

"**P**aul's not off the hook." Jerry caught the displeased look Symone sent from under her thick eyelashes. She wasn't happy with his decision. Fortunately, his job wasn't to make her happy. It was to keep her safe. "The interview left me with more questions than answers."

They'd logged onto the videoconference from the safe house's dining area late Saturday afternoon. Jerry could still smell the garlic, cumin, paprika, cheese and onions from the chili he'd made for lunch.

He and Symone were updating Zeke and Mal on their meeting with Paul earlier in the day. Both brothers wore crisp white shirts and jewel-toned ties, but they had taken off their suit jackets. Celeste had joined the videoconference from her office.

"I agree." Zeke's words came slowly as though he was processing the information Jerry, Symone and Celeste had shared with him. It was a lot. "I'm sure he believes he loved her. But there are numerous cases of spouses who'd professed to still be in love with the partners they killed."

Harsh but true.

Symone leaned forward, bringing her and her wildflower scent closer to Jerry. "Paul genuinely loved my mother. I don't have any doubt of that."

"Then I believe you." Celeste shrugged her shoulders. "Maybe it was a case of If-I-Can't-Have-Her-No-One-Can."

Symone spread her hands. "What does that have to do with the foundation?"

Celeste drummed her fingers against her desk. "I guess nothing, at least not on the surface. We need to know how long it would take someone who isn't on their heart medication to have an episode."

Mal broke his silence. "I asked Grace about that. She said the speed at which Odette's heart reacted to being off her heart medication would've depended on several factors, including her overall health and her body's response to the medication. But if she had to guess, Grace thought Odette's withdrawal from her prescription could've triggered a heart attack in a relatively short period of time, perhaps a week or two."

Symone drew a shaky breath. "And by the time we got her to the hospital, it was already too late."

Jerry squeezed her hand as it rested on the table beside his. "We're agreed that we'll keep Paul on the list."

Symone tilted her head. "No, we're not agreed. He had access and opportunity, but he didn't have motive. He has his own income separate from the foundation and it's quite comfortable. Now he's taking his wealth to North Carolina."

Jerry arched his eyebrows in surprise. He hadn't expected a high-society figure like Symone Bishop to paraphrase future NBA Hall of Famer LeBron James's 2010 quote about leaving the Cleveland Cavaliers and taking his talents to the Miami Heat. This was an unexpected side of the heiress.

"Let's compromise." Mal's words brought Jerry back to the meeting. "We'll keep Paul on the list but move him down. Have you scheduled your interview with Wesley Bragg?"

"Tomorrow at ten." Celeste looked up from her smartphone. "I'll meet you both at his house."

Jerry nodded. "One of our personal security consultants will again scout the area while we're meeting with Wesley. It's another layer of security."

Zeke inclined his head. "Good idea."

"Yes, good idea." Mal flipped through a multipage printout beside him. "Bragg has an interesting background. He's carrying a lot of personal debt."

Celeste raised her straight, ebony eyebrow. "I wonder why that would be."

Jerry was curious, too. "I look forward to asking him tomorrow."

Symone couldn't concentrate. She blamed that on the murder investigation hanging over her head. The varied schemes revealed over the past two days had sent her thoughts racing in half a dozen directions. Someone had killed her mother. That same person was most likely now threatening her. The board had scheduled a no-confidence vote against her—which made them suspects in her mother's murder. Her mother's husband also was a viable suspect, at least that's what Jerry kept saying. Her mother had filed for divorce from Paul—but hadn't told her.

In the meantime, she was hiding in an idyllic cabin in a lush, secluded woodland resort with an incredibly attractive bodyguard who cooked like a five-star chef.

What did it say about her lifestyle that she'd have to be in danger to get a date? Fate could be so cruel.

Her burner phone chirped, notifying Symone of an incoming call. She recognized Ellie's work cell phone number.

"Hello?" She rose from the desk in her bedroom.

"Oh, thank goodness!" Her admin's greeting rushed out on a relieved sigh.

"Ellie?" Symone crossed the room to sit on a corner of her bed. "What's the matter? Why are you calling me on a Saturday evening?"

Foundation employees may sometimes have to work long hours during the week, but her parents had prided themselves on ensuring their staff and board always spent holidays and weekends with their families.

"What?" Ellie's voice rose several octaves. "Symone, how could you ask me that? Someone's trying to kill you and I haven't heard from you since yesterday morning. I've been worried sick."

It wasn't completely true that her assistant hadn't heard from her in more than twenty-four hours. Symone had sent an email to staff and board members, explaining she would be working remotely and they could reach her via email or through a new phone number. Ellie must have read that email. How else would she have known the number for her secure phone?

Symone chose not to point that out. "I'm sorry you were worried."

"I'm not just your admin, Symone. We've worked closely together for almost a year now. I consider us to be friends." Ellie drew a deep breath as though trying to make herself relax. "I can't wait until this is over."

"That makes two of us." Three, counting Jerry.

Symone's eyes drifted toward their shared wall. He was probably looking forward to sleeping in his own bed. What was he doing right now? After the videoconference with Celeste, Zeke and Mal, they'd gone to their rooms.

She was supposed to be revising her report for the board. He'd mentioned some work he had to take care of as well.

"How are you?" Ellie's voice startled her.

Symone had almost forgotten she'd been on a call with her admin. "I'm fine, all things considered."

She rose, turning her back to the wall she shared with Jerry. Symone wandered to her secure laptop, which waited for her on the small cedarwood desk positioned between two large windows.

"Are you sleeping okay? How's your appetite?" Ellie's questions kept coming.

Symone smiled at her admin's fussing. "I'm getting some sleep."

"Are you there by yourself or is someone there with you? Where are you?" Frustration was seeping into Ellie's words.

Symone could understand. She was frustrated, too. It had only been two days, but already she was anxious for her life to return to normal. She could only pray they found the stalker/killer soon.

"I'm sorry, Ellie." Symone sat behind her desk and logged on to her email account. "I understand you're concerned, and I appreciate it. I really do. But the fewer people who know where I am, the better."

"What should I say if the board asks about you?" Her voice was tentative.

Symone shut her eyes. This situation couldn't have come at a worse time. Or maybe that was the point. If someone on the board wanted to ensure she was voted out as chair, then forcing her into hiding for her protection and thereby limiting her access to the board was an excellent way of achieving their goal.

Symone sighed, opening her eyes again. "I'm safe. That's all the board needs to know."

"What about Paul? Is he there with you?"

"We're both safe." Symone scanned her email inbox and noticed a message from Dr. Grace Blackwell. What was that about?

Ellie's sigh carried through the phone. "Good. I'm glad. That's what's important. Let's hope you both stay that way."

"Absolutely." Symone sat up, anxious to open Grace's email. "Ellie, I'm sorry. I should get going. Thank you for calling."

"Of course, but one last thing before I go." Her voice sped up. "Did you get my email with the new report numbers?"

"Yes, I see it here." The message had come in late Friday, about the time she'd fallen asleep in Jerry's arms. Symone shook her head to get rid of that thought. "Thank you so much for all of your hard work."

"You're very welcome, Symone. Stay safe."

"Thank you. You as well." Symone disconnected the call, then launched Grace's email.

Dear Symone,
Mal said it would be all right for me to send this email as long as you open it on either the secure laptop or the secure smartphone he provided to you.

I'm so very sorry to learn of your mother's passing and that her death appears to have been premeditated. I didn't have much interaction with your mother, but she impressed me during our brief conversations. I wish I'd gotten to know her better. She was a great champion for the health care industry.

Please know that I'm thinking of you during this difficult time. I'm giving you my phone number in case you need to talk. I'm here to listen. Just please remember to

only use the secure cell Mal gave you. Your safety is everyone's first priority.
With deepest condolences,
Grace

Symone blinked away tears. She was so grateful to Grace for reaching out to her. The other woman's simple, heartfelt message stated everything she needed to read to know she wasn't alone. She'd been feeling alone and lonely ever since her mother's death. Her mother had been her last blood relative. She'd been her business partner and her best friend. With Odette gone, Symone didn't have anyone to talk with, to confide in.

She read the phone number in Grace's email and tapped it into the secure cell phone.

Grace answered on the second ring. "Hello?"

Symone took a breath. "This is Symone Bishop. Is this Grace?"

There was a smile in the other woman's voice. "I'm so glad you called."

Symone's neck and shoulders relaxed. "Thank you for your email. Is this a good time to talk?"

Symone relaxed back against the warm brown, overstuffed sofa after dinner Saturday evening. Jerry sat on the sofa's other end. They'd been hidden in this safe house for a little more than a day and had found a routine that worked well, at least for their meals. He cooked while she set the table. They both cleaned the kitchen afterward. Then they wandered into the great room to relax and unwind for an hour or so.

Jerry shifted on the sofa cushion. "I've checked the

security system. Everything's fine. The video shows no one's approached the cabin. I'll check again before bed."

Symone's muscles eased, releasing the tension she hadn't known had settled in her neck and shoulders. "Thank you. I'm very grateful to you for monitoring the security system so diligently." Her eyes circled the spacious pine-and-cedar room with its fluffy tan sofa and armchairs. "If my car hadn't been bombed, I could pretend I was on vacation."

"You're right, although for you it would be a working vacation. How's your report for the board coming?" Jerry's interest surprised her.

Symone searched his dark eyes. Was he making polite conversation, or did he really want to know? She shrugged off her hesitation. It would be nice to talk about it with someone. "It's coming along slowly. Right now, all I have is an outline for the revisions. I have some ideas for changes to the application criteria. And Ellie's just forwarded the new figures from our investment firm."

Jerry shifted toward her on the sofa. "What exactly does the board want you to do?"

They want us to change the very essence of the foundation's mission statement.

Symone reeled in her aggravation and gathered her thoughts. "The board believes the foundation has been too conservative with our recent investment strategies and with the applications we've awarded. Members want us to increase the return on our investments and to approve more grant applications for broader-based health programs and products."

Jerry paused for several long seconds. Symone could feel his thoughts churning. She forced herself to remain still and return his intense regard.

Finally, he broke his silence. "What's in it for the members?"

Symone looked away. Stress and aggravation pressed down on her like unbearable weights. "The board wants more investments. The increased revenue would allow the foundation to provide more grants and to invest in additional projects."

It sounded like a reasonable proposal. Was her resistance to it unreasonable?

"But you think more money means more problems." Jerry made it a statement rather than a question.

Symone sent him a quick look before returning to her distracted study of the wall across the room. "Something like that. My grandfather created the foundation because so many of his loved ones had died from cancer, diabetes and heart conditions. He was devastated but determined to do something about it. He made it the foundation's mission to support medical research focused to preventing these diseases. He also was committed to finding cures and ensuring quality of life for people living with these illnesses."

"I read about your grandfather and the foundation's origin story on your website. Hearing it from you, though, makes the foundation's mission even more powerful because it's personal. Your grandfather sounds like a really impressive individual."

A slight smile curved Symone's lips. "I always thought he must have been larger than life. I'm sorry I never knew him. He died before I was born. He had pancreatic cancer."

"I'm so sorry." Jerry paused before continuing. "You don't seem sold on changing the foundation's investment or application strategies."

"I'm not." Symone pushed off the sofa to pace the room. After their meeting with Paul, she'd changed into powder blue shorts, white cotton T-shirt and taupe slipper socks. "It's risky. But maybe it's worth the risk? I don't know." She paused, staring down at the cold fireplace. "It breaks my heart that the diseases my grandfather was fighting to end took him and both of my parents from me. My father also died of pancreatic cancer. My mother died of heart disease. Yes, the board's strategy could provide more money to support research to treat and hopefully cure these diseases—or we could lose everything."

"There's a mission statement on the foundation's website."

Symone looked at Jerry over her shoulder. "Yes, my grandfather developed it."

Jerry stood, shoving his hands into the front pockets of his black pants. "Your grandfather's mission statement reads like a map for the foundation. You should use it to help you decide whether this next step that the board wants to take makes sense in terms of your grandfather's vision."

"My parents and I have always depended on my grandfather's mission statement to guide the foundation's decisions. That's been its touchstone for more than 40 years." Symone paced toward the bay window that overlooked the south side of the cabin.

"What's changed?" Jerry's tone suggested he already knew the answer.

The tint covering the windowpanes allowed her to enjoy the view while preventing anyone from seeing inside. Symone's attention lingered on the cabin's gray-stone-graveled walkway that led to a dirt path that disappeared into a forest of tall, stately, ancient maple and oak trees. From this angle, she couldn't see the river that ran along the resort ground's perimeter. Would she get a chance to walk beside it once this ordeal was over? She hoped so.

Symone turned to Jerry. He stood less than two yards from her. "The board changed. I realize that's significant for our investigation. But it also makes me wonder if it's time for the foundation to change."

"I know the foundation's important to you, of course. It's your family's legacy. But let's table the report for a sec." It was Jerry's turn to pace the spacious great room. Long, loose-legged strides brought him to the fireplace. "The board members aren't as committed to the foundation's mission statement anymore. So what's changed about the board? It has two new members, Wes Bragg, who we're meeting with tomorrow, and Xander Fence. Mal's doing a background check on him now."

Symone interrupted. "Our vendor already did a thorough background check on all of our members *and* both Wes and Xander have personal recommendations from people associated with the foundation."

Jerry slid a skeptical look in her direction as he crossed to the wall beside the bay window where Symone stood. "We're looking into their references as well."

Symone wanted to roll her eyes. With great effort, she did not. "You've already checked Wes's personal reference. It was from Paul."

"And Mal's doing a background check on Ellie." Jerry turned to pace in the opposite direction.

Symone was torn between defending her board, her staff and her vendor, and supporting Touré Security Group's efforts to keep her safe. The bottom line was her mother was dead because someone had tampered with her medication. Did she have confidence in the Touré brothers'— and Celeste Jarrett's—ability to help bring her mother's killer to justice?

Absolutely! She trusted them with her life. The matter

was resolved. She'd follow Touré Security Group's and Jarrett & Nichols Investigations's lead.

"Paul resigned from the foundation today. What does that mean for the board's vote in a couple of weeks?"

Symone took a moment to consider his question as she watched him walk past the fireplace. He was like a jaguar on the prowl—silent, unpredictable, dangerous. "For the vote itself, nothing would change. The board would still need a supermajority of the foundation's remaining eight voting members—seven on the board and one in administration— to remove me as chair. However, there would be one fewer person to speak on my behalf."

"Having fewer people in your corner is a concern, but at least it doesn't affect the vote count. They'd still need six on their side." Jerry turned to travel back across the room. "Who are the six members you think might vote against you?"

Symone shook her head, spreading her arms. "I really couldn't say. If you'd asked me three months ago, I wouldn't have thought anyone would vote against having a member of my family lead the foundation."

"But as you said, the board's changed." Jerry stopped in front of her. "So who do you think would vote against you now?"

Symone went back to her memories of the last board meeting and the discussion of the no-confidence vote. It wasn't hard to recall each member's reaction and what they said. "If I had to guess, I'd say Tina Gardner, the board president, then Julie Parke, Aaron Menéndez and Xander would support replacing me."

"That's four members." Jerry frowned. "Do you think the vote to replace you would be that close?" His voice was tight.

Symone felt his concern and drew strength and comfort from it. "I'm only guessing based on members' reactions during the last meeting. I hope Ellie and Wes will support me. Judging by their reactions, I think Keisha Lord and Kitty Lymon also will."

Jerry ran a hand over his thick, tight curls. A deep sigh expanded his muscled chest and lifted his broad shoulders. Symone sensed his thoughts racing. "What would happen if the vote ends in a tie?"

Symone spoke over her shoulder as she wandered back to the fireplace. "I'd remain the chair of my family's foundation."

"Then our side would have two chances to win, a simple majority of five votes in your favor or a tie." Jerry gave her a crooked smile.

Symone's breath lodged in her throat. "Uh-huh." She drew a breath. "I hadn't thought about that, but you're right. I still wish Paul would reconsider his resignation, at least until after the vote, as selfish as that might seem." She sighed as the other revelation from their earlier discussion with her stepfather returned to the forefront of her mind. "Why hadn't my mother told me she and Paul had discussed getting a divorce? Why hadn't I realized she'd been so unhappy with him?"

Jerry stepped forward, closing the distance between them. His voice was a gentle caress over her open emotional wounds. "I think the answer to both of those questions is she didn't want you to know."

"But why not?" She searched his kind, midnight eyes. His face was blurry through her unshed tears. "I'm her daughter. I thought we told each other everything."

Jerry reached out, cupping his right hand around her left upper arm. The warmth of his palm seeped into her muscles, soothing her. "There're probably so many reasons your mother hadn't had a chance to tell you she'd filed for divorce before she died. I'm sure she wanted to. She just didn't realize she was running out of time."

Lowering her eyes, Symone nodded. She rubbed tears from her eyes before looking up. "Thank you again for looking after me. I know I'm paying you and your brothers for your security services, but I feel so much safer knowing you guys and Celeste are involved in this case with me."

"You're wrong, Symone." Jerry dropped his hand to his side. "My brothers and I could've assigned your case to one of our security teams. We're each working on this case personally because we want to. I wanted to be here."

Jerry's words were like a dozen long-stemmed red roses. He and his brothers were standing by her because they cared. She really wasn't alone. She wanted to throw her arms around his neck and hold him close.

Instead, she forced herself to take a step back. "Thank you, Jerry. I'm going to work on that report for a couple of hours before turning in. Good night."

Jerry's well-wishes for the night followed her from the room. Symone concentrated on convincing her legs to carry her upstairs. She needed to identify her mother's killer/her stalker as soon as possible. It wasn't only her life that was in danger. As long as they were standing by her, the Touré brothers and Celeste also were targets.

Chapter 9

"You're Symone's bodyguards?" Wesley Bragg, one of the two new members of The Bishop Foundation Board of Directors, took Jerry's and Celeste's measure as they joined Symone and their host in Wes's living room Sunday morning.

They were meeting with Paul's lawyer at his home. The Cape Cod-style house was spacious with wide rooms and high ceilings. The living room's heavy, silver-and-black furnishings tempered the spill of natural light from the long, narrow front windows. The air carried the hint of lemon wax from the highly polished dark wood flooring.

Jerry returned Wes's regard. "Celeste Jarrett and I are working with the police to find the person behind the threats against Symone and Paul. Paul thinks the threats are connected to his lawsuits. He said you're handling that matter for him."

"That's right. It was my idea to sue Odette's doctor and the pharmaceutical company that manufactured her heart medicine." Wes managed to sound boastful and altruistic at the same time.

Symone interrupted him. "Paul told me you'd approached him with the idea the day after my mother's funeral."

Jerry couldn't tell whether Wes caught the hint of disapproval that chilled her words. He looked at Symone sitting politely between him and Celeste on the long, black leather sofa. She wore a modest blush, scoop-necked blouse and slim tan skirt suit with matching three-inch pumps. She'd once again accessorized with pearl earrings and a matching pearl necklace. The overall impression was cool and professional, but Jerry sensed it was a disguise masking a volcanic temper.

"Of course." Wes had the matching leather armchair to himself. "We needed to file the suit as soon as possible."

Celeste crossed her jean-clad legs. This pair was dark blue. She wore it with a square-necked black shell blouse. "Why were you so intent on suing them?"

Wes's expression was somber as he met Celeste's eyes. His thin lips were unsmiling. "You didn't see Paul when Odette died." He shifted his attention to Jerry. "He'd been in love with Odette for years, but he loved her more than Odette loved him." He looked at Symone. "Don't get me wrong, Odette liked Paul and enjoyed his company, but he knew she was still in love with your father. Did you know he'd proposed to her at least twice before she'd finally agreed to marry him?"

Symone nodded. "Yes, she told me."

Jerry could believe it. Symone said Langston Bishop had been larger than life. Like his parents. Her father be a tough act for anyone to follow, especially an introvert like Paul Kayple.

Wes shook his head. "At first, Paul had accepted that Odette would never love him as much as she'd loved your father but over time, it wore him down. When she died less than two years into their marriage, he was devastated."

"I know." Symone leaned back against the sofa. "We all were."

Wes's eyes widened as though he'd realized that as Paul was grieving the death of his wife, Symone was also grieving the death of her mother. "Of course. And that's the reason I offered to represent Paul in his lawsuits."

Celeste arched a straight eyebrow. She gave Wes a once-over. "Because he was heartbroken over Odette's death?"

Wes inclined his head. "That's right. I thought justice for Odette would bring him comfort and that was all I could offer him. Odette had contacted her doctor twice about her symptoms before her heart attack. Their first contact, he'd brushed her off. When she'd called the second time, he'd scheduled an appointment almost two weeks out. His lack of action shows he didn't take her concerns seriously. He should have urged her to come into his office immediately."

Jerry glanced at Symone. She was silent and still. Her temper showed in her thin lips and tight jaw. Underneath that subdued anger, he sensed her devastation. He searched Wes's innocent expression and replayed his altruistic words. He didn't buy the lawyer's act. He was capitalizing off Odette's death to make money to pay his debts.

Jerry gave the other man a curious look. "Are you sure your motivation for encouraging Paul to file these lawsuits wasn't the potential payday you'd get from suing a medical doctor and a large pharmaceutical company?"

Surprise wiped all expression from Wes's face. His lips parted and his eyes widened. "What do you mean?"

Jerry cocked his head. "We know you're in debt up to your eyeballs, Wes."

Celeste leaned forward, bracing her elbows on her thighs. "You're making child support and alimony payments to multiple ex-wives."

"Three of them." Jerry held up the index, middle and ring fingers of his right hand.

Celeste gestured around the room. "You also have mortgage payments. Your solo practice isn't doing well. Cases are slow. I get it. I run a business, too."

Jerry considered the older man. "Are you sure your financial situation isn't the real reason you convinced Paul to file the lawsuits?"

Wes's frown transformed from confusion to surprise. His eyes swept from Celeste and Jerry to settle on Symone. "You're checking up on me? Did Paul say something to you? Is he complaining about me?"

"What would he have to complain about?" Symone asked.

"Nothing." Wes's voice rose.

"Watch the tone, Wes." Jerry frowned over Wes's rudeness toward Symone. She didn't deserve that. He sensed her eyes on him.

"I'm sorry." Wes directed his apology to Symone, then divided a look between Jerry and Celeste. "You're right. I convinced Paul to sue because I need money. Business has been slow for a while. The few clients I've had are even slower to pay. Paul thought the extra money from my position on the board would help and he's right. It did help, but not enough. My mortgage payments and office rent alone wouldn't be so bad. It's the alimony and child support that are crushing me."

Symone crossed her right leg over her left and folded her arms below her chest. "We had my mother's medication tested. Her pills had been tainted with tetrahydrozoline."

Wes's bushy brown eyebrows knitted. "What are you saying?"

Symone pinned the other man with a hard look. "Someone poisoned my mother."

Wes's jaw dropped. "Symone, I'm so very sorry. But why would someone want to harm Odette? Everyone loved her."

Jerry turned his attention from Symone back to Wes. "That's what we're wondering. It would have to be someone who knew about Odette's prescription. Paul told us he'd mentioned Odette's heart condition to you."

Wes straightened on his chair. "You think *I* had something to do with Odette's death? I *absolutely* did *not*."

Jerry was tempted to believe his righteous outrage, but he knew the emotion could be faked. "As a member of the board, you'd be eligible to replace Symone as chair of the foundation if the board votes her out."

Wes's face flushed an angry red. "You think I'd kill Odette to take over the foundation?"

"Would you?" Celeste asked.

Wes leaned forward on his chair. "*No*, I would *not*. I don't have any interest in taking over the foundation. I have a law practice to run."

Jerry nodded. "You said yourself your practice isn't doing so well. You admitted you need cash for alimony and child support payments."

Wes's nostrils flared. "It'll turn around. The problem with the foundation is that the chair doesn't have control of the foundation. Not really. The way the bylaws are written, the chair's answerable to the board. No offense, Symone, but I don't envy you and I wouldn't want your job."

Celeste snorted. "You expect us to believe you?"

"It's the truth." Wes's voice was rough. "I'd rather pull out my fingernails than report to the narcissists on the foundation's board."

Symone gave a soft sigh. "I believe you."

Jerry's head jerked in her direction. "You do?"

"Yes." Symone nodded. "Because some days, I feel the same way."

Jerry turned back to Wes. Based on the board's plan to oust Symone, he could understand why she'd feel that way, but was that enough to dissuade Wes from taking Symone's job—especially if he needed the money?

Jerry read the skepticism in Celeste's eyes. He agreed with the private investigator. Wes was staying on the list.

He retrieved his cell phone from his front pants pocket. "Clear?" He sent the text to the security consultant stationed in a nondescript car across the street and down the block from Wes's house. The Touré Security Group agent was watching for suspicious cars, pedestrians and activities while he, Symone and Celeste interviewed Wes.

His phone chimed, alerting him to the consultant's reply. "Clear."

Jerry stood, returning his cell to his pants pocket. "Thanks for meeting with us, Wes. If we have any other questions, we'll be in touch." He waited for Symone and Celeste to stand before falling into step behind them.

"Of course." Wes escorted them to the front door. "Whatever I can do to help." He paused with his hand on the dark wood door's ancient bronze doorknob. He met Symone's eyes. "Paul really loved Odette even though he knew he might not have much time with her because of her heart condition. I think it made him even more anxious to marry her. He wanted as much time with her as possible."

Symone frowned as though unsure how to respond. "Thanks for your time, Wes."

Jerry was confused, too. Had Paul been anxious to marry Odette because he wanted as much time as he could get with her? Or had he married her for access to the foundation's money upon her demise? Paul's friend had just given them more evidence against him.

"Wes didn't kill my mother." Symone stared through the windshield as Jerry sped down U.S. 33 East late Sunday morning. Their safe house was about an hour south of Columbus.

Safe house. The term sounded more romantic than ominous. Was that because of her companion? Symone glanced at Jerry's clean, classically handsome profile as he sat behind the steering wheel of the rented smoke gray sedan. A sexy, pensive frown wrinkled his brow. He had a way of making the cramped interior seem cozy. The air held a hint of soap and mint. Symone took a quick breath to test it. Her body hummed restlessly.

She jerked her attention back to the scene outside. A gentle breeze nudged the few fluffy white clouds that dotted the bright cerulean blue sky. The thought of spending the rest of this beautiful, early summer day inside caused her stomach muscles to twist with regret.

"What makes you so sure he didn't kill her?" Jerry checked his rear and side mirrors before switching into the far-left lane.

He was switching lanes a lot. Was he an impatient driver? Or was he making sure they weren't being followed? Probably both. She'd noticed him scanning both sides of the street when they'd entered Wes's home and when they'd left. He'd done the same thing when they'd met with Paul the day before.

Symone returned her attention to the windshield. "You heard the way Wes talked about Paul's feelings for my mother. Wes and Paul have been close for years. He wouldn't kill his friend's wife."

The vehicle's interior vibrated with Jerry's skepticism. "Give someone a strong enough motive and they'll do anything. Money's a very strong motive."

"You want my opinion based on my experience with our suspects. With what I know about Wes and his relationship with Paul, I don't believe he's a threat." Symone's shrug was restless as she tried to put her feelings into words. "I've known Wes since before he joined the board. He's been to dinner with my mother and me. He was always talking about how proud he was of his children and things he was doing to bring in clients. I just can't imagine that person plotting to kill my mother."

Jerry maneuvered his way back to the far-right lane as they closed in on the exit to Ohio State Route 180 West. "He's been to your mother's house?"

"Yes." She frowned at his sharp tone.

"Was he there the month before your mother died?"

Symone made a quick calculation. "Yes. The four of us tried to get together for dinner at Mom and Paul's house the first Friday of the month. We all couldn't always make it, but we did that last Friday."

Jerry's intense eyes caught hers before returning to the traffic. "If he was in the house, he could've slipped away to replace your mother's prescription with the fake pills."

Symone was shaking her head before Jerry finished speaking. "I don't recall Wes disappearing. At least not for a lengthy period of time and not without an explanation."

"An explanation?"

Symone shifted on her seat to face him. "He may have excused himself to go to the bathroom or get something from his car."

Jerry flipped his right hand before returning it to the

steering wheel. "Either one of those excuses would've given him enough time to plant the pills."

Symone spread her hands. "How would he have known where my mother kept her medication?"

Jerry shrugged. "Most people keep their prescriptions in their nightstands."

That was true. "You heard him, though. He doesn't want to be chair. He said he'd rather pull out his fingernails than answer to the 'narcissistic' board. Even though I grew up with the foundation, I still get frustrated with the board. If someone doesn't have the same connection to the foundation that I have, the members can be a bit much."

Jerry checked his blind spot before exiting the state route. "Symone, I get that the idea that someone you know and thought you could trust would want to hurt you or especially your mother would be hard to deal with. But you have to remember this isn't about either of you. It's not personal. It's about the money."

Impatience made her skin crawl. "I understand that but when are we going to start removing people from our list so we can focus on viable suspects? I want to find my mother's killer, not continually debate the pros and cons of each candidate."

Jerry glanced at her before returning his attention to the traffic. "Wes *is* a viable suspect. He had motive, money. He had opportunity during the dinners. And for method, it wouldn't be hard for someone to get tetrahydrozoline." He turned right onto the main road that would take them back to the cabin resort.

How could she argue with that? He'd explained his reasoning so clearly and succinctly. And, even more frustrating, he'd made sense. Symone expelled a breath. Maybe she should ask him to explain the foundation's mission statement to the board.

Symone turned on her seat to face the windshield. "All right. I'll concede you've made some good points. Maybe we should keep Wes on the list, at least a little while longer. But I want to go on record that I don't believe he killed my mother. Call it a gut instinct."

Jerry sent her his wicked grin, the one that made her toes curl. "There's nothing wrong with following your gut. I do it all the time." He shrugged. "This time, our guts are on different sides of this issue."

"So we have Paul and Wes." Symone unclenched her teeth and shook her head. "It really bothers me that the two people with whom my mother and I were closest are the top suspects on this list."

"It bothers me, too." Jerry's voice was somber.

Symone blinked. "Thank you."

His empathy helped ease her wounded spirit. She didn't know what she'd expected from her first—and hopefully last—personal security consultant but Jerry was more than she could've imagined. They'd only known each other three days, but she trusted and respected him more than most of the people she'd known for years. It was the way he protected her with such single-mindedness. And the way he listened to her, paying attention to her voice and her body language. She even enjoyed their debates.

I wanted to be here.

Don't read into his words, Symone. It wasn't personal. It was about the assignment.

The sooner they found her mother's killer, the better. And then she and Jerry would part ways, never to see each other again. Disappointment felt like an elephant sitting on her lap.

* * *

Jerry's cell phone rang as he and Symone entered the safe house Sunday afternoon. They'd entered the cabin via the attached garage. The rented sedan's tinted windows and the garage provided cover in case someone was watching for them.

"What's up?" Jerry answered on the second ring, locking the breezeway door behind them.

Symone smiled at his casual greeting. He must've recognized the caller. She started to turn away to give him privacy, but he caught her hand.

"It's Mal and Zeke. They want me to put them on speaker." He tapped the screen without releasing her hand. "Okay. Go ahead."

"We have a problem." Mal's grim voice rose from the smartphone. Coming from the calmest Touré, the warning carried additional weight. "I can't find Dorothy Wiggans."

Symone's fingers tightened around Jerry's big, warm hand. *Oh, no.*

Jerry frowned. "The board member who'd recommended Xander Fence as her replacement?"

Dorothy "Dottie" Wiggans had served five full terms, the maximum amount of time, with the board. She was the last member to have worked with Langston Bishop. Symone pictured the woman. Dottie was a cross between Mary Poppins and Mrs. Santa Claus. The silver-haired septuagenarian was petite with laughing cornflower blue eyes and a riot of silver curls framing a pixie face.

Symone leaned closer to the cell phone. "Mal, what do you mean you 'can't find' her?"

"Someone filed a missing persons report for Dorothy Wiggans three months ago." Papers rustled just beneath Mal's words. Symone imagined the computer expert sifting through mountains of papers. "There hasn't been any activity on her credit cards or bank accounts since April. Her utilities have been shut off due to unpaid bills."

"April?" Jerry's eyes sharpened on Symone's face. "That's the same time your mother died."

He voiced the thought that had flashed across Symone's mind. What was happening? Was Dottie's disappearance somehow connected to her mother's murder? Symone's knees shook. Jerry helped her across the room to the soft, tan love seat. She dropped onto the left cushion.

Jerry settled beside her. "Are you okay?"

Symone nodded. "I'm fine. Thank you."

Zeke's voice came through the speaker. "Celeste's on her way to interview the neighbor who filed the police report. We've left messages for Eriq and Taylor."

"I've already reviewed the foundation's file on Xander." Mal jumped in. "I'm going over it again. And we've asked the foundation's background-check vendor for Dottie's file. In the meantime, what can you tell us about her?"

Symone's mind spun with the steps the brothers had already taken to find out what had happened to Dottie. "She was born and raised in Australia. Melbourne, I think. She'd immigrated to the United States in her twenties. She'd joined the board when my father was chair. She'd been a pathologist before she retired about five years ago. She'd never married. She didn't have any children, and she was the only member of her family in the United States. She'd told my father she was lonely and had a lot of time on her hands." Symone smiled. "She'd also been an amateur actor. She starred in musicals with a local community theater group. Even after she retired, she remained on the board. She would've been termed out this month. Board members are only allowed to serve five consecutive terms, which would be fifteen years."

Jerry shifted to face her. Their knees were inches apart. "Why did Dottie decide to leave before her term was up?"

"I was surprised by that, too." Symone spread her hands. "She told Paul she wanted to slow down. She was also going to visit her twin sister in Australia. Her sister was her only surviving relative after their older brother had died of cancer. They'd been estranged for years. Mom and I were thrilled that they were trying to reconcile."

"When and how did you receive her recommendation for Xander?" Mal asked.

Symone narrowed her eyes as she brought to mind the time frame. "It was late March, I think. A few weeks before Mom died. That's when Dottie called Paul. Paul was the foundation's board liaison at the time. She'd emailed her recommendation to him."

"Paul was the last person to speak with her?" Jerry's question was devoid of inflection.

Symone gave him a sharp look. She felt his suspicion toward her stepfather building. "My mother spoke with her also. She said Dottie sounded tired, so she didn't keep her very long."

Now Symone wished she'd followed up with Dottie. Both she and her mother had thought Dottie's abrupt departure had been uncharacteristic. She should've done more to learn what had been behind her decision. But she'd ignored her instincts and now she was learning Dottie had been missing for at least three months.

Zeke broke the brief silence. "What's your impression of Xander Fence?"

Symone shook her head although Zeke couldn't see her. "He doesn't say much during the board meetings. Neither does Wes. I thought that was because they're the newest members. They're still getting a feel for the organization and the board."

Jerry ran a hand over his hair. "We're going to have to step up our time frame for speaking with him."

Symone met his eyes. "I agree."

Zeke's sigh carried through the internet connection. "We'll contact you again as soon as we hear back from Celeste, Eriq and Taylor."

"Stay alert." Mal's voice was firm. "And, Symone, remember not to turn on your personal devices. The more we uncover in this case, the more certain I am that you were being tracked."

A chill flashed through her system. "I'll be careful."

Once Jerry had ended the call, Symone rose and looked down at him. "You were right to include Xander on our suspect list. I apologize for doubting you."

Jerry stood. "No apology necessary. I get it. You've known these people a lot longer than you've known me."

Then why do I trust you more?

Symone turned and walked toward the kitchenette. She needed a mug of tea to help settle her nerves. She felt trapped in a nightmare by unanswered questions that kept her from waking up. What had happened to Dottie? What role, if any, had Xander played in her disappearance? Did Paul have anything to do with this?

She clenched her fists. And the most terrifying question of all: Who else was involved?

Chapter 10

Jerry froze in the basement of the safe house early Monday morning. Symone stood in profile on a mauve yoga mat five or six yards from where he stood in the shadows of the staircase. She was clothed in a powder blue yoga tank and mid-thigh shorts that hugged her lean muscles and traced her firm curves. Surrounded by silence, she raised her slender arms above her head. Slowly, she bent forward from her waist and lowered her forehead to her thighs and her fingertips to the mat. She extended her legs behind her, first one, then the other, to form a plank. Her back was straight and her chin was lifted.

He was familiar with the yoga poses she was performing—sun salutation, cobra, planks. But it was the strength, grace and flexibility she exhibited that mesmerized him. She worked out in silence, but there was music to her movements. It was like watching a dance. Her stretches were long, well-balanced and fluid. Time stood still.

Jerry waited for Symone to finish before stepping forward out of the shadows. "That was impressive."

She must've jumped half a foot into the air. Her breath left her in a whoosh. She pressed her right hand against her heart as though trying to keep it from leaping out of her chest. "I didn't realize you were there." Breathless, nervous laughter escaped her parted lips.

"I'm so sorry." Jerry chuckled. "I didn't mean to startle you. I wanted to compliment you. That was an amazing workout."

Symone grinned up at him. Her chocolate eyes twinkled with good humor. "After seeing *your* workouts, I realize that's quite a compliment coming from you. Thank you."

She'd enjoyed watching him work out? Jerry hoped his grin wasn't as goofy as it felt.

Sweat slid over Symone's slender shoulders and trailed her toned arms. She squatted to roll her yoga mat. She was leaving. He wanted her to stay, at least a little while longer.

"Have you been practicing the self-defense moves we reviewed?"

Symone stood, carrying the mat to the far-left corner of the room where she'd left her matching yoga bag.

"Yes. I pantomime the steps a few times before my regular workout." She shoved her mat into the bag, zipped it, then leaned it against the corner before stepping forward to demonstrate the moves. "Solar plexus." She braced her legs, then drove her elbow into an imaginary solar plexus. "Instep." She ground her heel into a nonexistent instep. "Nose." She made a fist with her right hand, then punched backward over her shoulder. "Groin." She punched down with the same fist.

Jerry winced, imagining the impact. "Good. Now practice on me." He held out his left arm, palm out. "We're going for a real-world simulation but remember—pull your punches. You don't want to injure your personal security consultant."

Symone tossed him a cocky smile. "I'll be gentle."

Jerry chuckled. He hadn't met this Symone before. She was confident, in control. Even sexier. He liked this side of her. A lot.

She strode to him. When she was about an arm's length away, she turned her back to him and pretended to scroll through an imaginary cell phone. Nice touch.

Jerry came up from behind her. He wrapped his right arm around her lithe waist and clamped his left palm over her lush lips. Apparently startled, Symone flinched. The shift in her weight threw them both off-balance and they started to fall. Jerry snatched her to his chest and twisted his torso so Symone would land on top of him. Holding her close, he absorbed their impact as he landed on the padded flooring.

"Oh my gosh! Oh my gosh!" Symone rolled over on top of him. "Are you okay?" Her eyes had darkened with guilt and worry.

Jerry shook with laughter, causing Symone to bounce on his torso. His arms were loose around her waist. "I'm fine. How are you?"

"I'm so sorry." Her wide eyes searched his head and face as though she thought he was lying about being okay.

"As a self-defense technique, that maneuver needs a bit of work." He grinned up at her.

Symone's eyes met his. Amusement nudged away guilt and worry. "I hadn't expected you to grab me so aggressively."

"It was a *real-world* simulation. I had to sell it."

"You sold it a bit too well." Symone chuckled and her body moved against his.

Jerry knew the exact moment Symone realized she was lying on top of him. It was the millisecond after he became aware of her soft, warm body against his. Humor evaporated. Their bodies stilled. Their eyes locked. Air drained from the room as electricity arced around and between them.

Jerry was afraid to move, afraid the desire whispering in his ears would seep into his muscles and take control of him. It taunted him with commands he knew he couldn't obey.

Touch her.

Hold her.

Taste her.

His pulse raced. Jerry strained to ignore his body's orders. Sanity was a fading echo in the back of his mind.

She's out of your league.

She has to be able to trust you.

She's a client!

Jerry set his hands at her waist. He wanted to help her to her feet. He needed distance between them. He had to clear his mind.

His palms burned where they touched her skin. "Symone, I—"

She lowered her head and pressed her lips against his. Heat exploded in his gut like a shot from a cannon. His muscles stiffened in surprise, then relaxed in welcome.

Her lips were so soft and so warm. Her taste was sweet and spicy. Seemingly of its own accord, Jerry's right arm circled her waist to hold her closer to him. His left hand cupped the back of her head. Symone's palms slid over his chest to grip his shoulders. She shifted higher on his torso and angled her head to deepen their kiss. Jerry parted his lips. She accepted his invitation, sweeping her tongue inside his mouth to explore him. Symone moaned. He echoed the sound.

Sanity was once again shouting to be heard from somewhere far, far away. Its cautions were barely audible above the blood rushing in his head. *What are you doing? She's your client. You're betraying her trust. You come from different worlds.*

Those statements were true—but she felt so right in his arms.

Jerry drew Symone's tongue deeper into his mouth. His hands traced the lines of her firm, warm figure.

"Symone, you feel so good." He whispered the words against her lips.

"So do you." She tipped her head back and he trailed kisses along the length of her throat. "I want—"

Without warning, Symone scrambled off him. "Oh my gosh! Oh my gosh!" She surged to her feet. "I'm—I—Oh!" She rushed from the room.

What just happened?

Craning his neck, Jerry followed her flight until she disappeared up the stairs. Gritting his teeth, he dropped back against the padded flooring. He pressed his left forearm across his eyes and pounded his right fist against the ground. "Idiot! What have you done?"

"I'm sorry to say we found Dorothy Wiggans's body." Eriq's voice was heavy with grief. He and Taylor had joined the early morning videoconference. They appeared to be using a laptop in one of the police precinct's interrogation rooms. "She'd been a Jane Doe at the county morgue. The killer had suffocated her, probably with a pillow, then moved her body to a construction site on the far west side. Someone on the crew discovered her the next day."

"Oh, no." Symone's voice was muffled behind her palms. The temperature in the room felt as though it had dropped ten degrees. She shivered in reaction.

Taylor continued their report on Dottie. "Her neighbor identified Ms. Wiggans from the coroner's photos. Her body's already been cremated. The county has to either bury or cremate unclaimed bodies after sixty days."

Symone rubbed her arms, trying to get warm again. "I should've followed my instincts. I knew something was wrong. She wouldn't have stepped down before the end of her term. She's—she was—the kind of person who always completed a task. She was compulsive that way."

From his seat on her right, Jerry put his hand on her shoulder. His dark eyes were soft with empathy. "Don't blame yourself. You aren't the one who harmed her."

Symone's face burned with discomfort. She looked away. Jerry was distracting in an emerald polo shirt and black slacks. His midnight eyes were even more hypnotic since their kiss earlier that morning. What had she been thinking? That was the problem. She hadn't been. She'd acted on impulse, giving in to her feelings, to the moment. To the madness. But she hadn't been sorry. That's why she hadn't apologized. She would have been lying.

Breakfast had been awkward, to say the least. Jerry had made an effort to put her at ease. It was another example of his kindness and empathy. She'd been grateful to him, but her responses had still felt stilted and embarrassed.

"Jerry's right." Celeste swung back and forth on the black executive chair in her office. Her hazel brown eyes gleamed with anger. She wore another black T-shirt. This one was a V neck. "I'm sure her death is connected to this case. We'll find her killer."

"Thank you." Symone liked the other woman's confidence. Her certainty that they'd get justice for Dottie helped Symone refocus on their case. She drew a deep breath, catching the aroma of the coffee coming from the nearby kitchenette. And just beneath it, Jerry's soap-and-mint scent.

Celeste gave a curt nod, acknowledging Symone's words. "And we'll get started later this morning. Xander agreed to meet you, Jerry and me at the foundation."

"Keep us posted, CJ." Eriq's expression was still grim. The older detective wore a pale blue shirt beneath a black jacket. He'd complemented his outfit with his customary bolo tie. The silver slide clip was shaped like a white bass. "I want to close this cold case."

"Be careful." Zeke's tone betrayed a hint of concern. He looked professional in a white shirt and bronze tie. "Xander's now our top suspect. If he is the killer, we don't know how he'll react if he realizes we're onto him."

Celeste smirked. "This isn't my first barbecue, Zeke. Remember I was on the force with Eriq."

Zeke arched an eyebrow but otherwise remained silent. Symone wondered about their exchange and made a mental note to follow up with Jerry about it later.

"Thanks, Number One." Jerry's voice bounced with poorly masked amusement. "We'll be careful."

Symone still felt weighed down by grief. "I want to speak with Paul again."

"Why?" Celeste shrugged. "We just spoke with him Saturday."

Symone adjusted her glasses. "That was before we realized he and my mother were the last people from the foundation to speak with Dottie. He might be able to tell us something about her demeanor."

Jerry nodded his approval. "That's a good point. We'll circle back to Paul."

"Do you like him for these murders?" Taylor's crimson blouse made her large jade eyes pop. She'd gathered her wealth of honey blond hair into a ponytail that trailed down her back.

"It's hard to tell." Jerry dragged a hand over his tight dark curls. "As far as opportunity, Paul had access to Odette's medicine. But we believe the killer's motive is control of the foundation's money. Paul has his own wealth."

Celeste snorted. "Does anyone ever think they have enough money?"

Zeke gestured toward his monitor. "True, but Wes Bragg has a stronger motive. He actually needs money. And he knew about Odette's heart condition. As Jerry's pointed out, Wes could easily have tampered with her prescription during their last group dinner."

Mal turned his attention to Symone. Like Zeke, he wore a white shirt, but he'd paired it with a copper tie. "What do you think, Symone?"

She moved her shoulders restlessly. "I don't know what to think. I don't want to believe my mother had married a killer when she'd married Paul. I don't want to think she'd welcomed a murderer into her home each month when she invited Wes to dinner, either."

"No, there are no good options there." Celeste rubbed a pen between her palms. Her expression was thoughtful. "You know, they could be working together."

Symone had considered that idea herself. It made her feel sick. She wouldn't have stood by cluelessly while her mother had been surrounded by murderers. Would she? She would've known somehow that her mother had been in danger. Wouldn't she?

"We have two other suspects to interview, Xander and Ellie." Mal flipped through a short stack of printouts in front of him. "I'm almost done with Ellie's report. I should have it by tomorrow."

"Thanks, Mal." Jerry turned to Symone beside him. "Do you have any other questions or concerns?"

She shook her head. "No, thank you."

Jerry checked his watch. "If there's nothing else, I think we're done here. Celeste, Symone and I'll meet you at the foundation at ten. I've asked a couple of our consultants to stake out the area as added protection. They'll text me if they see anything suspicious."

Celeste nodded. "Good. I'll see you then." She left the videoconference without another word.

After wrapping up the meeting, Jerry quit the software application, logged off his system and closed the laptop. His movements seemed pensive and deliberate. He stood from the table and turned to Symone.

The skin on the back of her neck tingled. *Oh, boy.* Symone sensed an awkward encounter in her immediate future. She wasn't ready for it.

She popped off the cedar dining chair. "I'll get my purse."

His voice, deep and soft, stopped her. "May I have a moment of your time, please? We need to talk about our kiss."

No, we don't.

Symone briefly squeezed her eyes shut. Jerry stood between her and the staircase. Bummer. She took a breath and locked her knees.

"I'm sorry if I made you uncomfortable." Her hand on the table steadied her.

Jerry raised an eyebrow. "Did I seem uncomfortable?"

She hesitated. "I don't suppose you did."

Actually, he'd seemed very engaged. The memory of his responsiveness woke the butterflies in her stomach. It also made her feel powerful and confident.

Jerry sighed. He seemed as uneasy with this conversation as she was. That was small comfort. "Symone, you're a very beautiful woman. You're also my client. It's my job to keep you safe. It wouldn't be a good idea for us to become distracted by a personal relationship. This situation is too dangerous and we're already taking more risks than I think we should."

Symone cleared her throat and adjusted her glasses. "You're right. We should keep things between us strictly professional. Thank you for that."

She managed a smile as she strode past him on her way to the staircase. As she mounted the steps, one statement played on a loop in her mind, *Jerry Touré thinks I'm beautiful—very beautiful.*

"Symone, it's so good to see you." Ellie hurried across the foundation office's main room toward the entrance doors late Monday morning. Symone, Jerry and Celeste had just arrived.

Ellie's straight auburn tresses swung like a bell behind her slender shoulders. Her four-inch black stilettos were silent against the powder blue carpeting.

She came to a stop in front of Symone and searched her face with wide, dark blue eyes almost the exact shade as her knee-length coatdress. "How are you?"

Jerry could feel the excited vibrations radiating from the administrative assistant. Ellie must've really missed her boss. He half expected the older woman to pull Symone into a bone-crushing embrace.

"I'm fine, Ellie. Thank you. How are you?" In her understated cream skirt suit and matching pumps—how many pairs of shoes did she have?—Symone was several inches shorter than Ellie. Symone's poise and elegance made her stand out regardless of what she wore. At least, that was Jerry's opinion.

Ellie blew out a breath. "I've been a nervous wreck, worrying about you. But I'm so glad to see you looking

so well. Your bodyguard's taking excellent care of you."
She turned to Jerry and her sapphire earrings, a perfect
match to her necklace, swung from her earlobes. Her eyes
were warm with gratitude. "Thank you."

Jerry inclined his head. He appreciated her kind words
as well as her concern for her boss. What he really wanted,
though, was a lead to Symone's stalker. The sooner they
solved this case, the safer Symone would be. And then
she'd walk out of his life. He ignored the twisting pain of
regret in his chest and checked his watch. Xander should
be here in a couple of minutes.

Symone's smile was poise and elegance, as well as
warmth. "I don't know where you've found the time to
worry about me. You've been so busy with Paul *and* me
out of the office."

Ellie flashed a grin as her eyes took in the area. "It's a
good busy, if there's such a thing. And it makes the day
go faster."

"Yes, it does." Symone chuckled. "You're doing a wonderful job, Ellie. I appreciate all your efforts."

"I'm happy to do it." Ellie's expression grew somber.
"We were all sorry to learn that Paul's stepping down.
Thank you for sending that email. It was very thoughtful.
How do you feel about his leaving?"

Symone adjusted her glasses. "Of course I don't want him
to leave, but I understand his decision. With my mother's
death, he lost his only tangible connection to the foundation."

"That's a good point. I hadn't thought of that. Well,
you know I'll do everything I can to help make this transition easier for you." Ellie flicked looks at Jerry and Celeste before giving Symone an apologetic look. "Xander
called, Symone. He asked me to give you his regrets and

to explain something's come up. He's hoping the two of you can reschedule."

"*Something* came up?" Celeste wore gray jeans with her black cotton T-shirt and black jacket. Her lips were parted with surprise. Her eyes were wide with incredulity. "What was it?"

Ellie stepped back. Her brown eyebrows sprang up her pale cream forehead. "I don't know. He didn't tell me."

"It's all right, Ellie. Thank you." Symone gestured between Ellie and Celeste. "Eleanor Press, my administrative assistant. Celeste Jarrett of Jarrett and Nichols Private Investigations."

Ellie gaped at Symone. She lowered her voice. "A bodyguard *and* a private investigator? Symone, what's going on? Has something else happened?"

Symone's slender shoulders rose and fell with a sigh. She glanced at Jerry before responding. "Let's talk in the conference room."

"Sure, Symone." Ellie sounded uncertain, but she turned to lead the way back across the main room.

Symone followed her. Jerry came up the rear beside Celeste. Were they doing the right thing by interviewing Ellie now? They didn't have Mal's background report on her. He didn't like going in unprepared. They'd have to depend even more on Celeste's interview experience, and on Symone's familiarity with Ellie to determine whether the admin was being honest or whether she was withholding information. The problem was Symone had tunnel vision when it came to people she cared about. And she seemed to care a great deal about Ellie.

Once again, at almost every cubicle and workstation they passed, employees hailed Symone, eager to find out how she was, when she'd return full-time to the office and to update her on personal developments in their lives.

"For Pete's sake. Is it always like this?" Celeste's question snapped with impatience. "I feel like I'm at a political rally and Symone Bishop is the presumptive nominee."

"Really?" Jerry shrugged. "I think they're more like red carpet events for awards shows or movie premieres." Her staff adored her, and he could understand why. His chest felt close to bursting with pride.

Celeste grumbled as they stopped at another workstation. "Has the board seen these encounters? Because I seriously doubt they'd vote her out if they had. Her staff would mutiny."

"Good point." Another confirmation that the no-confidence vote was more about the foundation's money than its mission.

The conference room was quite small—and windowless. The cream walls displayed framed images of the foundation's logo, which looked like a bishop's chess piece with wings, and covers of its five most recent annual reports. The room held a hint of lavender, probably from the plug-in outlet device beside the walnut wood credenza in the back. Four sterling-silver-and-powder-blue-cushioned chairs surrounded the circular midsized walnut wood conversation table that dominated the space.

Jerry waited until Ellie, Celeste and Symone were seated before taking the last chair. Its back was to the door. From the perspective of a personal security consultant, Jerry acknowledged the arrangement wasn't his first choice, but it seemed unchivalrous to ask Ellie to switch with him.

"My mother didn't die of a heart attack, Ellie." Symone shifted to face her assistant. Ellie sat across the table from Jerry. "Someone tampered with her prescription."

Celeste had taken the chair to Jerry's left. "How well do you know Xander Fence?"

Ellie's eyes widened with surprise. "You think Xander did something to Odette's medicine?"

Celeste repeated her question. "How well do you know him?"

Ellie glanced back at Symone before returning her attention to Celeste. "Not well at all. I only know him through the board, but I heard he'd been highly recommended."

The admin seemed shaken. Was it because she'd just learned Odette had been murdered? Or was Celeste making her nervous? Celeste could be a little scary. Jerry would give Ellie that.

He sat back against his chair. "The former board member who'd recommended Xander was murdered shortly after the foundation received her referral."

"What?" Blood drained from Ellie's face.

Jerry pushed. "The timing of her death calls into question the validity of Xander's referral. We're doing another background check on him. That's one of the reasons we wanted to meet with him today. Are you sure there's nothing more you can tell us about the reason he canceled our meeting?"

Ellie's eyes stretched wide. "No, there's nothing. I told you what he told me."

"How did he sound when he called?" Jerry asked.

Ellie frowned as though trying to remember. "Like his normal self. Maybe distracted, busy. I don't know."

"You knew Odette had a heart condition, didn't you?" Celeste's question was abrupt.

"What?" Ellie gasped. "No, I didn't. I didn't know until Odette had already passed and Symone told me." She turned to her boss. Her voice was a whisper. Jerry strained to hear her words. "Symone, are you accusing me of killing your mother?"

Symone didn't flinch. "I'm trying to clear your name, Ellie. Jerry and Celeste are working with the police to find my mother's murderer."

Jerry didn't outwardly react to hearing Symone repeat the reason he gave her for keeping Paul's name on the suspect list. Inside, he was impressed. She was a quick study.

Ellie didn't look 100 percent convinced. She scowled at Celeste. "Well, I couldn't tamper with a prescription I didn't know existed, could I? So that blows a hole in your theory."

Not quite. "You've worked for the company for about nine months." Jerry remembered Symone mentioning that when he'd convinced her to give him an information dump on everyone on their suspect list.

Ellie turned her irritated attention to him. "That's right. Odette hired me and now I report to Symone."

He continued. "So you're in a position to replace Symone as the foundation chair, if the board votes her out."

Ellie's jaw dropped. Her eyes skated from Jerry to Symone and back. "That's absurd. And furthermore, you're wrong. Yes, I'm a voting member of the administration, but I wouldn't be the top candidate for foundation chair. I don't have the background, experience or enough time in my current position. And besides, I'm helping Symone with the report that's supposed to persuade the board to continue supporting her as chair. Why would I do that if I wanted her job?"

"To sabotage her so you could get her job." Celeste's response was dry.

Symone leaned forward to squeeze her assistant's shoulder. "Thank you for your time, Ellie. I'm sorry we've upset you, but I hope you understand our goal is to find my mother's killer." Symone rose from her chair. Jerry stood with her.

Ellie was shaky getting to her feet. "Of course. I do understand. And I'm so sorry your mother's death wasn't from natural causes. I hope her killer's brought to justice quickly."

"So do I." Symone glanced at Jerry, who'd stepped back so she could pass him. "Thank you."

Jerry and Celeste said goodbye to Ellie, then followed Symone from the room.

He pulled his cell phone from his front pants pocket. "Clear?" Jerry sent the text to one of the TSG guards on surveillance.

Her response came back. "Clear."

Jerry texted back. "Thanks." He smiled when he received her thumbs-up emoji. When they arrived at the suite's entrance, Jerry reached forward to open the door for Symone and Celeste.

Celeste grinned at him from over her shoulder. "You Touré brothers are living proof that chivalry's not dead." She pressed the elevator button before turning to Symone. "So? What does your gut tell you?"

Symone crossed her arms. "I don't think Ellie substituted my mother's pills."

Celeste looked crestfallen. Her bright eyes dimmed with disappointment. "I was sure we were on a roll with that one."

Jerry replayed parts of their interview in his head. "She couldn't be considered to replace Symone anyway. She hasn't been with the foundation long enough."

Symone looked up at him. "That part's not true."

"Really?" Hope flickered in Celeste's eyes.

The elevator doors opened. Symone dropped her arms and led them onboard. She pressed the button for the lobby. "If there are multiple new members on the board, you could request to be considered despite not having a year of leadership service. There are two new board members."

"Wes and Xander." Jerry's neck and shoulder muscles tightened with tension. "Too many things are happening at just the right time to threaten your position with the foundation. They can't all be coincidental."

"Hold on." Celeste held up her hands. "Is Ellie aware of the exception clause?"

Symone shrugged. "She is if she read the bylaws. But as she said, she doesn't have the qualifications. The board wouldn't vote her in."

"Unless she has another play to get control of the foundation's finances." The elevator doors opened onto the lobby. Jerry held them as Symone and Celeste walked off.

"Like what?" Celeste asked over her shoulder.

Jerry ran his hand over his hair. "Like bringing in a partner who does have the qualifications."

Chapter 11

"I promise I'll be vigilant." Symone led Jerry into the great room after dinner Monday evening, the end of their fourth day together.

Jerry had made chicken fajitas for dinner. The scents of the peppers, onions, olive oil and cheeses had followed them from the kitchen after he'd helped her clean up.

They'd gotten into the habit of spending an hour or so unwinding before turning in for the night. Symone enjoyed this time of the day. Even though they talked only about the case and foundation, she was getting to know Jerry through his questions, what he said and what he didn't say.

She settled onto the far end of the fluffy, brown sofa, expecting Jerry to take his customary position at the other end. She was disappointed when he chose the armchair closest to the dining area instead. Was the change in seating arrangements due to this morning's kiss?

"This is about more than 'vigilance,' Symone." Jerry held her eyes. "Xander is a strong suspect in your mother's murder. And there's a good chance he knows we're onto him."

"I'm sure that's the real reason he didn't show up to our meeting this morning." Symone was restless with anxiety. She doubted she'd be able to sleep tonight.

"Exactly." Jerry propped his right ankle on his left knee.

\

"If we question him, we don't know what he'll try. I'm also afraid he's not working alone."

A chill raced through Symone's system. "What makes you think that?" She was definitely not sleeping tonight.

"Like I said earlier, there are too many things happening at the same time for all of this to be a coincidence. And they all impact your tenure as foundation chair." Jerry counted off on his fingers. "Your mother's murdered. Dorothy Wiggans's murdered. Wes and Xander joined the board. One person can't pull all that off by themselves."

"That would require a lot of coordination for one person." Symone shook her head. "Switching my mother's pills. Hiding Dorothy's body. Stewarding Wes's and Xander's background checks."

"If Xander was involved, he must've had a partner, which means we're protecting you against two people."

"I understand." Symone shifted on the sofa to face Jerry, folding her left leg under her. "I promise to be careful when we go out and to pay attention to our surroundings during the rest of this investigation—just as I'm doing now."

Jerry considered her in silence for several moments. Was he questioning her integrity? The idea hurt.

"Eriq and Taylor should interview Xander without us. I'd be putting you in danger if we met with him. His partner could be nearby, waiting to kidnap you or worse."

Fear scattered Symone's thoughts. She struggled to sweep them back together. At least he wasn't questioning her honesty. Small victory. "You've had TSG guards surveilling the area while we interviewed the other suspects. They could do the same thing this time."

Jerry was shaking his head even while she spoke. "I'm sorry, Symone. It's too risky."

She winced from the stinging betrayal. Jerry knew how

important it was for her to confront her mother's killer. She wanted them to know she'd had an active role in getting justice for her mother. She wanted to look them in the eye and see the moment they realized they were going to be punished for what they did to her family.

"You're going back on your word. You agreed to let me participate in the interviews."

Jerry held up his hand. "I agreed with having you present as long as I was there. I'm not going to interview Xander, either. I'm going to be with you."

I'm going to be with you. Why were those six words so distracting?

Symone searched her mind for another solution. "You've taught me some self-defense techniques. I won't be completely helpless."

"Xander's partner—or partners—could have weapons, Symone." Jerry's eyes darkened with concern and regret. "I don't want to risk your life. Please try to understand. I don't want to deliver you to the people we think want to kill you."

Symone couldn't think of any other arguments that might persuade Jerry to her side—yet. "All right. Will Celeste be with Eriq and Taylor when they bring Xander in for questioning?"

"I'll ask them to invite her." Jerry's demeanor relaxed. The idea of her being in danger must have caused him more stress than she'd realized. "Thanks, Symone. I know backing off isn't easy for you. I appreciate your making this concession."

"You're welcome." She almost felt guilty for continuing to look for ways to change his mind.

Almost.

"How's your report coming?" Jerry's question broke

her concentration. It also changed the subject. Very clever of him.

She sighed. "It's moving a lot more slowly than I'd intended. The board wants me to be bold and to take risks, but that's not me. My whole life, I've been risk averse. I've always worked from a plan. My plans have plans. I don't know how to take risks."

Jerry chuckled. "You have to learn to trust your instincts."

Symone jerked her chin toward him. "You mean like you do? I've been meaning to ask how you knew someone had tampered with my mother's medication."

"I didn't." A slow smile curved his lips and flipped her stomach. "I was acting on instinct."

Symone swallowed to ease her dry throat. "My abilities aren't as finely honed as yours appear to be."

"I disagree." Jerry smiled into her eyes. "You have very good instincts."

Was he pulling her leg? "What makes you say that?"

Jerry arched a thick eyebrow. His expression was almost chastising. "You have impeccable manners, as though your parents sent you to a finishing school. Yet when you gave me a tour of the foundation, you never introduced me to anyone. I think that's because you instinctively knew you couldn't trust everyone in your organization."

"It was as though a little voice was whispering in my ear to be careful." Symone had been so tense that day. But now that she knew Jerry was on her side, she wasn't as anxious.

"Trust that little voice." He nodded his approval. "Just like today when you decided to interview Ellie in the conference room instead of your office. That was a good call. Your office could be bugged. My brothers and I haven't swept it."

Symone leaned back against the soft sofa cushions. "You make it sound so easy. 'Trust the little voice.'"

Jerry chuckled again. "It doesn't have to be hard."

"But that voice doesn't always want to talk to me."

"Or maybe you're not listening."

Symone rolled her eyes. "Okay, smart guy, share your secrets with me. How are you so comfortable taking risks?"

Jerry shrugged. "I don't know. It comes naturally to me. Risk is like a reflex to me. I've always trusted my gut—or at least I used to."

His smile faded. All at once, he seemed distant and cool, as though he'd been pulled back to a time and place she couldn't follow. His eyes drifted away from her. The restless energy that powered him seemed drained.

"What happened?" Symone's voice was a whisper. She was loath to intrude but desperate to know what had caused this change in him. "Why don't you trust your gut anymore?"

Jerry drew his eyes back to hers. The dark orbs seemed haunted. "Because I put my client in danger."

Jerry's mind recoiled from the memory and its paralyzing pain. He hated reliving that experience, which was the reason he avoided any mention of it at all costs.

Then why in the world had he brought it up with Symone? She was his client. Not his sister—thank goodness—his friend or his confessor. What had prompted him to share something so personal and damaging with her, something he hadn't even told his brothers?

His eyes moved over her tousled, golden brown tresses. They floated just above her slender shoulders, her round face, winged eyebrows, wide chocolate eyes and lush, pink lips.

What was it about her that made him want to unburden himself even more?

"What happened, Jerry?" Her voice was soft but insistent. "What's caused you not to trust yourself anymore?"

He stood and crossed to the fireplace. It took several deep breaths to calm the pulse pounding in his skull. It was July. The fireplace was cold. His mind projected the events of his past against its stone-and-wood surface like a movie trailer. "Nine months ago, my brothers and I accepted a contract to protect a pop star who was coming to Columbus. He was doing a concert here, one night only. But he was going to be in town for six nights." Six very long nights. "His father wanted round-the-clock security to protect his teenaged son from overzealous fans. Zeke, Mal and I didn't think it would be a complicated assignment. Our company's protected executives of billion-dollar industries and their families, state and federal politicians and their families, even international officials and their families. I thought one teenager—even with a legion of fans— shouldn't be more complicated than those assignments."

I'd been wrong.

"Did you treat the singer the same way you treated a visiting head of state?" Symone sounded puzzled.

"We use the same safety protocols whether you're the British prime minister or a D-list actor." Jerry spoke over his shoulder, though he still couldn't meet Symone's eyes. "It had been our parents' policy and it works."

"It's a good policy."

His restlessness pushed him to pace the room in front of the fireplace. "Yes, it is, and it would've worked this time except our client's son seemed to think our security services were a challenge he needed to beat. His first day, he tried to duck them at every opportunity—leaving the hotel, returning to the hotel, before and after concert rehearsals, at promotional stops, you name it."

"Oh, no." Symone's tone was thick with disappointment and disgust.

"Exactly." Jerry paced to the bay window. He paused to look out at the view from the side of the cabin. All he saw was the pop star's smug expression. "Our consultants are good, but he was treating his safety like a game."

"What did his father think?" Her voice was sharp with temper.

"He thought we should be able to control his son." Jerry turned from the window and paced past the fireplace to the dining area that separated the main room from the kitchenette and the rear entrance. "After the second day with the same crap, my brothers and I agreed to change the details. Instead of four two-person teams made up of younger agents who could relate to the charge, we assigned more seasoned agents who wouldn't put up with his pranks. I was with the overnight team, midnight to seven. I also checked in more frequently during the day."

"It's incredible that one kid caused so much havoc and his father—your client—didn't even care. He'd wanted a babysitter as much as a bodyguard. Did you consider canceling the contract?"

"No." Jerry dragged a hand over his hair. "We were contracted to provide a service. Our first reaction was to find a better way to deliver that service. But in retrospect, maybe we should've canceled the contract and returned our client's money. Because things went from bad to worse."

Symone groaned. "I'm afraid to ask."

Jerry slid his eyes her way. She looked interested and attentive. He didn't detect any judgment from her one way or the other. Her reaction was more than he'd hoped for.

He turned to continue pacing. "During my first shift, which was his third night here, I caught him climbing down his hotel room's balcony. Keep in mind, his room was on the fifth floor. To make it to the parking lot, he had to climb down four other balconies."

Symone interrupted. "Fortunately, you were waiting for him when he made it to the ground."

Jerry snorted. "With emergency services on speed dial in case he fell and broke his neck."

"Did his father at last step in?" She unfolded her leg from under her and sat forward.

"No, he just congratulated us on returning his son to his room." Jerry unclenched his teeth. "I was sure we were being pranked."

"I could understand why." Symone's winged eyebrows disappeared beneath her bangs. "Didn't your client share the hotel room with his son?"

Jerry nodded. "They had a suite with separate rooms and didn't spend a lot of time together."

She crossed her arms beneath her breasts. "Unbelievable."

Jerry's eyes locked with Symone's. He still didn't detect any judgment in her words, her voice or her body language. Nor did he feel any of the anguish, shame or guilt he'd carried for the past nine months.

"What is it?" Symone asked.

Jerry shook his head. "Nothing. I… Nothing." He shoved his hands into the front pockets of his dark gray cargo shorts.

"Is the singer's Spider-Man impersonation the reason you think you almost got him killed?"

"I wish it was." Jerry's eyes dropped to the main room's cedar flooring. "The next night, I got to the hotel early for the shift change. Our charge had already disappeared."

Symone's hand flew to her mouth. "Oh my goodness." Her words were muffled behind her palm.

Jerry's reaction at the time had been similar although not the same. "We calculated he had at least a twenty-minute head start on us. Of course, his father was furious—"

"What a hypocrite."

"I left my partner at the hotel room and took off to look for him. The client insisted on joining me—"

"Oh, *now* he wants to get involved."

Symone's constant interruptions were amusing—and reassuring. In an effort to be fair to his former client, Jerry was doing his best to leave out the types of editorial comments Symone was injecting. His charge's father had been a pain in his backside during their entire association. And his charge had been a spoiled, disrespectful, childish brat.

Jerry continued, trying not to smile. "As the client and I drove to the west side, I called Zeke and Mal to give them an update."

Symone's eyes widened with amazement. "How did you even know where to look for him?"

"The night I'd caught him climbing out of the hotel, I'd asked Mal to check the singer's computer to try to find out if he'd had a destination in mind."

Symone gave him a cheeky smile. "Was that your gut talking?"

Jerry chuckled. "Yes, it was. We weren't sure, but it seemed he was looking for illegal gambling clubs."

"You've *got* to be kidding me." Symone shook her head.

"I'm afraid not." But he wished he was. "Zeke and Mal met me and the client at the location. Luckily, we caught up with the charge before he entered the club."

"Oh, thank goodness." Symone exhaled. "Good job."

Jerry frowned. "Good job? He should never have been

able to slip past the guards. He should never have made it to that club. Anything could have happened to him. He was a kid. Those clubs are dangerous and attract dangerous people. At the very least, he could've been arrested."

Symone shook her head. "You're being too hard on yourself."

"No, I'm not. I knew he'd been looking for illegal gambling clubs. I withheld that information from the teams. All I told them was that he'd climbed down the balconies to the parking lot."

Symone threw up her hands. "Frankly, Jerry, that should have been enough to put everyone on high alert. But at the end of the day, the blame lays solely and squarely with your client and his bratty son. What did his father say when you found him?"

Jerry blew a breath. "He fired us on the spot."

Symone blinked. Her eyes stretched wide. "Unbelievable." She drew out the five syllables.

"I know." Jerry scrubbed his face with his palms. "That case was the first time in TSG's history that we've ever been fired. I can't risk putting my brothers and our company in that position ever again. My brothers don't blame me, but I blame myself. That's why I'm leaving our company."

"Jerry, no." Symone popped off the sofa. "Your charge put himself in that situation. You're not to blame."

He shrugged. "We could debate where to place the blame, but the bottom line is my charge could've been hurt because of me. That fact has shaken my self-confidence. Now, I'm second-guessing my every move."

Symone crossed to where he stood in front of the fireplace. She rested her hand on his upper arm and captured his eyes. "You couldn't be more wrong about your instincts. Yes, your client's son *could have been* hurt, but because of you, he *wasn't*. Your gut didn't fail you, Jerry. Because you trusted your instincts, you were able to prevent your charge from getting into trouble."

Tension Jerry hadn't realized had settled over him eased, releasing the muscles in his neck, shoulders and back. Symone's words were healing his self-inflicted wounds from the pop singer's case. They were cleansing his soul. She was looking at him as though he was some kind of hero. He wasn't. But she was making him feel like one.

Jerry struggled to clear his head. He was a professional. He needed to keep his distance from her. He couldn't become personally involved with a client. But in this moment, Symone wasn't his client. In this moment, she was the balm he desperately needed to become whole again. He knew he should take a step back. He should take several steps back. Instead, he stepped forward and covered her lips with his.

Symone had hoped she'd end up here again, kissing Jerry. She sighed and let her eyes drift closed. His scent, clean soap and fresh mint, surrounded her. It intoxicated her. She breathed deeply, filling her senses with it. His scent was an aphrodisiac, making her ache.

His tongue swept across her lips. She parted them, welcoming him in. Her arms eased up his torso. His hard muscles beneath her fingertips thrilled her. Her palms slid over his shoulders. She linked her fingers behind his neck. Symone pressed her body against his and deepened their kiss.

Jerry's arms wrapped around her waist, lifting her up on her toes and holding her even tighter against him. Her breasts were crushed against his chest. His hips were hard against hers. Symone moaned. Jerry's tongue caressed hers, encouraging her to taste him. She sucked him deeper into her mouth. Stroking his tongue, caressing his teeth. Every taste of him fueled the heat building inside her.

Symone couldn't be still. Her pulse was beating at the base of her throat. Her breath sped up. She pulled Jerry even closer to her. She whimpered when he broke their kiss, then sighed as his lips trailed down her neck. She tipped her head back to give him better access. His large hands cupped her hips against him. Symone gasped and trembled in his arms.

And then his warmth was gone.

Symone blinked her eyes open, trying to bring her surroundings back into focus. "What…?"

Jerry stepped back. "I apologize, Symone."

His voice was deep and rough. The sound did nothing to cool the desire building in her.

She was so confused. "Why? I…"

He shook his head. "As I told you this morning, you're my client. My job is to keep you safe. I'd never forgive myself if my distraction in any way jeopardized your well-being."

"But…"

"I'm sorry. I give you my word this won't happen again." Jerry turned and mounted the staircase.

Symone watched him disappear upstairs. What had just happened?

I give you my word this won't happen again.

That was depressing. And how dare he take all the credit for that kiss. She may be a bit out of practice in the dating scene, but she was fairly certain his reaction meant they wanted the same thing.

With her eyes still on the staircase, Symone squared

her shoulders. Being around Jerry was making her want to take risks. Good ones. Jerry could deny their attraction, if it made him feel better, but she was determined that they would indeed kiss again. And again.

Chapter 12

"Xander Fence is missing." Eriq made the announcement during their videoconference late Tuesday morning. The detective adjusted his bolo tie against his wine-red shirt. This tie had a copper slide clip shaped like a walleye.

Eriq and Taylor had joined the meeting from a police interrogation room again. It looked like the same room. The stains were familiar. Celeste was with them. Zeke and Mal sat at the conversation table in Zeke's office. Jerry was with Symone at the dinette table.

He still felt awkward around her after their kiss last night. His behavior had been inappropriate, unprofessional and inexcusable. Symone was beautiful, smart, funny and kind. But her attractive qualities didn't give him permission to make a pass at her, especially since she was a woman alone in a secluded cabin with a virtual stranger. That fact was an additional incentive to keep his hands to himself.

This morning, he'd gotten up earlier than usual to work out. Then he'd made sure he was out of the basement and back in his room before Symone arrived. This was his best option. He had to keep unnecessary contact with her to a minimum. Even now, the scent of her perfume was a distraction.

"He's missing?" Zeke glanced at Mal before returning his attention to his monitor. "When was he last seen?"

Frustrated, Jerry leaned into the table. Celeste, Eriq and Taylor were supposed to have interrogated Xander this morning. Identifying him as a strong suspect in Odette's murder and the threats against Symone was a big break for their investigation. Jerry had been counting on wrapping up the case today. He needed Symone to be safe.

Symone sat straighter on her chair. Confusion furrowed her brow. "Ellie said he'd called her yesterday morning."

"He could've been calling from anywhere." Mal frowned. He wore a dark gray shirt and black tie.

Celeste's black cotton T-shirt almost blended into the room's dark walls. Her hair fell in waves over her slim shoulders. "According to the file we received from the service that does the foundation's background checks, he works for GWI Investments. We went to the company. No one's heard of him."

"What?" Symone narrowed her eyes in thought. "But our vendor confirmed he worked there when they did a background check on him."

Jerry turned to Symone. "You need to have a conversation with your service. Remember, Mal found a bunch of red flags on Xander. Something seems off."

"My family has used them for decades." Clouds of concern and confusion swirled in Symone's dark eyes.

Jerry wanted to move heaven and earth to take her troubles away. "It may be time to consider a change."

"There's no *maybe* or *consider* about it." Celeste was abrupt. Her tone was irritated. "You need a company you can trust with something as important as background checks. It wasn't that Xander *no longer* worked there. He'd *never* worked there. Your vendor should've told you that."

Symone took off her glasses and rubbed her eyes. Jerry felt her confusion. "There must be a reason for these mistakes in Xander's file. Why would the service deliberately mislead us about Xander?" She put her glasses back on.

"You're right. We shouldn't jump to conclusions." Jerry was livid that a vendor Symone trusted may have been so dangerously sloppy, but he needed to be fair and not judge them before confronting them with these errors. "Let's discuss their report with them first."

"But for now, get ready for more bad news." Taylor wore a blue-green button-down blouse. "After we struck out at the investment company, Eriq, Celeste and I went to his condo. The property manager let us in. It looked as though he'd packed in a hurry and his car was gone."

Celeste drummed her fingers on the interrogation room's table. The sound was a low steady roll. "The place looked like a tornado had swept through it."

Zeke looked disgusted. He crossed his arms over his tan shirt, which he wore with a brown tie. "What did the manager say about him?"

"The usual." Eriq shrugged. "Good tenant. Quiet. Kept to himself. Rarely saw him."

Mal was doing his best sphinx impersonation. "How long had he lived there?"

Taylor took that question. "Six months."

Mal nodded. "And he'd been on the board for three."

Symone took a sharp breath. Her eyes flew to Jerry's, then back to the monitor. "Do you think he relocated to Columbus just to take the foundation away from my family?"

Mal paused as though considering Symone's question and his answer. "I don't know. He may have lived somewhere else first. But the speed of his disappearance makes me think he'd been prepared to run."

Symone's eyes dropped to her hands. They were clasped so tightly on her lap. "This is a nightmare."

Her words were a whisper. Jerry didn't think she'd meant anyone to hear her. But he had and he didn't have the strength to keep his distance.

He placed his right hand on her clenched fists and squeezed them gently before letting her go. "You're not going through this alone."

Symone straightened her back and returned her attention to the meeting. "What's our next move?"

Eriq's voice was kind. "We've put a BOLO on Xander and his car."

Celeste interrupted. "The property manager gave us the make, model, color, year and license plate number she had on file."

"Perfect." Zeke's attention seemed to linger on Celeste. "Let's hope he hasn't switched vehicles."

"We still need to find his partner." Jerry balanced his forearm on the table. "I'm convinced he's not working alone. Especially now that we know someone fabricated his background report."

"Agreed," Mal said.

Zeke, Celeste, Eriq and Taylor echoed his response.

His eldest brother sat forward. His tone was somber. "It goes without saying you and Symone need to be even more vigilant. Xander knows we've identified him. He's desperate, and we don't know where he is."

Jerry gestured toward the monitor, encompassing everyone in the meeting. "You all need to be careful, too. We don't have any idea how much he knows about our investigation and who's involved."

Once the meeting was over, Jerry turned to Symone. "Are you okay?"

Symone looked up at him. Her shoulders were slumped. Her eyes were dark with grief. "If Xander is the killer, he's killed my mother and a dear family friend, convinced my vendor to issue a false background check and tried to kill me. And he's apparently working with someone else at my family's foundation. How deep does this scheme go?"

"I promise we'll find out." It was a promise he was determined to keep, but it didn't feel like enough.

"Thank you." Symone pushed herself to her feet. She stopped halfway to the staircase. "You and your brothers are really good at what you do. And you work well together. Don't let doubts left over from your case with the pop singer push you out of your family's business. Talk with your brothers. Let them know how you feel. If you leave, you'll regret it, probably for the rest of your life."

She turned and left the room, not giving Jerry a chance to respond. He didn't need to. Symone was right, but it was a conversation he wasn't looking forward to.

Jerry was still avoiding her. Symone stood from the desk in her room Wednesday evening where she'd been trying to work on her revised report for the board. It was difficult to concentrate, though. After two days, they still hadn't located Xander. They hadn't made any progress identifying his partner, either.

So they were going to be stuck in this safe house/romantic cabin in the woods a while longer. Should she be concerned that she wasn't more upset about that? She'd had her reservations about being secluded with Jerry at first. At the top of the list was the fact he was a slob. She would never get over the condition of his office. While at the cabin, though, he was making an effort to be tidy, proving there was hope for him.

Symone sighed and checked the time. It was a few minutes past seven. She couldn't focus on the board's report. In part because she and Jerry had already been in the cabin for six days.

And it had been two days since she and Jerry had kissed. Twice. Now he didn't seem to want to be in the same room with her. Symone wandered to the dressing table. She traced her fingers along the cool cedar frame of the rectangular mirror on top of it before strolling away.

Last night and tonight, Jerry had gone to his room after dinner instead of lingering to talk with her as they'd gotten into the habit of doing. It was hard not to take that personally. In fact, his repeated rejections of her attempts to spend time with him were chipping away at her self-esteem. He'd kissed her before. Why was he pushing her away now? She understood he wanted to be professional. How could she make it even clearer to him that she *wanted* his attention?

Should I put it in a memo?

Symone glanced toward the small desk tucked between the two long narrow bedroom windows where she'd set up the clean laptop Mal had given her as well as stacks of grant applications. She shook her head, dismissing the memorandum idea.

She'd enjoyed talking with Jerry not just because he was handsome, interesting, intelligent, funny and kind. It was also because she didn't have anyone else to talk with. Her parents had been her best friends. She'd spent most of her time with them. She had a couple of good friends but most were friendly acquaintances. It didn't matter, though. Symone couldn't call one of them up to chat. What would she say if they asked to get together with her at the end of the week or the weekend?

Sorry, I can't commit to a date. I'm in protective cus-

tody. Someone's trying to kill me to gain control of my family foundation's money.

That would be awkward.

Symone strolled to the bed on the other side of the room. She smoothed her hand over the soft tan cotton coverlet. There *was* one person she could call. Grace Blackwell was a friendly acquaintance. Symone admired her and her dedication to finding a cure for diabetes. As an added bonus, Grace had been through a similar situation and had worked with the Touré Security Group. She would have at least some idea of how Symone was feeling.

She pulled out the safe phone Mal had given her. She selected Grace's number from the list of recent calls. The other woman answered on the second ring.

"Hi, Grace. It's Symone. Are you free to talk?"

"Of course, Symone." There was a smile in Grace's voice. "How're you holding up?"

"I'm okay." She positioned a pillow against the headboard and half sat, half reclined on the left side of the bed. "But it's stressful, as I'm sure you remember."

"Oh, I remember." Grace sounded grim. There was a pinging sound in the background like metal hitting porcelain. The other woman must be making coffee or tea. "We shouldn't talk about the case, though. I recognized your number from the last time you called. I'm sure the phone's safe, but I don't want to take any chances. What else should we talk about?"

"Actually, I have some questions about Jerry." Symone's cheeks burned with embarrassment. She struggled to sound casual. "What's your impression of him?"

"Oh, no. Are you and Jerry getting along all right?" The scrape of a chair against hardwood flooring meant Grace was either shifting to stand up or sit down.

"Everything's fine." Her eyes strayed to the closed bedroom door. What was Jerry doing now? "He's very diligent about my safety. He, Celeste and his brothers are working hard on the investigation. I'm just curious about what he's like when he's not working a case."

Symone winced. Could she be any more obvious about her personal interest in her bodyguard?

"Ah. Yes, the Tourés are very attractive." Grace chuckled. Apparently, the answer to Symone's question was no, she couldn't be more obvious. "I don't know Jerry or Zeke well, but if you spend any time at all with them, you realize they have very distinct personalities. Mal hates being the center of attention. He'd rather sit back, ask questions and observe."

Symone nodded. She'd noticed that during their initial meeting. And Mal had been the same way during their videoconferences. He rarely spoke.

Grace continued. "Jerry's the exact opposite. He usually jumps in to fill the silences."

Symone laughed. "He does like to talk." But when it was just the two of them, he often listened. "What about Zeke?"

"Well, he talks more than Mal and he listens more than Jerry." Grace hummed. "He's the hardest one to read. He's more focused on his brothers and their company. But one thing the three of them have in common is that they're protective of and loyal to the people they love. They'd rather take the punch than have someone they care about get hurt."

"I know what you're saying." Symone had experienced that with Jerry. Literally. He'd used his body to shield her and Ellie when her car had exploded. And when she'd caused them to stumble during her last self-defense training, he'd twisted his body so she'd landed on him.

"Jerry's a natural charmer. He can't help himself. When

his protection detail with my grandmother ended, he broke a lot of hearts at the senior retirement community where she lives. Grandma's still talking about that." Grace and Symone laughed at the anecdote. "But he's first and foremost a professional. He's not going to start a relationship with his charge."

Symone sighed as disappointment weighed on her shoulders. "I know. He told me."

Why would the stars align for her to meet such a fascinating, exciting and attractive man when her life was in danger? What was Fate trying to tell her?

"Really?" Grace's voice dripped with curiosity. "How far have things progressed? No, don't answer that. I'm sorry for prying. Listen, if you want my advice—"

Symone jumped at Grace's offer. "I do. I've never felt this way before. This isn't about adrenaline or fear because of this situation. It's him. When I wake up in the morning, I can't wait to see him. I love listening to him and I love the way he listens to me."

Did she sound as goofy as she felt? Symone forced herself to stop talking.

Grace's soft sigh traveled their phone connection. "I know how you feel. My advice is to go after what you want. But, Symone, make sure it really is what you want. A lot of feelings will be involved. And if Jerry gives up his personal code to have a relationship with his charge, I'd hate for him to have his heart broken."

Symone heard the gentle warning in Grace's words. "Thank you, Grace. And I promise I won't break his heart."

She hoped hers wouldn't be broken, either.

Jerry activated his wireless headset Wednesday evening before choosing Mal's number in his cell phone. He planned to do a three-way conference call with his brothers. He would be more comfortable without video for the conversation he was about to have with them. He propped two pillows behind his back to half sit and half recline on his queen-size bed as he waited for the connection to go through.

He shared the wall behind him with Symone. Low murmurs and bursts of laughter carried through the drywall. Whom was she speaking with? Whoever it was had a great sense of humor. More merry laughter bounced into the room. It seeped into his chest, warming him. Jerry smiled. He loved her laugh. It was so carefree, like childhood memories of running through the lawn sprinklers with his brothers on a hot summer day.

"What's up?" Mal's voice came on the line. Jerry heard tapping in the background as though he'd caught the second Touré in the middle of a project, probably an internet search.

"Hey, Mal. Hold on. Let me get Zeke." Jerry selected his eldest brother's number.

Zeke picked up on the second ring. "Hi, Jer. Is everything okay?"

"It's all good, Number One. I've got Mal on the line with us. Listen, there's something I wanted to talk with you about."

"Okay." Mal's tapping stopped.

"What is it?" Zeke's words were shaded with concern.

Jerry took a breath. He could hear Symone's words again as though she was whispering in his ear. *Talk with your brothers. Let them know how you feel. If you leave, you'll regret it, probably for the rest of your life.*

Leaving his cell on the mattress, Jerry rose and crossed to one of the two long bedroom windows. It was still bright and sunny at seven o'clock on a July evening. The wide-open field of lush green grass ringed by maple, oak and birch trees beckoned him out. He'd accept the invitation—if he and Symone weren't hiding for their lives.

"I hadn't been considering leaving TSG because I wanted to start my own business. I was using that as a cover story because I didn't want to admit the truth, at least not out loud. I was going to leave because I didn't want to screw up TSG any more than I already have."

"What are you talking about?" Zeke's tone was incredulous.

"Wait. What?" Mal responded at the same time.

Jerry turned away from the window and sat on the edge of the bed. "I really messed up with that pop star c—"

Mal interrupted him. His tone was firm, boarding on harsh. "No, you did not."

"Mal's right, Jer. That kid didn't know what he was getting into with that crowd at the illegal gambling casino. If it wasn't for you, he would've ended up in jail or worse."

Jerry stared blindly at the hardwood flooring. He held his head in both hands. "That's why I should've acted sooner to make sure he didn't slip out of that hotel a second time."

"What were we supposed to do, Jer? Handcuff him to a chair?" Zeke sighed. "We took every ethical precaution open to us. At some point, the kid had to take responsibility for his own safety."

Mal interrupted. "Not climbing over hotel balconies or visiting underground casinos would've been good starts."

Zeke continued. "But he wasn't willing to do that, and his parent wasn't holding him accountable for his behavior."

Jerry stared at his cell phone where it lay on the coverlet. He imagined his brothers sitting on either side of it, discussing the pop star case fiasco with him. He appreciated everything they'd said. But then they'd never, ever blamed him for the botched assignment. So what had he expected them to say today?

"What bothers me most about that case is that I got us fired." He stood again, walking away from his phone to tour the cozy room. "For the first time in the history of TSG, our client fired us because I couldn't handle the job." His bark of laughter was hollow.

"Jer, why are you beating yourself up like this?" Zeke sounded as upset as Jerry felt. He sensed his older brother shaking his head. "We knew you were more upset about this case than you let on."

"Why didn't you talk with us sooner?" Mal asked.

Jerry stiffened. Setting his hands on his hips, he drew a deep breath. "I was embarrassed."

"What?" Mal exclaimed.

Zeke bit off a curse. "Come on, Jerry. We're your brothers."

"I know. I know. But, I mean, think about it." Jerry marched across the room. His voice sped up. "It's the first time ever in the history of our family-owned business that a client fires us and it's because of me. How would you have felt if it had been because of you?"

"You tell us." Mal made it sound like a challenge. "Pretend Zeke had been the one assigned to protect an immature, self-centered narcissist masquerading as a pop star. Imagine he'd gone through everything you went through. And in the end, instead of thanking Zeke for saving his son from the terrible ramifications of his very bad decisions, our client fires us. Think about it. Would you blame Zeke for what happened?"

Jerry had never played role reversal with this situation.

He'd been too busy running from the memory to make the effort. But to satisfy Mal, he considered the event from the perspective of someone else going through the experience.

It made a difference. "No, I wouldn't. Our client had been unreasonable."

"That's right," Zeke said. "And remember, after we refunded his money, his son gave the other security company the slip, went to the illegal gambling casino and got arrested. It hit the national news."

Mal snorted. "Damaged his record sales and his career."

Jerry shook his head as he returned to the bed. He would never wish bad luck on anyone, but he hoped father and son had learned a valuable lesson from that experience.

"What made you finally decide to discuss your concerns about that case with us?" Zeke asked.

Jerry paused, staring at the shared wall between him and Symone. "Not what, who. Symone encouraged me to confide in you. She said if I didn't, I'd regret it for the rest of my life."

"Good advice." Mal sounded impressed. "I'm glad you took it. You usually don't."

Zeke chuckled. "I'm glad, too. So does this mean you're staying with the company?"

Jerry grinned. He felt lighter, freer than he'd felt in months. "Yes, that's exactly what I mean. You're stuck with me."

"Yes!" Zeke and Mal responded at the same time.

Jerry's eyes lingered on the wall. He was overwhelmed thinking about what Symone had done for him. She'd cared enough to push him out of his comfort zone to prevent him from making the worst mistake of his life, leaving his family's company. No one outside of his family had ever shown such concern for him. Jerry dropped onto the mattress as his legs began to shake.

There was no longer any doubt in his mind. When this assignment was over, he wasn't going to be able to walk away from Symone. She'd become more than a client. She was a necessity.

Chapter 13

"I thought you might like some tea." Jerry's voice coming from her bedroom doorway Wednesday night startled Symone.

She jerked upright on the cedarwood chair and swung to face the threshold. After ending her conversation with Grace about an hour earlier, Symone had opened the door. She'd heard Jerry's laughter through the wall her bedroom shared with his. The sound had made her smile. It was so full and alive, reminding her of that feeling she had as a little girl when her father would push her swing until she'd swung so high, she'd thought she could touch the sky.

"Thank you." Symone stood and walked toward him. "Would you like to come in?" *Please say yes.*

Jerry stepped forward, offering her one of the cream porcelain mugs. "Sure. Thanks. What're you working on?"

Symone returned to her chair. "I'm reviewing proposals for health care programs and products looking for foundation grants. Again."

As she'd intended, Jerry smiled at her dry tone. "Are you looking for—what was it?—cutting-edge, innovative proposals for the board's approval?"

Symone nodded. "That's right."

"How's that coming?"

With her free hand, Symone took off her glasses, set them on the table behind her and rubbed her eyes. "Not well. When we went through this exercise the first time three months ago, my mother and I had identified proposals that were cutting-edge, innovative *and* reflected our mission statement." She gestured toward the papers stacked on the right side of her desk. "Very few of these proposals are cutting-edge or innovative, and none of them align with our mission."

Jerry nodded toward the proposals. Without her glasses, he was slightly out of focus. "That's a huge pile of papers. It sounds like you're wasting your time."

"It feels like I'm wasting my time." Symone sipped her tea.

"I don't understand." Jerry leaned his hips back against the dressing table. "If it's your family's foundation, why does the board get to call all the shots?"

Good question. "When my grandfather created the foundation, he wanted to make sure his descendants would be good stewards of the organization. He was afraid the chair, acting alone, could lose sight of the foundation's purpose. So he set up the board with oversight authority to make sure the foundation remained focused on its mission."

Jerry frowned. "But it's the board that's derailing the foundation."

"Is it? Or is it trying to respond to the next generation of health care needs?" She shrugged. "I'm not sure."

"It's derailing the foundation." Jerry's tone was unequivocal. He straightened from the table and faced her. "I spoke with my brothers a little while ago."

Symone blinked. His sudden segue confused her. "Is everything all right?" She put her half-empty mug on the table.

"Everything's fine." He drank his tea. "I took your advice and told them how I felt about the botched assignment."

Symone stilled, waiting for him to continue. When he didn't, she prompted him. "It must have gone well. I heard you laughing."

Jerry smiled as though remembering those parts of their conversation. "It went…very well. They don't blame me at all, and they helped me to stop blaming myself."

"I knew they wouldn't blame you." Symone sprang from her seat. Her breath left her in a whoosh. "That's wonderful. So are you staying with the company?"

Jerry nodded. "I am. And I want to thank you for convincing me to tell them how I felt. I'm so glad I took your advice."

"That's wonderful news." Symone hurried across the room to hug him. She wrapped her arms around his waist and pressed her left cheek to his chest. His warm, hard body made her restless. With her ear against his chest, Symone heard his heart skip, then speed up to a strong, steady rhythm.

Jerry's arms wrapped around her slowly. He pulled her closer. Symone snuggled into him, breathing his scent. A soft sigh escaped her. Here. Like this. She wished she could stop time to be here in Jerry's arms like this for just a moment or two. A day or two. Forever.

He pressed his face to the curve of her neck. Symone leaned her head back and arched into his body. Jerry moaned and tightened his arms around her.

She turned her head and whispered against his ear. "You and I know we're going to make love. What does it matter whether it happens next week—or now?"

Jerry pressed his hips against her. Symone gasped at the feel of his arousal.

* * *

Symone's words were like gasoline poured over the embers burning inside Jerry. Desire, all consuming, ignited inside him. His body's response was swift. His lips parted, covering hers. He swallowed her gasp of surprise. He swept his tongue inside her mouth in search of the sweetness he'd tasted before. He stroked, caressed and suckled her, feasting on her reactions. Symone moaned and his movements grew bolder. She gasped and he demanded even more. She was restless in his arms, fueling his need.

Jerry tightened his arms around her, drawing her closer to him. His breath caught in his throat as he felt her heat. His arousal swelled at her response to him. He stroked her waist, and she pressed her breasts against him. He cupped her hips, and she arched her body into his. Her arms wrapped around him and moved up his back. Her fingers traced his spine. Her palms curved around his hips. Every touch, every caress made him crave her.

Symone pulled his shirt from him and pressed him back onto the bed. Holding his eyes, she unbuttoned her blouse, revealing a nude demi-cup bra. Jerry's throat went dry. He swallowed. Symone dropped her blouse to the floor. Still holding his eyes, she shed her tan shorts. Her matching underpants were a wisp of material that hugged her slim hips and dipped low to frame her navel. Jerry's heart raced as his eyes traveled over her. Her limbs were long and toned. Her breasts were full, waist tight and stomach flat. Jerry's muscles tightened with a sweet ache.

"You're like a fantasy." His voice was raw. He was torn between staring at her forever and kissing her all over.

Symone smiled. A blush warmed her chest and rose up into her cheeks. "So are you," she whispered back.

She climbed onto the bed, straddled him and leaned forward for his kiss. Jerry opened his mouth to join his tongue with hers. He stroked into her. She took him deeper. His muscles shook. His pulse raced. His breath was ragged.

He felt her fingers at his hips as she unfastened his shorts. Jerry pulled his wallet from his pocket and tossed it beside him on the bed. Symone freed his mouth to pull the rest of his clothes off, dropping them to the floor with hers. She kissed and licked her way up his legs. When she reached his hips, Jerry gripped the coverlet. He watched her draw him into her mouth. His hips surged up. He squeezed his eyes shut. She traced his length with her tongue. He groaned deep in his throat. His mind went blank. Pleasure, warm and sweet, spread throughout his body. Symone's hands caressed his hips, waist and torso. Her fingers traced his thighs, his erection. Her nails skimmed across his abdomen. As the pressure tightened inside him, Jerry gripped her shoulders.

"Stop." His voice was a shaky whisper. He rolled over, tucking her under him. He managed a smile. "My turn."

Symone's reply was a moan. He drank the sound, sliding his hands beneath her to release her bra. He leaned back, bringing the scrap of clothing with him. "Beautiful."

Her nipples tightened before his eyes. He leaned forward and took one into his mouth.

Symone's lips parted on a soundless scream. Her skin heated. She pressed Jerry's head to her breast and arched closer to him. His tongue licked her skin. His teeth teased her nipples. With his left hand, Jerry fondled her other breast, cupping it and stroking the tip with his palm.

"Jerry. Jerry."

"Symone," he whispered in her ear.

She shivered beneath him. Jerry slid down her body, caressing every inch of her skin. A stroke. A lick. A nibble. A kiss. He stripped off her underpants. She spread her legs.

He paused, moving his eyes over her limbs, hips, breasts and face. "You are so beautiful."

"So are you." She lost her breath as she looked at him, standing at the foot of the bed. He was broad shoulders, slim hips and long, muscled thighs.

Holding her eyes, Jerry returned to the mattress. He lay between her legs and lifted her hips to his tongue.

"What?" Startled, Symone widened her eyes, then squeezed them shut as he touched her.

She pressed her head against the pillow and fisted the coverlet in her hands. Her hips pumped against Jerry's lips as he kissed and caressed her. Her nipples puckered. Her muscles tightened as she raced toward her climax. Symone stiffened, then trembled as wave after wave after wave of pleasure broke over her. She tossed against the mattress, pumping her hips.

Jerry lowered her. As echoes of her climax trembled between her legs, Symone watched Jerry pull a condom from his wallet and make quick work of putting it on. Positioning himself on top of her, Jerry kissed her deeply as he entered her with one strong stroke. His erection moved inside her, deep and full. Symone gasped as she felt her passion building again. Her nipples tightened. Her muscles strained. Her hips matched his rhythm. She pressed her fingers against his shoulders and wrapped her legs around his hips as she tensed against him.

"Jerry." She whispered his name against his neck.

"I'm here." He worked his hand between them. "I'm with you." He lowered his head to her breast. He drew her nipple into his mouth as he touched her.

Symone shattered. Her body bucked and trembled as

a second orgasm rocked her. Jerry's body stiffened in re-sponse. She held on tight as his hips arched into her. Then he relaxed.

Gathering Symone into his arms, Jerry rolled over, po-sitioning her on top of him, and brought her lips to his for a kiss.

Chapter 14

Symone woke early Thursday morning to find Jerry lying on his side and smiling sleepily beside her. She could get used to that. "Were you watching me sleep?"

His smile widened. "Good morning to you, too." His morning voice was deep and gruff. Sexy.

"Good morning." She tilted her head back on her pillow to look at him. Her eyes traced his mouth. Her body warmed as she remembered all the things those wonderful lips had done to her last night.

"Do you always smile in your sleep?"

She chuckled. "Are you trying to get me to say I was dreaming of you?"

"Were you?"

She laughed. "What an ego."

Symone took in his lean, sienna features. Except for his morning stubble and his slightly unkempt hair, he looked just as wonderful first thing in the morning as he did during the day. Her eyes dropped to his bare torso. Maybe better.

She felt alive. Her body hummed with energy. It had been months since she'd slept so well. Jerry's loving had helped her to forget the board, the conspiracy, the murders and the threats—at least for a while.

Beneath the covers, she rolled onto her back and

stretched her arms and legs. That's when she remembered they'd slept naked. It had seemed like a great idea last night. This morning, not so much. She was much more modest with the sunrise.

Symone's eyes swept the room. Her glasses were on the desk several feet away on her left. Her clothes were on the floor at the foot of the bed. Her robe was in the closet on the other side of Jerry on her right. And she was naked.

"Jerry?" She rolled her head on her pillow to look at him again.

"Symone?"

She heard the humor in his voice. He was in a good mood today. So was she. It had been a very good night.

Her skin heated with a blush. "Could you close your eyes?"

Confusion quickly cleared with realization. Jerry feigned surprise, widening his eyes and gasping. "Are you naked under there?"

Symone fought not to laugh. "You know that I am. Will you please close your eyes?"

"All right, but you have to promise to do the same when I get out of bed." He stole a kiss, then rolled onto his stomach and closed his eyes.

Symone hesitated as she traced his broad, hard back with her eyes. Her fingers itched to touch him. Instead, she pressed a kiss to his spine. His muscles rippled. She heard his sharp intake of breath. Symone smiled as she leaped out of bed and hurried to the closet for her powder pink satin robe. She shrugged into the garment, then tied the band around her waist. The wide sleeves hung over her wrists, but the hem ended midthigh.

"Okay, I'm decent."

Jerry rolled over and opened his eyes, folding his arms

behind his head. His midnight eyes caressed her. "You're much better than decent."

Symone liked the way he looked at her. He made her feel strong, desirable and wanted. She smiled. She didn't think she could stop smiling. "Do you want me to look away so you can get out of bed?"

Jerry stretched. The muscles in his arms flexed as he raised them above his head. The sheet slipped down his waist. Symone watched, mesmerized, as his pecs contracted.

He flashed a grin. "Do you want to look away?"

Before she could answer, he tossed the sheet aside and climbed out on the other side of the bed. Symone couldn't stop her eyes from feasting on him. Jerry was unapologetic physical excellence. Broad shoulders, narrowing to a trim waist and slim hips. Long, powerful thighs and calves. Flat stomach and molded chest.

"Stop. You'll make me blush." Jerry circled the bed.

Her eyes flew to his. He was looking at her with a wicked smile. Desire glinted in his eyes. Her nipples tightened in response.

Symone kept her voice light. "I doubt you're capable of blushing." She gave him a cheeky look as she turned away. "I'll race you to the exercise room."

Jerry caught her hand to stop her. "What will I get when I win?"

Symone stepped closer to him. His scent brought back a sweet ache. She lowered her voice. "What will you give me when *I* win?"

His slow smile curled his lips—and her toes. "Whatever you'd like."

She chuckled. "Then I think we'll both win."

* * *

Symone half sat, half reclined on Jerry's bed late Thursday morning reviewing the stack of rejected foundation grant applications. Jerry was at his desk across the room, searching the internet for clues that could led them to Xander or Xander's associates. The silence was deep, but comfortable.

She watched him in silence for a moment. After their exercise, he'd changed into a brick red polo shirt, black cargo shorts, tube socks and sneakers. The bold colors looked wonderful on him. As though he sensed her eyes on him, Jerry looked over his shoulder at her.

Startled and embarrassed to have been caught staring, Symone said the first thing that popped into her mind. "Any luck?"

"Not yet." Jerry shifted on the chair to face her better. His voice was tight with irritation. "And I'm having trouble finding anything about him beyond five years ago. It's as though Xander Fence didn't exist before then."

"For Pete's sake." Symone removed her glasses and rubbed her eyes. How many more discrepancies in Xander's identity were they going to find? "Our vendor who does the background checks has a lot of explaining to do. I left a message for them earlier, asking them to call me."

"Good idea." Jerry nodded his approval. "I'd like to take part in that conversation, if you don't mind. They might say something that could help us learn more about Xander, his partner and their plan to take over the foundation."

Symone suppressed a shiver. "Of course. I'd appreciate your joining me. You might think of additional questions to ask."

Hearing Jerry put it that way—*their plan to take over the foundation*—frightened Symone. It sounded sinister, but it was true. Their investigation had uncovered a complicated, multipronged plan to take control of the foundation from her family. Symone still couldn't believe longtime board members could be involved.

Jerry inclined his head toward the stack of applications on the bed beside her. "How about you? How's the application review going?"

Symone put her glasses back on. "I'd rather be training with you." She exchanged a smile with him.

"You did well today."

Hours earlier, Symone had done power yoga while Jerry lifted weights. She'd run the treadmill and he'd kickboxed. Then they'd worked on her self-defense training. This time, she didn't trip him when she'd practiced freeing herself from her would-be abductor. He'd also taught her to flip a person over her shoulder.

Then they'd made love while they'd showered. Her body still hummed with the memory.

"Thank you." Symone's smile faded. "I haven't found any winners in this pile of applications, at least not yet. Of the ones I've taken another look at so far, I would be compromising myself and the foundation if I selected any of them."

"I'm sorry, Symone." Jerry stared at the flooring with narrowed eyes. "What would happen if you didn't select a program or product from among these applications?"

Symone shrugged, shaking her head. "The board would factor that into their no-confidence vote, which means it wouldn't go well for me. They asked me to pick a different grant applicant and to revise our investment strategy for the new fiscal year. If I fail to do either or both of those things, they'll vote me out and replace me with someone who will."

Jerry frowned, gesturing toward the stack of papers beside her. "Even though these applicants don't meet the mission criteria?"

"I'm afraid so." Symone lowered her voice. "That's my greatest fear, that I'll lose The Bishop Foundation—the organization my grandfather established. You know how important family legacies are."

"Yes, I do." Jerry's voice was dry. "We don't want to be the ones who lose them."

"No, we don't." Symone heard the tension in her voice. "But the board's adamant that it wants to take more risks, with or without me." She looked at the application in her hand. "More and more, it looks like it will have to be without me. There's more than one way to lose a legacy, and that includes compromising its integrity."

Jerry broke the tense silence. "Symone, I know this is hard. There's a lot at stake. But just for a moment, stop thinking and just feel."

Symone's brow furrowed. She didn't understand. "Feel what exactly?"

Jerry leaned forward, bracing his elbows on his legs. "What do you want for the foundation?"

"What do I want? I want a new board." Symone swallowed the nervous laughter that bubbled up her throat.

Jerry spread his hands. "If that's what you want, then go for it. You're already facing the worst that could happen, losing your family's foundation."

Symone blinked. "You're serious?"

"Of course I am." Jerry shrugged. "Why not go on the offensive?"

Symone considered Jerry's expression. He really was serious—and he had a point. The worst-case scenario was already on the table. Why not go out fighting?

She slipped off the bed. "You know what? I'm going to take your advice and go for it. It's a risk, but it's a risk worth taking. I'll start by reviewing the foundation's bylaws."

Jerry stood. "Perfect. Good luck. Let me know what you find."

"I will." Symone gathered the application folders and hurried to her room. Excitement powered her muscles. She had the beginnings of a plan. Granted, it was impetuous, and she was still putting it together, but it was the start of her taking a stand.

Symone rushed into her room and made a beeline for her desk. She deposited the files beside her laptop, then pulled the burner phone from the pocket of her knee-length, pleated lavender dress. She sighed. The foundation lawyer's number was in her personal phone. She dug through her purse for her cell, turned it on, then scrolled through her contacts list until she came to Percy Jeffries's information.

The law offices of Jeffries & Henderson PLLC had represented The Bishop Foundation before the organization had opened its doors. Symone's grandfather had worked with Percy's father until the other man's retirement. The foundation had started working with Percy once he took over his father's interest in the firm more than ten years earlier. Percy had become a good friend as well as their lawyer.

She tapped his direct-dial number into her burner cell. Symone was surprised when he answered on the first ring. She'd been expecting his voice mail. "Percy, it's Symone. How are you?"

She pictured the solicitor, seated behind his desk. Percy was a few years older than her father would've been if he were still alive. He was about her height and solidly built with close-cropped, salt-and-pepper hair. The lawyer was always impeccably dressed in dark three-piece suits. Faint lines creased his brown skin across his brow and on either side of his thin lips.

"Symone." His booming voice carried through the connection. "It's so nice to hear from you. I'm fine. How are you managing?"

"I'm fine, thank you, but I'd like your help with something, please." She wandered to the window. "I'm not in my office. Could you send me a copy of the foundation's bylaws via email?"

"Of course. Is there a problem?"

She heard typing in the background as though he was dropping everything to accommodate her request. Symone smiled. That was Percy. She should've thought to call him sooner.

Symone started to turn away from the window. "I—"

"Hang up!" Jerry burst into her room. "Hang up the phone! Now!"

Symone's eyes stretched wide. "Percy, I've got to go." She hung up on his frantic questions. "What's wrong?"

"We're being tracked." Jerry grabbed her cell phone from her hand. He turned it off and pocketed it. "We've gotta go. Now."

Chapter 15

"Get your things. We're out of here in ten." Jerry's sharp warning rang in her ears.

Symone ran around her bedroom in the formerly safe house. Her heart galloped in her throat as she grabbed shoes and a suitcase. "How do you know we're being tracked?"

She shoved her feet into her white canvas shoes, then dashed back to her desk. She heard Jerry opening and closing doors and drawers, and tossing things. A zipper opened.

"I got an alert on my cell phone." His voice was tense and breathless as he shouted back. "Hurry, Symone. We're taking only what we pack in ten minutes. Everything else is left behind."

"I'm hurrying." Her hands shook as she turned off her clean computer and shoved it into its case. With sweating palms, she threw grant applications and fistfuls of underwear, bras, sock, blouses and skirts into a suitcase. She zipped it closed, then raced to meet Jerry in the hallway. Her breaths were coming too fast. "Ready."

Without a word, he grabbed her suitcase with his free hand and led her on the flight down the stairs and into the garage. She circled the rented sedan while he threw their cases into the trunk.

"Where are we going?" She settled onto the passenger

seat and connected her seat belt. Her pulse drummed in her ears.

"I don't know yet." He climbed behind the steering wheel and fastened his seat belt as he activated the automatic garage door opener.

Symone half expected to see a force of masked gunmen surrounding them in the yard.

Jerry backed the car out of the garage. His eyes made rapid sweeps of the area as he drove above the speed limit out of the resort.

"Why are we going this way?" Symone searched their surroundings through the windshield and side window.

"This exit leads to an isolated road." Jerry lifted his left hip to free an access keycard from his back shorts pocket. "There's only one way into the resort. This access lets you out, but it won't let you back in."

For the past six days, they'd been using the complex's front gates to exit and enter. Now they were traveling in the opposite direction. The condition of the trail grew worse the farther they traveled. The rental car bounced and rocked with increasing frequency. The asphalt surface had broken and deteriorated over the years. After a few miles, it disappeared, leaving behind depressions, ruts and cracks caused by water erosion. No one had been motivated to fix this section of the trail, which was strange since the rest of the resort was so well maintained. Perhaps the road's condition was a deliberate attempt to dissuade visitors from exploring this part of the resort.

A pristine wrought iron gate rose from the ground at the end of the dirt path. This seemed to confirm Symone's suspicion about the road's poor condition being a deterrent. Jerry made the briefest stop to wave his keycard in front of an electronic door lock. The gate retracted. Jerry drove through as soon as there was enough space for the car to clear. He turned the vehicle toward Ohio State Route 180, east to Columbus. They were going home. She wasn't sure how she felt about that. Home was where the danger had started. It also meant the end of their sanctuary.

Symone stole a look at Jerry in her peripheral vision. His expression was the grimmest she'd seen since they'd started this case. "It's because I turned on my cell phone, isn't it?"

"Yes." His stark response sent a chill through her. Symone wanted to kick herself. He continued. "It's my fault. I didn't do enough to emphasize the seriousness of this situation. I should've scared you more."

He was blaming himself for her mistake. Classic Jerry. That was the same thing he'd done with the uncontrollable pop star. Symone didn't want to be in the same category as that emotionally stunted child. Jerry's taking responsibility for her irresponsible act magnified Symone's guilt and shame.

"You've kept me adequately afraid." Telling her people were determined to kill her was scary enough. "I wasn't thinking. This is entirely my fault, not yours and I'm so very sorry. I can't apologize enough."

"It's my job to keep you alive. And keeping you alive is what we have to focus on."

Symone gave him a sharp look. What was he implying? Was he ending their love affair as it was starting? To her, this wasn't just about great sex. In less than a week, Jerry Touré had stolen her heart. Was he going to pretend it was something else? Was their relationship a mere breach of protocol that needed to be rectified?

She forced her attention back to the windshield and briefly closed her eyes. One problem at a time. The issue that had them running from assassins should take precedence.

"How much damage do you think I've done to our safety?" She hated that her carelessness had not only endangered her—it had also threatened Jerry.

"We won't know until we're sure we're not being followed." Jerry repeatedly checked the rearview mirror. He also scanned the cars in front of him. This part of the state route was one lane in either direction. "I'm taking us to Mal's house. His security system's even better than mine and Zeke's."

Like Jerry, Symone kept scanning their surroundings. She felt crushed with guilt over not turning off her cell phone earlier. "Will he mind?"

Jerry glanced at her. "No. He'll understand. I'll let him know once we get there. For now, I need to make sure we're not followed and that I get you there safe and sound."

Symone corrected him. "*We* need to make sure *we* arrive safe and sound." His lack of response wasn't encouraging. "I don't want to put anyone else in danger. What else can I do to keep us safe?"

Jerry paused as though thinking. "I don't know yet. I'd turned off your cell phone and left it in my room at the safe house."

Symone raised her eyebrows. "Oh. Okay. That makes sense." She'd probably never look at another cell phone the same way again.

"Once we get to Mal's, I'll hold on to your laptop. It's what I should've done with both of your devices from the beginning."

"All right." She clenched her hands together on her lap. "You have every right to be upset with me."

He cut her off. "I'm not upset with you."

Hmm. He had a strange way of showing it.

Symone let that pass. She cleared her throat. "I really am sorry for my stupid mistake. You and Mal told me repeatedly not to use my cell phone. You said someone was using it to track my location. You both told me the risk. I only meant to turn it on for a minute, but I got distracted when Percy answered the call so quickly. It was stupid and thoughtless. I truly am sorry."

Jerry shook his head. He vibrated with impatience. "Stop apologizing. It's not your fault. It's mine. I should've made sure you knew not to take any chances. I should've taken the battery out of your phone. I should've taken your phone. I was stupid to have left it with you. You're my charge, my responsibility."

Symone's heart sank. She studied the clean, sharp lines of his profile. "I'm your charge?"

Jerry kept his eyes on the road. "That's right. I shouldn't have allowed our relationship to get personal. *I'm* the professional. I should've known better."

Symone caught her breath. "All right."

She turned back to the windshield, blinking to ease the sting in her eyes. She was his *charge*, someone he was obliged to care for. Then, at the first opportunity, he would leave. Like Paul. With her mother's death, she had to get used to being on her own. It was good that she'd found out now before she fell any deeper in love with a fantasy.

Jerry pulled his rental into Mal's driveway late Thursday morning. He was tense and tired after driving an hour from the cabin resort to his brother's home in northwest Columbus, but he was certain they hadn't been followed. He turned off the engine and shifted to look at Symone on the passenger seat beside him. She'd leaned forward to study the exterior of Mal's house. It was the home in which he and his brothers had grown up. What did she think of it?

For most of their journey, she'd been quiet. What had she been thinking about? What was she thinking about now? Was she nervous about being back in Columbus and within reach of the people who were threatening her?

"We'll be safe here." Jerry waited for her to look at him before he continued. Her chocolate eyes were cool. "The resort was safer because it's farther away. But Mal's got a very secure system. It's the latest technology."

Her smile was polite. "Thank you." She went back to looking at Mal's house.

Jerry pulled out his cell phone and selected Mal's number. "I'll put Mal on speaker."

His brother answered right away. "What's up?"

"Mal, I'm with Symone. We have you on speaker. We're outside of your house. Symone's phone was on. The stalker tried to use the connection to track us."

Mal chewed a curse. "Are you both all right?"

"Yes, we're good." Jerry glanced at Symone.

She started to lean toward him, then seemed to catch herself. "I'm so sorry, Mal."

"What matters is that you're both safe," he said. "Hold on. I'll get Zeke."

Less than two minutes later, Zeke joined the call. "Are you sure you're both okay?"

Jerry sat back on the driver's seat. He heard typing in the background as though Mal had gone back to work. "We're sure but we need a new safe house."

"Use mine." Mal continued working his computer keyboard.

Jerry smiled. "I was hoping you'd say that. Thanks."

Symone pressed against the passenger seat. "Thank you, Mal. It's very kind of you."

"No problem." Mal's typing stopped. "I tried to trace the hacker, but I couldn't find the signal. They must've shut off the program."

Jerry nodded. "Thanks for trying."

"Of course." Mal paused. "And, Jerry, remember—no food in the living room."

Jerry rolled his eyes. "It was one time, Mal." He and his brothers wrapped up their conversation.

"What was that about?" Symone asked. "Why doesn't Mal want you eating in his living room?"

"Mal holds grudges." Jerry scanned their surroundings. "Let's go in. I'll get our bags after I show you around."

Mal's two-story home was an American Craftsman model with white siding and gray stone. Small holly scrubs bordered the well-tended lawn and led visitors up a winding concrete path. Three wide concrete steps carried Jerry and Symone up to the porch and to the chestnut wood door. Jerry unlocked the door and deactivated the alarm before inviting Symone in.

She looked around the open floor plan. "This is a beautiful home."

Jerry pictured Odette and Paul's house. It was spacious and stately despite Paul's horrible decorating style. He was sure Symone's family home had been just as grand. "It's a modest space compared to what you're probably used to, but we enjoyed growing up here."

Her eyes widened with excitement. "This is your family home? It's wonderful."

"Thank you." He turned toward the staircase. "I'll take you upstairs."

Jerry turned right at the top of the stairs. "You can take this guest room. I'll make up the bed after the tour."

Symone moved past him. She stood in the middle of the spacious square room. Two windows allowed plenty of natural light in. A dressing table and matching nightstands were made of teakwood. Vibrant, jewel-toned sectional rugs were laid on the polished hardwood floor around the queen-size bed.

"It's so bright and welcoming." She glanced out one of the windows, then turned to the rest of the room. "Whose room was this?"

"It was originally Zeke's. I took it over when he moved onto OSU's campus." Two years later, he'd joined his older brother at The Ohio State University, where their arguments had become legendary. Mal had wisely attended Ohio University to get away from the brothers' constant fights. "I'll be in Mal's old room across the hall."

Her eyes widened on the framed colored-pencil image beside the closet. She crossed to it. "This is beautiful. Antrim Lake." She adjusted her glasses as she leaned in to read the artist's name. "It's Zeke's work?" She looked at the other two drawings in the room. "Park of Roses. Scioto River. Did he do the paintings in your conference room?"

"Yes, he did." Jerry's chest filled with pride. He enjoyed her reaction to his brother's talent.

Symone smiled. "Your brother's a wonderful artist. I thought you'd bought those pieces from a gallery."

"The agency doesn't have that kind of money." Jerry was going to enjoy sharing Symone's comment with Zeke and especially Mal. "I'm sorry there isn't a desk in the room, but you can work in the dining room or kitchen."

Symone shrugged. "I'm used to working in bed."

"Okay." Jerry nodded. "Are you ready to see the rest of the house?"

"Yes, please." Her brown eyes gleamed with excitement. Over seeing his family home?

Jerry escorted her to Mal's office. He stopped in front of the iPad, which stood on a short, black metal file cabinet. "This device is connected to a twenty-four-hour home security system. The screen displays real-time video feeds from the six cameras stationed around the perimeter of the house. Mal and I'll watch it closely."

"Thank you." Symone's eyes swept the office, pausing on Mal's project board, computers and bookcases. "It's wonderful that you grew up in a big family. Even though your parents are no longer with you, you still have your brothers. You're not alone."

Symone's back stiffened. Her eyes widened as though she was surprised that she'd spoken the words out loud. She turned and walked out of room, stopping in front of another door.

Jerry paused beside her. He wanted to reach out to her, take her hand and assure her she wasn't alone. He wanted to wrap his arms around her until the loneliness left her eyes. He crushed those instincts. His feelings for Symone were what got them into this latest mess in the first place.

He nudged the door open. "This is the guest bathroom. I'll get us fresh towels later."

Symone assessed the turquoise decor and blue ceramic tiling. "Mal's very tidy. If I didn't know someone lived here, I'd think this was a display home."

Jerry chuckled. "I'll have to tell him you said that."

Symone spun toward him. Her lips were parted in shock. "Don't you dare."

Jerry grinned, staring into her big brown eyes before

forcing himself to turn away. He nodded toward the end of the hall. "That's Mal's bedroom. He has an adjoining bathroom, so we'll have this one to ourselves. Last stop is the basement."

He took her through the living and dining rooms, and the kitchen on their way to the basement. "Washer and dryer." He gestured toward the laundry units in the corner, then drew her attention to the treadmill, elliptical machine, old-school weight bench and black vinyl boxing bag. "Exercise equipment."

Symone's eyebrows disappeared beneath her bangs. "You Tourés really take your fitness seriously."

"We have to." Jerry shrugged. "Our clients' lives depend on it."

Symone nodded. "Thank you. And thank you so much for allowing me to stay with you and your brother. Hopefully, you won't have to put up with me much longer."

Put up with me... "What's that supposed to mean?" Jerry followed Symone up the basement stairs to the kitchen. Her steps were so fast. Was she running from him?

"I'm your client. Your charge." She didn't stop at the kitchen. She continued through the dining and living rooms, speaking over her shoulder. The flirty skirt of her lavender dress swung at him like a chiding finger. "You have a job to do and once you're done, you'll move on to the next."

"Symone, you hired my brothers and me to protect you. Your safety is our priority." Jerry appealed to her back as he followed her up the main stairs to the top floor. "We have to focus on keeping you safe. We can't risk being distracted. We need to find the people who killed your mother and who are trying to kill you."

Symone turned in the doorway of her guest room. Her

frown questioned him. "You want to put our relationship on pause until after the investigation?"

He saw the spark of hope in her brown eyes. It almost weakened him. He wanted so badly to give in to his need for her—but that was only a delay. He could never make her happy. They were just too different. "Symone, I don't think that would be a good idea."

Hurt replaced the hope in her eyes. "Why not?"

Jerry closed his eyes briefly. He didn't have the strength for this. Ending things with Symone was like cutting off his arm. "Let's stick to the case."

"No." She shook her head. "I need to understand how it's possible for you to make love with me this morning and now act like we're barely more than strangers."

He dropped his eyes to the hardwood flooring. "Symone, you and I wouldn't fit. We're from two different worlds."

"Are we?" Symone tilted her head. "I'm from Earth. Where do you think you're from?"

Jerry rolled his eyes. "You know what I mean. We're too different."

"You're going to have to do better than that, Jerry." She crossed her arms over the lavender bodice of her dress. "How are we so very different?"

He gestured between them. "For example, my family and I are struggling to keep our security business open. Your family founded a multimillion-dollar foundation to advance medical research. You're pearls and designer suits. I don't even wear a tie."

She released her arms. "Are you really that shallow?" Her eyes widened with amazement. "You're loyalty and courage, and doing what's right. You inspire *me* to be courageous. You give me hope that there are more people like you and your brothers in this world."

She was giving him that look again, as though he was some sort of hero. She made him want to live up to those expectations, so he'd actually be worthy of her regard.

Jerry ran a hand over his hair. "I'm sorry, Symone. I wish I could give you what you need, but I can't."

"Can't? Or won't?" Her eyes glowed with temper as she looked him over. "How do you do that, Jerry?"

He frowned. "Do what?"

"Turn your emotions on and off. One moment you care…the next, you really don't."

"Symone—"

"I was thinking about you on the drive over here." Her full lips twisted in a cynical smile. He didn't recognize her. "You blame yourself if your charges put themselves in danger like I did by leaving my personal cell phone on, or like that spoiled teenaged singer did by sneaking out of his hotel room to go to an illegal gambling hole. Everybody thinks you're doing that because it's your case so you're in total control. If there's any finger-pointing to be done, then by golly, they should point their fingers at you because that's where they belong."

By golly? "If I take point on a case, then yes, everything to do with that case is my responsibility. How's that a bad thing?"

Symone started shaking her head before he'd finished speaking. "But that's not the reason, Jerry. Maybe you've tricked yourself into believing it is, but it's not."

He folded his arms across his chest. "Then tell me, Symone. You know me so well. Why do I accept responsibility if things go south on my case?"

"You're not blaming yourself for everything and anything that goes wrong on a case because of some over-developed sense of responsibility." She stepped closer to him, holding his eyes. "Blaming yourself is your way of running from your emotions."

"What?" Where had that come from? "What are you—?"

Symone continued as though she hadn't heard his interruption. Her face flushed. Her body vibrated with agitation. "You treat yourself like a machine—like an android—because you don't want to feel."

"That's ridi—"

Her words sped up. "You're afraid that if you feel, you'll get hurt and that's probably the only risk in your entire life that you don't want to take."

Through her unshed tears, Jerry could see the hurt and anger in her eyes. His heart shattered in his chest.

His head spun. His ears rang. Symone's words were like a punch in the face from a heavyweight champion. "You're wrong." His voice was raw, even to his ears.

"Am I?" She stepped backward into the room. "We'll do this your way, Jerry. This is a job. I'm your charge. You're my bodyguard. When this is over—and I pray it will be soon—I'll write you a check and we'll never have to see each other again."

"Wait, Symone, I—" He didn't know what he was going to say. He only knew he didn't want their conversation to end like this.

"I have work to do. Could you bring up my bags, please? Thank you." She closed the door between them.

Jerry stared at it as thoughts, snatches of conversations and images of Symone's tear-filled eyes spun in his mind. She wasn't going to open the door. She wasn't going to hear him out. She'd made it clear she was done talking with him, at least about their personal relationship. He forced his legs to turn and walk away.

He'd made so many mistakes with this case. He should've taken Symone's personal cell phone from her. He shouldn't have gotten involved with a charge. And he never should've fallen in love with a woman who was out of his league.

Chapter 16

"Thanks again for cooking, Jer." Mal finished his spaghetti and meatballs. Seated at the head of the table, he lowered his knife and fork to the cream porcelain plate and sipped his ice water.

"It was delicious. Thank you." Symone avoided his eyes as she lowered her blue-tinted acrylic glass.

Jerry took a deep drink of water to ease his dry throat. "You're both welcome. I'm glad you enjoyed it. Dinner is the least I can do, Mal, since you're letting us stay here without any notice."

Jerry and Symone were still in the clothes they'd worn when they'd run from the safe house. Mal was wearing the business casual gray slacks, blue shirt and gray tie he'd worn to work.

Symone gave Mal a warm smile. "I can't thank you enough."

Mal waved away their words. "No problem. I'm glad you came here."

"I feel like we're putting you out." Symone dropped her eyes to her nearly empty plate. "It was *my* thoughtless actions that caused the change in plans." She stroked moisture from her water glass with the tips of her long, slender fingers.

Jerry remembered the feel of her hands on his skin. Her

touch had made his body burn. He grabbed his glass and drained the last of his water.

Mal looked from Symone to him and back. His brother had masked his expression, but Jerry could tell Mal had picked up on the tension between him and Symone. The voice in his head spewed a string of curses.

Dinner had been a comfortable experience for the most part. Symone had asked Mal about the search for Xander—nothing new to report—and their search for his possible accomplice—no leads yet. Conversation had flowed between Symone and Mal, and Jerry and Mal, but Jerry's exchanges with Symone had been stilted. Mal would've had to have been in a deep sleep to miss it. His brother never missed anything.

Mal gave Symone an empathetic smile. "There's no such thing as a perfect plan. That's why we have backups and safeguards like the alert on Jerry's phone in case we need to make changes in the middle of an investigation."

"You explained that so well, Mal." She adjusted her glasses. Her expression was thoughtful. "Instead of looking for someone to blame, your explanation acknowledges that it's humanly impossible to be in complete control all the time. Thank you."

"Sure." Mal's response was neutral. But Jerry knew his brother. On the inside, Mal was laughing at him.

For Pete's sake.

Jerry drew a calming breath, catching the scents of tomato sauce, oregano, garlic and Parmesan cheese from their meal. He forced his stiff facial muscles into a professional smile. "Bottom line—TSG believes the burden of adjusting our original plans lies with us, not our clients."

"Or your charges." Symone looked through him. Her detachment cut like a blade.

Mal coughed as though his drink had gone down the wrong pipe. He caught his breath after a moment. "Speaking of making adjustments, I'll work from home until the killer is caught. That way, I can be additional protection for you, Symone."

"Thank you. I would really like that." Her smile was like the sun coming out.

Jerry felt the burn. Did she think they'd need a buffer going forward? Thinking about the tension between them during dinner, she may be right. "Thanks, Mal."

Symone adjusted her glasses again. "I'm a little embarrassed to be causing all this trouble."

Mal shook his head. "Your safety isn't trouble, Symone. It's our priority."

Symone stood to gather her place setting. "That's what Jerry said. Several times."

Jerry stood more abruptly than he'd intended. He put his hands on Symone's dishes to stop her from clearing the table. "I'll take care of that."

Her eyes fell short of his. "That's not fair. You cooked. I'll do the cleanup."

Mal rose from the table. "Jerry's right. We've got this."

Symone hesitated. "All right, if you insist. I've got some work to do anyway. Thank you, gentlemen. I'll wish you good night now."

"Sleep well," Mal responded.

"Night." Jerry watched her disappear at the staircase. A weight pressed against his chest as he thought about all the meals they'd shared and how they'd worked in perfect sync to clean up afterward. Kitchen patrol had never been so enjoyable.

Mal carried his dishes to the sink. "What's up?"

Jerry followed him, carrying Symone's place setting. "What do you mean?"

Mal turned to him. His brother was maybe an inch taller than him. Wonder Woman had her Lasso of Truth. Mal had his direct stare. He pinned Jerry with it now. "Don't pretend, Jer. When I got home, I thought I'd set my air conditioner too low. That was before I'd seen either of you. And you made spaghetti and meatballs."

Jerry frowned. "So what?"

Mal arched a thick dark eyebrow. "It's your go-to comfort food. What did you argue about? Was it the case—or something else?"

Jerry's gaze fell. He lowered his voice, hoping Symone wouldn't hear them talking about her. "Things got personal at the cabin. Neither of us expected anything to happen, but… She's amazing. Shy and bold. Intense and funny. Super smart and kind. You should see the way her employees react to her. It's like a Beyoncé concert—or at least the way I imagine a Beyoncé concert."

Mal smiled. "She's great. I know. I've spoken with her, too. What happened?"

Jerry leaned his hips against the white-and-silver marble countertop beside the sink. He folded his arms under his chest. "I let myself get distracted. I lost my focus, and the killer almost tracked her to the safe house."

His gut filled with ice each time he thought about what could've happened if he hadn't received the alert that the killer had connected with Symone's phone.

"That's not what happened."

Jerry's eyes shot to Mal's. "Yes, it is."

Mal shook his head. "Symone made an honest mistake and you're using it to put distance between you because you think you're falling in love." He returned to the dining room to continue clearing the table.

Jerry didn't *think* he was falling in love—he was afraid he was already there. He followed Mal. "How could I be in love? We've only known each other a week."

"Mom and Dad said it was love at first sight for them. It was the same for me with Grace." Mal collected the water pitcher.

Love at first sight? Jerry almost dropped his dishes. "Symone and I are too different. She comes from generations of wealth. Mom and Dad were retired military."

Their parents had met while serving in the Marine Corps.

"This is about you and Symone, not your extended families." Mal loaded the dishwasher.

Jerry considered the back of Mal's clean-shaven head. His plain-spoken brother was always honest with him regardless of how much the truth might hurt. "Do you think I run away from my feelings because I'm afraid of getting hurt?"

"Yes." Mal spoke over his shoulder.

That stung. "I disagree."

Mal continued packing the dishwasher. "You're allowed."

"Symone and I wouldn't last. She barely uses contractions and says things like, 'Our bylaws mandate.'" Jerry put his dishes in the sink, ready for Mal to load them.

"And you're a slob." Mal straightened from the dishwasher. "Do you want to give a relationship with her a chance or not?"

Jerry thought about his time with Symone at the cabin. They were strangers to each other in an unfamiliar environment, running for their lives. Their circumstances had been unusual to say the least but the week they'd spent together had been incredible.

"Of course I do." Jerry's voice was hoarse. "But I have to face facts. The time Symone and I spent in the cabin, that wasn't real. What if she agrees to continue our relationship in the real world and then realizes I don't belong there?"

Mal shrugged. "What if she realizes you do?"

Jerry shook his head as he turned to walk away. *Only in my dreams.*

"Symone! I was worried about you. What happened?" Percy answered her call after the first ring early Friday morning.

Symone half sat, half reclined on the bed in Zeke's old room. Her thoughts raced. She couldn't tell The Bishop Foundation's lawyer and longtime family friend the truth about what happened yesterday—*The person who's trying to kill me was tracking my cell phone*—but she owed him an explanation. "I'm so sorry, Percy. I had a sudden emergency."

"It must have been a matter of life and death." His tone was dry.

"Aren't they always?" She hoped her humor sounded natural.

Percy chuckled. "Before I forget, you should call Ellie after we talk. When I didn't hear back from you yesterday, I called her to ask if she'd spoken with you. I'm afraid I scared her. She asked if I knew where you were and who you were with. Of course I didn't. But I told her whoever heard from you first should make sure to ask you to contact the other one."

Symone stared at the teakwood dressing table across the room without seeing it. She wished Percy hadn't involved

Ellie in yesterday's events. She understood why he had. She probably would have done the same. Symone would deal with Ellie, but that would have to wait until later. "I'll give her a call. Thank you."

"Wonderful." Percy sighed. "Now, how can I help you, my dear?"

Symone swung her legs off the mattress and rose from the bed. The sectional rug was soft beneath her bare feet. Like the safe house, Mal had covered all the windows in his home with one-way tinted screens. Still, the room received enough sunlight that Symone had chosen to leave the overhead lamps off.

She wandered to the wall beside the closet to study Zeke's colored-pencil framed drawing of Antrim Lake. The image was from the perspective of the dock overlooking the free-form lake. It was soothing. Zeke was incredibly talented.

A couple of hours ago, she'd risked a trip to Mal's basement to exercise. She'd hoped to arrive early enough to avoid Jerry. He seemed to have had the same hope. They'd arrived at the same time. Mal was meeting up with Zeke for their usual six-mile run around Antrim Lake. Jerry, however, remained inside. The killer knew Jerry and Symone were together. If Jerry was seen in the neighborhood, the killer would've known Symone was nearby. While exercising, Symone tried to ignore him, but it would've been easier to ignore the sun.

After cleaning up and dressing in a cream blouse and tangerine culottes, she'd made this call to Percy. "Thank you for sending me a copy of the foundation's bylaws."

"Of course. It's my pleasure." Beneath Percy's voice, the pinging sound of metal hitting porcelain was a strong hint the lawyer was enjoying a mug of coffee. "Did it provide the information you were hoping for?"

"I'm not sure." Symone returned to the bed where she'd left her printout of the bylaws. She'd marked several passages with yellow highlighter. "That's why I'm calling. Could you pull up a copy to follow along with me?"

"I can. Give me a moment." Rapid tapping broke the brief silence. "I've got it. What questions can I help you with?"

"Could you explain Article Two, Section Three? I can read a prospectus and spreadsheets, but legalese is too much for me." She waited for Percy to find the section she referenced.

"Ah, this language deals with the board." His tone was distracted as though he was skimming it in preparation for her questions. "What would you like to ask, my dear?"

"I want to be clear on the separation of powers between the board and the chair, and the specific responsibilities board members have."

Percy hesitated. "Is everything okay, Symone?"

No, everything's not okay. "I just want a better understanding of the board's responsibilities to the chair and the foundation. Section Three requires each member of the board to bring concerns about the foundation to the chair, members of the administration and other board members in a timely manner. Am I understanding that correctly?"

"Yes, you are." Percy sounded like a proud professor. "Your grandfather thought of it as a check on the board."

Jerry was right. Her grandfather had included in the bylaws checks on the foundation's board as well as the chair. "What does it require of the board?"

"That section requires *any* member who had a complaint about *any* aspect of the foundation to bring their concerns to the entire leadership team—chair, vice chair, administrative assistant and board members—in a timely manner. Your grandfather was adamant about that. He didn't want the members to go off in secret to complain about the foundation, then ambush him during a meeting. He dealt with enough of that in the corporate world."

Grandpa, I could kiss you. "How do the bylaws define a 'timely manner'?"

"It's quarterly." A clicking sound carried from Percy's end of the line as he moved through the electronic file. "Article Five, Section One explains that the leadership team will close out all old business each quarter. My father and your grandfather referred to it as the speak-now-or-forever-hold-your-peace section."

Symone flipped through her printout of the bylaws. It would have been helpful if her grandfather and Percy's father had created an index. She made a mental note to request one, perhaps after the board meeting that would decide her fate with the foundation.

"Found it. Thank you." She highlighted the passage. "Is there a penalty if a board member breaks any of these rules? If they meet separately to discuss their concerns or if they don't bring their concerns to leadership in a timely manner?"

"Oh, absolutely." Percy chuckled. "Your grandfather was big on enforcement. Penalties for various infractions—missing board meetings, missing leadership votes, discussing foundation business without authorization, et cetera—are all described under Article Thirteen, Section Six, Disciplinary Measures."

Symone flipped through more pages, searching for Article Thirteen, Section Six. "I can't believe you remember where all of this information appears in this document." Percy's laughter made her smile. She got to the pertinent section and skimmed the text. *Gotcha!* "This is just what I need. Thank you, Percy."

"Anytime, my dear. Call me if there's anything else I can do for you."

"Oh, I will." Symone gave Percy her best, asking him to give her love to his family, then ended the call.

She took a few moments to review the Disciplinary Measures more thoroughly before she remembered her promise to call Ellie. She filed the bylaws, then entered her administrative assistant's phone number by memory.

Her admin answered on the first ring. "This is Eleanor Press. May I help you?"

"Ellie, it's Symone—"

"Symone! Where have you been?" Ellie's voice rose several octaves. Symone winced. "We've been so worried about you. Percy said you disconnected the call abruptly."

"I'm fine, Ellie. I'm sorry you were worried." Symone paced the room. It was more spacious than her bedroom in the cabin. She stopped to again admire Zeke's original drawings of the Scioto River and the Park of Roses.

"But where are you?" The other woman sounded frustrated.

Symone smiled at her fussing. "Ellie, you know I can't tell you that."

Ellie exhaled a heavy sigh. "Symone, with all due respect, how much longer is this going to continue? It's been more than a week. What's taking Touré Security Group so long? Do they even know what they're doing?"

Symone's muscles stiffened. It surprised her how much her admin's criticism of Jerry and his brothers bothered her. Her face heated with anger.

"Yes, they do know what they're doing." Her tone was curt. "They have my complete trust and respect."

"How can you say that?" Ellie seemed equal parts angry and incredulous. "You barely know these men. What have they learned from their investigation?"

Her temper strained for release. Symone made an effort to keep it in check. "I don't owe you an explanation or update. Do you have any issues relating to the foundation you need to discuss with me?"

Ellie's sigh was softer. She brought her voice under control. "I'm sorry, Symone. I'm worried about you. And I'm running a lot of interference with the board. It's very stressful. They want to know when you'll be back in the office full-time."

"Once we find the person who killed my mother and who's threatening me." Symone turned back to the bed, and the folders, printouts and charts strewn across it. "Is there anything else?"

"How's the report coming? Do you need any more information?"

"It's almost completed." Symone settled back against the bed's headboard. She lifted her laptop's lid and re-awakened the device.

"Really?" Ellie sounded pleasantly surprised. "Great. Do you want me to review it for you?"

Symone shook her head although Ellie couldn't see her. "No, I can handle it. In fact, I'd better get back to—"

Ellie interrupted. "I'm sorry, Symone. I didn't mean to upset you. I'm just worried about you."

Symone forced herself to relax. Ellie had apologized. She was irritated but accepting the other woman's apology and moving on was the right and mature thing to do. "There's no need to be worried, but thank you. Email if you need me. And don't let the board get to you. Tell them to call me if they need to discuss my return to the office."

She and Ellie ended their conversation cordially. The board must really be putting pressure on her admin. Symone tossed the burner phone beside her on the mattress. Once things returned to normal, she'd encourage Ellie to take a few weeks off.

"Eleanor Press and Xander Fence are fugitives." Mal dropped the bombshell at the start of the team's videoconference late Friday morning. Working from home, he wore a cream polo shirt, navy cargo shorts and athletic socks. "They're wanted by the FBI for bank, insurance and wire fraud."

Symone's mind went blank. "What?" She was seated to Mal's right at his circular blond wood dining table.

"Wait a minute. What?" Jerry spoke at the same time. Seated on Mal's left, he was similarly dressed as his brother in a jade polo shirt and black shorts.

"Excuse me?" Zeke spoke from the small blond wood conversation table in his office. He looked like the corporate executive he was in a white dress shirt and magenta tie.

"Now we know who Xander's partner is." Celeste sat beside Zeke, sipping coffee. The private investigator was wearing another black cotton T-shirt. "How'd you discover that?"

Mal lowered his pen to his notepad and leaned back against his chair. "When we searched farther than five years back, we lost the trail on Ellie and Xander. That made me suspect those were fake names. I used the trial facial recognition program we'd ordered—"

Jerry corrected him. "The one *you'd* ordered, geek."

Mal slid his brother a look but didn't take the bait. "We couldn't find anything on Xander beyond five years ago because his identity didn't exist. His real name is Norris

Hall. Hall and Dorothy Wiggans belonged to the same community theater group."

Symone's eyes flew to Mal's. "That's how he learned about the foundation."

"Apparently." Mal nodded. "As for Ellie, her identity is stolen. Her real name is Bonnie Rae." A few clicks on his laptop allowed Mal to share his screen. He uploaded two images. "These are Hall's and Rae's FBI wanted photos."

Zeke nodded. "Impressive work, Mal. Thank you."

Celeste squinted at the computer screen. "I agree. Good job."

Jerry patted Mal's shoulder. "You've got skills, Mal."

"Thank you." Symone could only stare at the images on the screen. Instead of Ellie's auburn hair and jade eyes, Bonnie Rae was a brown-eyed brunette. So was Norris Hall. Symone felt sick.

She stared at Mal but didn't see him. His voice was muffled beneath the pulse roaring in her ears. Her lips were parted, but her mind was blank. She didn't have the words.

Jerry leaned forward to catch Symone's attention from Mal's other side. His movement shattered her trance. "Are you all right?"

Symone shook her head. Her fingers trembled as she smoothed the shorts of her tangerine culottes. "I've worked with her for more than nine months. I never once suspected she was anyone other than who she said she was." She turned to meet Jerry's eyes. "And she killed my mother."

"We don't know that yet," Zeke said.

"Yes, we do." Celeste gestured in Symone's direction. "As the foundation's admin, she worked closely with Symone, Odette and Paul. She probably overheard snatches of conversation that could've included information about

Odette's heart condition. She could access Symone's phone and laptop to plant the bugs."

Zeke spread his hands. "All good points, but we can't jump to conclusions."

Celeste shrugged. The movement was jerky with impatience. "Okay. If it makes you feel better, we'll pretend two plus two doesn't equal four—yet."

Jerry addressed Symone. "You really need to talk with your background check services vendor."

"You're right." Anger chased the chill from Symone's blood. She waved a hand toward the computer screen. "Ellie or Bonnie or whatever she calls herself had access to all our bank account information and financial documents. I just spoke with her."

Celeste lowered her coffee mug. "Today? What about?"

Symone clenched her hands. "She wanted to know where I was. Of course, I didn't tell her. I thought she was being protective. It never occurred to me she could be Xander's partner—or a fugitive from the law. She also asked about the report for the special board meeting."

Zeke rubbed his eyes. "We have to take this to Eriq and Taylor." He dropped his hand. "They can bring Bonnie Rae in for questioning."

Jerry nodded. "She probably knows where Xander is."

"Please excuse me." Symone stood and started toward the stairs. Her legs felt shaky. "I have to call the foundation's lawyer and ask him to remove Ellie's—Bonnie's—access to the foundation's accounts."

Seconds after Symone ended her call with Percy, Jerry knocked on the open door to her guest room. The look on his face made her stomach drop. His expression was almost as grave as it had been when he'd broken the news that her mother had been murdered.

Leaning against the nearby dressing table, she dropped the burner cell into her pocket and braced herself for whatever he had to say. "What's happened?"

"There's been an accident." He paused. "Paul's in the hospital."

Symone's knees shook. If it wasn't for the dresser, she would have ended up on the floor. Her only thought was to get to her stepfather. Fast.

Chapter 17

"What happened to Paul?" Symone slid forward on the car's back passenger seat. She strained to keep panic from her voice and gory images from her mind. Mal was navigating his black SUV on the twenty-minute drive to Mount Carmel St. Ann's in northeast Columbus Friday morning.

Jerry turned sideways on the front passenger seat to see her. "Eriq called Zeke. Paul was hit by a car in a shopping center parking lot."

"Oh, my—" Symone covered her gasp with her right hand. "How is he?" Her palm muffled her words.

Jerry took a breath. "He was still unconscious when the ambulance arrived."

Dropping her hands, Symone closed her eyes. "Why didn't I insist he accept protection? I should have insisted." She felt Jerry's hand, warm and strong, cover hers where they rested on her lap. Her eyes popped open.

Jerry held them. "You tried to get him to change his mind, but you couldn't force him. TSG had an agent watching him, but from a distance. She was the one who called the ambulance and provided a description of the car."

Symone eased her hands free of Jerry's and sat back against the smoke gray cloth interior. Her skin was cold where she'd lost his touch. "Thank you for that."

Silence settled in the vehicle. The tension around her was like an inflatable ball, pressing against her as it swelled. Symone chased images of Paul's broken body from her mind. Desperate for a distraction, she concentrated on the view through the side window. Treetops were interspersed with shopping centers featuring upscale restaurants, fast-food stops, specialty stores and movie theaters. These neighborhoods were homes to warehouses, discount shops, gas stations and parking lots. And in the distance, the silhouette of the downtown skyline loomed.

Symone drew a calming breath. Mal's SUV smelled like vinyl cleaner, soap and pine needles. Jerry had been using a rental during the case. What kind of car did he own and what did it smell like? Probably coffee, fast food— and mints.

Mal merged onto Interstate 270 toward downtown Columbus. The sluggish traffic put her patience to the test.

She checked her watch, then looked up at the back of Jerry's tight curls and Mal's clean-shaven head. "I thought I was the killer's target? Why would they attack Paul, especially since we announced his resignation from the foundation?"

"I thought that was strange." Mal's response was almost inaudible.

Symone caught the look that passed between the brothers. She narrowed her eyes. "Are you using me as bait?"

"I'm sorry." Jerry shifted on his seat to look at her again. "We think the killer's getting impatient and is trying to draw you out. Eriq and Taylor agree with us."

"They're at the hospital." Mal changed lanes, moving closer to the exit in preparation of getting off the interstate. "Zeke updated them on Ellie's and Xander's real identities."

Symone removed her glasses to rub both eyes. "If you're going to set a trap with me as the target, you could have at least told me."

Mal glanced at her in the rearview mirror. "It was Jerry's idea, but I'm sorry, too."

"You have enough on your mind with Paul's accident." Jerry held her eyes. "I wouldn't put you in harm's way if I wasn't sure you'd be safe with Mal, Eriq, Taylor and me."

Symone adjusted her glasses. "You want to use me as bait. I want to see Paul. We both get what we want. Just next time, tell me."

"I'm hoping there won't be a next time." Jerry faced forward.

"So am I." Mal's voice was grim.

Symone's eyes brushed over the back of Jerry's head before she turned away. Once they solved this case, would her life have to be in danger before she saw him again?

Eriq and Taylor met them in the hospital lobby and brought them up to Paul's room. Symone's tension eased a bit when she saw the uniformed police officer stationed outside his room. The young man was chatting with a nurse who looked to be about his age. They made a good-looking couple.

Symone gave Eriq and Taylor a smile of gratitude. "Thank you for providing him with protection."

"Of course." Taylor wore a black, scoop-necked blouse and cream slacks. "He came to for a little while, but he's sleeping again now." She gestured toward the nurse who'd joined them. "Becky's one of the nurses assigned to your stepfather."

The young woman was about Symone's height. She returned her handshake with a firm grip. Her hot pink, short-sleeved top and matching pants clashed with her wealth of red curls. Her hair framed her peaches-and-cream complexion. Her brown eyes sparkled when she smiled. Symone instantly felt she could trust the medical professional.

Becky's voice was soft and kind as she explained Paul's condition. "Your stepfather has a headache. He doesn't show signs of a concussion, though. He has a few cracked ribs, some cuts and bruises. He's in pain, but the good news is we don't believe any of his injuries will lead to permanent damage."

"That *is* good news." But Symone couldn't stop worrying. "Would it be possible for me to see him? I won't stay long."

Becky shook her head. "He's sleeping, which is exactly what he needs. We don't think he should be disturbed yet. But we're going to check on him again in another hour. You could see him then."

An hour? That long? Symone sighed, gritting her teeth. "All right. Thank you and thank you for taking care of him."

"You're welcome." Becky smiled. "I'm familiar with The Bishop Foundation. Thank *you* for everything you do." She left before Symone could respond.

"All right, then." Eriq pulled out his notepad. "The TSG agent assigned to Paul told the officers at the scene it looked like the driver aimed for your stepfather." He gave Symone an apologetic look. "The driver struck him and kept going as though they were fleeing the scene. Other witnesses corroborated the agent's statement. We also have part of the license plate and a description of the car—a silver hatchback."

Symone froze. "A silver hatchback?"

Eriq smoothed his bolo tie. The copper slide clip was shaped like a walleye. He wore it with a white shirt and navy slacks. "We're way ahead of you. We checked for cars registered under Ellie Press and Xander Fence. We know Ellie owns a silver hatchback and the first three letters of her plate match witnesses' reports, GZH."

Jerry looked to Symone. "This hit-and-run's similar to the second threat against you and Paul."

Symone's eyes strayed toward Paul's room. Something didn't make sense. "When did the hit-and-run happen?"

Eriq flipped through pages filled with notes.

Taylor found the information in her book first. "About nine."

"That's right." Eriq nodded, stabbing a page in his book. "Why?"

"I was on the phone with Ellie—Bonnie, whoever—a little after nine." Symone frowned. She looked from Eriq and Taylor to Jerry and Mal. "I called her at the office. She answered the phone right away and we spoke for several minutes." She turned back to the detectives. "That may have been Ellie's car, but she couldn't have been driving it. She was on the phone with me."

Jerry's muscles tightened with surprise. He crossed his arms over his jade polo shirt. "Xander Fence."

"He's resurfaced." Like Jerry, Mal crossed his arms over his cream shirt.

"*He* must be the one trying to draw Symone out." Jerry addressed Eriq and Taylor. "We don't know if he's going to look like Xander or Norris." Will he be a green-eyed blond or a brown-eyed brunette?

Eriq gestured toward the officer outside Paul's door. "We gave Officer Mallard pictures of both suspects and their alternate identities."

Symone adjusted her glasses. "But if they're partners,

why would Xander try to frame Ellie for the hit-and-run? What's the benefit?"

Taylor shrugged. "He must be setting her up to take the fall. You've heard the saying there's no honor among thieves."

Eriq turned to Symone. "You said you were speaking with Ellie at the time of the hit-and-run. What did you talk about?"

Symone gave the detectives a succinct summary of her conversation with her admin-cum-FBI-fugitive. It was the same information she'd given him and his brothers earlier. Jerry watched her sharing the exchange with Eriq and Taylor. Her recap was clear and concise. Her voice was warm and soothing. Her arms were as graceful as a dancer's as she used them to talk. She was beautiful.

The four of them plus Officer Mallard stationed outside Paul's door were partially blocking the hallway. However, from the way Symone's eyes kept straying to Paul's room as though her stepfather would appear in the doorway, Jerry was sure she wouldn't willingly move to a more comfortable location. Her continued care and concern for her stepfather impressed Jerry. He'd been surprised and disappointed when Paul had deserted Symone after being told she was the killer's target. However, Symone remained by her stepfather's side when he was in danger. She didn't hold a grudge. She was motivated by decency and doing the right thing. Another reason he was in love with her.

After Symone brought the detectives up to speed on her conversation with Ellie, Jerry turned to them. "We need a favor."

Eriq gave the three of them a suspicious look. "What is it?"

At the same time, Taylor smiled. "Of course."

Eriq scowled at his partner.

Asking for this favor was worth the risk of rejection. If his plan worked, it would ensure Symone's safety and get Ellie/Bonnie and Xander/Norris out of her life for good.

Jerry continued. "Let Zeke and Mal watch your interview with Ellie. They could research her answers for connections to Xander or help us find him before he finds us."

Eriq seemed skeptical. "And where would you be?"

Jerry turned to Symone. She was watching him as though he was a stranger. That hurt. He worked through the pain. "Symone and I will search Ellie's office for anything that would connect her and/or Xander to Odette's murder, the threats against Symone and Paul, or maybe even Dorothy Wiggans's death. Maybe we'll even find something that lets us know where Xander is. But we'll have to do this after hours when the employees have gone."

"It's a good plan." Mal nodded in approval.

"Yes." Symone sounded surprised. "It's a very good plan."

Taylor turned to Eriq. "I agree. Teaming up with Zeke, Mal, Jerry and Symone would save us a ton of legwork on the back end, especially if Jerry and Symone find something in Ellie's office."

Eriq hesitated. "But if this hit-and-run is just for Xander to get to Symone, is it really a good idea for just the two of you to go off on your own?"

Symone squared her shoulders. "We'll be careful. Don't worry."

Eriq shrugged. "Well, if you're not worried, I'm not worried." He shifted his attention to Jerry. "Let's do it."

"Great." Jerry felt a surge of success. If they found evidence linking Ellie and Xander to these crimes, and could arrest both of them, they could close this case tonight and Symone would be safe. He turned to Mal. "Let's get Zeke."

Mal held up his cell phone. "I'll let him know we're coming."

Jerry turned to Symone. "Are you with me?"

"Always." Her eyes seemed drawn to Paul's room one final time before she led the way to the bank of elevators.

Always. He wished that word wasn't so out of reach.

Symone unlocked the side door that led from the parking lot to the lobby of the building that housed The Bishop Foundation Friday evening. With the longer summer days, the sun was still out although the temperature had dropped. Thankfully.

"This building's lack of security is insulting." Jerry seemed frustrated again by the lack of cameras. He held the door open for her.

Symone locked her knees in preparation for walking past his warmth and scent. She watched as he looked over his shoulder toward the parking lot, and up and down the sidewalk. His tension eased. Apparently, they hadn't been followed. Good.

Jerry joined Symone inside, making sure the door locked behind them. Then he submitted the lobby to the same scrutiny he'd given the building's exterior. Overhead lights were on all over the main floor. Symone suspected the extra electricity was the property manager's concession to safety. Of course, the company passed the cost of the all-night utility usage back to its tenants, including the foundation.

Symone led them to the elevators. "You said as much previously." She pressed the Up button, then gave him a smile. "In fact, you criticized the security one week ago today, the first day we met."

Heat shifted in his eyes. Symone caught her breath. His look reminded her of their night—and morning—of intimacy. Her skin tingled as though he'd touched her.

Jerry broke eye contact, shifting his attention to the elevator bank behind her. "We're the only two people here. It's not safe. Do you work here by yourself after hours?"

The elevator's arrival claimed Symone's attention. She entered the car and waited for Jerry to join her before pressing the button for the seventh floor. "I have the feeling that if I answer yes, you'll be disappointed."

"It's not safe, Symone," he repeated. "Promise me—"

Symone waited but Jerry didn't finish his thought. Was he going to ask her to promise him she wouldn't come to the building after hours? She clenched her fists at her side. Was he toying with her? Was she his charge and nothing more? Were they friends? She gave him a once-over from the corner of her eyes. She remembered what he looked like without clothes. There was no way they could ever be just friends.

The elevator doors opened, depositing them in the anteroom outside The Bishop Foundation.

Symone crossed to the suite's entrance. She sensed Jerry behind her. It was her turn to avoid his eyes. "I'll email the property manager in the morning about requesting an estimate from TSG."

Jerry held the door for her again. "We'd appreciate the contract, but this is about keeping you safe."

Safe from murderers, burglars and assailants. Symone was grateful for that. Was there a service that could keep her heart safe from him?

"This way." Symone gestured to the offices at the end

of the hall. "Ellie's office is beside mine." She caught his smile. "What's funny?"

"Nothing." But his smile remained. "This will be the first time I'll be able to walk this hall with you without members of your staff stopping you every three feet to say hello and tell you about their families."

Symone chuckled. "Those are some of the best parts of my day."

"I can tell. I hope you're able to prevent the board from voting you out."

Her joy vanished. "So do I." A few more steps brought her to Ellie's office. She pulled out her keys again. "We lock all the offices at the end of the day as a safety precaution. I have a master key that opens every room in the suite, though."

She unlocked the door and crossed the threshold into Ellie's spacious area. Like Symone's, Ellie's room was furnished in heavy, dark wood pieces, including a desk, bookcase, credenza and conversation table. The single window behind the navy blue executive chair welcomed a wealth of natural light.

Jerry looked around. "Your office is bigger."

Symone circled the desk. "What are we looking for?"

Jerry crossed to the credenza. "Anything that she's not supposed to have. A folder. A recording device. A checkbook for the foundation. An envelope taped to the bottom of a drawer." He looked over his shoulder at her. "I saw that one in a movie."

Symone wished he'd stop being so charming. She opened the center drawer and found pens, pencils, rubber bands and thumbtacks. Nothing seemed suspicious. "You were impressive earlier. When did you become a planner?"

"I've recently learned planning has its benefits." Jerry

flipped through the files in Ellie's credenza. His movements were practiced and efficient. This wasn't his first search.

She shook her head. "As a lifelong planner, I agree. I'm just surprised you've admitted it. You once told me you thought planning was a waste of time."

"People can change." His words were low, reluctant. Completing his examination of the credenza, Jerry moved on to the bookcase. The shelves held a dictionary, a thesaurus, medical industry journals and project binders, among other things.

"Hmm." *Would that include changing their minds about getting involved with their "charges"?* Symone pulled out the center drawer and turned it over. "There's no hidden envelope."

Jerry searched the credenza's exterior. "Keep looking. We need to find something that could help prove Ellie and Xander were involved in a conspiracy to defraud the foundation."

The desk had four other drawers. Symone moved on to the one at the top left. She found scissors, binder clips and a ruler. Bending over, she managed to wiggle the drawer free of its rollers. She turned it over—and gasped. "There's an envelope taped to the bottom of this drawer."

Two long strides brought Jerry to her side. "What is it?"

Symone turned the drawer upside down on the desk's surface so she could access the package. It was a nine-by-twelve manila booklet envelope. The return address belonged to the company that processed the foundation's background checks.

"It's addressed to me. Why did Ellie hide it?" She pulled the envelope free of the drawer and opened it. Inside was a thick stack of papers.

Jerry read over her shoulder. "It's the background check for Xander."

"Except this one comes with a recommendation to deny his membership to the board." Symone flipped through the pages. "Ellie intercepted the report and switched the real one with the one she'd falsified."

The quiet click sent ice through Symone's system. She looked up and found a gun pointed at her. Just beneath the sound of her pulse galloping in her ears, she heard Xander's voice.

"I'll take that envelope, please."

Chapter 18

"Norris Hall, I presume." Jerry's voice mocked him. He paraphrased the famous quote, substituting Norris's name for Dr. Livingstone. His bravado in the face of a gun wielded by a serial killer almost sent Symone into cardiac arrest.

Norris stood just inside the door to Ellie's office. He wore the curly blond wig and dark green contacts he'd established as his look for Xander. But tonight, he'd made a wardrobe change. Instead of an expensive three-piece suit and Italian shoes, he wore black sweats and sneakers.

"We haven't been formally introduced." Xander's thin lips parted in a smile—or maybe it was a sneer. He held the gun as though it was an extension of his hand.

Symone's mouth was too dry to swallow. She set the report on Ellie's desk and clenched her hands to stop them from shaking.

"Jeremiah Touré." Jerry's smile was cold. His eyes were sharp. "By which name would you prefer we call you, Xander Fence or Norris Hall?"

Jerry stood beside Symone, back straight, shoulders squared, legs braced. He'd shifted closer to the desk as though once again shielding her with his body—his body that seemed to be always in motion. Then why was he so still now? He could probably disarm the other man in two moves.

"Xander will be fine." His shrug caused the gun to shift just a bit.

Symone's knees almost buckled. She leaned her thighs against the desk, braced her hands on its surface and drew a shaky breath. The bitter scent enveloping her was fear.

Turning to Jerry, she widened her eyes, *Disarm him.*

He looked her over, then returned his attention to the man with the gun.

What did that mean? Her muscles shook from a disabling mixture of confusion, fear and anger.

Jerry cocked his head. "Do you prefer Xander because Norris is wanted by the FBI? Fraud, right? Bank, wire, insurance and a few others."

Xander's smile faded. "You've done your research."

Symone couldn't take this chatter any more. This wasn't going according to their plan. They were supposed to get in, get evidence, then get out. She hadn't envisioned being held at gunpoint. Perhaps she should have thought of that. But right now, she was having trouble controlling her breathing and she couldn't think straight.

"You killed my mother." Her voice was raw.

Xander shrugged again. "Collateral damage, I'm afraid."

Symone saw red. She wanted to climb over the desk and choke the feigned sympathy from his face.

Jerry shifted forward. "What was Dorothy Wiggans? Why did you kill her?"

"Step. Back." Xander pointed the gun at Jerry's head. He lowered it to Symone's chest when Jerry returned to her side. "You know about Dottie? Boy, you *are* good. I needed Dottie's spot on the board to make the plan work."

"Why are you doing this?" Her voice was more demanding than she'd expected. Anger was giving her strength.

Xander raised his eyebrows. "For money, of course. The foundation has lots of it."

Symone's temper was overtaking her fear. "Board members are paid a percentage of the profits from the products we invest in."

"I want more." He sounded so reasonable while making his unreasonable demand.

Symone concentrated on her breathing. She needed to collect her wits. "Defrauding my family's foundation won't be as easy as you think. We have safeguards in place."

"Like that safeguard?" Xander nodded toward the manila envelope in front of Symone. "*You* should be surprised by how easily I took control of your foundation. In less than a month, I convinced a simple majority of your board members to challenge your leadership. You've lost your company. Your stepfather left you. *You* should've left when I asked you to. But no. Instead, you decided to involve an innocent man in trying to protect your precious foundation. It's your fault he's going to die."

Symone turned to Jerry and again widened her eyes. *Please, do something.*

Again he looked at her, then away.

She didn't understand. She'd seen his strenuous workouts. His reflexes were fast. His punches were powerful. Why wasn't he using those skills on Xander now? Symone was certain he could disarm the other man in two moves, three tops. What was holding him back?

You are.

Symone's eyes had opened. Jerry was holding back because he was afraid the gun would go off in the struggle and she'd be hit by a stray bullet.

Think. Think. Think. What can I do to get us out of dan-

ger? "Do you really think killing me and Jerry will give you control of my family's foundation?"

How do I take myself out of the equation?

"My brothers and the police know what you've done." Jerry shifted his stance. "The detectives in charge of this investigation are interrogating Ellie right now."

"Ellie. That fool." Xander spit out his words. "She's become a liability."

Take myself out of the equation. Of course! Symone deliberately looked past Xander as though there was someone in the hallway behind him, then hurriedly returned her attention to him. He narrowed his eyes at her.

Symone cleared her throat. "Is that the reason you tried to frame Ellie for the hit-and-run that almost killed my stepfather?"

Xander gave a mirthless laugh. "You ask too many questions."

Now or never.

Symone looked past Xander. "Help us!" She shouted, infusing her words with all the fear and desperation in her body.

She saw Xander spin around to confront an enemy who wasn't there, turning his back to the adversary in the room. She saw Jerry leap at Xander.

Symone threw herself under the table. Digging her burner cell from the pocket of her culottes, she dialed emergency services.

"9-1-1. What is your emergency?"

"An armed shooter has broken into The Bishop Foundation. Please send help." She gave the foundation's address, then disconnected the call.

"Symone!" Jerry was breathless. "You can come out now."

She crawled out from under the table. Straightening,

she brushed off her clothes, then took a moment to get her breathing under control. Jerry stood a distance from the table. He held the gun aimed at Xander. The other man lay on his back at Jerry's feet. His arms were raised above his head.

"The police are on the way." Her voice shook slightly. The adrenaline that had kept her going through this threat was quickly draining. Forcing her legs to move, she circled the desk and headed toward the door. "I'll get something to restrain him." She hoped to find something suitable in their supply closet.

Jerry watched her walk toward him. He gave her a crooked grin. "Great improv."

She smiled into his eyes. "Thank you. Great save."

His expression softened. "We make a good team."

"I know." Symone continued past him.

She'd always known they were better together. They hadn't had to put their lives on the line to convince her. It was Jerry who'd encouraged her to push back against her board's attempt to oust her. She'd urged Jerry to tell his brothers the real reason he wanted to leave their company. Even their arguments over the suspects in their investigation had helped them arrive at the truth about her mother's murder, and Xander and Ellie's scheme.

But what difference did all that make when Jerry was certain they were from different worlds?

"She screamed 'Help us,' as though the world was coming to an end." Jerry hadn't shared details like that with Taylor when he'd given the detective his statement earlier at the precinct. But in his family home—now Mal's home—surrounded by his brothers and Symone, Grace and Celeste late Friday night, he needed to share the fear, anger, uncertainty and, yes, humor of the experience. He could smile about it now—barely—but he'd almost had a stroke when Symone had drawn Xander's attention to herself with her scream. He shut out the images of what could've gone wrong before he passed out.

Celeste turned to Symone. "What made you shout 'Help us'?"

Jerry looked at Symone seated beside him on the love seat. His heart clenched with concern. She seemed exhausted. It was as though she'd used the last of her adrenaline to file her report with Eriq and now she was coasting on fumes. Or perhaps the hot, sweet chamomile tea Mal and Grace had made for the group had something to do with it. Jerry was a little tired himself. The tea's herbal scent wafted up to him.

Symone spread her arms. "I was afraid if I shouted 'Get him,' Xander would think I was referring to Jerry."

Dry chuckles floated around the room. Mal and Grace leaned against each other as they sat on the near corner of the sofa like the lovebirds they were. Celeste had taken the far end of the sofa. Zeke had pulled one of the dining chairs into the living room and positioned it beside her. There was something going on between those two. Celeste had impressed him. Jerry was rooting for his brother's happiness.

Symone had all but collapsed beside Jerry. He'd wanted to see to her comfort, curl his left arm around her shoulder and tuck her into him. But he couldn't, not if he'd meant what he'd said when he'd told her they didn't have a future together.

Jerry turned his head, smiling into Symone's sleepy chocolate eyes. "Those weren't your only two options."

"Those were the only ones that came to my mind at the

time." Symone's voice was low and breathy. Was it fatigue? Or something else, something he'd foolishly rejected?

Zeke raised his mug toward her. "Thank you for choosing the one most likely to keep my brother alive."

Mal nodded. "Yes, good choice, Symone."

Symone blushed as Jerry, Grace and Celeste echoed Zeke's and Mal's gratitude.

His brothers were making light of it now, but it was obvious from the looks on their faces when he'd walked into the precinct with Symone that they'd heard what had happened. He hoped never to cause them that much anguish again.

Grace cradled her mug between her palms. "For Xander and Ellie, it was just about the money?"

Jerry nodded. "It was a confidence scam."

Mal interrupted. "All of their crimes were confidence scams. They'd earn people's trust, then take their money."

"True." Jerry brought an image of their arrest report, which Mal had provided, to mind. "Xander had gained the board's acceptance and convinced a simple majority of them to call for a no-confidence vote against Symone."

Symone shook her head with disgust. "Which he'd done with indecent speed."

Jerry continued. "Then he'd need a supermajority to vote her out."

"Wow." Celeste's eyes widened. "Do you think he would've gotten the supermajority?"

Symone adjusted her glasses. "I don't know. During our last board meeting, I could tell a few still supported me but a couple were unsure."

Grace sighed. "That was too close. It would be a great

loss for the health care industry if The Bishop Foundation ever lost the clarity of mission your family brings to it."

"Thank you." Symone nodded. "I agree."

Grace frowned. "But Ellie seems to have been the key to this plan." She shifted to look at Mal. "Xander wouldn't have been able to get a hold on the foundation without Ellie so how did she get in?"

"Identity theft," Mal said. "It took me a little while to find the connection—"

Jerry interrupted. "No one stays hidden from Mal for long."

Mal smiled. "Bonnie Rae had stolen the real Eleanor Press's identity so her background would be approved. But, according to Ellie, Xander was afraid they'd be pushing their luck if he also stole someone's identity. So they submitted a fraudulent background check for him instead."

"I was curious about something." Celeste leaned forward, resting her forearms on her lap. Zeke's eyes were drawn to her beside him. "Why did Xander think Ellie had become a liability?"

Symone rubbed her thumbs over her warm porcelain mug. "Because she refused to destroy the actual background report the foundation's vendor provided, which recommended *against* adding Xander to the board."

Jerry watched Symone's thumbs caress her mug. "Ellie was using it as leverage to keep Xander in line. She was afraid he'd cut her out of the money or make her the fall guy for their scheme."

Zeke gestured with his mug of tea. "That report is evidence of Xander and Ellie's conspiracy to defraud the foundation."

Celeste drank more of her tea. "Symone, how do you feel now that Xander and Ellie are in custody?"

* * *

Symone paused, considering her answer. How did she feel? Destroyed, alone, afraid.

She met Celeste's eyes. She tried, but failed, to strip the emotion from her voice. "It doesn't bring my mother back. They destroyed my family and for what? They were *never* going to gain control of The Bishop Foundation's accounts." She paused, blinking away tears and trying to steady her voice. "However, I'm glad I was able to confront them. That was so important to me. And I'm very grateful to all of you—Grace, Mal, Zeke, Celeste and Jerry—for helping me get justice for my mother. It means a lot. Thank you doesn't feel like enough. I'll never forget it. I promise."

"We're glad we were able to help you," Mal said.

Zeke nodded. "Absolutely. This was important. And thank you is more than enough."

Jerry's hand settled softly on her shoulder, drawing her attention to him. "Your family deserves justice. We were happy to help."

Silence settled over the room. Symone thought of her mother. She would have liked Jerry. She would have liked all the Touré brothers. Symone wished she hadn't had to meet them under these circumstances. Xander and Ellie had taken so much from her—her mother, her trust in her board members, her stepfather. And while The Bishop Foundation was out of immediate danger, she was facing a lot of heavy lifting to repair the damage the confidence scammers had done and to rebuild the foundation.

Grace broke the silence. She sent a smile around the living room. "It seems like the five of you wrapped up this case with a great big bow. This was a complicated—and dangerous—investigation, but you closed it in just one week. Congratulations."

"Thanks." Celeste sat back against her chair. "It was a long, hard week. But I agree with Grace. You Tourés run a tight ship."

"Thank you, Celeste." Zeke shifted on his chair to face her. "I knew you'd be a great addition to the team. I—we—enjoyed working with you."

Symone sensed the chemistry between Zeke and Celeste. She was sure everyone in the room did, including those two. They'd make a good couple. At least Zeke didn't seem as clueless as his youngest brother. Her eyes drifted toward Jerry before she dragged them back to the rest of the group.

Celeste looked at Zeke. "I enjoyed working with you, too. I hope we can do it again sometime." She stood, collecting her purse from the sofa. "It's late. I should get home. Great job, everyone. Thanks for the tea and chat. Have a good weekend."

"I should leave, too." Symone rose from the love seat. "The case is over—"

Celeste turned to her. "Do you want a ride?"

Jerry shot to his feet. "No!"

Startled Symone spun toward him. "Actually, I would like—"

Jerry interrupted again. "Celeste, it's too far out of your way and, as you said, it's late."

Symone's shoulders sagged. She would've loved some time alone to chat with the other woman but Jerry was right. It was too much to ask.

"Thank you for your offer, Celeste." She turned to collect her purse, which she'd left on the love seat. "I'll call a car service."

Jerry caught her hand. His fingers were long and warm as they wrapped around hers. "Wait. Why? All your stuff's upstairs. Why don't you stay the night and I'll take you home in the morning?"

Because I don't want to drag out this goodbye. I'd rather rip the bandage off tonight and wake up with a fresh start in the morning.

She turned her head but didn't quite meet his eyes. "The case is over, and I don't want to impose."

Jerry stiffened as though he'd read more into her protest than she'd intended. "You're not imposing, Symone. Right, Mal?"

"Not at all." Mal's reply was immediate and sincere. "Please stay."

"You seem tired, Symone," Grace added. "Why don't you go up to bed and Jerry will take you home in the morning."

Symone hesitated for a heartbeat or two. She was exhausted. It had been a long and emotional seven days. The group seemed determine to add another night. Fine, she'd go up to bed, shut her door and pretend her heart wasn't breaking.

She turned her back to Jerry. "Thank you for your hospitality, Mal. I'll take your advice and go up to bed. It's been a long day."

She watched Celeste leave, then bid Jerry, Zeke, Mal and Grace good night before dragging herself up to sleep. Just one more night. Then, in the morning, she'd start rebuilding the foundation and her heart.

"Thank you again for driving me home." Symone sent a brief look toward Jerry as he took State Route 33 to Upper Arlington early Saturday morning. She wanted to sear the image of his strong, clean profile onto her memory, but it hurt too much to let her eyes linger. "I'm going to put 'buy a new car' on top of my to-do list since Xander and Ellie bombed mine. I'll have to get a rental for the time being, though. Actually, there are a lot of things on the top of my to-do list."

Like stop talking.

But Jerry's silence was making her nervous. These were the last few minutes they'd ever spend together. What was he thinking about? Had he realized pushing her away was a mistake? She stared blindly at his dashboard. Or was he thinking about returning this rental car?

"I'm sure you have a plan for getting through all of your tasks in a timely manner." The smile in his voice tugged at her heart.

"And I promise to keep my word about asking my building manager to get a proposal from TSG." They'd earned the recommendation. And although she was paying for their services, she felt she owed them more.

"Thank you." Jerry stopped at a red light. "My brothers and I appreciate that."

Symone swallowed the lump in her throat. "I'm glad things worked out for you and your brothers, and that you've decided to continue working with your family's company. Family's important."

"I agree." Jerry glanced at her. "Speaking of family, have you gotten an update on Paul's condition?"

"I spoke with one of the nurses this morning. He was still asleep when I called. I'm picking him up after I get the rental."

"Is that the reason you wanted to leave so early today?" Jerry continued through the intersection after the light finally turned green. "Because you're picking up Paul?"

His question was like a punch to the heart. "No, Jerry. I'm leaving because there's no reason for me to stay."

When the silence settled into the car this time, Symone ignored it. Traffic on this Saturday morning was brisk. She watched the sunlight fall like diamonds on the Scioto River. Thick old trees and overgrown underbrush framed its banks.

"Are you ready for your board meeting next Monday?" This time Jerry broke the silence.

She nodded, keeping her attention on the scenery through the windshield. "I believe so."

"You'll be great." He made the turn onto Fishinger Road. "The foundation would be in trouble without you."

"Thank you." She risked another look in his direction. "That's kind of you to say. If I am able to pull this off, it will be thanks to you."

"No." His tone was firm. "Your success is all you, Symone. No one else."

She looked at him in surprise. "Thank you."

Jerry shook his head. "You don't have to thank me. You're stronger than you think. You're smart and capable and kind. You just need to have more confidence in yourself."

Symone struggled to keep her jaw from dropping. "You sound like my mother."

Jerry laughed. "Then your mother was even smarter than I imagined her to be."

Symone's laughter joined his. "She was very smart— and strong, capable, kind and confident." She hesitated. "She would have liked you."

A flush rose up Jerry's neck and settled in his cheeks. "My parents would've liked you as well."

Then why doesn't their son want to take a chance on us?

Instead of asking the question aloud, Symone directed Jerry to her house. He pulled into her winding stone driveway, bordered on both sides by well-manicured lawns, evergreen bushes and stubby, short trees.

Jerry turned off the engine and stared at her stone Tudor-style home. "Wow."

Symone stiffened. "I grew up here. When my mother and Paul bought their new home, I bought this house from her. She gave me a good deal."

She felt Jerry calculating the differences in square footage and costs between their childhood homes. To him, this would be a tangible reminder of their differences.

Symone shifted to face him as she unclenched her teeth. "Thank you for bringing me home." Looking into his eyes, she saw him pulling away. It hurt.

"You're welcome." He gave her a distracted smile. "It was my pleasure." He popped the trunk, then unfolded himself from the driver's seat.

Symone followed him to the back of the rental car. "I can get my bag. Thank you."

"I'll get it." His response was final. "And I'll have the rest of your belongings from the safe house brought to you by Monday."

"Thank you." In retrospect, she was embarrassed that she'd taken both of her bags to the safe house. Carrying all those clothes around probably made her seem like a diva, which may have given Jerry even more reason not to get involved with her.

With a mental shrug, Symone led him to her maple wood front door. "Would you like to come in for some coffee?" She held her breath, waiting for his answer.

"Thanks, but I'd better get moving. Like you, I've got a lot of stuff to take care of today."

She'd expected that response. Disappointment was like bile in her throat. Symone unlocked her door and pushed it wide open. Jerry reached around her to set her suitcase just inside the entrance. She noticed he avoided looking around. Was that because he didn't want the memory of her home?

Symone straightened her back and squared her shoulders. She braced her legs. "Thank you again for everything. I'll never forget what you've done for me and my family's legacy." *Or what you've meant to me.*

Jerry nodded. "It's been an honor. If there's anything we can do for you in the future, please let us know." His eyes swept her face as though committing her features to memory.

She was doing the same with his. "I hope I won't need you to keep me alive in the future."

He smiled. "I hope so, too."

Symone stepped back and offered him her right hand. "Good luck with TSG. Please give your brothers my best."

Jerry looked from Symone's face to her hand. He lifted his eyes to hers. She saw a light shift in them.

Symone's breath left her lungs with a whoosh as Jerry pulled her into his arms. He pressed his mouth to hers and swept his tongue between her lips. The moan rose from her gut. Her thighs tensed as her body began a slow burn. She sucked his tongue as memories of their lovemaking— never far away—rushed back to her. She tightened her arms around his shoulders. Jerry held her closer. His right hand slid down her back to press her hips to his. Symone felt his arousal.

She moaned again and pulled her mouth from his. "Jerry, I—"

And then he released her. Without a backward glance, Jerry strode to his rental car as though some crazy ex-girlfriend was chasing after him. He reversed out of the driveway and disappeared.

The tears came without warning. Symone stumbled into her home and shut the door. Her sobs grew louder as she crumbled to the floor and curled into a ball.

Jerry, I love you.

Chapter 19

"I thought you could use some moral support." Paul stood in the threshold of Symone's office early Monday morning, minutes before the special board meeting to hold the no-confidence vote for Symone.

She rose behind her desk and crossed to him. "It's good to see you, Paul. You look well."

In the ten days since Xander had struck Paul with Ellie's car, the cuts and bruises had faded significantly. Despite the discomfort of fractured ribs, Paul was dressed formally in a dark blue tie, dark blue pin-striped, three-piece suit and snow white shirt.

Symone had been taking him to his follow-up medical visits. Both Paul and his older brother were disappointed by this delay in Paul's relocating to North Carolina. For their sake, she hoped Paul had a speedy recovery. But she was grateful for the distraction of her stepfather's presence.

"I feel better every day." Paul leaned against the doorway. "What about you? Are you ready for the meeting?"

"Considering I'm on my way to it now, I hope I am." Symone's tone was dry.

She collected her manila meeting folder and six plain white standard business envelopes printed with The Bishop Foundation logo. Each one was addressed to a remaining board member.

"Yes, I'm certain you are." Paul watched her approach him. "You seem more assertive and bolder since that horrible mess with Xander and Ellie." He hesitated. "You seem sadder, too."

Symone stopped beside him. "I'm just anxious to get this meeting over with." *And I'm missing Jerry. Terribly.*

"Remember, no matter what happens, you've given it your best effort. You always do. Your parents were so proud of you."

"Thank you, Paul. That means a lot." She led him into the hallway, then linked her arm with his to provide him with support as they walked to the boardroom. Along the way, they picked up Jackie Emery, Symone's temporary administrative assistant, who would be taking the board meeting minutes in Ellie's place.

Symone led them into the empty room. Her watch showed they had seven minutes to wait. Board members slowly trickled in.

Tina Grand called the meeting to order at exactly 10:00 a.m. She read from what appeared to be a prepared statement. "Due to changes in the board membership, the board agrees to cancel this special meeting for a no-confidence vote for our foundation chair. The board also apologizes to our foundation chair for any perceived lack of support this scheduled vote may have signaled."

Preferring not to hold a grudge, Symone sent a smile around the table. "Apology accepted."

"Thank you, Madam Chair." Tina glowed with relief. "So, if there are no further matters, the meeting will be adjourned."

Symone looked around the table. When no one else stirred, she addressed the board. "Madam President, I have a matter for discussion. This pertains to several articles in our bylaws." She passed photocopies of the specific bylaw articles around the table. She shared her copy with Paul. "Let's start with Article Two, Section Three. This article requires each member of the board to bring concerns about the foundation to the chair, members of the administration and other board members in a timely manner."

She looked around the table. Symone saw dawning concern in the members' stiffening features and widening eyes. "In other words, if you were concerned about the manner in which my mother or I were handling the foundation's accounts, you were required to tell us much sooner than six years after my father's death."

Tina flipped through the copies. "The penalty for a member not reporting concerns in a timely manner is removal from the board?" Her voice ended in a squeak. "I was not even aware of these rules." She looked around the table. "Was anyone aware of them?"

Murmurs of dismay and confusion circled the table.

Symone's disappointment lay like a brick in her stomach. "That's the problem. None of you are committed to the foundation, not the way it needs you to be. We need board members who will be real partners. Members who are as enthusiastic about our mission as I am."

Kitty humphed. "We made a mistake, but we've apologized. I don't think there's any reason for you to take it to such drastic measures."

Symone stood and circled the table, delivering her personalized letters to the members. "Please don't misunderstand. I appreciate your apology. This action is not a reflection of my personal feelings. If this was a personal decision, I wouldn't dissolve this board." *Or at least I wouldn't remove most of you.* "I'm doing what's best for the foundation."

"I just got here." Wesley looked from Paul to Symone. "Isn't there like a probationary period? I could really use the money from serving on this board."

That was the kind of attitude from members that got them into this situation in the first place. "I'm afraid there isn't a probationary period."

Keisha's sigh was low with resignation. "I've enjoyed being part of this organization, but you're right. Every one of us had an obligation to bring the investment and grant approval process concerns to you immediately."

"Thank you, Keisha." Symone returned to her seat. "The envelope has information about the separation process. If you have any questions about the process or your compensation package, please feel free to contact the foundation lawyer, Percy Jeffries. His business card is in your envelope."

Julie sat back against her chair. "I'm disappointed, but I understand your decision. What's the process for reapplying?"

Symone frowned. "I'll have to research that, Julie. This is a new development for the foundation."

"I'd like to know about that, too," Aaron said. "I'd like to recommit to the foundation."

"Thank you, Aaron. That's nice to know." Symone turned to a blank page in her notebook. "I'll let everyone know about the reapplication process. If there aren't any other questions, we can conclude this final meeting of this year's board."

Tina glowered at her from the other end of the table. "The meeting is concluded."

The older woman swept out of the room without another word. The other members wished Symone well before departing.

Paul turned to her. "Congratulations, Symone. You've won."

"I don't feel like I've won." Symone watched the members and Jackie disappear beyond the conference room doors. "For the first time in the history of my family's foundation, we don't have a board."

"You had to follow the bylaws or risk setting a bad precedent." Seated on her right, Paul reached over and patted her shoulder. "But these changes you're implementing almost make me want to stay."

Symone felt a spark of hope. "You were in the administration, but if you'd like to be on the board, you're always welcome."

Paul shook his head, but there was a wistful quality to his smile. "Thank you, but I think I'd better leave. The foundation, our home, everything has too many memories of Odette for me to stay."

Symone felt that, too. But Columbus was her home and she'd rather live with those memories of her parents than without them. She stood and linked her arm with Paul's. "I understand. But if you change your mind, let me know."

Paul cleared his throat. "I really loved your mother, but Langston Bishop was a tough act to follow." He paused. "You know, there's something about Jerry Touré that reminds me of your father."

"I agree." Symone swallowed a sigh, thinking of Jerry. He was exciting. Larger than life. The ten days they'd been apart hadn't helped to diminish her feelings for him. Symone had a feeling even a year apart wouldn't make a difference.

"We've come to see for ourselves." Mal crossed the threshold into Jerry's house late Monday morning.

Jerry frowned at his brother's back. "To see what?"

Zeke strode in after Mal. "You've taken a three-day weekend to clean your house. We're here to document this event with photos, videos and interviews."

"Ha. Ha." Jerry locked his door. He was dressed in a baggy gray T-shirt and black canvas shorts. His feet were bare. Both Zeke and Mal wore dark business suits with jewel-toned shirts and ties.

Jerry had been cleaning for almost four hours today. He'd had trouble sleeping last night, but this morning, instead of being tired, he was filled with nervous energy. He'd channeled that momentum into cleaning his basement. He'd begun this unusual cleaning spree Saturday and had already cleaned the top and main floors of his two-story home. His house now smelled like furniture polish, floor wax and window cleaner.

Reluctantly, he trailed after his brothers, who'd made a beeline for his kitchen. This entire situation had shades of their childhood, good-natured taunting at his expense. At some point, wouldn't they have to outgrow that?

Jerry washed his hands at the kitchen sink. "Do you guys want coffee?"

He wandered to his coffee machine to prepare the brew although he didn't need the caffeine. Breakfast might be a good idea, though. All he'd had was an apple.

"I didn't know you had black-and-white marble countertops." Mal ran one large hand over his kitchen counter.

"You're in my way, Mal." Jerry's eyes strayed toward the clock across the room. It was after ten. Was the foundation's board still meeting? What was happening? Had they voted? Would they still vote after everything that had happened? He needed to know.

Jerry measured the water for the carafe, then poured it into the machine.

"Wow. I don't think I've ever seen this floor." Zeke stared at the hardwood beneath his feet. Jerry had polished it yesterday.

"Yes, you have." Jerry measured the grounds for the coffee. "You and Mal helped me put it in." He turned to face his brothers through the kitchen pass-through.

Zeke and Mal sat at Jerry's round, blond wood dining table. They'd taken off their jackets and hooked them over the backs of their chairs.

Zeke gave Jerry a narrow-eyed stare as though he could decipher all of Jerry's thoughts. "What's this really about, Jer?"

Jerry crossed his arms and leaned back against the kitchen counter. "What do you mean?"

Mal rubbed his forehead with the tips of his right fingers. "Not this again."

Zeke rested his right ankle on his left knee. "Jer, you took a vacation day to clean. For you, that's a cry for help."

Mal stretched his legs in front of him and crossed them at his ankles. "You've been uncharacteristically quiet and withdrawn since we closed Symone's case. Do you want to talk about it?"

Jerry glanced again at the clock on the wall across the room. A few more minutes had crawled past. "The Bishop Foundation's Board is meeting right now to decide whether to keep Symone as chair or replace her."

Zeke's eyebrows jumped up his forehead. "Are they going through with that vote? They were taking their orders from a confidence scammer."

"Have you spoken with Symone recently?" Mal asked.

Jerry's eyes dropped to the cream floor tiles in his narrow kitchen. "I haven't spoken with her since I brought her home." That was ten days ago. Ten very long days.

Zeke arched an eyebrow. "Not even to thank her for referring us to her building manager? Getting that contract would've been a perfect excuse to call."

Jerry ran a hand over his hair. "I'm not looking for excuses to call her. I'm trying to figure out how to function without having her in my life."

"Why?" his brothers asked in unison.

Jerry paced the kitchen. "I've told you. She's out of my league. You should see the house she grew up in. You could fit each of our homes inside of it."

Zeke shifted on his seat, exchanging a look with Mal. "What does the size of a house have to do with whether the two of you are compatible?"

Jerry's stomach roiled with frustration. His skin crawled with it. His brothers should understand how he felt. They'd grown up in the same home. In contrast, they'd seen Symone, with her pearls, expensive suits and matching shoes.

He swallowed his pride and admitted to the fear that plagued his mind and heart. "I can't give her the kind of lifestyle she's used to."

Mal arched an eyebrow. "Did she ask you to?"

Jerry swept out his arm. "Not yet, but—"

Zeke considered him with narrowed eyes and a furrowed brow. "So your plan is to picture a relationship with Symone, then fast-forward to some imaginary breakup?"

Put like that, Jerry admitted his behavior sounded pretty foolish.

Mal shook his head. "Jer, talk with Symone. Let *her* be the one to decide if you're good enough for her."

What if her answer is no?

"Do you remember what Mom told us after Dad died?"

Zeke asked. "Losing someone hurts like hell, but the time you spend with them makes it worth it."

Mal nodded his agreement. "She's right. When Grace broke up with me in Chicago, I thought I'd never get over the pain. But I didn't for one moment ever regret being with her."

Jerry thought about his time with Symone. What his mother and Mal said made sense. Even if Symone turned him away, he'd still have those memories. He'd like the chance to make even more.

"All right." Jerry strode out of the kitchen. "I'll ask Symone to take a chance on me." He hesitated. "But first I'll need a plan."

Symone sat at her desk Monday afternoon, doing what she did best, especially when she was stressed and overwhelmed. She was making a list. Topping the list was revising the screening process for employees and board members. She needed a replacement for Ellie, preferably someone who wasn't a fugitive from the FBI. She had to replace the board.

And she had to call Jerry.

She couldn't stop thinking about him. She felt him in her dreams. He whispered to her throughout her day. She was craving mints. And sometimes she would see him at random places around the city. Those sightings hurt worst of all because when she approached him, he'd turn out to be someone else.

Symone dropped her head into her hands. This had to stop. She had to convince him to give them a chance. He was being unreasonable.

Symone sat up and adjusted her glasses. She took a breath before reaching for her cell phone beside the landline on her desk. She didn't know what to say if he answered the call. She would wing it and hope for the best.

A knock on her open office door broke her concentration. Symone looked up. "Jerry?"

Good grief. Was she dreaming again? He looked so real. He stood in her threshold in a gunmetal gray suit, maroon shirt and black tie. His right hand was still pressed against the door. His left hand held a bouquet of long-stemmed red roses.

His smile was uncertain. "You don't look like someone celebrating reclaiming control of her family's foundation."

He was really here? The pulse at the base of her throat broke into a sprint. "How did you know about that?"

Jerry crossed her threshold and closed her door. His loose-limbed strides brought him to her desk. "I spoke with Paul. Congratulations." The caution clouding his eyes belied the smile curving his lips.

"Thank you." Symone was beginning to believe he really was in her office. Her eyes dropped to the bouquet. "Are those for me?" The scent of the roses filled her office. She'd much rather smell him.

"Yes." He extended them to her.

"Thank you." Symone took them and buried her face in the roses. "They're beautiful."

The bouquet was really here. Maybe the man was, too. Her heart felt ready to burst from her chest. She couldn't stop smiling.

"Symone—" He came around her desk, offered her his hand and helped her to her feet. He drew a breath. "Symone, when I look at you, I see someone with intelligence, courage, integrity and kindness."

Her pulse fluttered like a butterfly in her throat. She set

the bouquet on her desk. "Not a bank account?" Her voice was a whisper.

Jerry shook his head. "No. I used that as an excuse to push you away because I thought I wasn't good enough. But being 'good enough' isn't about a bank account. It's about what's in here." He pressed her hand against his heart. Its beat was strong and steady against her palm.

She raised her eyes to his face. His image was blurry through her tears. "Why didn't you tell me this before?"

His throat muscles flexed before he could answer. "I was afraid." His chuckle was wry humor. "I can confront an armed serial killer, but the thought of disappointing you makes me shake in my shoes."

Symone laughed. She pressed her palm against his chest again. "You could never disappoint me, Jerry. From the first day we met, you've been saving me. I love planning with you. I love being spontaneous with you. I love arguing with you. And I absolutely love falling in love with you."

Jerry's heart slammed against her palm. He lowered his forehead to hers and exhaled. "I love falling in love with you, too."

Symone gasped. "You do?"

He nodded, his forehead rubbing against hers. "I cleaned my house."

Symone's lips parted. "Jerry," she breathed.

He lifted his head to look at her. His smile was uncertain. "I'd planned to come to your office and take you to lunch. Then, I'd plead my case to you."

Symone beamed up at him. "I prefer acting on impulse." She rose up on her toes and kissed him.

* * * * *

Romantic Suspense

Danger. Passion. Drama.

Available Next Month

A Colton Kidnapping Justine Davis
Hotshot's Dangerous Liaison Lisa Childs

Stalker In The Storm Carla Cassidy
Undercover Heist Rachel Astor

 LOVE INSPIRED

Chasing Justice Valerie Hansen
Searching For Evidence Carol J. Post

Larger Print

 LOVE INSPIRED

Shielding The Innocent Target Terri Reed
Kidnapped In Montana Sharon Dunn

Larger Print

 LOVE INSPIRED

In Need Of Protection Jill Elizabeth Nelson
Hidden Mountain Secrets Kerry Johnson

Larger Print

Keep reading for an excerpt of a new title
from the Intrigue series,
CONARD COUNTY: MURDEROUS INTENT
by Rachel Lee

Prologue

Krystal Metcalfe loved to sit on the porch of her small cabin in the mornings, especially when the weather was exceptionally pleasant. With a fresh cup of coffee and its delightful aroma mixing with those of the forest around, she found internal peace and calm here.

Across a bubbling creek that ran before her porch, her morning view included the old Healey house. Abandoned about twenty years ago, it had been steadily sinking into decline. The roof sagged, wood planks had been silvered by the years and there was little left that looked safe or even useful. Krystal had always anticipated the day when the forest would reclaim it.

Then came the morning when a motor home pulled up beside the crumbling house and a large man climbed out. He spent some time investigating the old structure, inside and out. Maybe hunting for anything he could reclaim? Would that be theft at this point?

She lingered, watching with mild curiosity but little concern. At some level she had always supposed that someone would express interest in the Healey land itself. It wasn't easy anymore to find private land on the edge of US Forest, and eventually the "grandfathering" that had left the Healey family their ownership would end because of lack of occupancy. Regardless, it wasn't exactly a large piece of land, unlikely to be useful to most, and the Forest Service would let it return to nature.

Less of that house meant more of the forest devouring the eyesore. And at least the bubbling of the creek passing through the canyon swallowed most of the sounds that might be coming from that direction now that the man was there. And it sure looked like he might be helping the destruction of that eyesore.

But then came another morning when she stepped out with her coffee and saw a group of people, maybe a dozen, camped around the ramshackle house. That's when things started to become noisy despite the sound baffling provided by the creek.

A truck full of lumber managed to make its way up the remaining ruined road on that side of the creek and dumped a load that caused Krystal to gasp. Rebuilding? Building bigger?

What kind of eyesore would she have to face? Her view from this porch was her favorite. Her other windows and doors didn't include the creek. And all those people buzzing around provided an annoying level of activity that would distract her.

Then came the ultimate insult: a generator fired up and drowned any peaceful sound that remained, the wind in the trees and the creek both.

That did it. Maybe these people were squatters who could be driven away. She certainly doubted she'd be able to write at all with that roaring generator. Her cabin was far from soundproofed.

After setting her coffee mug on the railing, she headed for the stepping stones that crossed the creek. For gen-

erations they'd been a path between two friendly families until the Healeys had departed. As Krystal crossed,
she sensed people pulling back into the woods. Creepy.
Maybe she ought to reconsider this trip across the creek.
But her backbone stiffened. It usually did.

She walked around the house, now smelling of freshly
cut wood, sure she'd have to find *someone*.

Then she found the man around the back corner. Since
she was determined not to begin this encounter by yell-
ing at the guy, she waited impatiently until he turned and
saw her. He leaned over, turning the generator to a lower
level, then simply looked at her.

He wore old jeans and a long-sleeved gray work shirt.
A pair of safety goggles rode the top of his head. A dust
mask hung around his neck. Workmanlike, which only
made her uneasier.

Then she noticed more. God, he was gorgeous. Tall,
large, broad-shouldered. A rugged, angular face with turquoise eyes that seemed to pierce the green shade of the
trees. The forest's shadow hid the creek that still danced
and sparkled in revealed sunlight behind her.

This area was a green cavern. One she quite liked.

Finally he spoke, clearly reluctant to do so. "Yes?"

"I'm Krystal Metcalfe. I live in the house across the
creek."

One brief nod. His face remained like granite. Then
slowly he said, "Josh Healey."

An alarm sounded in her mind. Then recognition made
her heart hammer because this might be truly bad news.
"This is Healey property, isn't it?" Of course it was. Not
a bright question from her.

A short nod.

"Are you going to renovate this place?"

"Yes."

God, this was going to be like pulling teeth, she thought irritably. "I hope you're not planning to cut down many trees."

"No."

Stymied, as it became clear this man had no intention of beginning any conversation, even one as casual as talking about the weather, she glared. "Okay, then. Just take care of the forest."

She turned sharply on her heel without another word and made her way across the stepping stones to her own property. Maybe she should start drinking her morning coffee on the front porch of her house on the other side from the creek.

She was certainly going to have to go down to Conard City to buy a pair of ear protectors or go mad trying to do her own work when that generator once again revved up.

Gah!

Josh Healey had watched Krystal Metcalfe coming round the corner of his new building. Trouble? She sure seemed to be looking for it.

She was cute, pretty, her blue eyes as bright as the summer sky overhead. But he didn't care about that.

What he cared about were his troops, men and women who were escaping a world that PTSD and war had ripped from them. People who needed to be left alone to find balance within themselves and with group therapy. Josh, a psychologist, had brought them here for that solitude.

Now he had that neighbor trying to poke her nose into his business. Not good. He knew how people reacted to the mere idea of vets with PTSD, their beliefs that these people were unpredictable and violent.

But he had more than a dozen soldiers to protect and he was determined to do so. If that woman became a problem, he'd find a way to shut her down.

It was *his* land after all.

Chapter One

No.

Nearly a year later, that one word still sometimes re-sounded in Krystal Metcalfe's head. One of the few words and nearly the last word Josh Healey had spoken to her.

A simple question. Several simple questions, and the only response had been single syllables. Well, except for his name.

The man had annoyed her with his refusal to be neighborly, but nothing had changed in nearly a year. Well, except for the crowd over there. A bunch of invaders.

At least Josh Healey hadn't scalped the forest.

Krystal loved the quiet, the peace, the view from her private cabin at the Wyoming-based Mountain Artists' Retreat in the small community of Cash Creek Canyon. She was no temporary resident, unlike guests in the other cabins, but instead a permanent one as her mother's partner in this venture.

She thought of this cabin and the surrounding woods as her Zen Space, a place where she could always center herself, could always find the internal quiet that unleashed wandering ideas, some of them answers to questions her writing awoke in her.

But lately—well, for nearly a year in fact—this Zen

Space of hers had been invaded. Across the creek, within view from her porch, a fallen-down house had been renovated by about a dozen people, then surrounded by a rustic stockade.

What the hell? A fence would have done if they wanted some privacy, but a stockade, looking like something from a Western movie?

Well, she told herself as she sat on her porch, maybe it wasn't as ugly as chain-link or an ordinary privacy fence might have been. It certainly fit with the age of the community that had always been called Cash Creek Canyon since a brief gold rush in the 1870s.

But still, what the hell? It sat there, blending well enough with the surrounding forest, but weird. Overkill. Unnecessary, as Krystal knew from having spent most of her life right here. Nothing to hide from, nothing to hide. Not around here.

Sighing, she put her booted feet up on her porch railing and sipped her coffee, considering her previous but brief encounters with the landowner, Josh Healey.

Talk about monosyllabic! She was quite sure that she hadn't gotten more than a word from him in all this time. At least not the few times she had crossed the creek on the old stepping stones.

The Healey house had been abandoned like so many along Cash Creek as life on the mountainside had become more difficult. For twenty years, Krystal had hoped the house's steady decay would finally collapse the structure, restoring the surrounding forest to its rightful ownership.

Except that hadn't happened and she couldn't quite help getting irritated from the day a huge motor home had moved in to be followed by trucks of lumber, a noisy generator and a dozen or so men and women who camped in tents as they restored the sagging house. A year since then and she was still troubled by the activity over there.

The biggest question was why it had happened. The next question was what had brought the last owner of the property back here with a bunch of his friends to fill up the steadily shrinking hole in the woods.

No answers. At least none from Josh Healey. None, for that matter, from the Conard County sheriff's deputies who patrolled the community of Cash Creek Canyon. They knew no more than anyone: that it was a group residence.

The privacy of that stockade was absolute. At least the damn noise had quieted at last, leaving the Mountain Artists' Retreat in the kind of peace its residents needed for their creative work.

For a while it had seemed that the retreat might die from the noise, even with the muffling woods around. That had not happened, and spring's guests had arrived pretty much as usual, some new to the community, others returning visitors.

Much as she resented the building that had invaded her Zen Space, Krystal had to acknowledge a curiosity that wouldn't go away. A curiosity about those people. About the owner, who would say nothing about why he had brought them all there.

Some kind of cult?

That question troubled her. But what troubled her more was how much she enjoyed watching Josh Healey laboring around that place. Muscled. Hardworking. And entirely too attractive when he worked with his shirt off.

Dang. On the one hand she wanted to drive the man away. On the other she wanted to have sex with him. Wanted it enough to feel a tingling throughout her body.

How foolish could she get?

ACROSS THE CREEK, Josh Healey often noticed the woman who sat on her porch in the mornings drinking coffee. He knew her name because she had crossed the creek a few times: Krystal Metcalfe, joint owner of the artists' retreat. A pretty package of a woman, but he had no time or interest in such things these days.

Nor did he have any desire to share the purpose of his compound. It had been necessary to speak briefly with a deputy who hadn't been that curious. He imagined word had gotten around some, probably with attendant rumors, but no one out there in the community of Cash Creek Canyon, or beyond it in Conard City or County, had any need to know what he hoped he was accomplishing. And from what he could tell, no one did.

Nor did anyone have a need to know the reentry problems being faced by his ex-military residents.

Least of all Krystal Metcalfe, who watched too often and had ventured over here with her questions. Questions she really had no right to ask.

So when he saw her in the mornings, he shrugged it off. She had a right to sit on her damn porch, a right to watch whatever she could see…although the stockade fencing had pretty much occluded any nosy viewing.

But sometimes he wondered, with private amusement, just how she would respond if he crossed that creek and questioned her. Asked *her* about the hole in the woods created by her lodge and all the little cabins she and her mother had scattered through the forest.

Hah! She apparently felt she took care of her environment but he could see at least a dozen problems with her viewpoint. Enough problems that his own invasion seemed paltry by comparison.

As it was, right now he had more than a dozen vets, a number that often grew for a while, who kept themselves busy with maintaining the sanctuary itself, with cooking, with gardening. And a lot of time with group therapy, helping each other through a very difficult time, one that had shredded their lives. All of them leaving behind the booze and drugs previously used as easy crutches.

Some of his people left when they felt ready. New ones arrived, sometimes more than he had room for but always welcomed.

Most of the folks inside, male and female, knew about Krystal Metcalfe, and after he explained her harmless curiosity to them, they lost their suspicion, lost their fear of accusations.

Because his people *had* been accused. Every last one of them had been accused of something. It seemed society had no room for the detritus, the *problems*, their damn war had brought home.

He sighed and shook his head and continued around the perimeter of the large stockade. Like many of his folks here, he couldn't relax completely.

It always niggled at the back of his mind that someone curious or dangerous might try to get into the stockade. Exactly the thing that he'd prevented by building it this way in the first place.

But still the worry wouldn't quite leave him. His own remnant from a war.

He glanced at Krystal Metcalfe one last time before he rounded the corner. She appeared to be absorbed in a tablet.

Good. Her curiosity had gone far enough.

NEW RELEASES

**Four sisters. One surprise will.
One year to wed.**

Don't miss these two volumes of
Wed In The Outback!

When Holt Waverly leaves his flourishing outback estate to his four daughters, it comes to pass that without an eldest son to inherit, the farm will be entailed to someone else…unless all his daughters are married within the year!

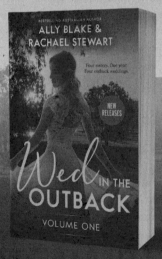

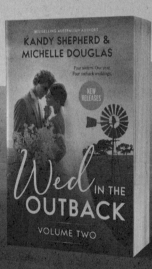

May 2024

July 2024